"**A** book of immense ambition, learning, and scope, *Quicksilver* is often brilliant and occasionally astonishing in its evocation of a remarkable time and place . . . There is much beauty and insight in Stephenson's novel . . . *Quicksilver* has wit, ambition, and . . . moments of real genius."

Washington Post Book World

"**I**ntoxicating . . . hilarious . . . An epic . . . nod to the unrivaled genius, creativity, and discovery of the Baroque period . . . Stephenson, always in control, manages a more than equitable balance of hallowed history and hearty histrionics to honor a healthy contribution of all those involved in that dazzling era."

San Diego Union-Tribune

"**R**ollicking good fun . . . Historical fiction driven by the history of ideas . . . Mr. Stephenson is a magnificent chronicler of the Information Age."

Wall Street Journal

"*Quicksilver* infuses old-school science and engineering with a badly needed dose of swashbuckling adventure, complete with a professor-versus-the-pirates battle at sea. Who knew the Natural Philosophers were so cool?"

Slate

"*Quicksilver* captures the spirit of discovery with Stephenson's relentlessly dry sense of humor . . . Not merely a period piece but a book very much about today . . . With its insights into our modern world, the book should appeal to everyone who wonders where technology is taking us . . . With a plot that . . . offers political intrigue, religious corruption, and spirited characters, *Quicksilver* just might be what puts Stephenson on the map for good."

Denver Rocky Mountain News

"*Quicksilver* does not rely on fictional technology to drive its story. Instead, it feeds its engine with philosophy, court intrigue, economics, and the wars, plagues, and natural disasters of the era . . . Everyone who's anyone in late seventeenth-century or early eighteenth-century Europe and North America shows up in the story . . . Stephenson clearly never intended *Quicksilver* to be one of those meticulously accurate historical novels that capture ways of thought of times gone by. Instead, it explores the philosophic concerns of today . . . The novel does this through thrillingly clever, suspenseful, and amusing plot twists."

New York Times Book Review

"The great trick of *Quicksilver* is that it makes you ponder concepts and theories you initially think you'll never under- stand, and its greatest pleasure is that Stephenson is such an enthralling explainer . . . He throws in lots of sex, violence, and puns that are 'funny in a painful way' . . . Stephenson has set himself up as the Lord of the Baroque and he's going for broke."

Entertainment Weekly

"**A** story of science, revolution, and scientific revolution . . . [Stephenson] has one of those rare, fluid minds that push the boundaries of brilliance. With exuberant, intoxicating prose, he has written a lusty adventure tale that also seems to be scientifically accurate . . . Stephenson has created fictitious characters and imagined real ones who pulse with life and whom we really care about . . . A book that you don't want to end."

St. Paul Pioneer Press

"**T**ogether, the books of **The Baroque Cycle** form a sublime, immersive, brain-throttlingly complex marvel of a novel that will keep scholars and critics occupied for the next 100 years . . . Despite its size, and the often daunting density of its ideas and complexity of its plots, [it] remains highly readable. It's the sort of work that quickly becomes an obsession . . . A reader's feast, featuring pirates and courtesans, palaces and prisons, Whigs and Tories, narrow escapes and gruesome executions, exotic islands and dank sewers, science and alchemy. Really, there's something for everyone."

Toronto Star

"**W**onderfully inventive . . . Stephenson brings to life a cast of unforgettable characters in a time of breathtaking genius and discovery."

Contra Costa Time

"**The Baroque Cycle** is great fun that never seems to end."

Columbus Dispatch

"**A**rguably the most ambitious literary offering in this century . . . **[The Baroque Cycle]** spills over with historical, social, architectural, and scientific minutiae. It is Dickensian potboiler and Baroque reader smashed into one hefty and masterfully paced [tale] told . . . by a maddeningly talented writer . . . It is a triumph."

Virginian Pilot

"**A** tremendous gift to his fans, who will delve into a richly imagined world of intrigue, science, and plenty of name-dropping . . . *Quicksilver* is a vast narrative that sweeps through a time of tremendous development in science, math, and discovery, not to mention a period of tremendous upheaval in the English monarchy . . . Stephenson's fantastic attention to detail is matched with lyrical descriptions and at times dark humor . . . It's a big world, and there's plenty of explaining to do. If *Quicksilver* is anything by which to judge, Stephenson is just the author to offer it."

Kansas City Star

"**S**tephenson has been compared . . . to Charles Dickens, Thomas Pynchon, Don DeLillo, William Gibson, Michael Crichton, and Isaac Asimov, which suggests what a broad range he covers . . . *Quicksilver* is both a whopping . . . historical epic, filled with the usual trappings . . . and a detail-packed history of science."

Atlanta Journal-Constitution

Books by
Neal Stephenson

THE DIAMOND AGE
SNOW CRASH
ZODIAC
CRYPTONOMICON
QUICKSILVER
THE KING OF THE VAGABONDS
ODALISQUE
ANATHEM
REAMDE

NEAL STEPHENSON

QUICKSILVER

THE BAROQUE CYCLE #1

HARPER

An Imprint of HarperCollinsPublishers

Quicksilver: The Baroque Cycle #1 was originally published in hardcover and trade paperback as part of the overall novel, *Quicksilver: Volume One of the Baroque Cycle* by Neal Stephenson.

Map of 1667 London reproduced with changes courtesy of Historic Urban Plans, Inc.

Refracting sphere illustration from the facsimile edition of Robert Hooke's *Philosophical Experiments and Observations,* edited by W. Derham. Published by Frank Cass & Co., Ltd., London, 1967.

Flea illustration from Robert Hooke's 1665 *Micrographia* reprinted by permission of Octavo, www.octavo.com.

HARPER

An Imprint of HarperCollins*Publishers*
10 East 53rd Street
New York, New York 10022-5299

Copyright © 2003 by Neal Stephenson
Excerpt from *King of the Vagabonds* copyright © 2003 by Neal Stephenson
Maps by Nick Springer
Family trees created by Lisa Gold; illustrated by Jane S. Kim
ISBN: 978-0-06-083316-9

First Harper mass market printing: August 2012
First HarperTorch mass market printing: February 2006
First Perennial paperback printing: October 2004
First William Morrow hardcover printing: October 2003

HarperCollins® and Harper® are registered trademarks of HarperCollins Publishers.

Printed in the United States of America

Visit Harper paperbacks on the World Wide Web at www.harpercollins.com

10 9 8 7 6 5 4

To the woman upstairs

✧

Acknowledgments

❦

A WORK LIKE THIS ONE hangs in an immense web of dependencies that cannot be done justice by a brief acknowledgments page. Such a project would be inconceivable were it not for the efforts of scholars and scientists dating back to the era of Wilkins and Comenius, and extending into the present day. Not to say as much would be unjust. But in a work of fiction, which necessarily strays from historical and scientific truth, acknowledgments can backfire. Serious scholars mentioned below should be applauded for their good work, never blamed for my tawdry divagations.

The project would not have happened at all were it not for serendipitous conversations several years ago with George Dyson and Steven Horst.

The following scholars (again in alphabetical order) have published work that was essential to the completion of this project. While eager to give them due credit, I am aware that they may be chagrined by my work's many excursions from historical truth. Readers who want to know what really happened should buy and read their books, while blaming the errors herein on me: Julian Barbour, Gale E. Christianson, A. Rupert Hall, David Kahn, Hans Georg Schulte-Albert, Lee Smolin, Richard Westfall, D. T. Whiteside.

Particular mention must go to Fernand Braudel, to whose work this book may be considered a discursive footnote. Many other scholarly works were consulted during this project, and space does not permit mentioning them here. Of particular note is Sir Winston Spencer Churchill's six-volume biography of Marlborough, which people who are *really* interested in this period of history should *read,* and people who think that *I* am too long-winded should *weigh.*

Special thanks to Béla and Gabriella Bollobás, Doug Carlston, and Tomi Pierce for providing me with access to places I could not have seen (Bollobás) or worked in (Carlston/Pierce) otherwise. George Jewsbury and Catherine Durandin and Hugo Durandin DeSousa provided timely assistance. Greg Bear lent me two books; I promise to return them! And for talking to me about gunpowder, and listening equably to the occasional rant about Alchemy, thanks to Marco Kaltofen, P. E., of the Natick Indian Plantation and Needham West Militia Companies.

Helping in many ways to make this possible on the publishing end, and exhibiting superhuman patience, were Jennifer Hershey, Liz Darhansoff, Jennifer Brehl, and Ravi Mirchandani.

Jeremy Bornstein, Alvy Ray Smith, and Lisa Gold read the penultimate draft and supplied useful commentary. The latter two, along with the cartographer Nick Springer, participated in creation of maps, diagrams, and family trees. More detail is to be found on the website BaroqueCycle.com.

Contents

Invocation

State your intentions, Muse. I know you're there.
Dead bards who pined for you have said
You're bright as flame, but fickle as the air.
My pen and I, submerged in liquid shade,
Much dark can spread, on days and over reams
But without you, no radiance can shed.
Why rustle in the dark, when fledged with fire?
Craze the night with flails of light. Reave
Your turbid shroud. Bestow what I require.

But you're not in the dark. I do believe
I swim, like squid, in clouds of my own make,
To you, offensive. To us both, opaque.
What's constituted so, only a pen
Can penetrate. I have one here; let's go.

Gunfleet House

Comstock House

PICCADILLY

ST. JAMES' STREET

St. James' Palace

PALL MALL

ST. MARTIN'S LANE

Covent
Garden

St. Martin-
in-the-Fields

THE STRAND

LeFebure's

CHARING
CROSS

The New
Exchange

Holbein
Gate

KING STREET

King St. Gate

Whitehall
Palace

Westminster

LONDON

Based on a map made after the Fire of 1666 and attributed to Robert Hooke, Royal Surveyor and Fellow of the Royal Society.

The part of London destroyed in the Fire is unshaded.

BOOK ONE

Quicksilver

Those who assume hypotheses as first principles of their speculations . . . may indeed form an ingenious romance, but a romance it will still be.
—ROGER COTES,
PREFACE TO SIR ISAAC NEWTON'S
Principia Mathematica,
SECOND EDITION, 1713

Boston Common

ENOCH ROUNDS THE CORNER JUST as the executioner raises
the noose above the woman's head. The crowd on the Common stop praying and sobbing for just as long as Jack Ketch
stands there, elbows locked, for all the world like a carpenter heaving a ridge-beam into place. The rope clutches a
disk of blue New England sky. The Puritans gaze at it and,
to all appearances, think. Enoch the Red reins in his borrowed horse as it nears the edge of the crowd, and sees that
the executioner's purpose is not to let them inspect his knot-
work, but to give them all a narrow—and, to a Puritan, tan-
talizing—glimpse of the portal through which they all must
pass one day.

Boston's a dollop of hills in a spoon of marshes. The road
up the spoon-handle is barred by a wall, with the usual gallows outside it, and victims, or parts of them, strung up or
nailed to the city gates. Enoch has just come that way, and
reckoned he had seen the last of such things—that thenceforth it would all be churches and taverns. But the dead men
outside the gate were common robbers, killed for earthly
crimes. What is happening now on the Common is of a more
Sacramental nature.

The noose lies on the woman's gray head like a crown.
The executioner pushes it down. Her head forces it open like
an infant's dilating the birth canal. When it finds the widest
part it drops suddenly onto her shoulders. Her knees pimple

the front of her apron and her skirts telescope into the platform as she makes to collapse. The executioner hugs her
with one arm, like a dancing-master, to keep her upright, and
adjusts the knot while an official reads the death warrant.
This is as bland as a lease. The crowd scratches and shuffles.
There are none of the diversions of a London hanging: no
catcalls, jugglers, or pickpockets. Down at the other end of
the Common, a squadron of lobsterbacks drills and marches
round the base of a hummock with a stone powder-house
planted in its top. An Irish sergeant bellows—bored but in-
dignant—in a voice that carries forever on the wind, like the
smell of smoke.

He's not come to watch witch-hangings, but now that
Enoch's blundered into one it would be bad form to leave.
There is a drum-roll, and then a sudden awkward silence. He
judges it very far from the worst hanging he's ever seen—no
kicking or writhing, no breaking of ropes or unraveling of
knots—all in all, an unusually competent piece of work.

He hadn't really known what to expect of America. But
people here seem to do things—hangings included—with a
blunt, blank efficiency that's admirable and disappointing at
the same time. Like jumping fish, they go about difficult
matters with bloodless ease. As if they were all born knowing things that other people must absorb, along with færy-
tales and superstitions, from their families and villages.
Maybe it is because most of them came over on ships.

As they are cutting the limp witch down, a gust tumbles
over the Common from the North. On Sir Isaac Newton's
temperature scale, where freezing is zero and the heat of the
human body is twelve, it is probably four or five. If Herr
Fahrenheit were here with one of his new quicksilver-filled,
sealed-tube thermometers, he would probably observe
something in the fifties. But this sort of wind, coming as it
does from the North in the autumn, is more chilling than any
mere instrument can tell. It reminds everyone here that if
they don't want to be dead in a few months' time, they have
firewood to stack and chinks to caulk. The wind is noticed

by a hoarse preacher at the base of the gallows, who takes it to be Satan himself, come to carry the witch's soul to hell, and who is not slow to share this opinion with his flock. The preacher is staring Enoch in the eye as he testifies.

Enoch feels the heightened, chafing self-consciousness that is the precursor to fear. What's to prevent them from trying and hanging *him* as a witch?

How must he look to these people? A man of indefinable age but evidently broad experience, with silver hair queued down to the small of his back, a copper-red beard, pale gray eyes, and skin weathered and marred like a blacksmith's ox-hide apron. Dressed in a long traveling-cloak, a walking-staff and an outmoded rapier strapped 'longside the saddle of a notably fine black horse. Two pistols in his waistband, prominent enough that Indians, highwaymen, and French raiders can clearly see them from ambuscades (he'd like to move them out of view, but reaching for them at this moment seems like a bad idea). Saddlebags (should they be searched) filled with instruments, flasks of quicksilver, and stranger matters—some, as they'd learn, quite dangerous— books in Hebrew, Greek, and Latin pocked with the occult symbols of Alchemists and Kabalists. Things could go badly for him in Boston.

But the crowd takes the preacher's ranting not as a call to arms but a signal to turn and disperse, muttering. The red-coats discharge their muskets with deep hissing booms, like handfuls of sand hurled against a kettledrum. Enoch dismounts into the midst of the colonists. He sweeps the robe round him, concealing the pistols, pulls the hood back from his head, and amounts to just another weary pilgrim. He does not meet any man's eye but scans their faces sidelong, and is surprised by a general lack of self-righteousness.

"God willing," one man says, "that'll be the last one."

"Do you mean, sir, the last witch?" Enoch asks.

"I mean, sir, the last hanging."

Flowing like water round the bases of the steep hills, they migrate across a burying ground on the south edge of the

Common, already full of lost Englishmen, and follow the witch's corpse down the street. The houses are mostly of wood, and so are the churches. Spaniards would have built a single great cathedral here, of stone, with gold on the inside, but the colonists cannot agree on anything and so it is more like Amsterdam: small churches on every block, some barely distinguishable from barns, each no doubt preaching that all of the others have it wrong. But at least they can muster a consensus to kill a witch. She is borne off into a new burying ground, which for some reason they have situated hard by the granary. Enoch is at a loss to know whether this juxtaposition—that is, storing their Dead, and their Staff of Life, in the same place—is some sort of Message from the city's elders, or simple bad taste.

Enoch, who has seen more than one city burn, recognizes the scars of a great fire along this main street. Houses and churches are being rebuilt with brick or stone. He comes to what must be the greatest intersection in the town, where this road from the city gate crosses a very broad street that runs straight down to salt water, and continues on a long wharf that projects far out into the harbor, thrusting across a ruined rampart of stones and logs: the rubble of a disused sea-wall. The long wharf is ridged with barracks. It reaches far enough out into the harbor that one of the Navy's very largest men-of-war is able to moor at its end. Turning his head the other way, he sees artillery mounted up on a hill-side, and blue-coated gunners tending to a vatlike mortar, ready to lob iron bombs onto the decks of any French or Spanish galleons that might trespass on the bay.

So, drawing a mental line from the dead criminals at the city gate, to the powder-house on the Common, to the witch-gallows, and finally to the harbor defenses, he has got one Cartesian number-line—what Leibniz would call the Ordi-nate—plotted out: he understands what people are afraid of in Boston, and how the churchmen and the generals keep the place in hand. But it remains to be seen what can be plotted in the space above and below. The hills of Boston are skirted by endless flat marshes that fade, slow as twilight, into Harbor or River, providing blank empty planes on which men with ropes and rulers can construct whatever strange curves they phant'sy.

Enoch knows where to find the Origin of this coordinate system, because he has talked to ship's masters who have visited Boston. He goes down to where the long wharf grips the shore. Among fine stone sea-merchants' houses, there is a brick-red door with a bunch of grapes dangling above it. Enoch goes through that door and finds himself in a good tavern. Men with swords and expensive clothes turn round to look at him. Slavers, merchants of rum and molasses and tea and tobacco, and captains of the ships that carry those things. It could be any place in the world, for the same tavern is in London, Cadiz, Smyrna, and Manila, and the same men are in it. None of them cares, supposing they even know, that witches are being hanged five minutes' walk away. He is much more comfortable in here than out there; but he has not come to be comfortable. The particular sea-captain he's looking for—van Hoek—is not here. He backs out before the tavern-keeper can tempt him.

Back in America and among Puritans, he enters into narrower streets and heads north, leading his horse over a rickety wooden bridge thrown over a little mill-creek. Flotillas of shavings from some carpenter's block-plane sail down the stream like ships going off to war. Underneath them the weak current nudges turds and bits of slaughtered animals down towards the harbor. It smells accordingly. No denying there is a tallow-chandlery not far upwind, where beast-grease not fit for eating is made into candles and soap.

"Did you come from Europe?"

He had *sensed* someone was following him, but *seen* nothing whenever he looked back. Now he knows why: his doppelgänger is a lad, moving about like a drop of quicksilver that cannot be trapped under the thumb. Ten years old, Enoch guesses. Then the boy thinks about smiling and his lips part. His gums support a rubble of adult teeth shouldering their way into pink gaps, and deciduous ones flapping like tavern signs on skin hinges. He's closer to eight. But cod and corn have made him big for his age—at least by London standards. And he is precocious in every respect save social graces.

Enoch might answer, *Yes, I am from Europe, where a boy addresses an old man as "sir," if he addresses him at all*. But he cannot get past the odd nomenclature. "Europe," he repeats, "is that what you name it here? Most people *there* say *Christendom*."

"But we have Christians *here*."

"So this *is* Christendom, you are saying," says Enoch, "but, obviously to you, I've come from somewhere *else*. Perhaps Europe *is* the better term, now that you mention it. Hmm."

"What do other people call it?"

"Do I look like a schoolmaster to you?"

"No, but you talk like one."

"You know something of schoolmasters, do you?"

"Yes, sir," the boy says, faltering a bit as he sees the jaws of the trap swinging toward his leg.

"Yet here it is the middle of Monday—"

"The place was empty 'cause of the Hanging. I didn't want to stay and—"

"And what?"

"Get more ahead of the others than I was already."

"If you are ahead, the correct thing is to *get used to it*— not to make yourself into an imbecile. Come, you belong in school."

"School is where one learns," says the boy. "If you'd be so kind as to answer my question, sir, then I should be learning something, which would mean I *were* in school."

The boy is obviously dangerous. So Enoch decides to accept the proposition. "You may address me as Mr. Root. And you are—?"

"Ben. Son of Josiah. The tallow-chandler. Why do you laugh, Mr. Root?"

"Because in most parts of Christendom—or Europe—tallow-chandlers' sons do not go to grammar school. It is a peculiarity of . . . your people." Enoch almost let slip the word *Puritans.* Back in England, where Puritans are a memory of a bygone age, or at worst streetcorner nuisances, the term serves well enough to lampoon the backwoodsmen of Massachusetts Bay Colony. But as he keeps being reminded here, the truth of the matter is more complex. From a coffeehouse in London, one may speak blithely of Islam and the Mussulman, but in Cairo such terms are void. Here Enoch is in the Puritans' Cairo. "I shall answer your question," Enoch says before Ben can let fly with any more. "What do people in other parts call the place I am from? Well, Islam—a larger, richer, and in most ways more sophisticated civilization that hems in the Christians of Europe to the east and the south—divides all the world into only three parts: their part, which is the *dar al-Islam*; the part with which they are friendly, which is the *dar as-sulh,* or House of Peace; and everything else, which is the *dar al-harb*, or House of War. The latter is, I'm sorry to say, a far more apt name than Christendom for the part of the world where most of the Christians live."

"I know of the war," Ben says coolly. "It is at an end. A Peace has been signed at Utrecht. France gets Spain. Austria gets the Spanish Netherlands. We get Gibraltar, Newfoundland, St. Kitts, and—" lowering his voice "—the slave trade."

"Yes—the *Asiento.*"

"Ssh! There are a few here, sir, opposed to it, and they are dangerous."

"You have Barkers here?"

"Yes, sir."

Enoch studies the boy's face now with some care, for the chap he is looking for is a sort of Barker, and it would be useful to know how such are regarded hereabouts by their less maniacal brethren. Ben seems cautious, rather than contemptuous.

"But you are speaking only of *one* war—"

"The War of the Spanish Succession," says Ben, "whose cause was the death in Madrid of King Carlos the Sufferer."

"I should say that wretched man's death was the *pretext,* not the cause," says Enoch. "The War of the Spanish Succession was only the second, and I pray the last, part of a great war that began a quarter of a century ago, at the time of—"

"The Glorious Revolution!"

"As some style it. You *have* been at your lessons, Ben, and I commend you. Perhaps you know that in that Revolution the King of England—a Catholic—was sent packing, and replaced by a Protestant King and Queen."

"William and Mary!"

"Indeed. But has it occurred to you to wonder *why* Protestants and Catholics were at war in the first place?"

"In our studies we more often speak of wars *among* Protestants."

"Ah, yes—a phenomenon restricted to England. That is natural, for your parents came here because of such a conflict."

"The Civil War," says Ben.

"Your side won the Civil War," Enoch reminds him, "but later came the Restoration, which was a grievous defeat for your folk, and sent them flocking hither."

"You have hit the mark, Mr. Root," says Ben, "for that is just why my father Josiah quit England."

"What about your mother?"

"Nantucket-born sir. But her father came here to escape from a wicked Bishop—a loud fellow, or so I have heard—"

"Finally, Ben, I have found a limit to your knowledge. You are speaking of Archbishop Laud—a terrible oppressor of Puritans—as some called your folk—under Charles the First. The Puritans paid him back by chopping off the head of that same Charles in Charing Cross, in the year of our lord sixteen hundred and forty-nine."

"Cromwell," says Ben.

"Cromwell. Yes. He had something to do with it. Now,

Ben. We have been standing by this millstream for rather a long while. I grow cold. My horse is restless. We have, as I said, found the place where your erudition gives way to ignorance. I shall be pleased to hold up my end of our agreement—that is, to teach you things, so that when you go home to-night you may claim to Josiah that you were in school the whole day. Though the schoolmaster may give him an account that shall conflict with yours. However, I do require certain minor services in return."

"Only name them, Mr. Root."

"I have come to Boston to find a certain man who at last report was living here. He is an old man."

"Older than you?"

"No, but he might *seem* older."

"How old is he, then?"

"He watched the head of King Charles the First being chopped off."

"At least threescore and four then."

"Ah, I see you have been learning sums and differences."

"And products and dividends, Mr. Root."

"Work this into your reckonings, then: the one I seek had an excellent view of the beheading, for he was sitting upon his father's shoulders."

"Couldn't have been more than a few years old then. Unless his father was a sturdy fellow indeed."

"His father was sturdy in a sense," says Enoch, "for Archbishop Laud had caused his ears and his nose to be cut off in Star Chamber some two decades before, and yet he was not daunted, but kept up his agitation against the King. Against all Kings."

"He was a Barker." Again, this word brings no sign of contempt to Ben's face. Shocking how different this place is from London.

"But to answer your question, Ben: Drake was not an especially big or strong man."

"So the son on his shoulders was small. By now he should

be, perhaps, threescore and eight. But I do not know of a Mr. Drake here."

"Drake was the father's *Christian* name."

"Pray, what then is the name of the family?"

"I will not tell you that just now," says Enoch. For the man he wants to find might have a very poor character among these people—might already have been hanged on Boston Common, for all Enoch knows.

"How can I help you find him, sir, if you won't let me know his name?"

"By guiding me to the Charlestown ferry," Enoch says, "for I know that he spends his days on the north side of the River Charles."

"Follow me," says Ben, "but I hope you've silver."

"Oh yes, I've silver," says Enoch.

THEY ARE SKIRTING A KNOB of land at the north end of the city. Wharves, smaller and older than the big one, radiate from its shore. The sails and rigging, spars and masts to his starboard combine into a tangle vast and inextricable, as characters on a page must do in the eyes of an unlettered peasant. Enoch does not see van Hoek or *Minerva*. He begins to fear that he shall have to go into taverns and make inquiries, and spend time, and draw attention.

Ben takes him direct to the wharf where the Charlestown Ferry is ready to shove off. It is all crowded with hanging-watchers, and Enoch must pay the waterman extra to bring the horse aboard. Enoch pulls his purse open and peers into it. The King of Spain's coat of arms stares back at him, stamped in silver, variously blurred, chopped, and mangled. The Christian name varies, depending on which king reigned when each of these coins was hammered out in New Spain, but after that they all say D. G. HISPAN ET IND REX. By the grace of God, of Spain and the Indies, King. The same sort of bluster that all kings stamp onto their coins.

Those words don't matter to anyone—most people can't read them anyway. What does matter is that a man standing in a cold breeze on the Boston waterfront, seeking to buy passage on a ferry run by an Englishman, cannot pay with the coins that are being stamped out by Sir Isaac Newton in the Royal Mint at the Tower of London. The only coinage here is Spanish—the same coins that are changing hands, at this moment, in Lima, Manila, Macao, Goa, Bandar Abbas, Mocha, Cairo, Smyrna, Malta, Madrid, the Canary Islands, Marseilles.

The man who saw Enoch down to the docks in London months ago said: "Gold knows things that no man does."

Enoch churns his purse up and down, making the coins-fragments fly, hoping to spy a single pie-slice—one-eighth of a Piece of Eight, or a bit, as they are called. But he already knows he's spent most of his bits for small necessaries along the road. The smallest piece he has in his purse right now is half of a coin—four bits.

He looks up the street and sees a blacksmith's forge only a stone's throw away. Some quick work with a hammer and that smith could make change for him.

The ferryman's reading Enoch's mind. He couldn't see into the purse, but he could hear the massive gonging of whole coins colliding, without the clashing tinkle of bits. "We're shoving off," he is pleased to say.

Enoch comes to his senses, remembers what he's doing, and hands over a silver semicircle. "But the boy comes with me," he insists, "and you'll give him passage back."

"Done," says the ferryman.

This is more than Ben could have hoped for, and yet he *was* hoping for it. Though the boy is too self-possessed to say as much, this voyage is to him as good as a passage down to the Caribbean to go a-pirating on the Spanish Main. He goes from wharf to ferry without touching the gangplank.

Charlestown is less than a mile distant, across the mouth of a sluggish river. It is a low green hill shingled with long slender hay-mows limned by dry-stone fences. On the slope facing toward Boston, below the summit but above the endless tidal flats and cattail-filled marshes, a town has occurred: partly laid out by geometers, but partly growing like ivy.

The ferryman's hefty Africans pace short reciprocating arcs on the deck, sweeping and shoveling the black water of the Charles Basin with long stanchion-mounted oars, minting systems of vortices that fall to aft, flailing about one another, tracing out fading and flattening conic sections that Sir Isaac could probably work out in his head. *The Hypothesis of Vortices is pressed with many difficulties.* The sky's a matted reticule of taut jute and spokeshaved tree-trunks. Gusts make the anchored ships start and jostle like nervous horses hearing distant guns. Irregular waves slap curiously at the lapping clinkers of their hulls, which are infested with barefoot jacks paying pitch and oakum into troublesome seams. The ships appear to glide this way and that as the ferry's movement plays with the parallax. Enoch, who has the good fortune to be a bit taller than most of the other passengers, hands the reins to Ben and excuses his way around the ferry's deck trying to read the names.

He knows the ship he's looking for, though, simply by recognizing the carved Lady mounted below the bowsprit: a gray-eyed woman in a gilded helmet, braving the North Atlantic seas with a snaky shield and nipples understandably erect. *Minerva* hasn't weighed anchor yet—that's lucky— but she is heavy-laden and gives every appearance of being just about to put to sea. Men are walking aboard hugging baskets of loaves so fresh they're steaming. Enoch turns back toward the shore to read the level of the tide from a barnacled pile, then turns the other way to check the phase and altitude of the moon. Tide will be going out soon, and *Minerva* will probably want to ride it. Enoch finally spies van Hoek standing on the foredeck, doing some paperwork on the top of a barrel, and through some kind of action-at-a-distance wills him to look up and notice him, down on the ferry.

Van Hoek looks his way and stiffens.

Enoch makes no outward sign, but stares him in the eye

long enough to give him second thoughts about pushing for a hasty departure.

A colonist in a black hat is attempting to make friends with one of the Africans, who doesn't speak much English—but this is no hindrance, the white man has taught himself a few words of some African tongue. The slave is very dark, and the arms of the King of Spain are branded into his left shoulder, and so he is probably Angolan. Life has been strange to him: abducted by Africans fiercer than he, chained up in a hole in Luanda, marked with a hot iron to indicate that duty had been paid on him, loaded onto a ship, and sent to a cold place full of pale men. After all of that, you'd think that nothing could possibly surprise him. But he's astonished by whatever this Barker is telling him. The Barker's punching at the air and becoming quite exercised, and not just because he is inarticulate. Assuming that he has been in touch with his brethren in London (and that is a very good assumption), he is probably telling the Angolan that he, and all of the other slaves, are perfectly justified in taking up arms and mounting a violent rebellion.

"Your mount is very fine. Did you bring him from Europe?"

"No, Ben. Borrowed him in New Amsterdam. New *York,* I mean."

"Why'd you sail to New York if the man you seek's in Boston?"

"The next America-bound ship from the Pool of London happened to be headed thither."

"You're in a terrible hurry, then!"

"I shall be in a terrible hurry to toss you over the side if you continue to draw such inferences."

This quiets Ben, but only long enough for him to circle round and probe Enoch's defenses from another quarter: "The owner of this horse must be a very dear friend of yours, to lend you such a mount."

Enoch must now be a bit careful. The owner's a gentleman of quality in New York. If Enoch claims his friendship, then proceeds to make a bloody hash of things in Boston, it could deal damage to the gentleman's repute. "It is not so much that he is a friend. I'd never met him until I showed up at his door a few days ago."

Ben can't fathom it. "Then why'd he even admit you to his house? By your leave, sir, looking as you do, and armed. Why'd he lend you such a worthy stallion?"

"He let me in to his house because there was a riot underway, and I requested sanctuary." Enoch gazes over at the Barker, then sidles closer to Ben. "Here is a wonder for you: When my ship reached New York, we were greeted by the spectacle of thousands of slaves—some Irish, the rest Angolan—running through the streets with pitchforks and firebrands. Lobsterbacks tromping after them in leapfrogging blocks, firing volleys. The white smoke of their muskets rose and mingled with the black smoke of burning warehouses to turn the sky into a blazing, spark-shot melting-pot, wondrous to look at but, as we supposed, unfit to support life. Our pilot had us stand a-loof until the tide forced his hand. We put in at a pier that seemed to be under the sway of the redcoats."

"Anyway," Enoch continues—for his discourse is beginning to draw unwanted notice—"that's how I got in the door. He lent me the horse because he and I are Fellows in the same Society, and I am here, in a way, to do an errand for that Society."

"Is it a Society of Barkers, like?" asks Ben, stepping in close to whisper, and glancing at the one who's proselytizing the slave. For by now Ben has taken note of Enoch's various pistols and blades, and matched him with tales his folk have probably told him concerning that fell Sect during their halcyon days of Cathedral-sacking and King-killing.

"No, it is a society of philosophers," Enoch says, before the boy's phant'sies wax any wilder.

"Philosophers, sir!"

Enoch had supposed the boy should be disappointed. Instead he's thrilled. So Enoch was correct: the boy's dangerous.

"*Natural* Philosophers. Not, mind you, the other sort—"

"Unnatural?"

"An apt coinage. *Some* would say it's the unnatural philosophers that are to blame for Protestants fighting Protestants in England and Catholics everywhere else."

"What, then, is a Natural Philosopher?"

"One who tries to prevent his ruminations from straying, by hewing to what can be observed, and proving things, when possible, by rules of logic." This gets him nowhere with Ben. "Rather like a Judge in a Court, who insists on facts, and scorns rumor, hearsay, and appeals to sentiment. As when your own Judges finally went up to Salem and pointed out that the people there were going crazy."

Ben nods. Good. "What is the name of your Clubb?"

"The Royal Society of London."

"One day I shall be a Fellow of it, and a Judge of such things."

"I shall nominate you the moment I get back, Ben."

"Is it a part of your code that members must lend each other horses in time of need?"

"No, but it is a rule that they must pay dues—for which there is *ever* a need—and this chap had not paid his dues in many a year. Sir Isaac—who is the President of the Royal Society—looks with disfavor on such. I explained to the gentleman in New York why it was a Bad Idea to land on Sir Isaac's Shit List—by your leave, by your leave—and he was so convinced by my arguments that he lent me his best riding-horse without further suasion."

"He's a beauty," Ben says, and strokes the animal's nose. The stallion mistrusted Ben at first for being small, darting, and smelling of long-dead beasts. Now he has accepted the boy as an animated hitching-post, capable of performing a few services such as nose-scratching and fly-shooing.

The ferryman is more amused than angry when he discovers a Barker conspiring with his slave, and shoos him away. The Barker identifies Enoch as fresh meat, and begins trying to catch his eye. Enoch moves away from him and pretends to study the approaching shore. The ferry is maneuvering around a raft of immense logs drifting out of the estuary, each marked with the King's Arrow—going to build ships for the Navy.

Inland of Charlestown spreads a loose agglomeration of hamlets conjoined by a network of cowpaths. The largest cowpath goes all the way to Newtowne, where Harvard College is. But most of it just looks like a forest, smoking without being burned, spattered with muffled whacks of axes and hammers. Occasional musket shots boom in the distance and are echoed from hamlet to hamlet—some kind of system for relaying information across the countryside. Enoch wonders how he's ever going to find Daniel in all that.

He moves toward a talkative group that has formed on the center of the ferry's deck, allowing the less erudite (for these must be Harvard men) to break the wind for them. It is a mix of pompous sots and peering quick-faced men basting their sentences together with bad Latin. Some of them have a dour Puritan look about them, others are dressed in something closer to last year's London mode. A pear-shaped, red-nosed man in a tall gray wig seems to be the Don of this jury-rigged College. Enoch catches this one's eye and lets him see that he's bearing a sword. This is not a threat, but an assertion of status.

"A gentleman traveler from abroad joins us. Welcome, sir, to our humble Colony!"

Enoch goes through the requisite polite movements and utterances. They show a great deal of interest in him, a sure sign that not much new and interesting is going on at Harvard College. But the place is only some three-quarters of a century old, so how much can really be happening there? They want to know if he's from a Germanic land; he says not really. They guess that he has come on some Alchemical errand, which is an excellent guess, but wrong. When it is polite to do so, he tells them the name of the man he has come to see.

He's never heard such scoffing. They are, to a man, pained that a gentleman should've crossed the North Atlantic, and now the Charles Basin, only to spoil the journey by meeting with *that* fellow.

"I know him not," Enoch lies.

"Then let us prepare you, sir!" one of them says. "Daniel Waterhouse is a man advanced in years, but the years have been less kind to him than you."

"He is correctly addressed as Dr. Waterhouse, is he not?"

Silence ruined by stifled gurgles.

"I do not presume to correct any man," Enoch says, "only to be sure that I give no offense when I encounter the fellow in person."

"Indeed, he is accounted a Doctor," says the pear-shaped Don, "but—"

"Of what?" someone asks.

"Gears," someone suggests, to great hilarity.

"Nay, nay!" says the Don, shouting them down, in a show of false goodwill. "For all of his gears are to no purpose without a *primum mobile,* a source of motive power—"

"The Franklin boy!" and all turn to look at Ben.

"Today it might be young Ben, tomorrow perhaps little Godfrey Waterhouse will step into Ben's shoes. Later perhaps a rodent on a tread-mill. But in any case, the *vis viva* is conducted into Dr. Waterhouse's gear-boxes by—what? Anyone?" The Don cups a hand to an ear Socratically.

"Shafts?" someone guesses.

"Cranks!" another shouts.

"Ah, excellent! Our colleague Waterhouse is, then, a Doctor of—what?"

"Cranks!" says the entire College in unison.

"And so devoted is our Doctor of Cranks to his work that he quite sacrifices himself," says the Don admiringly. "Going many days uncovered—"

"Shaking the gear-filings from his sleeves when he sits down to break bread—"

"Better than pepper—"

"And cheaper!"

"Are you, perhaps, coming to join his Institute, then?"

"Or foreclose on't?" Too hilarious.

"I have heard of his Institute, but know little of it," Enoch Root says. He looks over at Ben, who has gone red in the neck and ears, and turned his back on all to nuzzle the horse.

"Many learned scholars are in the same state of ignorance—be not ashamed."

"Since he came to America, Dr. Waterhouse has been infected with the local influenza, whose chief symptom is causing men to found new projects and endeavours, rather than going to the trouble of remedying the old ones."

"He's not entirely satisfied with Harvard College then!?" Enoch says wonderingly.

"Oh, no! He has founded—"

"—and *personally endowed*—"

"—and laid the cornerstone—"

"—corner-log, if truth be told—"

"—of—what does he call it?"

"The Massachusetts Bay Colony Institute of Technologickal Arts."

"Where might I find Dr. Waterhouse's Institute?" Enoch inquires.

"Midway from Charlestown to Harvard. Follow the sound of grinding gears 'til you come to America's smallest and smokiest dwelling—"

"Sir, you are a learned and clear-minded gentleman," says the Don. "If your errand has aught to do with Philosophy, then is not Harvard College a more fitting destination?"

"Mr. Root is a Natural Philosopher of note, sir!" blurts Ben, only as a way to prevent himself bursting into tears. The way he says it makes it clear he thinks the Harvard men are of the Unnatural type. "He is a Fellow of the Royal Society!"

Oh, dear.

The Don steps forward and hunches his shoulders like a conspirator. "I beg your pardon, sir, I did not know."

"It is quite all right, really."

"Dr. Waterhouse, you must be warned, has fallen quite under the spell of Herr Leibniz—"

"—him that stole the calculus from Sir Isaac—" someone footnotes.

"—yes, and, like Leibniz, is infected with Metaphysickal thinking—"

"—a throwback to the Scholastics, sir—notwithstanding Sir Isaac's having exploded the old ways through very clear demonstrations—"

"—and labors now, like a possessed man, on a Mill—designed after Leibniz's principles—that he imagines will discover new truths through *computation*!"

"Perhaps our visitor has come to exorcise him of Leibniz's daemons!" some very drunk fellow hypothesizes.

Enoch clears his throat irritably, hacking loose a small accumulation of yellow bile—the humour of anger and ill-temper. He says, "It does Dr. Leibniz an injustice to call him a mere metaphysician."

This challenge produces momentary silence, followed by tremendous excitement and gaiety. The Don smiles thinly and squares off. "I know of a small tavern on Harvard Square, a suitable venue in which I could disabuse the gentleman of any misconceptions—"

The offer to sit down in front of a crock of beer and edify these wags is dangerously tempting. But the Charlestown waterfront is drawing near, the slaves already shortening their strokes; *Minerva* is fairly straining at her hawsers in eagerness to catch the tide, and he must have results. He'd rather get this done discreetly. But that is hopeless now that Ben has unmasked him. More important is to get it done *quickly*.

Besides, Enoch has lost his temper.

He draws a folded and sealed Letter from his breast pocket and, for lack of a better term, brandishes it.

The Letter is borrowed, scrutinized—one side is inscribed "Doktor   Waterhouse—Newtowne—Massachusetts"—and flipped over. Monocles are quarried from velvet-lined pockets for the Examination of the Seal: a lump of red wax the size of Ben's fist. Lips move and strange mutterings occur as parched throats attempt German.

All of the Professors seem to realize it at once. They jump back as if the letter were a specimen of white phosphorus that had suddenly burst into flame. The Don is left holding it. He extends it towards Enoch the Red with a certain desperate pleading look. Enoch punishes him by being slow to accept the burden.

"Bitte, mein herr . . ."

"English is perfectly sufficient," Enoch says. "Preferable, in fact."

At the fringes of the robed and hooded mob, certain near-sighted faculty members are frantic with indignation over not having been able to read the seal. Their colleagues are muttering to them words like "Hanover" and "Ansbach."

A man removes his hat and bows to Enoch. Then another.

They have not even set foot in Charlestown before the dons have begun to make a commotion. Porters and would-be passengers stare quizzically at the approaching ferry as they are assailed with shouts of "Make way!" and broad waving motions. The ferry's become a floating stage packed with bad actors. Enoch wonders whether any of these men really supposes that word of their diligence will actually make its way back to court in Hanover, and be heard by their future Queen. It is ghoulish—they are behaving as if Queen Anne were already dead and buried, and the Hanovers on the throne.

"Sir, if you'd only *told* me 'twas Daniel Waterhouse you sought, I'd have taken you *to* him without delay—and without all of this *bother.*"

"I erred by not confiding in you, Ben," Enoch says.

Indeed. In retrospect, it's obvious that in such a small town, Daniel would have noticed a lad like Ben, or Ben would have been drawn to Daniel, or both. "Do you know the way?"

"Of course!"

"Mount up," Enoch commands, and nods at the horse. Ben needn't be asked twice. He's up like a spider. Enoch follows as soon as dignity and inertia will allow. They share the saddle, Ben on Enoch's lap with his legs thrust back and wedged between Enoch's knees and the horse's rib-cage. The horse has, overall, taken a dim view of the Ferry and the Faculty, and bangs across the plank as soon as it has been thrown down. They're pursued through the streets of Charlestown by some of the more nimble Doctors. But Charlestown doesn't *have* that many streets and so the chase is brief. Then they break out into the mephitic bog on its western flank. It puts Enoch strongly in mind of another swampy, dirty, miasma-ridden burg full of savants: Cambridge, England.

"INTO YONDER COPPICE, then ford the creek," Ben suggests. "We shall lose the Professors, and perhaps find Godfrey. When we were on the ferry, I spied him going thither with a pail."

"Is Godfrey the son of Dr. Waterhouse?"

"Indeed, sir. Two years younger than I."

"Would his middle name, perchance, be William?"

"How'd you know that, Mr. Root?"

"He is very likely named after Gottfried Wilhelm Leibniz."

"A friend of yours and Sir Isaac's?"

"Of mine, yes. Of Sir Isaac's, no—and therein lies a tale too long to tell now."

"Would it fill a book?"

"In truth, 'twould fill *several*—and it is not even finished yet."

"When shall it be finished?"

"At times, I fear *never*. But you and I shall hurry it to its final act to-day, Ben. How much farther to the Massachusetts Bay Colony Institute of Technologickal Arts?"

Ben shrugs. "It is halfway between Charlestown and Harvard. But close to the river. More than a mile. Perhaps less than two."

The horse is disinclined to enter the coppice, so Ben tumbles off and goes in there afoot to flush out little Godfrey. Enoch finds a place to ford the creek that runs through it, and works his way round to the other side of the little wood to find Ben engaged in an apple-fight with a smaller, paler lad.

Enoch dismounts and brokers a peace, then hurries the boys on by offering them a ride on the horse. Enoch walks ahead, leading it; but soon enough the horse divines that they are bound for a timber building in the distance. For it is the *only* building, and a faint path leads to it. Thenceforth Enoch need only walk alongside, and feed him the odd apple.

"The sight of you two lads scuffling over apples in this bleak gusty place full of Puritans puts me in mind of something remarkable I saw a long time ago."

"Where?" asks Godfrey.

"Grantham, Lincolnshire. Which is part of England."

"How long ago, to be exact?" Ben demands, taking the empiricist bit in his teeth.

"That is a harder question than it sounds, for the way I remember such things is most disorderly."

"Why were you journeying to that bleak place?" asks Godfrey.

"To stop being pestered. In Grantham lived an apothecary, name of Clarke, an indefatigable pesterer."

"Then why'd you go *to* him?"

"He'd been pestering me with letters, wanting me to deliver certain necessaries of his trade. He'd been doing it for years—ever since sending letters had become possible again."

"What made it possible?"

"In my neck of the woods—for I was living in a town in Saxony, called Leipzig—the peace of Westphalia did."

"1648!" Ben says donnishly to the younger boy. "The end of the Thirty Years' War."

"At *his* end," Enoch continues, "it was the removal of the King's head from the rest of the King, which settled the Civil War and brought a kind of peace to England."

"1649," Godfrey murmurs before Ben can get it out. Enoch wonders whether Daniel has been so indiscreet as to regale his son with decapitation yarns.

"If Mr. Clarke had been pestering you *for years*, then you must have gone to Grantham in the middle of the 1650s," Ben says.

"How can you be that old?" Godfrey asks.

"Ask your father," Enoch returns. "I am still endeavouring to answer the question of *when* exactly. Ben is correct. I couldn't have been so rash as to make the attempt before, let us say, 1652; for, regicide notwithstanding, the Civil War did not really wind up for another couple of years. Cromwell smashed the Royalists for the umpteenth and final time at Worcester. Charles the Second ran off to Paris with as many of his noble supporters as had not been slain yet. Come to think of it, I *saw* him, and them, at Paris."

"Why *Paris*? That were a *dreadful* way to get from Leipzig to Lincolnshire!" says Ben.

"Your geography is stronger than your history. What do you phant'sy would be a *good* way to make that journey?"

"Through the Dutch Republic, of course."

"And indeed I *did* stop there, to look in on a Mr. Huygens in the Hague. But I did not *sail* from any Dutch port."

"Why not? The Dutch are ever so much better at sailing than the French!"

"But what was the first thing that Cromwell did after winning the Civil War?"

"Granted all men, even Jews, the right to worship wheresoever they pleased," says Godfrey, as if reciting a catechism.

"Well, naturally—that was the whole *point*, wasn't it? But other than *that*—?"

"Killed a great many Irishmen," Ben tries.

"True, too true—but it's not the answer I was looking for. The answer is: the Navigation Act. And a sea-war against the Dutch. So you see, Ben, journeying via Paris might have been *roundabout*, but it was infinitely *safer*. Besides, people

in Paris had been pestering me, too, and they had more
money than Mr. Clarke. So Mr. Clarke had to *get in line,* as
they say in New York."

"Why were so many pestering you?" asks Godfrey.

"Rich Tories, no less!" adds Ben.

"We did not begin calling such people Tories until a good
bit later," Enoch corrects him. "But your question is apt:
what did *I* have in Leipzig that was wanted so badly, alike by
an apothecary in Grantham and a lot of Cavalier courtiers
sitting in Paris waiting for Cromwell to grow old and die of
natural causes?"

"Something to do with the Royal Society?" guesses Ben.

"Shrewd try. Very close to the mark. But this was in the
days before the Royal Society, indeed before Natural Philosophy as we know it. Oh, there were a few—Francis Bacon,
Galileo, Descartes—who'd seen the light, and had done all
that they could to get everyone else to attend to it. But in
those days, most of the chaps who were curious about how
the world worked were captivated by a rather different approach called Alchemy."

"My daddy hates Alchemists!" Godfrey announces—very
proud of his daddy.

"I believe I know *why.* But this is 1713. Rather a lot has
changed. In the æra I am speaking of, it was Alchemy, or
nothing. I knew a lot of Alchemists. I peddled them the
stuff they needed. Some of those English cavaliers had dabbled in the Art. It was the gentlemanly thing to do. Even the
King-in-Exile had a laboratory. After Cromwell had beaten
them like kettledrums and sent them packing to France,
they found themselves with nothing to pass the years except—" and here, if he'd been telling the story to adults,
Enoch would've listed a few of the ways they *had* spent
their time.

"Except what, Mr. Root?"

"Studying the hidden laws of God's creation. Some of
them—in particular John Comstock and Thomas More Anglesey—fell in with Monsieur LeFebure, who was the

apothecary to the French Court. They spent rather a lot of time on Alchemy."

"But wasn't it all stupid nonsense, rot, gibberish, and criminally fraudulent nincompoopery?"

"Godfrey, you are living proof that the apple does not fall far from the tree. Who am I to dispute such matters with your father? Yes. 'Twas all rubbish."

"Then why'd you go to Paris?"

"Partly, if truth be told, I wished to see the coronation of the French King."

"Which one?" asks Godfrey.

"The same one as now!" says Ben, outraged that they are having to waste their time on such questions.

"The big one," Enoch says, "*the* King. Louis the Fourteenth. His formal coronation was in 1654. They anointed him with angel-balm, a thousand years old."

"Eeeyew, it must have stunk to high heaven!"

"Hard to say, in France."

"Where would they've gotten such a thing?"

"Never mind. I am drawing closer to answering the question of when. But that was not my whole reason. Really it was that *something was happening.* Huygens—a brilliant youth, of a great family in the Hague—was at work on a pendulum-clock there that was astonishing. Of course, pendulums were an old idea—but he did something simple and beautiful that fixed them so that they would actually tell time! I saw a prototype, ticking away there in that magnificent house, where the afternoon light streamed in off the Plein—that's a sort of square hard by the palace of the Dutch Court. Then down to Paris, where Comstock and Anglesey were toiling away on—you're correct—stupid nonsense. They truly wanted to learn. But they wanted the brilliance of a Huygens, the audacity to invent a whole new discipline. Alchemy was the only way they knew of."

"How'd you cross over to England if there was a sea-war on?"

"French salt-smugglers," says Enoch, as if this were self-evident. "Now, many an English gentleman had made up his mind that staying in London and dabbling with Alchemy was safer than riding 'round the island making war against Cromwell and his New Model Army. So I'd no difficulty lightening my load, and stuffing my purse, in London. Then I nipped up to Oxford, meaning only to pay a call on John Wilkins and pick up some copies of *Cryptonomicon*."

"What is that?" Ben wants to know.

"A very queer old book, dreadfully thick, and full of nonsense," says Godfrey. "Papa uses it to keep the door from blowing shut."

"It is a compendium of secret codes and cyphers that this chap Wilkins had written some years earlier," says Enoch. "In those days, he was Warden of Wadham College, which is part of the University of Oxford. When I arrived, he was steeling himself to make the ultimate sacrifice in the name of Natural Philosophy."

"He was beheaded?" Ben asks

Godfrey: "Tortured?"

Ben: "Mutilated, like?"

"No: he married Cromwell's sister."

"But I thought you said there *was* no Natural Philosophy in those days," Godfrey complains.

"There *was*—once a week, in John Wilkins's chambers at Wadham College," says Enoch. "For that is where the Experimental Philosophical Clubb met. Christopher Wren, Robert Boyle, Robert Hooke, and others you ought to have heard of. By the time I got there, they'd run out of space and moved to an apothecary's shop—a less flammable environment. It was that apothecary, come to think of it, who exhorted me to make the journey north and pay a call on Mr. Clarke in Grantham."

"Have we settled on a year yet?"

"I'll settle on one now, Ben. By the time I reached Oxford, that pendulum-clock I'd seen on the table of Huygens's house in the Hague had been perfected, and set into motion. The first clock worthy of the name. Galileo had timed his experiments by counting his pulse or listening to musicians; but after Huygens we used clocks, which—according to some—told *absolute* time, fixed and invariant. God's time. Huygens published a book about it later; but the clock first began to tick, and the Time of Natural Philosophy began, in the year of Our Lord—"

⚭

1655

⚓

For between true science and erroneous doctrines, ignorance is in the middle.
—HOBBES, *Leviathan*

IN EVERY KINGDOM, empire, principality, archbishopric, duchy, and electorate Enoch had ever visited, the penalty for transmuting base metals into gold—or trying to—or, in some places, even thinking about it—was death. This did not worry him especially. It was only one of a thousand excuses that rulers kept handy to kill inconvenient persons, and to carry it off in a way that made them look good. For example, if you were in Frankfurt-on-Main, where the Archbishop-Elector von Schönborn and his minister and sidekick Boyneburg were both avid practitioners of the Art, you were probably safe.

Cromwell's England was another matter. Since the Puritans had killed the king and taken the place over, Enoch didn't go around that Commonwealth (as they styled it now) in a pointy hat with stars and moons. Not that Enoch the Red had ever been that kind of alchemist anyway. The old stars-

and-moons act was a good way to farm the unduly trusting. But the need to raise money in the first place seemed to call into question one's own ability to turn lead into gold.

Enoch had made himself something of an expert on longevity. It was only a couple of decades since a Dr. John Lambe had been killed by the *mobile* in the streets of London. Lambe was a self-styled sorcerer with high connections at Court. The Mobb had convinced themselves that Lambe had conjured up a recent thunderstorm and tornado that had scraped the dirt from graves of some chaps who had perished in the last round of Plague. Not wishing to end up in Lambe's position, Enoch had tried to develop the knack of edging around people's perceptions like one of those dreams that does not set itself firmly in memory, and is flushed into oblivion by the first thoughts and sensations of the day.

He'd stayed a week or two in Wilkins's chambers, and attended meetings of the Experimental Philosophical Clubb. This had been a revelation to him, for during the Civil War, practically nothing had been heard out of England. The savants of Leipzig, Paris, and Amsterdam had begun to think of it as a rock in the high Atlantic, overrun by heavily armed preachers.

Gazing out Wilkins's windows, studying the northbound traffic, Enoch had been surprised by the number of private traders: adventuresome merchants, taking advantage of the cessation of the Civil War to travel into the country and deal with farmers in the country, buying their produce for less than what it would bring in a city market. They mostly had a Puritan look about them, and Enoch did not especially want to ride in their company. So he'd waited for a full moon and a cloudless night and ridden up to Grantham in the night, arriving before daybreak.

THE FRONT OF CLARKE'S HOUSE was tidy, which told Enoch that Mrs. Clarke was still alive. He led his horse round into the stable-yard. Scattered about were cracked mortars and crucibles, stained yellow and vermilion and silver. A columnar furnace, smoke-stained, reigned over coal-piles. It was littered with rinds of hardened dross raked off the tops of crucibles—the fœces of certain alchemical processes, mingled on this ground with the softer excrement of horses and geese.

Clarke backed out his side-door embracing a brimming chamber-pot.

"Save it up," Enoch said, his voice croaky from not having been used in a day or two, "you can extract much that's interesting from urine."

The apothecary startled, and upon recognizing Enoch he nearly dropped the pot, then caught it, then wished he had dropped it, since these evolutions had set up a complex and dangerous sloshing that must be countervailed by gliding about in a bent-knee gait, melting foot-shaped holes in the frost on the grass, and, as a last resort, tilting the pot when whitecaps were observed. The roosters of Grantham, Lincolnshire, who had slept through Enoch's arrival, came awake and began to celebrate Clarke's performance.

The sun had been rolling along the horizon for hours, like a fat waterfowl making its takeoff run. Well before full daylight, Enoch was inside the apothecary's shop, brewing up a potion from boiled water and an exotic Eastern herb. "Take an amount that will fill the cup of your palm, and throw it in—"

"The water turns brown already!"

"—remove it from the fire or it will be intolerably bitter. I'll require a strainer."

"Do you mean to suggest I'm expected to taste it?"

"Not just *taste* but *drink*. Don't look so condemned. I've done it for months with no effect."

"Other than *addiction,* t'would seem."

"You are too suspicious. The Mahrattas drink it to the exclusion of all else."

"So I'm right about the addiction!"

"It is nothing more than a mild stimulant."

"Mmm . . . not all that bad," Clarke said later, sipping cautiously. "What ailments does it cure?"

"None whatsoever."

"Ah. That's different, then . . . what's it called?"

"*Cha,* or *chai,* or *the,* or *tay.* I know a Dutch merchant who has several tons of it sitting in a warehouse in Amsterdam . . ."

Clarke chuckled. "Oh, no, Enoch, I'll not be drawn into some foreign trading scheme. This tay is inoffensive enough, but I don't think Englishmen will ever take to anything so outlandish."

"Very well, then—we'll speak of other commodities." And, setting down his tay-cup, Enoch reached into his saddle-bags and brought out bags of yellow sulfur he'd collected from a burning mountain in Italy, finger-sized ingots of antimony, heavy flasks of quicksilver, tiny clay crucibles and melting-pots, retorts, spirit-burners, and books with woodcuts showing the design of diverse furnaces. He set them up on the deal tables and counters of the apothecary shop, saying a few words about each one. Clarke stood to one side with his fingers laced together, partly for warmth, and partly just to contain himself from lunging toward the goods. Years had gone by, a Civil War had been prosecuted, and a King's head had rolled in Charing Cross since Clarke had touched some of these items. He imagined that the Continental adepts had been penetrating the innermost secrets of God's creation the entire time. But Enoch knew that the alchemists of Europe were men just like Clarke—hoping, and dreading, that Enoch would return with the news that some English savant, working in isolation, had found the trick of refining, from the base, dark, cold, essentially fœcal matter of which the World was made, the Philosophick Mercury— the pure living essence of God's power and presence in the world—the key to the transmutation of metals, the attainment of immortal life and perfect wisdom.

Enoch was less a merchant than a messenger. The sulfur and antimony he brought as favors. He accepted money in order to pay for his expenses. The important cargo was in his mind. He and Clarke talked for hours.

Sleepy thumping, footfalls, and piping voices sounded from the attic. The staircase boomed and groaned like a ship in a squall. A maid lit a fire and cooked porridge. Mrs. Clarke roused herself and served it to children—too many of them. "Has it been that long?" Enoch asked, listening to their chatter from the next room, trying to tally the voices.

Clarke said, "They're not ours."

"Boarders?"

"Some of the local yeomen send their young ones to my brother's school. We have room upstairs, and my wife is fond of children."

"Are you?"

"Some more than others."

The young boarders dispatched their porridge and mobbed the exit. Enoch drifted over to a window: a lattice of hand-sized, diamond-shaped panes, each pane greenish, warped, and bubbled. Each pane was a prism, so the sun showered the room with rainbows. The children showed as pink mottles, sliding and leaping from one pane to another, sometimes breaking up and recombining like beads of mercury on a tabletop. But this was simply an exaggeration of how children normally looked to Enoch.

One of them, slight and fair-haired, stopped squarely before the window and turned to peer through it. He must have had more acute senses than the others, because he knew that Mr. Clarke had a visitor this morning. Perhaps he'd heard the low murmur of their conversation, or detected an unfamiliar whinny from the stable. Perhaps he was an insomniac who had been studying Enoch through a chink in the wall as Enoch had strolled around the stable-yard before dawn. The boy cupped his hands around his face to block out peripheral sunlight. It seemed that those hands were splashed with colors. From one of them dangled some kind of little project, a toy or weapon made of string.

Then another boy called to him and he spun about, too eagerly, and darted away like a sparrow.

"I'd best be going," Enoch said, not sure why. "Our

brethren in Cambridge must know by now that I've been in Oxford—they'll be frantic." With steely politeness he turned aside Clarke's amiable delaying-tactics, declining the offer of porridge, postponing the suggestion that they pray together, insisting that he really needed no rest until he reached Cambridge.

His horse had had only a few hours to feed and doze. Enoch had borrowed it from Wilkins with the implicit promise to treat it kindly, and so rather than mounting into the saddle he led it by the reins down Grantham's high street and in the direction of the school, chatting to it.

He caught sight of the boarders soon enough. They had found stones that needed kicking, dogs that needed fellowship, and a few late apples, still dangling from tree-branches. Enoch lingered in the long shadow of a stone wall and watched the apple project. Some planning had gone into it—a whispered conference between bunks last night. One of the boys had clambered up into the tree and was shinnying out onto the limb in question. It was too slender to bear his weight, but he phant'sied he could bend it low enough to bring it within the tallest boy's jumping-range.

The little fair-haired boy adored the tall boy's fruitless jumping. But he was working on his own project, the same one Enoch had glimpsed through the window: a stone on the end of a string. Not an easy thing to make. He whirled the stone around and flung it upwards. It whipped around the end of the tree-branch. By pulling it down he was able to bring the apple within easy reach. The tall boy stood aside grudgingly, but the fair boy kept both hands on that string, and insisted that the tall one have it as a present. Enoch almost groaned aloud when he saw the infatuation on the little boy's face.

The tall boy's face was less pleasant to look at. He hungered for the apple but suspected a trick. Finally he lashed out and snatched it. Finding the prize in his hand, he looked searchingly at the fair boy, trying to understand his motives, and became unsettled and sullen. He took a bite of the apple as the other watched with almost physical satisfaction. The boy who'd shinnied out onto the tree-limb had come down, and now managed to tease the string off the branch. He examined the way it was tied to the stone and decided that suspicion was the safest course. "A pretty lace-maker you are!" he piped. But the fair-haired boy had eyes only for his beloved.

Then the tall boy spat onto the ground, and tossed the rest of the apple over a fence into a yard where a couple of pigs fought over it.

Now it became unbearable for a while, and made Enoch wish he had never followed them.

The two stupid boys dogged the other one down the road, wide eyes traveling up and down his body, seeing him now for the first time—seeing a little of what Enoch saw. Enoch heard snatches of their taunts—"What's on your hands? What'd you say? Paint!? For what? Pretty pictures? What'd you say? For furniture? I haven't seen any furniture. Oh, *doll* furniture!?"

Being a sooty empiric, what was important to Enoch was not these tedious details of specifically *how* the boy's heart got broken. He went to the apple tree to have a look at the boy's handiwork.

The boy had imprisoned the stone in a twine net: two sets of helices, one climbing clockwise, the other anti-clockwise, intersecting each other in a pattern of diamonds, just like the lead net that held Clarke's window together. Enoch didn't suppose that this was a coincidence. The work was irregular at the start, but by the time he'd completed the first row of knots the boy had learned to take into account the length of twine spent in making the knots themselves, and by the time he reached the end, it was as regular as the precession of the zodiac.

Enoch then walked briskly to the school and arrived in time to watch the inevitable fight. The fair boy was red-eyed and had porridge-vomit on his chin—it was safe to assume he'd been punched in the stomach. Another schoolboy—

there was one in every school—seemed to have appointed himself master of ceremonies, and was goading them to action, paying most attention to the smaller boy, the injured party and presumed loser-to-be of the fight. To the surprise and delight of the community of young scholars, the smaller boy stepped forward and raised his fists.

Enoch approved, so far. Some pugnacity in the lad would be useful. Talent was not rare; the ability to survive having it was.

Then combat was joined. Not many punches were thrown. The small boy did something clever, down around the tall boy's knees, that knocked him back on his arse. Almost immediately the little boy's knee was in the other's groin, then in the pit of his stomach, and then on his throat. And then, suddenly, the tall boy was struggling to get up—but only because the fair-haired boy was trying to rip both of his ears off. Like a farmer dragging an ox by his nose-ring, the smaller boy led the bigger one over to the nearest stone wall, which happened to be that of Grantham's huge, ancient church, and then began to rub his prisoner's face against it as though trying to erase it from the skull.

Until this point the other boys had been jubilant. Even Enoch had found the early stages of the victory stirring in a way. But as this torture went on, the boys' faces went slack. Many of them turned and ran away. The fair-haired boy had flown into a state of something like ecstasy—groping and flailing like a man nearing erotic climax, his body an insufficient vehicle for his passions, a dead weight impeding the flowering of the spirit. Finally an adult man—Clarke's brother?—banged out through a door and stormed across the yard between school and church in the tottering gait of a man unaccustomed to having to move quickly, carrying a cane but not touching the ground with it. He was so angry that he did not utter a word, or try to separate the boys, but simply began to cut air with the cane, like a blind man fending off a bear, as he got close. Soon enough he maneuvered within range of the fair boy and planted his feet and bent to his work, the cane producing memorable whorling noises cut off by pungent whacks. A few brown-nosers now considered it safe to approach. Two of them dragged the fair boy off of his victim, who contracted into a fetal position at the base of the church wall, hands open like the covers of a book to enfold his wrecked face. The schoolmaster adjusted his azimuth as the target moved, like a telescope tracking a comet, but none of his blows seemed to have been actually felt by the fair boy yet—he wore a look of steadfast, righteous triumph, much like Enoch supposed Cromwell must have shown as he beheld the butchering of the Irish at Drogheda.

The boy was dragged inside for higher punishments. Enoch rode back to Clarke's apothecary shop, reining in a silly urge to gallop through the town like a Cavalier.

Clarke was sipping tay and gnawing biscuits, already several pages into a new alchemical treatise, moving crumb-spattered lips as he solved the Latin.

"Who is he?" Enoch demanded, coming in the door.

Clarke elected to play innocent. Enoch crossed the room and found the stairs. He didn't really care about the name anyway. It would just be another English name.

The upstairs was all one odd-shaped room with low adze-marked rafters and rough plaster walls that had once been whitewashed. Enoch hadn't visited many children's rooms, but to him it seemed like a den of thieves hastily abandoned and stumbled upon by a plodding constable, filled with evidence of many peculiar, ingenious, frequently unwise plots and machinations suddenly cut short. He stopped in the doorway and steadied himself. Like a good empiric, he had to see all and alter nothing.

The walls were marked with what his eyes first took to be the grooves left behind by a careless plasterer's trowel, but as his pupils dilated, he understood that Mr. and Mrs. Clarke's boarders had been drawing on the walls, apparently with bits of charcoal fetched out of the grate. It was plain to see which pictures had been drawn by whom. Most were caricatures learned by rote from slightly older children. Others—generally closer to the floor—were maps of insight, manifestoes of intelligence, always precise, sometimes beautiful. Enoch had been right in supposing that the boy had excellent senses. Things that others did not see at all, or chose not to register out of some kind of mental obstinacy, this boy took in avidly.

There were four tiny beds. The litter of toys on the floor was generally boyish, but over by one bed there was a tendency toward ribbons and frills. Clarke had mentioned one of the boarders was a girl. There was a dollhouse and a clan of rag dolls in diverse phases of ontogeny. Here there'd been a meeting of interests. There was doll furniture ingeniously made by the same regular mind and clever hands that had woven the net round the stone. The boy had made stalks of grass into rattan tables, and willow twigs into rocking-chairs. The alchemist in him had been at work copying recipes from that old corrupter of curious youths, Bates's *The Mysteries of Nature & Art,* extracting pigments from plants and formulating paints.

He had tried to draw sketches of the other boys while they were sleeping—the only time they could be relied on to hold still and not behave abominably. He did not yet have the skill to make a regular portrait, but from time to time the Muse would take hold of his hand, and in a fortunate sweep of the arm he'd capture something beautiful in the curve of a jaw-bone or an eyelash.

There were broken and dismantled parts of machines that Enoch did not understand. Later, though, perusing the notebook where the boy had been copying out recipes, Enoch found sketches of the hearts of rats and birds that the boy had apparently dissected. Then the little machines made sense. For what was the heart but the model for the perpetual motion machine? And what was the perpetual motion machine but Man's attempt to make a thing that would do what the heart did? To harness the heart's occult power and bend it to use.

The apothecary had joined him in the room. Clarke

looked nervous. "You're up to something clever, aren't you?" Enoch said.

"By that, do you mean—"

"He came your way by chance?"

"Not precisely. His mother knows my wife. I had seen the boy."

"And seen that he had promise—as how could you not."

"He lacks a father. I made a recommendation to the mother. She is steady. Intermittently decent. Quasi-literate . . ."

"But too thick to know what she has begotten?"

"Oh my, yes."

"So you took the boy under your wing—and if he's shown some interest in the Art you have not discouraged it."

"Of course not! He could be the one, Enoch."

"He's not the one," Enoch said. "Not the one you are thinking of. Oh, he will be a great empiricist. He will, perhaps, be the one to accomplish some great thing we have never imagined."

"Enoch, what can you possibly be talking about?"

It made his head ache. How was he to explain it without making Clarke out to be a fool, and himself a swindler? "Something is happening."

Clarke pursed his lips and waited for something a little more specific.

"Galileo and Descartes were only harbingers. Something is happening now—the mercury is rising in the ground, like water climbing up the bore of a well."

Enoch couldn't get Oxford out of his mind—Hooke and Wren and Boyle, all exchanging thoughts so quickly that flames practically leaped between them. He decided to try another tack. "There's a boy in Leipzig like this one. Father died recently, leaving him nothing except a vast library. The boy began reading those books. Only six years old."

"It's not unheard-of for six-year-olds to read."

"German, Latin, and Greek?"

"With proper instruction—"

"That's just it. The boy's teachers prevailed on the mother

to lock the child out of the library. I got wind of it. Talked to the mother, and secured a promise from her that little Gottfried would be allowed free run of the books. He taught himself Latin and Greek in the space of a year."

Clarke shrugged. "Very well. Perhaps little Gottfried is the one."

Enoch then should've known it was hopeless, but he tried again: "We are empiricists—we scorn the Scholastic way of memorizing old books and rejecting what is new—and that is good. But in pinning our hopes on the Philosophick Mercury we have decided in advance what it is that we seek to discover, and that is never right."

This merely made Clarke nervous. Enoch tried yet another tack: "I have in my saddlebags a copy of *Principia Philosophica,* the last thing Descartes wrote before he died. Dedicated to young Elizabeth, the Winter Queen's daughter . . ."

Clarke was straining to look receptive, like a dutiful university student still intoxicated from last night's recreations at the tavern. Enoch remembered the stone on the string, and decided to aim for something more concrete. "Huygens has made a clock that is regulated by a pendulum."

"Huygens?"

"A young Dutch savant. Not an alchemist."

"Oh!"

"He has worked out a way to make a pendulum that will always go back and forth in the same amount of time. By connecting it to the internal workings of a clock, he has wrought a perfectly regular time-piece. Its ticks divide infinity, as calipers step out leagues on a map. With these two— clock and calipers—we can measure both extent and duration. And this, combined with the new method of analysis of Descartes, gives us a way to describe Creation and perhaps to predict the future."

"Ah, I see!" Clarke said. "So this Huygens—he is some kind of astrologer?"

"No, no, no! He is neither astrologer nor alchemist. He is something new. More like him will follow. Wilkins, down in

Oxford, is trying to bring them together. Their achievements may exceed those of alchemists." If they did not, Enoch thought, he'd be chagrined. "I am suggesting to you that this little boy may turn out to be another one like Huygens."

"You want me to steer him away from the Art?" Clarke exclaimed.

"Not if he shows interest. But beyond that do not steer him at all—let him pursue his own conclusions." Enoch looked at the faces and diagrams on the wall, noting some rather good perspective work. "And see to it that mathematics is brought to his attention."

"I do not think that he has the temperament to be a mere computer," Clarke warned. "Sitting at his pages day after day, drudging out tables of logarithms, cube roots, cosines—"

"Thanks to Descartes, there are other uses for mathematics now," Enoch said. "Tell your brother to show the boy Euclid and let him find his own way."

THE CONVERSATION MIGHT NOT HAVE gone precisely this way. Enoch had the same way with his memories as a ship's master with his rigging—a compulsion to tighten what was slack, mend what was frayed, caulk what leaked, and stow, or throw overboard, what was to no purpose. So the conversation with Clarke might have wandered into quite a few more blind alleys than he remembered. A great deal of time was probably spent on politeness. Certainly it took up most of that short autumn day. Because Enoch didn't ride out of Grantham until late. He passed by the school one more time on his way down towards Cambridge. All the boys had gone home by that hour save one, who'd been made to stay behind and, as punishment, scrub and scrape his own name off the various windowsills and chair-backs where he'd inscribed it. These infractions had probably been noticed by Clarke's brother, who had saved them up for the day when the child would need particular discipline.

The sun, already low at mid-afternoon, was streaming into the open windows. Enoch drew up along the northwest side of the school so that anyone who looked back at him would see only a long hooded shadow, and watched the boy work for a while. The sun was crimson in the boy's face, which was ruddy to begin with from his exertions with the scrub-brush. Far from being reluctant, he seemed enthusiastic about the job of erasing all traces of himself from the school—as if the tumbledown place was unworthy to bear his mark. One windowsill after another came under him and was wiped clean of the name I. NEWTON.

Newtowne, Massachusetts Bay Colony

OCTOBER 12, 1713

> How are these Colonies of the *English* increas'd and improv'd, even to such a Degree, that some have suggested, tho' not for Want of Ignorance, a Danger of their revolting from the *English* Government, and setting up an Independency of Power for themselves. It is true, the Notion is absurd, and without Foundation, but serves to confirm what I have said above of the real Encrease of those Colonies, and of the flourishing Condition of the Commerce carried on there.
>
> —DANIEL DEFOE, *A Plan of the English Commerce*

SOMETIMES IT SEEMS AS IF *everyone's* immigrating to America—sailing-ships on the North Atlantic as thick as watermen's boats on the Thames, more or less wearing ruts in the sea-lanes—and so, in an idle way, Enoch supposes that his appearance on the threshold of the Massachusetts Bay Colony Institute of Technologickal Arts will come as no surprise at all to its founder. But Daniel Waterhouse nearly swallows his teeth when Enoch walks through the door, and it's not just because the hem of Enoch's cloak knocks over a great teetering stack of cards. For a moment Enoch's afraid that some sort of apoplectic climax is in progress, and that Dr. Waterhouse's final contribution to the Royal Society, after nearly a lifetime of service, will be a traumatically deranged cardiac muscle, pickled in spirits of wine in a crystal jug. The Doctor spends the first minute of their interview frozen halfway between sitting and standing, with his mouth open and his left hand on his breastbone. This might be the beginnings of a courteous bow, or a hasty maneuver to conceal, beneath his coat, a shirt so work-stained as to cast aspersions on his young wife's diligence. Or perhaps it's a *philosophick* enquiry, viz. checking his own pulse—if so, it's good news, because Sir John Floyer just invented the practice, and if Daniel Waterhouse knows of it, it means he's been keeping up with the latest work out of London.

Enoch takes advantage of the lull to make other observations and try to judge empirically whether Daniel's as unsound as the faculty of Harvard College would have him believe. From the Doctors' jibes on the ferry-ride, Enoch had expected nothing but cranks and gears. And indeed Waterhouse does have a mechanic's shop in a corner of the—how will Enoch characterize this structure to the Royal Society? "Log cabin," while technically correct, calls to mind wild men in skins. "Sturdy, serviceable, and in no way extravagant laboratory making ingenious use of indigenous building materials." There. But anyway, most of it is given over not to the hard ware of gears, but to softer matters: cards. They are stacked in slender columns that would totter in the breeze from a moth's wings if the columns had not been jammed together into banks, stairways, and terraces,

the whole formation built on a layer of loose tiles on the dirt
floor to (Enoch guesses) prevent the card-stacks from wick-
ing up the copious ground-water. Edging farther into the
room and peering round a bulwark of card-stacks, Enoch
finds a writing-desk stocked with blank cards. Ragged gray
quills project from inkpots, bent and broken ones crosshatch
the floor, bits of down and fluff and cartilage and other bird-
wreckage form a dandruffy layer on everything.

On pretext of cleaning up his mess, Enoch begins to pick
the spilled cards off the floor. Each is marked at the top with
a rather large number, always odd, and beneath it a long row
of ones and zeroes, which (since the last digit is always 1, in-
dicating an odd number) he takes to be nothing other then
the selfsame number expressed in the binary notation lately
perfected by Leibniz. Underneath the number, then, is a
word or short phrase, a different one on each card. As he
picks them up and re-stacks them he sees: *Noah's Ark;
Treaties terminating wars; Membranophones (e.g., mirli-
tons); The notion of a classless society; The pharynx and its
outgrowths; Drawing instruments (e.g., T-squares); The
Skepticism of Pyrrhon of Elis; Requirements for valid mar-
itime insurance contracts; The Kamakura* bakufu; *The fal-
lacy of Assertion without Knowledge; Agates; Rules
governing the determination of questions of fact in Roman
civil courts; Mummification; Sunspots; The sex organs of
bryophytes (e.g., liverwort); Euclidean geometry—homo-
theties and similitudes; Pantomime; The Election & Reign
of Rudolf of Hapsburg; Testes; Nonsymmetrical dyadic relations; the Investiture Controversy; Phosphorus; Traditional impotence remedies; the Arminian heresy;* and—

"Some of these strike one as being too complicated for
monads," he says, desperate for some way to break the ice.
"Such as this—'The Development of Portuguese Hegemony
over Central Africa.'"

"Look at the number at the top of that card," Waterhouse
says. "It is the product of five primes: one for *development,*

one for *Portuguese,* one for *Hegemony,* one for *Central,* and one for *Africa.*"

"Ah, so it's not a monad at all, but a composite."

"Yes."

"It's difficult to tell when the cards are helter-skelter. Don't you think you should organize them?"

"According to what scheme?" Waterhouse asks shrewdly.

"Oh, no, I'll not be tricked into *that* discussion."

"No linear indexing system is adequate to express the multi-dimensionality of knowledge," Dr. Waterhouse reminds him. "But if each one is assigned a unique number—prime numbers for monads, and products of primes for composites—then organizing them is simply a matter of performing computations . . . *Mr. Root.*"

"Dr. Waterhouse. Pardon the interruption."

"Not at all." He sits back down, finally, and goes back to what he was doing before: running a long file back and forth over a chunk of metal with tremendous sneezing noises. "It is a welcome diversion to have you appear before me, so unlooked-for, so *implausibly well-preserved,*" he shouts over the keening of the warm tool and the ringing of the work-piece.

"Durability is preferable to the alternative—but not always convenient. Less hale persons are forever sending me off on errands."

"Lengthy and tedious ones at that."

"The journey's dangers, discomforts, and tedium are more than compensated for by the sight of you, so productively occupied, and in such good health." Or something like that. This is the polite part of the conversation, which is not likely to last much longer. If he had returned the compliment, Daniel would have scoffed, because no one would say he's well preserved in the sense that Enoch is. He looks as old as he ought to. But he's wiry, with clear, sky-blue eyes, no tremors in his jaw or his hands, no hesitation in his speech once he's over the shock of seeing Enoch (or, per-

haps, *anyone*) in his Institute. Daniel Waterhouse is almost
completely bald, with a fringe of white hair clamping the
back of his head like wind-hammered snow on a tree-trunk.
He makes no apologies for being uncovered and does not
reach for a wig—indeed, appears not to *own* one. His eyes
are large, wide and staring in a way that probably does nothing to improve his reputation. Those orbs flank a hawkish
nose that nearly conceals the slot-like mouth of a miser biting down on a suspect coin. His ears are elongated and have
grown a radiant fringe of lanugo. The imbalance between his
organs of input and output seems to say that he sees and
knows more than he'll say.

"Are you a colonist now, or—"

"I'm here to see you."

The eyes stare back, knowing and calm. "So it is a social
visit! That is heroic—when a simple exchange of letters is
so much less fraught with seasickness, pirates, scurvy, mass
drownings—"

"Speaking of letters—I've one here," Enoch says, taking
it out.

"Great big magnificent seal. Someone dreadfully important must've written it. Can't say how impressed I am."

"Personal friend of Dr. Leibniz."

"The Electress Sophie?"

"No, the other one."

"Ah. What does Princess Caroline want of me? Must be
something appalling, or else she wouldn't've sent you to
chivvy me along."

Dr. Waterhouse is embarrassed at having been so startled
earlier and is making up for it with peevishness. But it's fine,
because it seems to Enoch that the thirty-year-old Waterhouse hidden inside the old man is now pressing outward
against the loose mask of skin, like a marble sculpture in-
forming its burlap wrappings.

"Think of it as coaxing you forward. Dr. Waterhouse!
Let's find a tavern and—"

"We'll find a tavern—after I've had an answer. What does she want of me?"

"The same thing as ever."

Dr. Waterhouse shrinks—the inner thirty-year-old recedes, and he becomes just an oddly familiar-looking gaffer. "Should've known. What other use is there for a broken-down old computational monadologist?"

"It's remarkable."

"What?"

"I've known you for—what—thirty or forty years now, almost as long as you've known Leibniz. I've seen you in some unenviable spots. But in all that time, I don't believe I've ever heard you whine, until just then."

Daniel considers this carefully, then actually laughs. "My apologies."

"Not at all!"

"I thought my work would be appreciated here. I was going to establish what, to Harvard, would've been what Gresham's College was to Oxford. Imagined I'd find a student body, or at least a protégé. Someone who could help me build the Logic Mill. Hasn't worked out that way. All of the mechanically talented sorts are dreaming of steam-engines. Ludicrous! What's wrong with water-wheels? Plenty of rivers here. Look, there's a little one right between your feet!"

"Engines are naturally more interesting to the young."

"You needn't tell me. When I was a student, a *prism* was a wonder. Went to Sturbridge Fair with Isaac to buy them—little miracles wrapped in velvet. Played with 'em for months."

"This fact is now widely known."

"Now the lads are torn every direction at once, like a prisoner being quartered. Or eighthed, or sixteenthed. I can already see it happening to young Ben out there, and soon it'll happen to my own boy. 'Should I study mathematics? Euclidean or Cartesian? Newtonian or Leibnizian calculus? Or should I go the empirical route? Will it be dissecting animals

then, or classifying weeds, or making strange matters in crucibles? Rolling balls down inclined planes? Sporting with
electricity and magnets?' Against that, what's in my shack
here to interest them?"

"Could this lack of interest have something to do with that
everyone knows the project was conceived by Leibniz?"

"I'm not doing it his way. His plan was to use balls running down troughs to represent the binary digits, and pass
them through mechanical gates to perform the logical operations. Ingenious, but not very practical. I'm using pushrods."

"Superficial. I ask again: could your lack of popularity
here be related to that all Englishmen believe that Leibniz is
a villain—a plagiarist?"

"This is an unnatural turn in the conversation, Mr. Root.
Are you being devious?"

"Only a little."

"You and your Continental ways."

"It's just that the priority dispute has lately turned vi-
cious."

"Knew it would happen."

"I don't think you appreciate just how unpleasant it is."

"You don't appreciate how well I know Sir Isaac."

"I'm saying that its repercussions may extend to here, to
this very room, and might account for your (forgive me for
mentioning this) solitude, and slow progress."

"Ludicrous!"

"Have you seen the latest flying letters, speeding about
Europe unsigned, undated, devoid of even a printer's mark?
The anonymous reviews, planted, like sapper's mines, in the
journals of the savants? Sudden unmaskings of hitherto un-
named 'leading mathematicians' forced to own, or deny,
opinions they have long disseminated in private correspondence? Great minds who, in any other era, would be making
discoveries of Copernican significance, reduced to acting as
cat's-paws and hired leg-breakers for the two principals?
New and deservedly obscure journals suddenly elevated to
the first rank of learned discourse, simply because some

lackey has caused his latest stiletto-thrust to be printed in its back pages? Challenge problems flying back and forth across the Channel, each one fiendishly devised to prove that Leibniz's calculus is the original, and Newton's but a shoddy counterfeit, or vice versa? Reputations tossed about on points of swords—"

"No," Daniel says. "I moved here to get away from European intrigues." His eyes drop to the Letter. Enoch can't help looking at it, too.

"It is purely an anomaly of fate," Enoch says, "that Gottfried, as a young man, lacking means, seeking a position—anything that would give him the simple freedom to work—landed in the court of an obscure German Duke. Who through intricate and tedious lacework of marryings, couplings, dyings, religious conversions, wars, revolutions, miscarriages, decapitations, congenital feeble-mindedness, excommunications, *et cetera* among Europe's elite—most notably, the deaths of all seventeen of Queen Anne's children—became first in line to the Throne of England and Scotland, or Great Britain as we're supposed to call it now."

"*Some* would call it fate. Others—"

"Let's not get into *that*."

"Agreed."

"Anne's in miserable health, the House of Hanover is packing up its pointed helmets and illustrated beer-mugs, and taking English lessons. Sophie may get to be Queen of England yet, at least for a short while. But soon enough, George Louis will become Newton's King and—as Sir Isaac is still at the Mint—his boss."

"I take your point. It is most awkward."

"George Louis is the embodiment of awkwardness—he doesn't care, and scarcely knows, and would probably think it amusing if he did. But his daughter-in-law the Princess—author of this letter—in time likely to become Queen of England herself—is a friend of Leibniz. And yet an admirer of Newton. She wants a reconciliation."

"She wants a dove to fly between the Pillars of Hercules. Which are still runny with the guts of the previous several peace-makers."

"It's supposed that you are different."

"Herculean, perhaps?"

"Well . . ."

"Do you have any idea why I'm different, Mr. Root?"

"I do not, Dr. Waterhouse."

"The tavern it is, then."

BEN AND GODFREY ARE SENT back to Boston on the ferry. Daniel scorns the nearest tavern—some sort of long-running dispute with the proprietor—so they find the highway and ride northwest for a couple of miles, drawing off to one side from time to time to let drovers bring their small herds of Boston-bound cattle through. They arrive at what used to be the capital of Massachusetts, before the city fathers of Boston out-maneuvered it. Several roads lunge out of the wilderness and collide with one another. Yeomen and drovers and backwoodsmen churn it up into a vortex of mud and manure. Next to it is a College. Newtowne is, in other words, paradise for tavern-keepers, and the square (as they style it) is lined with public houses.

Waterhouse enters a tavern but immediately backs out of it. Looking into the place over his companion's shoulder, Enoch glimpses a white-wigged Judge on a massive chair at the head of the tap-room, a jury empaneled on plank benches, a grimy rogue being interrogated. "Not a good place for a pair of idlers," Waterhouse mumbles.

"You hold *judicial proceedings* in *drinking-houses*!?"

"Poh! That judge is no more drunk than any magistrate of the Old Bailey."

"It is perfectly logical when you put it that way."

Daniel chooses another tavern. They walk through its brick-red door. A couple of leather fire-buckets dangle by the entrance, in accordance with safety regulations, and a bootjack hangs on the wall so that the innkeeper can take his guests' footwear hostage at night. The proprietor is bastioned in a little wooden fort in the corner, bottles on shelves behind him, a preposterous firearm, at least six feet long, leaning in the angle of the walls. He's busy sorting his customers' mail. Enoch cannot believe the size of the planks that make up the floor. They creak and pop like ice on a frozen lake as people move around. Waterhouse leads him to a table. It consists of a single slab of wood sawn from the heart of a tree that must have been at least three feet in diameter.

"Trees such as these have not been seen in Europe for hundreds of years," Enoch says. He measures it against the length of his arm. "Should have gone straight to Her Majesty's Navy. I am shocked."

"There is an exemption to that rule," Waterhouse says, showing for the first time a bit of good humor. "If a tree is blown down by the wind, anyone may salvage it. In consequence of which, Gomer Bolstrood, and his fellow Barkers, have built their colonies in remote places, where the trees are very large—"

"And where freak hurricanoes often strike without warning?"

"And without being noticed by any of their neighbors. Yes."

"Firebrands to furniture-makers in a single generation. I wonder what old Knott would think."

"Firebrands *and* furniture-makers," Waterhouse corrects him.

"Ah, well . . . If my name were Bolstrood, I'd be happy to live anywhere that was beyond the reach of Tories and Archbishops."

Daniel Waterhouse rises and goes over to the fireplace, plucks a couple of loggerheads from their hooks, and thrusts them angrily into the coals. Then he goes to the corner and speaks with the tavern-keeper, who cracks two eggs into two

mugs and then begins throwing in rum and bitters and molasses. It is sticky and complicated—as is the entire situation
here that Enoch's gotten himself into.

There's a similar room on the other side of the wall, re-
served for the ladies. Spinning wheels whirr, cards chafe
against wool. Someone begins tuning up a bowed instrument. Not the old-fashioned viol, but (judging from its
sound) a violin. Hard to believe, considering where he is.
But then the musician begins to play—and instead of a
Baroque minuet, it is a weird keening sort of melody—an
Irish tune, unless he's mistaken. It's like using watered silk
to make grain sacks—the Londoners would laugh until tears
ran down their faces. Enoch goes and peers through the
doorway to make sure he's not imagining it. Indeed, a girl
with carrot-colored hair is playing a violin, entertaining
some other women who are spinning and sewing, and the
women and the music are as Irish as the day is long.

Enoch goes back to the table, shaking his head. Daniel
Waterhouse slides a hot loggerhead into each mug, warming
and thickening the drinks. Enoch sits down, takes a sip of
the stuff, and decides he likes it. Even the music is beginning
to grow on him.

He cannot look in any direction without seeing eyeballs
just in the act of glancing away from them. Some of the
other patrons actually run down the road to *other* taverns to
advertise their presence here, as if Root and Waterhouse
were a public entertainment. Dons and students saunter in
nonchalantly, as if it's normal to stand up in mid-pint and
move along to a different establishment.

"Where'd you get the idea you were escaping from intrigue?"

Daniel ignores this, too busy glaring at the other customers.

"My father, Drake, educated me for one reason alone,"
Daniel finally says. "To assist him in his preparations for the
Apocalypse. He reckoned it would occur in the year 1666—

Number of the Beast and all that. I was, therefore, produced in 1646—as always, Drake's timing was carefully thought out. When I came of age, I would be a man of the cloth, with the full university education, well versed in many dead classical languages, so that I could stand on the Cliffs of Dover and personally welcome Jesus Christ back to England in fluent Aramaic. Sometimes I look about myself—" he waves his arm at the tavern "—and see the way it turned out, and wonder whether my father could possibly have been any more wrong."

"I think this is a good place for you," Enoch says. "Nothing here is going according to plan. The music. The furniture. It's all contrary to expectations."

"My father and I took in the execution of Hugh Peters—Cromwell's chaplain—in London one day. We rode straight from that spectacle to Cambridge. Since executions are customarily held at daybreak, you see, an industrious Puritan can view one and yet get in a full day's hard traveling and working before evening prayers. It was done with a knife. Drake wasn't shaken at all by the sight of Brother Hugh's intestines. It only made him that much more determined to get me into Cambridge. We went there and called upon Wilkins at Trinity College."

"Hold, my memory fails—wasn't Wilkins at *Oxford*? Wadham College?"

"Anno 1656 he married Robina. Cromwell's sister."

"*That* I remember."

"Cromwell made him Master of Trinity College in Cambridge. But of course that was undone by the Restoration. So he only served in that post for a few months—it's no wonder you've forgotten it."

"Very well. Pardon the interruption. Drake took you up to Cambridge—?"

"And we called on Wilkins. I was fourteen. Father went off and left us alone, secure in the knowledge that this man—Cromwell's Brother-in-Law, for God's sake!—would lead me down the path of righteousness—perhaps explicate some Bible verses about nine-headed beasts with me, perhaps pray for Hugh Peters."

"You did neither, I presume."

"You must imagine a great chamber in Trinity, a gothickal stone warren, like the underbelly of some ancient cathedral, ancient tables scattered about, stained and burnt alchemically, beakers and retorts clouded with residues pungent and bright, but most of all, *the books*—brown wads stacked like cordwood—more books than I'd ever seen in one room. It was a decade or two since Wilkins had written his great *Cryptonomicon.* In the course of that project, he had, of course, gathered tomes on occult writing from all over the world, compiling all that had been known, since the time of the Ancients, about the writing of secrets. The publication of that book had brought him fame among those who study such things. Copies were known to have circulated as far as Peking, Lima, Isfahan, Shahjahanabad. Consequently more books *yet* had been sent to him, from Portuguese crypto-Kabbalists, Arabic savants skulking through the ruins and ashes of Alexandria, Parsees who secretly worship at the altar of Zoroaster, Armenian merchants who must communicate all across the world, in a kind of net-work of information, through subtle signs and symbols hidden in the margins and the ostensible text of letters so cleverly that a competitor, intercepting the message, could examine it and find nothing but trivial chatter—yet a fellow-Armenian could extract the vital *data* as easy as you or I would read a hand-bill in the street. Secret code-systems of Mandarins, too, who because of their Chinese writing cannot use cyphers as we do, but must hide messages in the position of characters on the sheet, and other means so devious that whole lifetimes must have gone into thinking of them. All of these things had come to him because of the fame of the *Cryptonomicon,* and to appreciate my position, you must understand that I'd been raised, by Drake and Knott and the others, to believe that every word and character of these books was Satanic. That, if I were to so much as lift the cover of one of these books, and expose my eyes to the occult characters within, I'd be sucked down into Tophet just like that."

"I can see it made quite an impression on you—"

"Wilkins let me sit in a chair for half an hour just to soak the place in. Then we began mucking about in his chambers, and set fire to a tabletop. Wilkins was reading some proofs of Boyle's *The Skeptical Chemist*—you should read it sometime, Enoch, by the way—"

"I'm familiar with its contents."

"Wilkins and I were idly trying to reproduce one of Boyle's experiments when things got out of hand. Fortunately no serious damage was done. It wasn't a serious fire, but it accomplished what Wilkins wanted it to: wrecked the mask of etiquette that Drake had set over me, and set my tongue a-run. I must have looked as if I'd gazed upon the face of God. Wilkins let slip that, if it was an actual *education* I was looking for, there was this thing down in London called Gresham's College where he and a few of his old Oxford cronies were teaching Natural Philosophy *directly,* without years and years of tedious Classical nincompoopery as prerequisite.

"Now, I was too young to even think of being devious. Even had I practiced to be clever, I'd have had second thoughts doing it in *that* room. So I simply told Wilkins the truth: I had no interest in religion, at least as a profession, and wanted only to be a natural philosopher like Boyle or Huygens. But of course Wilkins had already discerned this. 'Leave it in my hands,' he said, and winked at me.

"Drake would not hear of sending me to Gresham's, so two years later I enrolled at that old vicar-mill: Trinity College, Cambridge. Father believed that I did so in fulfillment of his plan for me. Wilkins meanwhile had come up with his own plan for my life. And so you see, Enoch, I am well accustomed to others devising hare-brained plans for how I am to live. That is why I have come to Massachusetts, and why I do not intend to leave it."

"Your intentions are your own business. I merely ask that you read the letter," Enoch says.

"What sudden event caused you to be sent here, Enoch? A falling-out between Sir Isaac and a young protégé?"

"Remarkable guesswork!"

"It's no more a guess than when Halley predicted the return of the comet. Newton's bound by his own laws. He's been working on the second edition of the *Principia* with that young fellow, what's-his-name . . ."

"Roger Cotes."

"Promising, fresh-faced young lad, is he?"

"Fresh-faced, beyond doubt," Enoch says, "promising, until . . ."

"Until he made some kind of a misstep, and Newton flew into a rage, and flung him into the Lake of Fire."

"Apparently. Now, all that Cotes was working on—the revised *Principia Mathematica* and some kind of reconciliation with Leibniz—is ruined, or at least stopped."

"Isaac never cast me into the Lake of Fire," Daniel muses. "I was so young and so obviously innocent—he could never think the worst of me, as he does of everyone else."

"Thank you for reminding me! Please." Enoch shoves the letter across the table.

Daniel breaks the seal and hauls it open. He fishes spectacles from a pocket and holds them up to his face with one hand, as if actually fitting them over his ears would imply some sort of binding commitment. At first he locks his elbow to regard the whole letter as a work of calligraphic art, admiring its graceful loops and swirls. "Thank God it's not written in those barbarous German letters," he says. Finally the elbow bends, and he gets down to actually reading it.

As he nears the bottom of the first page, a transformation comes over Daniel's face.

"As you have probably noted," Enoch says, "the Princess, fully appreciating the hazards of a trans-Atlantic voyage, has arranged an insurance policy . . ."

"A posthumous bribe!" Daniel says. "The Royal Society

is infested with actuaries and statisticians nowadays—drawing up tables for those swindlers at the 'Change. You must have 'run the numbers' and computed the odds of a man my age surviving a voyage across the Atlantic; months or even years in that pestilential metropolis; and a journey back to Boston."

"Daniel! We most certainly did not 'run the numbers.' It's only reasonable for the Princess to insure you."

"At this amount? This is a pension—a *legacy*—for my wife and my son."

"Do you have a pension now, Daniel?"

"What!? Compared to this, I have nothing." Flicking one nail angrily upon a train of zeroes inscribed in the heart of the letter.

"Then it seems as if Her Royal Highness is making a persuasive case."

Waterhouse has just, at this instant, realized that very soon he is going to climb aboard ship and sail for London. That much can be read from his face. But he's still an hour or two away from admitting it. They will be difficult hours for Enoch.

"Even without the insurance policy," Enoch says, "it would be in your best interests. Natural philosophy, like war and romance, is best done by young men. Sir Isaac has not done any creative work since he had that mysterious catastrophe in '93."

"It's not mysterious to *me*."

"Since then, it's been toiling at the Mint, and working up new versions of old books, and vomiting flames at Leibniz."

"And you are advising me to emulate *that*?"

"I am advising you to put down the file, pack up your cards, step back from the workbench, and consider the future of the revolution."

"What revolution can you possibly be talking about? There was the Glorious one back in '88, and people are nattering on about throwing one here, but . . ."

"Don't be disingenuous, Daniel. You speak and think in a

language that did not exist when you and Sir Isaac entered Trinity."

"Fine, fine. If you want to call it a revolution, I won't quibble."

"That revolution is turning on itself now. The calculus dispute is becoming a schism between the natural philosophers of the Continent and those of Great Britain. The British have far more to lose. Already there's a reluctance to use Leibniz's techniques—which are now more advanced, since he actually bothered to disseminate his ideas. Your difficulties in starting the Massachusetts Bay Colony Institute of Technologickal Arts are a symptom of the same ailment. So do not lurk on the fringes of civilization trifling with cards and cranks, Dr. Waterhouse. Return to the core, look at first causes, heal the central wound. If you can accomplish that, why, then, by the time your son is of an age to become a student, the Institute will no longer be a log cabin sinking into the mire, but a campus of domed pavilions and many-chambered laboratories along the banks of the River Charles, where the most ingenious youth of America will convene to study and refine the art of automatic computation!"

Dr. Waterhouse is favoring him with a look of bleak pity usually directed toward uncles too far gone to know they are incontinent. "Or at least I might catch a fever and die three days from now and provide Faith and Godfrey with a comfortable pension."

"There's that added inducement."

To be a European Christian (the rest of the world might be forgiven for thinking) was to build ships and sail them to any and all coasts not already a-bristle with cannons, make landfall at river's mouth, kiss the dirt, plant a cross or a flag, scare the hell out of any indigenes with a musketry demo', and—having come so far, and suffered and risked so much—unpack a shallow basin and scoop up some muck from the river-bottom. Whirled about, the basin became a vortex, shrouded in murk for a few moments as the silt rose into the current like dust from a cyclone. But as that was blown away by the river's current, the shape of the vortex was revealed. In its middle was an eye of dirt that slowly disintegrated from the outside in as lighter granules were shouldered to the outside and cast off. Left in the middle was a huddle of nodes, heavier than all the rest. Blue eyes from far away attended to these, for sometimes they were shiny and yellow.

Now, 'twere easy to call such men stupid (not even broaching the subjects of greedy, violent, arrogant, *et cetera*), for there was something wilfully idiotic in going to an unknown country, ignoring its people, their languages, art, its beasts and butterflies, flowers, herbs, trees, ruins, *et cetera,* and reducing it all to a few lumps of heavy matter in the center of a dish. Yet as Daniel, in the tavern, tries to rake together his early memories of Trinity and of Cambridge, he's chagrined to find that a like process has been going on within his skull for half a century.

The impressions he received in those years had been as infinitely various as what confronted a Conquistador when he dragged his longboat up onto an uncharted shore. *Bewilderment,* in its ancient and literal sense of being cast away in a trackless wild, was the lot of the explorer, and it well described Daniel's state of mind during his first years at Trinity. The analogy was not all that far-fetched, for Daniel had matriculated just after the Restoration, and found himself among young men of the Quality who'd spent most of their lives in Paris. Their clothing struck Daniel's eye much as the gorgeous plumage of tropical birds would a black-robed Jesuit, and their rapiers and daggers were no less fatal than the fangs and talons of jungle predators. Being a pensive chap, he had, on the very first day, begun trying to make sense of it—to get to the bottom of things, like the explorer who turns his back on orang-utans and orchids to jam his pan into the mud of a creek bed. Naught but swirling murk had been the result.

In years since he has rarely gone back to those old memories. As he does now, in the tavern near Harvard College, he's startled to find that the muddy whirl has been swept away. The mental pan has been churning for fifty years, sorting the dirt and sand to the periphery and throwing it off. Most of the memories are simply gone. All that remain are a few wee nuggets. It's not plain to Daniel why *these* impressions have stayed, while others, which seemed as or more important to him at the time they happened, have gone away. But if the gold-panning similitude is faithful, it means that these memories matter more than the ones that have flown. For gold stays in the pan's center because of its density; it has more matter (whatever that means) in a given extent than anything else.

The crowd in Charing Cross, the sword falling silently on the neck of Charles I: this is his first nugget. Then there's nothing until some months later when the Waterhouses and their old family friends the Bolstroods went on a sort of holiday in the country to demolish a cathedral.

Nugget: In silhouette against a cathedral's rose window, a bent, black wraith lumbering, his two arms a pendulum, a severed marble saint's head swinging in them. This was Drake Waterhouse, Daniel's father, about sixty years old.

Nugget: The stone head in flight, turning to look back in surprise at Drake. The gorgeous fabric of the window drawn inwards, like the skin on a kettle of soup when you poke a spoon through it—the glass falling away, the transcendent vision of the window converted to a disk of plain old blue-green English hillside beneath a silver sky. This was the English Civil War.

Nugget: A short but stout man, having done with battering down the gilded fence that Archbishop Laud had built around the altar, dropping his sledgehammer and falling into an epileptic fit on the Lord's Table. This was Gregory Bolstrood, about fifty years old at the time. He was a preacher. He called himself an Independent. His tendency to throw fits had led to rumors that he barked like a dog during his three-hour sermons, and so the sect he'd founded, and Drake had funded, had come to be known as the Barkers.

Nugget: A younger Barker smiting the cathedral's organ with an iron rod—stately pipes being felled like trees, polished boxwood keys skittering across the marble floor. This was Knott Bolstrood, the son of Gregory, in his prime.

BUT THESE ARE ALL FROM his early childhood, before he'd learned to read and think. After that his young life had been well-ordered and (he's surprised to see in retrospect) interesting. Adventurous, even. Drake was a trader. After Cromwell had won and the Civil War ended, he and young Daniel traveled all over England during the 1650s buying the local produce low, then shipping it to Holland where it could be sold high. Despite much of the trade being illegal (for Drake held it as a religious conviction that the State had no business imposing on him with taxes and tariffs, and considered smuggling not just a good idea but a sacred observance), it was all orderly enough. Daniel's memories of that time—to the extent he still has any—are as prim and simple as a morality play penned by Puritans. It was not until the Restoration, and his going off to Trinity, that all became confused again, and he entered into a kind of second toddlerhood.

Nugget: The night before Daniel rode up to Cambridge to begin his four-year Cram Session for the End of the World, he slept in his father's house on the outskirts of London. The bed was a rectangle of stout beams, a piece of canvas stretched across the middle by a zigzag of hairy ropes, a sack of straw tossed on, and half a dozen Dissenting preachers snoring into one another's feet. Royalty was back, England had a King, who was called Charles II, and that King had courtiers. One of them, John Comstock, had drawn up an Act of Uniformity, and the King had signed it—with one stroke of the quill making all Independent ministers into unemployed heretics. Of course they had all converged on Drake's house. Sir Roger L'Estrange, the Surveyor of the

Press, came every few days and raided the place, on the suspicion that all those idle Phanatiques must be grinding out handbills in the cellar.

Wilkins—who for a brief while had been Master of Trinity—had secured Daniel a place there. Daniel had phant'sied that he should be Wilkins's student, his protégé. But before Daniel could matriculate, the Restoration had forced Wilkins out. Wilkins had retired to London to serve as the minister of the Church of St. Lawrence Jewry and, in his spare time, to launch the Royal Society. It was a lesson for Daniel in just how enormously a plan could go awry. For Daniel had been living in London, and could have spent as much time as he pleased with Wilkins, and gone to all the meetings of the Royal Society, and learnt everything he might have cared to know of Natural Philosophy simply by walking across town. Instead he went up to Trinity a few months after Wilkins had left it behind forever.

Nugget: On the ride up to Cambridge he passed by roadside saints whose noses and ears had been hammered off years ago by enraged Puritans. Each one of them, therefore, bore a marked resemblance to Drake. It seemed to him that each one turned its head to watch him ride past.

Nugget: A wench with paint on her face, squealing as she fell backwards onto Daniel's bed at Trinity College. Daniel getting an erection. This was the Restoration.

The woman's weight on his legs suddenly doubled as a boy half her age, embedded in a flouncing spray of French lace, fell on top of her. This was Upnor.

Nugget: A jeweled duelling-sword clattering as its owner dropped to hands and knees and washed the floor with a bubbling fan of vomit. "Eehhr," he groaned, rising up to a kneeling position and letting his head loll back on his lace collar. Candle-light shone in his face: a bad portrait of the King of England. This was the Duke of Monmouth.

Nugget: A sizar with a mop and a bucket, trying to clean

up the room—Monmouth and Upnor and Jeffreys and all of the other fellow-commoners calling for beer, sending him scurrying down to the cellar. This was Roger Comstock. Related, distantly, to the John Comstock who'd written the Act of Uniformity. But from a branch of the family that was at odds with John's. Hence his base status at Trinity.

Daniel had his own bed at Trinity, and yet he could not sleep. Sharing the great bed in Drake's house with smelly Phanatiques, or sleeping in common beds of inns while traveling round England with his father, Daniel had enjoyed great unbroken slabs of black, dreamless sleep. But when he went off to University he suddenly found himself sharing his room, and even his bed, with young men who were too drunk to stand up and too dangerous to argue with. His nights were fractured into shards. Vivid, exhausting dreams came through the cracks in between, like vapors escaping from a crazed vessel.

His first coherent memory of the place begins on a night like that.

⚜

College of the Holy and Undivided Trinity, Cambridge

1661

⚜

The Dissenters are destitute of all decorations that can please the outward Senses, what their Teachers can hope for from humane Assistance lies altogether in their own endeavours,

and they have nothing to strengthen their
Doctrine with (besides what they can say for it)
but probity of Manners and exemplary Lives.

—*The Mischiefs That Ought Justly
to Be Apprehended from a
Whig-Government*, ANONYMOUS,
ATTRIBUTED TO BERNARD MANDEVILLE, 1714

SOME SORT OF COMMOTION in the courtyard below. Not the
usual revels, or else he wouldn't have bothered to hear it.

Daniel got out of bed and found himself alone in the
chamber. The voices below sounded angry. He went to the
window. The tail of Ursa Major was like the hand of a cœlestial clock, and Daniel had been studying how to read it. The
time was probably around three in the morning.

Beneath him several figures swam in murky pools of
lanthorn-light. One of them was dressed as men always had
been, in Daniel's experience, until very recently: a black
coat and black breeches with no decorations. But the others
were flounced and feathered like rare birds.

The one in black seemed to be defending the door from
the others. Until recently, everyone at Cambridge had
looked like him, and the University had been allowed to exist only because a godly nation required divines who were
fluent in Greek and Latin and Hebrew. He was barring the
door because the men in lace and velvet and silk were trying
to bring a wench in with them. And hardly for the first time!
But this man, apparently, had seen one wench too many, and
resolved to make a stand.

A scarlet boy flourished in the midst of the lanthorn-
light—a writhing bouquet of tassels and flounces. His arms
were crossed over his body. He drew them apart with a sharp
ringing noise. A rod of silver light had appeared in each of
his hands—a long one in his right, a short one in his left. He
drew into a crouch. His companions were all shouting;

Daniel could not make out the words, but the feelings expressed were a welter of fear and joy. The black-clad fellow drew out a sword of his own, something dull and clanging, a heavier spadroon, and the scarlet boy came at him like a boiling cloud, with lightning darting out of the center. He fought as animals fight, with movements too quick for the eye to follow, and the man in black fought as men fight, with hesitations and second thoughts. He had a great many holes in him very soon, and was reduced to a heap of somber, bloody clothing on the green grass of the courtyard, shifting and rocking, trying to find a position that was not excruciatingly painful.

All of the Cavaliers ran away. The Duke of Monmouth picked the wench up over his shoulder like a sack of grain and carried her off at a dead run. The scarlet boy tarried long enough to plant a boot on the dying man's shoulder, turn him over onto his back, and spit something into his face.

All round the courtyard, shutters began to slam closed.

Daniel threw a coat over himself, pulled on a pair of boots, got a lanthorn of his own lit, and hurried downstairs. But it was too late for hurrying—the body was already gone. The blood looked like tar on the grass. Daniel followed one dribble to the next, across the green, out the back of the college, and onto the Backs—the boggy floodplain of the river Cam, which wandered around in back of the University. The wind had come up a bit, making noise in the trees that nearly obscured the splash. A less eager witness than Daniel could have claimed he'd heard nothing, and it would have been no lie.

He stopped then, because his mind had finally come awake, and he was afraid. He was out in the middle of an empty fen, following a dead man toward a dark river, and the wind was trying to blow out his lanthorn.

A pair of naked men appeared in the light, and Daniel screamed.

One of the men was tall, and had the most beautiful eyes Daniel had ever seen in a man's face; they were like the eyes of a painting of the Pieta that Drake had once flung onto a bonfire. He looked towards Daniel as if to say, *Who dares scream?*

The other man was shorter, and he reacted by cringing. Daniel finally recognized him as Roger Comstock, the sizar. "Who's that?" this one asked. "My lord?" he guessed.

"No man's lord," Daniel said. "It is I. Daniel Waterhouse."

"It's Comstock and Jeffreys. What are you doing out here in the middle of the night?" Both of the men were naked and soaked, their long hair draggling and seeping on their shoulders. Yet even Comstock seemed at ease compared to Daniel, who was dry, clothed, and equipped with a lanthorn.

"I might ask the same of you. Where are your clothes?"

Jeffreys now stepped forward. Comstock knew to shut up.

"We doffed our clothing when we swam the river," Jeffreys said, as if this should be perfectly obvious.

Comstock saw the hole in that story as quickly as Daniel did, and hastily plugged it: "When we emerged, we found that we had drifted for some distance downstream, and were unable to find them again in the darkness."

"Why did you swim the river?"

"We were in hot pursuit of that ruffian."

"Ruffian!?"

The outburst caused a narrowing of the beautiful eyes. A look of mild disgust appeared on Jeffreys's face. But Roger Comstock was not above continuing with the conversation: "Yes! Some Phanatique—a Puritan, or possibly a Barker— he challenged my Lord Upnor in the courtyard just now! You must not have seen it."

"I did see it."

"Ah." Jeffreys turned sideways, caught his dripping penis between two fingers, and urinated tremendously onto the ground. He was staring toward the College. "The window of your and My Lord Monmouth's chamber is awkwardly located—you must have leaned out of it?"

"Perhaps I leaned out a bit."

"Otherwise, how could you have seen the men duelling?"

"Would you call it duelling, or murdering?"

Once again, Jeffreys appeared to be overcome with queasiness at the fact that he was having a conversation of any sort with the likes of Daniel. Comstock put on a convincing display of mock astonishment. "Are you claiming to have witnessed a murder?"

Daniel was too taken aback to answer. Jeffreys continued to jet urine onto the ground; he had produced a great steaming patch of it already, as if he intended to cover his nakedness with a cloud. He furrowed his brow and asked, "Murder, you say. So a man has died?"

"I . . . I should suppose so," Daniel stammered.

"Hmmm. . . . *supposing* is a *dangerous* practice, when you are supposing that an Earl has committed a capital crime. Perhaps you'd better show the dead body to the Justice of the Peace, and allow the coroner to establish a cause of death."

"The body is gone."

"You say *body*. Wouldn't it be *correct* to say, *wounded man*?"

"Well . . . I did not personally verify that the heart had stopped, if that is what you mean."

"Wounded man would be the *correct* term, then. To me, he seemed very much a *wounded* man, and not a *dead* one, when Comstock and I were pursuing him across the Backs."

"Unquestionably not dead," Comstock agreed.

"But I saw him lying there—"

"From your window?" Jeffreys asked, finally done pissing.

"Yes."

"But you are not looking out your window *now,* are you, Waterhouse?"

"Obviously not."

"Thank you for telling me what is *obvious*. Did you leap out of your window, or did you walk down stairs?"

"Down stairs, of course!"

"Can you see the courtyard from the staircase?"

"No."

"So as you descended the stairs, you lost sight of the wounded man."

"Naturally."

"You really haven't the faintest idea, do you, Waterhouse, of what happened in the courtyard during the interval when you were coming down stairs?"

"No, but—"

"And despite this ignorance—ignorance utter, black, and entire—you presume to accuse an Earl, and personal friend of the King, of having committed—what was it again?"

"I believe he said *murder,* sir," Comstock put in helpfully.

"Very well. Let us go and wake up the Justice of the Peace," Jeffreys said. On his way past Waterhouse he snatched the lanthorn, and then began marching back towards the College. Comstock followed him, giggling.

First Jeffreys had to get himself dried off, and to summon his own sizar to dress his hair and get his clothes on—a gentleman could not go and visit the Justice of the Peace in a disheveled state. Meanwhile Daniel had to sit in his chamber with Comstock, who bustled about and cleaned the place with more diligence than he had ever shown before. Since Daniel was not in a talkative mood, Roger Comstock filled in the silences. "Louis Anglesey, Earl of Upnor—pushes a sword like a demon, doesn't he? You'd never guess he's only fourteen! It's because he and Monmouth and all that lot spent the Interregnum in Paris, taking their pushing-lessons at the Academy of Monsieur du Plessis, near the Palais Cardinal. They learned a very French conception of honor there, and haven't quite adjusted to England yet—they'll challenge a man to a duel at the slightest offence—real or phant'sied. Oh, now, don't look so stricken, Mr. Waterhouse—remember that if that fellow he was duelling with is found, and is found to be dead, and his injuries found to be the cause of his death, and those injuries are found to've been inflicted by My Lord Upnor, and not in a duel *per se* but in an unprovoked assault, and if a jury can be persuaded to overlook the faults in your account—in a word, if he is successfully prosecuted for this hypothetical murder—then you won't have to worry about it! After all, if he's guilty, then he can't very well claim you've dishonored him with the accusation, can he? Nice and tidy, Mr. Waterhouse. Some of his friends might be quite angry with you, I'll admit—oh, no, Mr. Waterhouse, I didn't mean it in the way you think. *I* am not your enemy—remember, I am of the Golden, not the Silver, Comstocks."

It was not the first time he'd said something like this. Daniel knew that the Comstocks were a grotesquely large and complicated family, who had begun popping up in minor roles as far back as the reign of King Richard Lionheart, and he gathered that this Silver/Golden dichotomy was some kind of feud between different branches of the clan. Roger Comstock wanted to impress on Daniel that he had nothing in common, other than a name, with John Comstock: the aging gunpowder magnate and arch-Royalist, and now Lord Chancellor, who had been the author of the recent Declaration of Uniformity—the act that had filled Drake's house with jobless Ranters, Barkers, Quakers, *et cetera*. "Your people," Daniel said, "the Golden Comstocks, as you dub them—pray, what are they?"

"I beg your pardon?"

"High Church?" Meaning Anglicans of the Archbishop Laud school, who according to Drake and his ilk were really no different from Papists—and Drake believed that the Pope was literally the Antichrist. "Low Church?" Meaning Anglicans of a more Calvinist bent, nationalistic, suspicious of priests in fancy clothes. "Independents?" Meaning ones who'd severed all ties with the Established Church, and made up their own churches as it suited them. Daniel did not venture any further down the continuum, for he had already shot well beyond Roger Comstock's limits as a theologian.

Roger threw up his hands and said merely, "Because of the unpleasantness with the Silver branch, recent generations of the Golden Comstocks have spent rather a lot of time in the Dutch Republic."

To Daniel, the Dutch Republic meant God-fearing places like Leiden, where the pilgrims had sojourned before going to Massachusetts. But it presently came clear that Roger was talking about Amsterdam. "There are all sorts of churches in Amsterdam. Cheek by jowl. Strange as it must sound, this habit has quite worn off on us over the years."

"Meaning what? That you've become used to preserving your faith despite being surrounded by heretics?"

"No. Rather, it's as if I've got an Amsterdam inside of my head."

"A *what* !?"

"Many different sects and faiths that are always arguing with one another. A Babel of religious disputation that never dies down. I have got used to it."

"You believe *nothing* !?"

Further debate—if listening to Roger's ramblings could be considered such—was cut off by the arrival of Monmouth, who strolled in looking offensively relaxed. Roger Comstock had to make a fuss over him for a while—jacking his boots off, letting his hair down, getting him undressed. Comstock supplied entertainment by telling the tale of chasing the killer Puritan across the Backs and into the River Cam. The more the Duke heard of this story, the more he liked it, and the more he loved Roger Comstock. And yet Comstock made so many ingratiating references to Waterhouse that Daniel began to feel that he was still part of the same merry crew; and Monmouth even directed one or two kindly winks at him.

Finally Jeffreys arrived in a freshly blocked wig, fur-lined cape, purple silk doublet, and fringed breeches, a ruby-handled rapier dangling alongside one leg, and fantastical boots turned down at the tops so far that they nearly brushed the ground. Looking, therefore, twice as old and ten times as rich as Daniel, even though he was a year younger and probably broke. He led the faltering Daniel and the implacably cheerful Comstock down the staircase—pausing there for a while to reflect upon the total impossibility of anyone's see-

ing the courtyard from it—and across Trinity's great lawn
and out the gate into the streets of Cambridge, where water-
filled wheel-ruts, reflecting the light of dawn, looked like
torpid, fluorescent snakes. In a few minutes they reached the
house of the Justice of the Peace, and were informed that he
was at church. Jeffreys therefore led them to an alehouse,
where he was soon engulfed in wenches. He caused drink
and food to be brought out. Daniel sat and watched him tear
into a great bloody haunch of beef whilst downing two pints
of ale and four small glasses of the Irish drink known as
Usquebaugh. None of it had any effect on Jeffreys; he was
one of those who could become staggeringly drunk and yet
only wax quieter and calmer.

The wenches kept Jeffreys occupied. Daniel sat and knew
fear—not the abstract fear that he dutifully claimed to feel
when preachers spoke of hellfire, but a genuine physical sensation, a taste in his mouth, a sense that at any moment, from
any direction, a blade of French steel might invade his vitals
and inaugurate a slow process of bleeding or festering to
death. Why else would Jeffreys have led him to this den? It
was a perfect place to get murdered.

The only way to get his mind off it was to talk to Roger
Comstock, who continued with strenuous but completely
pointless efforts to ingratiate himself. He circled round one
more time to the topic of John Comstock, with whom—it
could not be said too many times—he had nothing in common. That he had it on good authority that the gunpowder
turned out by Comstock's mills was full of sand, and that it
either failed entirely to explode, or else caused cannons to
burst. Why everyone, save a few self-deluding Puritans, now
understood that the defeat of the first King Charles had occurred not because Cromwell was such a great general, but
because of the faulty powder that Comstock had supplied to
the Cavaliers. Daniel—scared to death—was in no position
to understand the genealogical distinctions between the so-
called Silver and Golden Comstocks. The upshot was that
Roger Comstock seemed, in some way, to want to be his

friend, and was trying desperately hard to be just that, and indeed was the finest fellow that a fellow could possibly be, while still having spent the night dumping the corpse of a murder victim into a river.

The ringing of church-bells told them that the Justice of the Peace was probably finished with his breakfast of bread and wine. But Jeffreys, having made himself comfortable here, was in no hurry to leave. From time to time he would catch Daniel's eye and stare at him, daring Daniel to stand up and head for the door. But Daniel was in no hurry, either. His mind was seeking an excuse for doing nothing.

The one that he settled on went something like this: Upnor would be Judged—for good—five years from now when Jesus came back. What was the point of having the secular authorities sit in judgment on him now? If England were still a holy nation, as it had been until recently, then prosecuting Louis Anglesey, Earl of Upnor, would have been a fitting exercise of her authority. But the King was back, England was Babylon, Daniel Waterhouse and the hapless Puritan who'd died last night were strangers in a strange land, like early Christians in pagan Rome, and Daniel would only dirty his hands by getting into some endless legal broil. Best to rise above the fray and keep his eye on the year sixteen hundred and sixty-six.

So it was back to the College of the Holy and Undivided Trinity without saying a word to the Justice of the Peace. It had begun to rain. When Daniel reached the college, the grass had been washed clean.

THE DEAD MAN'S BODY was found two days later, tangled in some rushes half a mile down the Cam. He was a Fellow of Trinity College, a scholar of Hebrew and Aramaic who had been slightly acquainted with Drake. His friends went round making inquiries, but no one had seen a thing.

There was a rowdy funeral service in a primitive church that had been established in a barn five miles from Cambridge. *Exactly* five miles. For the Act of Uniformity stated,

among other things, that Independents could not gather
churches within five miles of any Established (i.e., Anglican) parish church, and so a lot of Puritans had been busy
with compasses and maps lately, and a lot of bleak real estate had changed hands. Drake came up, and brought with
him Daniel's older half-brothers, Raleigh and Sterling.
Hymns were sung and homilies delivered, affirming that the
victim had gone on to his eternal reward. Daniel prayed,
rather loudly, to be delivered from the seething den of rep-
tiles that was Trinity College.

Then, of course, he had to suffer advice from his elders.
First, Drake took him aside.

Drake had long ago adjusted to the loss of his nose and
ears, but all he had to do was turn his face in Daniel's direction to remind him that what he was going through at Trinity
wasn't so bad. So Daniel hardly took in a single word of
what Drake said to him. But he gathered that it was something along the lines of that coming into one's chambers
every night to find a different whore, services already paid
for, slumbering in one's bed, constituted a severe temptation
for a young man, and that Drake was all in favor of it—seeing it as a way to hold said young man's feet to the eternal
fire and find out what he was made of.

Implicit in all of this was that Daniel would pass the test.
He could not bring himself to tell his father that he'd already
failed it.

Second, Raleigh and Sterling took Daniel to an extremely rural alehouse on the way back into town and told
him that he must be some kind of half-wit, not to mention
an ingrate, if he was not in a state of bliss. Drake and his
first clutch of sons had made a very large amount of money
despite (come to think of it, *because of*) religious persecu-
tion. Among that ilk, the entire point of going to Cambridge was to rub elbows with the fine and the mighty. The
family had sent Daniel there, at great expense (as they
never tired of reminding him), and if Daniel occasionally
woke up to find the Duke of Monmouth passed out on top

of him, it only meant that all of *their* dreams had come true.

Implicit was that Raleigh and Sterling did *not* believe that the world was coming to an end in 1666. If true, this meant that Daniel's excuse for not ratting on Upnor was void.

The whole incident was then apparently forgotten by everyone at Trinity except Waterhouse and Jeffreys. Jeffreys ignored Daniel for the most part, but from time to time he would, for example, sit across from him and stare at him all through dinner, then pursue him across the lawn afterwards: "I can't stop looking at you. You are fascinating, Mr. Waterhouse, a living and walking incarnation of cravenness. You saw a man murdered, and you did *nothing* about it. Your face glows like a hot branding-iron. I want to brand it into my memory so that as I grow old, I may look back upon it as a sort of Platonic ideal of cowardice.

"I'm going into law, you know. Were you aware that the emblem of justice is a scale? From a beam depend two pans. On one, what is being weighed—the accused party. On the other, a standard weight, a polished gold cylinder stamped with the assayer's mark. You, Mr. Waterhouse, shall be the standard against which I will weigh all guilty cowards.

"What sort of Puritanical sophistry did you gin up, Mr. Waterhouse, to justify your inaction? Others like you got on a ship and sailed to Massachusetts so that they could be apart from us sinners, and live a pure life. I ween you are of the same mind, Mr. Waterhouse, but sailing on a ship across the North Atlantic is not for cowards, and so you are here. I think that you have withdrawn into a sort of Massachusetts of the mind! Your body's here at Trinity, but your spirit has flown off to some sort of notional Plymouth Rock—when we sit at High Table, you phant'sy yourself in a wigwam ripping drumsticks from a turkey and chewing on Indian corn and making eyes at some redskinned Indian lass."

THIS SORT OF THING LED to Daniel's spending much time going for walks in Cambridge's gardens and greens, where, if he chose his route carefully, he could stroll for a quarter of an hour without having to step over the body of an unconscious young scholar, or (in warmer weather) make apologies for having stumbled upon Monmouth, or one of his courtiers, copulating with a prostitute *al fresco*. More than once, he noticed another solitary young man strolling around the Backs. Daniel knew nothing of him—he had made no impression upon the College whatsoever. But once Daniel got in the habit of looking for him, he began to notice him here and there, skulking around the edges of University life. The boy was a sizar—a nobody from the provinces trying to escape from the lower class by taking holy orders and angling for a deaconage in some gale-chafed parish. He and the other sizars (such as Roger Comstock) could be seen descending on the dining-hall after the upper classes—pensioners (e.g., Daniel) and fellow-commoners (e.g., Monmouth and Upnor)—had departed, to forage among their scraps and clean up their mess.

Like a pair of comets drawn together, across a desolate void, by some mysterious action at a distance, they attracted each other across the greens and fells of Cambridge. Both were shy, and so early they would simply fall into parallel trajectories during their long strolls. But in time the lines converged. Isaac was pale as star-light, and so frail-looking that no one would've guessed he'd live as long as he had. His hair was exceptionally fair and already streaked with silver. He already had protruding pale eyes and a sharp nose. There was the sense of much going on inside his head, which he had not the slightest inclination to share with anyone else. But like Daniel, he was an alienated Puritan with a secret interest in natural philosophy, so naturally they fell in together.

They arranged a room swap. Another merchant's son eagerly took Daniel's place, viewing it as a move up the world's ladder. The College of the Holy and Undivided Trinity did not segregate the classes as rigidly as other colleges, so it was permitted for Isaac and Daniel to chum together. They shared a tiny room with a window looking out over the town—for Daniel, a great improvement over the courtyard view, so fraught with bloody memories. Musket-balls had been fired in through their window during the Civil War, and the bullet-holes were still in the ceiling.

Daniel learned that Isaac came from a family prosperous by Lincolnshire standards. His father had died before Newton was even born, leaving behind a middling yeoman's legacy. His mother had soon married a more or less affluent cleric. She did not sound, from Isaac's description, like a doting mum. She'd packed him off to school in a town called Grantham. Between her inheritance from the first marriage and what she'd acquired from the second, she easily could have sent him to Cambridge as a pensioner. But out of miserliness, or spite, or some hostility toward education in general, she'd sent him as a sizar instead—meaning that Isaac was obliged to serve as some other student's boot-polisher and table-waiter. Isaac's dear mother, unable to humiliate her son from a distance, had arranged it so that some other student—it didn't matter which—would do it in her stead. In combination with that Newton was obviously far more brilliant than Daniel was, Daniel was uneasy with the arrangement. Daniel proposed that they make common cause, and pool what they had, and live together as equals.

To Daniel's surprise, Isaac did not accept. He continued to perform sizar's work, without complaint. By any measure, his life was much better now. They'd spend hours, days, in that chamber together, spending candles by the pound and ink by the quart, working their separate ways through Aristotle. It was the life that both of them had longed for. Even so, Daniel thought it strange that Isaac would help him in the mornings with his clothing, and devote a quarter of an hour, or more, to dressing his hair. Half a century later, Daniel could remember, without vanity, that he had been a handsome enough young man. His hair was thick and long, and Isaac learned that if he combed it in a particular way he could bring out a certain natural wave, up above Daniel's forehead. He would not rest, every morning, until he had accomplished this. Daniel went along with it uneasily. Even then, Isaac had the air of a man who could be dangerous when offended, and Daniel sensed that if he declined, Isaac would not take it well.

So it went until one Whitsunday, when Daniel awoke to find Isaac gone. Daniel had gone to sleep well after midnight, Isaac as usual had stayed up later. The candles were all burned down to stubs. Daniel guessed Isaac was out emptying the chamber-pot, but he didn't come back. Daniel went over to their little work-table to look for evidence, and found a sheet of paper on which Isaac had drawn a remarkably fine portrait of a sleeping youth. An angelic beauty. Daniel could not tell whether it was meant to be a boy or a girl. But carrying it to the window and looking at it in day-light, he noticed, above the youth's brow, a detail in the hair. It served as the cryptological key that unlocked the message. Suddenly he recognized himself in that page. Not as he really was, but purified, beautified, perfected, as though by some alchemical refinement—the slag and dross raked away, the radiant spirit allowed to shine forth, like the Philosophick Mercury. It was a drawing of Daniel Waterhouse as he might have looked if he had gone to the Justice of the Peace and accused Upnor and been persecuted and suffered a Christlike death.

Daniel went down and eventually found Isaac bent and kneeling in the chapel, wracked with agony, praying desperately for the salvation of his immortal soul. Daniel could not but sympathize, though he knew too little of sin and too little of Isaac to guess what his friend might be repenting for. Daniel sat nearby and did a little praying of his own. In time, the pain and fear seemed to ebb away. The chapel filled up. A service was begun. They took out the Books of Common Prayer and turned to the page for Whitsunday. The priest intoned: "What is required of them who come to the Lord's Supper?" They answered, "To examine themselves whether they repent of their former sins, steadfastly purporting to lead a new life." Daniel watched Isaac's face as he spoke this catechism and saw in it the same fervor that always lit up

Drake's mangled countenance when he really thought he was on to something. Both of them took communion. *This is the Lamb of God who takes away the sins of the world.*

Daniel watched Isaac change from a tortured wretch, literally writhing in spiritual pain, into a holy and purified saint. Having repented of their former sins—steadfastly purporting to lead new lives—they went back up to their chamber. Isaac pitched that drawing into the fire, opened up his note-book, and began to write. At the head of a blank page he wrote *Sins committed before Whitsunday 1662* and then began writing out a list of every bad thing he'd ever done that he could remember, all the way back to his childhood: wishing that his stepfather was dead, beating up some boy at school, and so forth. He wrote all day and into the night. When he had exhausted himself he started up a new page entitled *Since Whitsunday 1662* and left it, for the time being, blank.

Meanwhile, Daniel turned back to his Euclid. Jeffreys kept reminding him that he had failed at being a holy man. Jeffreys did this because he supposed it was a way of torturing Daniel the Puritan. In fact, Daniel had never wanted to be a preacher anyway, save insofar as he wanted to please his father. Ever since his meeting with Wilkins, he had wanted only to be a Natural Philosopher. Failing the moral test had freed him to be that, at a heavy price in self-loathing. If Natural Philosophy led him to eternal damnation, there was nothing he could do about it anyway, as Drake the predestinationist would be the first to affirm. An interval of years or even decades might separate Whitsunday 1662 and Daniel's arrival at the gates of Hell. He reckoned he might as well fill that time with something he at least found interesting.

A month later, when Isaac was out of the room, Daniel opened up the note-book and turned to the page headed *Since Whitsunday 1662*. It was still blank.

He checked it again two months later. Nothing.

At the time he assumed that Isaac had simply forgotten about it. Or perhaps he had stopped sinning! Years later,

Daniel understood that neither guess was true. Isaac Newton had stopped believing himself capable of sin.

This was a harsh judgment to pass on anyone—and the proverb went *Judge not lest ye be judged.* But its converse was that when you were treating with a man like Isaac Newton, the rashest and cruelest judge who ever lived, you must be sure and swift in your own judgments.

⚜️

Boston, Massachusetts Bay Colony

OCTOBER 12, 1713

☙

> Others apart sat on a Hill retir'd,
> In thoughts more elevate, and reason'd high
> Of Providence, Foreknowledge, Will and Fate
> —MILTON, *Paradise Lost*

LIKE A GOOD CARTESIAN who measures everything against a fixed point, Daniel Waterhouse thinks about whether or not to go back to England while keeping one eye, through a half-closed door, on his son: Godfrey William, the fixed stake that Daniel has driven into the ground after many decades' wanderings. At an arbitrary place on a featureless plain, some would argue, but now the Origin of all his considerations. Sir Isaac would have it that all matter is a sort of permanent ongoing miracle, that planets are held in their orbits, and atoms in their places, by the immanent will of God, and looking at his own son, Daniel can hardly bear to think oth-

erwise. The boy's a coiled spring, the potential for generations of American Waterhouses, though it's just as likely
he'll catch a fever and die tomorrow.

In most other Boston houses, a slave woman would be
looking after the boy, leaving the parents free to discourse
with their visitor. Daniel Waterhouse does not own slaves. The
reasons are several. Some of them are even altruistic. So little
Godfrey sits on the lap, not of some Angolan negress, but of
their neighbor: the daft but harmless Mrs. Goose, who comes
into their home occasionally to do the one thing that she apparently *can* do: to entertain children by spouting all manner
of nonsensical stories and doggerel that she has collected or
invented. Meanwhile Enoch is off trying to make arrangements with Captain van Hoek of the *Minerva*. This has freed
Daniel and Faith and the young Rev. Wait Still Waterhouse* to
discuss what is the best way to respond to the startling invitation from Princess Caroline of Ansbach. Many words are said,
but they make no more impact on Daniel than Mrs. Goose's
incoherent narratives about cutlery leaping over cœlestial
bodies and sluttish hags living in discarded footwear.

Wait Still Waterhouse says something like, "You're sixty-
seven, it's true, but you have your health—many have lived
much longer."

"If you avoid large crowds, sleep well, nourish yourself—"
Faith says.

"Lon-don Bridge is fal-ling down, fal-ling down, fal-ling
down . . . ," sings Mrs. Goose.

"My mind has never felt quite so much like an arrangement of cranks and gears," Daniel says. "I decided what I
was going to do quite some time ago."

"But people have been known to change their minds—"
says the reverend.

"Am I to infer, from what you just said, that you are a Free
Will man?" Daniel inquires. "I really am shocked to find that

---

*Son of Praise-God W., son of Raleigh W., son of Drake—hence, some sort
of nephew to Daniel.

in a Waterhouse. What are they teaching at Harvard these days? Don't you realize that this Colony was founded by people fleeing from those who backed the concept of Free Will?"

"I don't fancy that the Free Will question really had very much to do with the founding of this Colony. It was more a rebellion against the entire notion of an Established church—be it Papist or Anglican. It is true that many of those Independents—such as our ancestor John Waterhouse—got their doctrine from the Calvinists in Geneva, and scorned the notion, so cherished by the Papists and the Anglicans, of Free Will. But this alone would not have sufficed to send them into exile."

"I get it not from Calvin but from Natural Philosophy," Daniel says. "The mind is a machine, a Logic Mill. That's what I believe."

"Like the one you have been building across the river?"

"A good deal more effective than that one, fortunately."

"You think that if you made yours better, it could do what the human mind does? That it could have a soul?"

"When you speak of a soul, you phant'sy something above and beyond the cranks and gears, the dead matter, of which the machine—be it a Logic Mill or a brain—is constructed. I do not believe in this."

"Why not?"

Like many simple questions, this one is difficult for Daniel to answer. "Why not? I suppose because it puts me in mind of Alchemy. This soul, this extra thing added to the brain, reminds me of the Quintessence that the Alchemists are forever seeking: a mysterious supernatural presence that is supposed to suffuse the world. But they can never seem to find any. Sir Isaac Newton has devoted his life to the project and has nothing to show for it."

"If your sympathies do not run in that direction, then I know better than to change your mind, at least where Free Will versus Predestination is concerned," says Wait Still. "But I know that when you were a boy you had the privilege of sitting at the knee of men such as John Wilkins, Gregory

Bolstrood, Drake Waterhouse, and many others of Independent sympathies—men who preached freedom of conscience. Who advocated Gathered, as opposed to Established, churches. The flourishing of small congregations. Abolition of central dogma."

Daniel, still not quite believing it: "Yes . . ."

Wait Still, brightly: "So what's to stop me from preaching Free Will to *my* flock?"

Daniel laughs. "And, as you are not merely glib, but young, handsome, and personable, converting many to the same creed—including, I take it, my own wife?"

Faith blushes, then stands up and turns around to hide it. In the candle-light, a bit of silver glints in her hair: a hair-pin shaped like a caduceus. She has gotten up on the pretext of going to check on little Godfrey, even though Mrs. Goose has him well in hand.

In a small town like Boston, you'd think it would be impossible to have a conversation about anything without being eavesdropped on. Indeed, the whole place was set up to make it so—they deliver the mail, not to your house, but to the nearest tavern, and if you don't come round and pick it up after a few days the publican will open it up and read it aloud to whomever is in attendance. So Daniel had assumed that Mrs. Goose would be listening in on the whole conversation. But instead she is completely absorbed in her work, as if telling yarns to a boy were more important than this great Decision that Daniel is wrestling with, here at damn near the end of his long life.

"It's quite all right, my dear," Daniel says to the back of Faith's bodice. "Having been raised by a man who believed in Predestination, I'd much rather that my boy was raised by a Free Will woman." But Faith leaves the room.

Wait Still says, "So . . . you believe God has predestined you to sail for England tonight?"

"No—I'm not a Calvinist. Now, you're baffled, Reverend, because you spent too much time at Harvard reading old books about the likes of Calvin and Archbishop Laud, and are still caught up in the disputes of Arminians versus Puritans."

"What should I have been reading, Doctor?" said Wait Still, making a bit too much of a show of flexibility.

"Galileo, Descartes, Huygens, Newton, Leibniz."

"The syllabus of your Institute of Technologickal Arts?"

"Yes."

"Didn't know that you touched on matters of theology."

"That was a bit of a jab—no, no, quite all right! I rather liked it. I'm pleased by the display of backbone. I can see clearly enough that you'll end up raising my son." Daniel means this in a completely non-sexual way—he had in mind that Wait Still would act in some avuncular role—but from the blush on Wait Still's face he can see that the role of stepfather is more likely.

This, then, would be a good time to change the subject to abstract technical matters: "It all comes from first principles. Everything can be measured. Everything acts according to physical laws. Our minds included. My mind, that's doing the deciding, is already set in its course, like a ball rolling down a trough."

"Uncle! Surely you are not denying the existence of souls—of a Supreme Soul."

Daniel says nothing to this.

"Neither Newton nor Leibniz would agree with you," Wait Still continues.

"They're afraid to agree with me, because they are important men, and they would be destroyed if they came out and said it. But no one will bother to destroy *me*."

"Can we not influence your mental machine by arguments?" asks Faith, who has returned to stand in the doorway.

Daniel wants to say that Wait Still's best arguments would be about as influential as boogers flicked against the planking of a Ship of the Line in full sail, but sees no reason to be acrimonious—the whole point of the exercise is to be remembered well by those who'll stay in the New World, on the theory that as the sun rises on the eastern fringe of

America, small things cast long shadows westwards. "The future is as set as the past," he says, "and the future is that I'll climb on board the *Minerva* within the hour. You can argue that I should stay in Boston to raise my son. Of course, I should like nothing better. I should, God willing, have the satisfaction of watching him grow up for as many years as I have left. Godfrey would have a flesh-and-blood father with many conspicuous weaknesses and failings. He'd hold me in awe for a short while, as all boys do their fathers. It would not last. But if I sail away on *Minerva,* then in place of a flesh-and-blood Dad—a fixed, known quantity—he'll have a phant'sy of one, infinitely ductile in his mind. I can go away and imagine generations of Waterhouses yet unborn, and Godfrey can imagine a hero-father better than I can really be."

Wait Still Waterhouse, an intelligent and decent man, can see so many holes in this argument that he is paralyzed by choices. Faith, a better mother than wife, who has a better son than a husband, encompasses a vast sweep of compromises with a pert nod of the head. Daniel gathers up his son from Mrs. Goose's lap—Enoch calls in a hired coach—they go to the waterfront.

> So I saw in my dream that the man began to run. Now he had not run far from his own door, but his wife and children perceiving it began to cry after him to return: but the man put his fingers in his ears, and ran on crying, "Life, life, eternal life." So he looked not behind him, but fled towards the middle of the plain.
>
> —JOHN BUNYAN, *The Pilgrim's Progress*

MINERVA HAS ALREADY WEIGHED ANCHOR, using the high tide to widen the distance between her keel and certain obstructions near the Harbor's entrance. Daniel is to be rowed out to join her in a pilot's boat. Godfrey, who is half asleep, kisses his old Dad dutifully and watches his departure like a dream—that's good, as he can tailor the memory later to suit his changing demands—like a suit of clothes modified every six months to fit a growing frame. Wait Still stands by Faith's side, and Daniel can't help thinking they make a lovely couple. Enoch, that home-wrecker, remains on the end of the wharf, guiltily apart, his silver hair glowing like white fire in the full moon-light.

A dozen slaves pull mightily at the oars, forcing Daniel to sit down, lest the boat shoot out from under his feet and leave him floundering in the Harbor. Actually he does not sit as much as sprawl and get lucky. From shore it probably looks like a pratfall, but he knows that this ungainly moment will be edited from The Story that will one day live in the memories of the American Waterhouses. The Story is in excellent hands. Mrs. Goose has come along to watch and memorize, and she has a creepy knack for that kind of thing, and Enoch is staying, too, partly to look after the physical residue of the Massachusetts Bay Colony Institute of Technologickal Arts, but also partly to look after The Story and see that it's shaped and told to Daniel's advantage.

Daniel weeps.

The sounds of his sniffling and heaving drown out nearly everything else, but he becomes aware of some low, strange music: the slaves have begun to sing. A rowing-song? No, that would have a lumbering, yo-ho-ho sort of rhythm, and this is much more complicated, with beats in the wrong places. It must be an Africk tune, because they have meddled with some of the notes, made them flatter than they should be. And yet it's weirdly Irish at the same time. There is no shortage of Irish slaves in the West Indies, where these men first fell under the whip, so that might explain it. It is (musicological speculations aside) an entirely sad song, and Daniel knows why: by climbing aboard this boat and breaking down in sobs, he has reminded each one of these Africans of the day when he was taken, in chains, off the coast of Guinea, and loaded aboard a tall ship.

Within a few minutes they are out of view of the Boston wharves, but still surrounded by land: the many islets, rocks, and bony tentacles of Boston Harbor. Their progress is watched by dead men hanging in rusty gibbets. When pirates are put to death, it is because they have been out on the high seas violating Admiralty law, whose jurisdiction extends only to the high-tide mark. The implacable logic of the Law dictates that pirate-gallows must, therefore, be erected in the intertidal zone, and that pirate-corpses must be washed three times by the tide before they are cut down. Of course mere death is too good for pirates, and so the sentence normally calls for their corpses to be gibbeted in locked iron cages so that they can never be cut down and given a Christian burial.

New England seems to have at least as many pirates as honest seamen. But here, as in so many other matters, Providence has smiled upon Massachusetts, for Boston Harbor is choked with small islands that are washed by high tides, providing vast resources of pirate-hanging and -gibbeting real estate. Nearly all of it has been put to use. During the daytime, the gibbets are obscured by clouds of hungry birds. But it's the middle of the night, the birds are in Boston and Charlestown, slumbering in their nests of plaited pirate-hair. The tide is high, the tops of the reefs submerged, the supports rising directly out of the waves. And so as the singing slaves row Daniel out on what he assumes will be his last voyage, scores of dessicated and skeletonized pirates, suspended in midair above the moonlit sea, watch him go by, as a ceremonial honor-guard.

It takes better than an hour to catch *Minerva,* just clearing the Spectacle Island shallows. Her hull is barrel-shaped and curves out above them. A pilot's ladder is deployed. The ascent isn't easy. Universal gravitation is not his only opponent. Rising waves, sneaking in from the North Atlantic, bounce him off the hull. Infuriatingly, the climb brings back all manner of Puritanical dogma he's done his best to forget—the ladder becomes Jacob's, the boat of sweaty black slaves Earth, the Ship Heaven, the sailors in the moonlit rig-

ging Angels, the captain none other than Drake himself, ascended these many years, exhorting him to climb faster.

Daniel leaves America, becoming part of that country's
stock of memories—the composted manure from which it's
sending out fresh green shoots. The Old World reaches down
to draw him in: a couple of lascars, their flesh and breath
suffused with saffron, asafœtida, and cardamom, lean over
the rail, snare his cold pale hands in their warm black ones,
and haul him in like a fish. A roller slides under the hull at
the same moment—they fall back to the deck in an orgiastic
tangle. The lascars spring up and busy themselves drawing
up his equipage on ropes. Compared to the little boat with
the creaking and splashing of its oars and the grunting of the
slaves, *Minerva* moves with the silence of a well-trimmed
ship, signifying (or so he hopes) her harmony with the
forces and fields of nature. Those Atlantic rollers make the
deck beneath him accelerate gently up and down, effort-
lessly moving his body—it's like lying on a mother's bosom
as she breathes. So Daniel lies there spreadeagled for a
while, staring up at the stars—white geometric points on a
slate, gridded by shadows of rigging, an explanatory net-
work of catenary curves and Euclidean sections, like one of
those geometric proofs out of Newton's *Principia Mathematica.*

College of the Holy and Undivided Trinity, Cambridge
1663

❦

An Ideot may be taught by Custom to Write
and Read, yet no Man can be taught Genius.
— *Memoirs of the Right Villanous*
John Hall, 1708

DANIEL HAD GONE OUT for a time in the evening, and met
with Roger Comstock at a tavern, and witnessed to him, and
tried to bring him to Jesus. This had failed. Daniel returned
to his chamber to find the cat up on the table with its face
planted in Isaac's dinner. Isaac was seated a few inches
away. He had shoved a darning-needle several inches into
his eyeball.

Daniel screamed from deep down in his gut. The cat, mor-
bidly obese from eating virtually all of Isaac's meals, fell off
the table like a four-legged haggis, and trudged away. Isaac
did not flinch, which was probably a good thing. Daniel's
scream had no other effects on business as usual at Trinity
College—those who weren't too impaired to hear it probably assumed it was a wench playing hard-to-get.

"In my dissections of animals' eyes at Grantham, I often
marveled at their perfect sphericity, which, in bodies that
were otherwise irregular grab-bags of bones, tubes, skeins

and guts, seemed to mark them out as apart from all the other organs. As if the Creator had made those orbs in the very image of the heavenly spheres, signifying that one should receive light from the other," Isaac mused aloud. "Naturally, I wondered whether an eye that was *not* spherical would work as well. There are practical as well as theologic reasons for spherical eyes: one, so that they can swivel in their sockets." There was some tension in his voice—the discomfort must have been appalling. Tears streamed down and spattered on the table like the exhaust from a water-clock— the only time Daniel ever saw Isaac weep. "Another practical reason is simply that the eyeball is pressurized from within by the aqueous humour."

"My God, you're not bleeding the humour from your eyeball—?"

"Look more carefully!" Isaac snapped. "Observe—don't imagine."

"I can't bear it."

"The needle is not *piercing* anything—the orb is perfectly intact. Come and see!"

Daniel approached, one hand clamped over his mouth as if he were abducting himself—he did not want to vomit on the open Waste-Book where Isaac was taking notes with his free hand. Upon a closer look he saw that Isaac had inserted the darning-needle not into the eyeball itself but into the lubricated bearing where the orb rotated in its socket—he must've simply pulled his lower eyelid way down and probed between it and the eyeball until he'd found a way in. "The needle is blunt—it is perfectly harmless," Isaac grunted. "If I could trouble you for a few minutes' assistance?"

Now supposedly Daniel was a student, attending lectures and studying the works of Aristotle and Euclid. But in fact, he had over the last year become the one thing, aside from the Grace of God, keeping Isaac Newton alive. He'd long since stopped asking him such annoying, pointless questions as "Can you remember the last time you put food into your mouth" or "Don't you suppose that a nap of an hour or two, once a night, might be good?" The only thing that really worked was to monitor Isaac until he physically collapsed on the table, then haul him into bed, like a grave-robber transporting his goods, then pursue his own studies nearby and keep one eye on him until consciousness began to return, and then, during the moments when Isaac still didn't know what day it was, and hadn't gone off on some fresh train of thought, shove milk and bread at him so he wouldn't starve all the way to death. He did all of this voluntarily—sacrificing his own education, and making a burnt offering of Drake's tuition payments—because he considered it his Christian duty. Isaac, still in theory his sizar, had become his master, and Daniel the attentive servant. Of course Isaac was completely unaware of all Daniel's efforts—which only made it a more perfect specimen of Christlike self-abnegation. Daniel was like one of those Papist fanatics who, after they died, were found to've been secretly wearing hair-shirts underneath their satin vestments.

"The diagram may give you a better comprehension of the design of tonight's experiment," Isaac said. He'd drawn a cross-sectional view of eyeball, hand, and darning-needle in his Waste Book. It was the closest thing to a work of art he had produced since the strange events of Whitsunday last year—since that date, only equations had flowed from his pen.

"May I ask *why* you are doing this?"

"Theory of Colors is part of the Program," Isaac said—referring (Daniel knew) to a list of philosophical questions Isaac had recently written out in his Waste Book, and the studies he had pursued, entirely on his own, in hopes of answering them. Between the two young men in this room—Newton with his Program and Waterhouse with his God-given responsibility to keep the other from killing himself—neither had attended a single lecture, or had any contact with actual members of the faculty, in over a year. Isaac continued, "I've been reading Boyle's latest—*Experiments and Considerations Touching Colors*—and it occurred to me: he uses his eyes to make all of his observations—his eyes are therefore instruments, like telescopes—but does he really understand how those instruments work? An astronomer who did not understand his lenses would be a poor philosopher indeed."

Daniel might have said any number of things then, but what came out was, "How may I assist you?" And it was not just being a simpering toady. He was, for a moment, gobsmacked by the sheer presumption of a mere student, twenty-one years old, with no degree, calling into question the great Boyle's ability to make simple observations. But in the next moment it occurred to Daniel for the first time: What if Newton was right, and all the others wrong? It was a difficult thing to believe. On the other hand, he *wanted* to believe it, because *if* it were true, it meant that in failing to attend so many lectures he had missed precisely *nothing,* and in acting as Newton's manservant he was getting the best education in natural philosophy a man could ever have.

"I need you to draw a reticule on a leaf of paper and then hold it up at various measured distances from my cornea— as you do, I'll move the darning needle up and down—creating greater and lesser distortions in the shape of my eyeball—I say, I'll do that with one hand, and take notes of what I see with the other."

So the night proceeded—by sunrise, Isaac Newton knew more about the human eye than anyone who had ever lived, and Daniel knew more than anyone save Isaac. The experiment could have been performed by anyone. Only one person had actually done it, however. Newton pulled the needle out of his eye, which was blood-red, and swollen nearly shut. He turned to another part of the Waste Book and began wrestling with some difficult math out of Cartesian analysis while Daniel stumbled downstairs and went to church. The sun turned the stained-glass windows of the chapel into matrices of burning jewels.

Daniel saw in a way he'd never seen anything before: his mind was a homunculus squatting in the middle of his skull, peering out through good but imperfect telescopes and listening-horns, gathering observations that had been distorted along the way, as a lens put chromatic aberrations into all the light that passed through it. A man who peered out at the world through a telescope would assume that the aberration was *real,* that the stars actually *looked* like that—what false assumptions, then, had natural philosophers been making about the evidence of their senses, until last night? Sitting in the gaudy radiance of those windows hearing the organ play and the choir sing, his mind pleasantly intoxicated from exhaustion, Daniel experienced a faint echo of what it must be like, *all the time,* to be Isaac Newton: a permanent ongoing epiphany, an endless immersion in lurid radiance, a drowning in light, a ringing of cosmic harmonies in the ears.

⚓

Aboard Minerva, *Massachusetts Bay*

OCTOBER 1713

⚕

DANIEL BECOMES AWARE that someone is standing over him as he lies on the deck: a stubby red-headed and -bearded man with a lit cigar in his mouth, and spectacles with tiny circular lenses: it's van Hoek, the captain, just checking to see whether his passenger will have to be buried at sea to-morrow. Daniel sits up, finally, and introduces himself, and van Hoek says very little—probably pretending to know less English than he really does, so Daniel won't be coming to his cabin and pestering him at all hours. He leads Daniel aft along *Minerva*'s main deck (which is called the upperdeck, even though, at the ends of the ship, there other other decks above it) and up a staircase to the quarter-deck and shows him to a cabin. Even van Hoek, who can be mistaken for a stout ten-year-old if you see him from behind, has to crouch to avoid banging his head on the subtly arched joists that support the poop deck overhead. He raises one arm above his head and steadies himself against a low beam—touching it not with a hand, but a brass hook.

Even though small and low-ceilinged, the cabin is perfectly all right—a chest, a lantern, and a bed consisting of a wooden box containing a canvas sack stuffed with straw. The straw is fresh, and its aroma will continue to remind Daniel of the green fields of Massachusetts all the way to England. Daniel strips off just a few items of clothing, curls up, and sleeps.

When he wakes up, the sun is in his eyes. The cabin has a small window (its forward bulkhead is deeply sheltered under the poop deck and so it is safe to put panes of glass there). And since they are sailing eastwards, the rising sun shines into it directly—along the way, it happens to beam directly through the huge spoked wheel by which the ship is steered. This is situated just beneath the edge of that same poop deck so that the steersman can take shelter from the weather while enjoying a clear view forward down almost the entire length of *Minerva*. At the moment, loops of rope have been cast over a couple of the handles at the ends of the wheel's spokes and tied down to keep the rudder fixed in one position. No one is at the wheel, and it's neatly dividing the red disk of the rising sun into sectors.

College of the Holy and Undivided Trinity, Cambridge

1664

✣

IN THE GREAT COURT of Trinity there was a sundial Isaac Newton didn't like: a flat disk divided by labeled spokes with a gnomon angling up from the center, naïvely copied from Roman designs, having a certain Classical elegance, and always wrong. Newton was constructing a sundial on a south-facing wall, using, as gnomon, a slender rod with a ball on the end. Every sunny day the ball's shadow would trace a curve across the wall—a slightly different curve every day, because the tilt of the earth's axis slowly changed through the seasons. That sheaf of curves made a fine set of astronomical data but not a usable timepiece. To tell time, Isaac (or his faithful assistant, Daniel Waterhouse) had to make a little cross-tick at the place the gnomon's shadow stood when Trinity's bell (always just a bit out of synchronization with King's) rang each of the day's hours. In theory, after 365 repetitions of this daily routine, each of the curves would be marked with ticks for 8:00 A.M., 9:00 A.M., and so on. By connecting those ticks—drawing a curve that passed through all of the eight o'clock ticks, another through all of the nine o'clock ticks, and so on—Isaac produced a second family of curves, roughly parallel to one another and roughly perpendicular to the day curves.

One evening, about two hundred days and over a thousand cross-ticks into this procedure, Daniel asked Isaac why he found sundials so interesting. Isaac got up, fled the room, and ran off in the direction of the Backs. Daniel let him be for a couple of hours and then went out looking for him. Eventually, at about two o'clock in the morning, he found Isaac standing in the middle of Jesus Green, contemplating his own long shadow in the light of a full moon.

"It was a sincere request for information—nothing more—I want you to convey to me whatever it is about sundials I've been too thick-headed to find very interesting."

This seemed to calm Isaac down, though he did not apologize for having thought the worst about Daniel. He said something along the lines of: "Heavenly radiance fills the æther, its rays parallel and straight and, so long as nothing is there to interrupt them, invisible. The secrets of God's creation are all told by those rays, but told in a language we do not understand, or even hear—the direction from which they shine, the spectrum of colors concealed within the light, these are all characters in a cryptogram. The gnomon—look at our shadows on the Green! *We* are the gnomon. We interrupt that light and we are warmed and illuminated by it. By stopping the light, we destroy part of the message without understanding it. We cast a shadow, a hole in the light, a ray of darkness that is shaped like ourselves—some might say that it contains no information save the profile of our own forms—but they are wrong. By recording the stretching and skewing of our shadows, we can attain part of the knowledge hidden in the cryptogram. All we need to make the necessary observations is a fixed regular surface—a plane—against which to cast the shadow. Descartes gave us the plane."

And so from then onwards Daniel understood that the point of this grueling sundial project was not merely to plot the curves, but to understand *why* each curve was shaped as it was. To put it another way, Isaac wanted to be able to walk up to a blank wall on a cloudy day, stab a gnomon into it, and draw all of the curves simply by *knowing* where the shadow *would* pass. This was the same thing as knowing where the sun would be in the sky, and that was the same as knowing where the earth was in its circuit around the sun, and in its daily rotation.

Though, as months went on, Daniel understood that Isaac wanted to be able to do the same thing even if the blank wall happened to be situated on, say, the moon that Christian Huygens had lately discovered revolving around Saturn.

Exactly how this might be accomplished was a question with ramifications that extended into such fields as: Would Isaac (and Daniel, for that matter) be thrown out of Trinity College? Were the Earth, and all the works of Man, nearing the end of a long relentless decay that had begun with the expulsion from Eden and that would very soon culminate in the Apocalypse? Or might things actually be getting *better,* with the promise of *continuing* to do so? Did people have souls? Did they have Free Will?

⚜

Aboard Minerva, *Massachusetts Bay*

OCTOBER 1713

☿

> Hereby it is manifest, that during the time men
> live without a common power to keep them all
> in awe, they are in that condition which is
> called war; and such a war, as is of every man,
> against every man. For WAR, consisteth not in
> battle only, or the act of fighting; but in a tract
> of time, wherein the will to contend by battle is
> sufficiently known.
>
> —HOBBES, *Leviathan*

NOW WALKING OUT ONTO the upperdeck to find *Minerva* sailing steadily eastwards on calm seas, Daniel's appalled that anyone ever doubted these matters. The horizon is a perfect line, the sun a red circle tracing a neat path in the sky and proceeding through an orderly series of color-changes, red-yellow-white. Thus Nature. *Minerva*—the human world—is a family of curves. There are no straight lines here. The decks are slightly arched to shed water and supply greater strength, the masts flexed, impelled by the thrust of the sails but restrained by webs of rigging: curve-grids like Isaac's sundial lines. Of course, wherever wind collects in a sail or water skims around the hull it follows rules that Bernoulli has set down using the calculus—Leibniz's version. *Minerva* is a congregation of Leibniz-curves navigating according to Bernoulli-rules across a vast, mostly water-covered sphere whose size, precise shape, trajectory through the heavens, and destiny were all laid down by Newton.

One cannot board a ship without imagining ship-wreck. Daniel envisions it as being like an opera, lasting several hours and proceeding through a series of Acts.

Act I: The hero rises to clear skies and smooth sailing. The sun is following a smooth and well-understood cœlestial curve, the sea is a plane, sailors are strumming guitars and carving *objets d'art* from walrus tusks, *et cetera,* while erudite passengers take the air and muse about grand philosophical themes.

Act II: A change in the weather is predicted based upon readings in the captain's barometer. Hours later it appears in the distance, a formation of clouds that is observed, sketched, and analyzed. Sailors cheerfully prepare for weather.

Act III: The storm hits. Changes are noted on the barometer, thermometer, clinometer, compass, and other instruments—cœlestial bodies are, however, no longer visible—the sky is a boiling chaos torn unpredictably by bolts—the sea is rough, the ship heaves, the cargo remains tied safely down, but most passengers are too ill or worried to think. The sailors are all working without rest—some of them sacrifice chickens in hopes of appeasing their gods. The rigging glows with St. Elmo's Fire—this is attributed to supernatural forces.

Act IV: The masts snap and the rudder goes missing. There is panic. Lives are already being lost, but it is not known how many. Cannons and casks are careering randomly about, making it impossible to guess who'll be alive and who dead ten seconds from now. The compass, barometer, *et cetera,* are all destroyed and the records of their readings swept overboard—maps dissolve—sailors are helpless—those who are still alive and sentient can think of nothing to do but pray.

Act V: The ship is no more. Survivors cling to casks and planks, fighting off the less fortunate and leaving them to drown. Everyone has reverted to a feral state of terror and misery. Huge waves shove them around without any pattern, carnivorous fish use living persons as food. There is no relief in sight, or even imaginable.

—There might also be an Act VI in which everyone was dead, but it wouldn't make for good opera so Daniel omits it.

Men of his generation were born during Act V* and raised in Act IV. As students, they huddled in a small vulnerable bubble of Act III. The human race has, actually, been in Act V for most of history and has recently accomplished the miraculous feat of assembling splintered planks afloat on a stormy sea into a sailing-ship and then, having climbed onboard it, building instruments with which to measure the world, and then finding a kind of regularity in those measurements. When they were at Cambridge, Newton was surrounded by a personal nimbus of Act II and was well on his way to Act I.

But they had, perversely, been living among people who were peering into the wrong end of the telescope, or something, and who had convinced themselves that the

---

*In England, the Civil War that brought Cromwell to power, and on the Continent, the Thirty Years' War.

opposite was true—that the world had once been a splendid, orderly place—that men had made a reasonably trouble-free move from the Garden of Eden to the Athens of Plato and Aristotle, stopping over in the Holy Land to encrypt the secrets of the Universe in the pages of the Bible, and that everything had been slowly, relentlessly falling apart ever since. Cambridge was run by a mixture of fogeys too old to be considered dangerous, and Puritans who had been packed into the place by Cromwell after he'd purged all the people he *did* consider dangerous. With a few exceptions such as Isaac Barrow, none of them would have had any use for Isaac's sundial, because it didn't look like an *old* sundial, and they'd prefer telling time wrong the Classical way to telling it right the new-fangled way. The curves that Newton plotted on the wall were a methodical document of their wrongness—a manifesto like Luther's theses on the church-door.

In explaining why those curves were as they were, the Fellows of Cambridge would instinctively use Euclid's geometry: the earth is a sphere. Its orbit around the sun is an ellipse—you get an ellipse by constructing a vast imaginary cone in space and then cutting through it with an imaginary plane; the intersection of the cone and the plane is the ellipse. Beginning with these primitive objects (viz. the tiny sphere revolving around the place where the gigantic cone was cut by the imaginary plane), these geometers would add on more spheres, cones, planes, lines, and other elements—so many that if you could look up and see 'em, the heavens would turn nearly black with them—until at last they had found a way to account for the curves that Newton had drawn on the wall. Along the way, every step would be verified by applying one or the other of the rules that Euclid had proved to be true, two thousand years earlier, in Alexandria, where everyone had been a genius.

Isaac hadn't studied Euclid that much, and hadn't cared enough to study him well. If he wanted to work with a curve he would instinctively write it down, not as an intersection of planes and cones, but as a series of numbers and letters: an algebraic expression. That only worked if there was a language, or at least an alphabet, that had the power of *expressing* shapes without literally *depicting* them, a problem that Monsieur Descartes had lately solved by (first) conceiving of curves, lines, *et cetera,* as being collections of individual points and (then) devising a way to express a point by giving its coordinates—two numbers, or letters *representing* numbers, or (best of all) algebraic expressions that could in principle be evaluated to *generate* numbers. This translated all geometry to a new language with its own set of rules: algebra. The construction of equations was an exercise in translation. By following those rules, one could create new statements that were true, without even having to think about what the symbols referred to in any physical universe. It was this seemingly occult power that scared the hell out of some Puritans at the time, and even seemed to scare Isaac a bit.

By 1664, which was the year that Isaac and Daniel were supposed to get their degrees or else leave Cambridge, Isaac, by taking the very latest in imported Cartesian analysis and then extending it into realms unknown, was (unbeknownst to anyone except Daniel) accomplishing things in the field of natural philosophy that his teachers at Trinity could not even *comprehend,* much less *accomplish*—they, meanwhile, were preparing to subject Isaac and Daniel to the ancient and traditional ordeal of examinations designed to test their knowledge of Euclid. If they failed these exams, they'd be branded a pair of dimwitted failures and sent packing.

As the date drew nearer, Daniel began to mention them more and more frequently to Isaac. Eventually they went to see Isaac Barrow, the first Lucasian Professor of Mathematics, because he was conspicuously a better mathematician than the rest. Also because recently, when Barrow had been traveling in the Mediterranean, the ship on which he'd been passenger had been assaulted by pirates, and Barrow had gone abovedecks with a cutlass and helped fight them off. As such, he did not seem like the type who would really care in what order students learned the material. They were right about that—when Isaac showed up one day, alarmingly late in his academic career, with a few shillings, and bought a copy of Barrow's Latin translation of Euclid, Barrow didn't seem to mind. It was a tiny book with almost no margins, but Isaac wrote in the margins anyway, in nearly microscopic print. Just as Barrow had translated Euclid's Greek into the universal tongue of Latin, Isaac translated Euclid's ideas (expressed as curves and surfaces) into Algebra.

Half a century later on the deck of *Minerva,* that's all Daniel can remember about their Classical education; they took the exams, did indifferently (Daniel did better than Isaac), and were given new titles: they were now scholars, meaning that they had scholarships, meaning that Newton would not have to go back home to Woolsthorpe and become a gentleman-farmer. They would continue to share a chamber at Trinity, and Daniel would continue to learn more from Isaac's idle musings than he would from the entire apparatus of the University.

ONCE HE'S HAD THE OPPORTUNITY to settle in aboard *Minerva,* Daniel realizes it's certain that when, God willing, he reaches London, he'll be asked to provide a sort of affidavit telling what he knows about the invention of the calculus. As long as the ship's not moving too violently, he sits down at the large dining-table in the common-room, one deck below his cabin, and tries to organize his thoughts.

> Some weeks after we had received our Scholarships, probably in the Spring of 1665, Isaac Newton and I decided to walk out to Stourbridge Fair.

Reading it back to himself, he scratches out *probably in* and writes in *certainly no later than.*

Here Daniel leaves much out—it was Isaac who'd an-

nounced he was going. Daniel had decided to come along to
look after him. Isaac had grown up in a small town and never
been to London. To him, Cambridge was a big city—he was
completely unequipped for Stourbridge Fair, which was one
of the biggest in Europe. Daniel had been there many times
with father Drake or half-brother Raleigh, and knew what
not to do, anyway.

> The two of us went out back of Trinity and began to
> walk downstream along the Cam. After passing by the
> bridge in the center of town that gives the City and
> University their name, we entered into a reach along
> the north side of Jesus Green where the Cam describes
> a graceful curve in the shape of an elongated S.

Daniel almost writes *like the integration symbol used in
the calculus.* But he suppresses that, since that symbol, and
indeed the term *calculus*, were invented by Leibniz.

> I made some waggish student-like remark about this
> curve, as curves had been much on our minds the pre-
> vious year, and Newton began to speak with confi-
> dence and enthusiasm—demonstrating that the ideas
> he spoke of were not extemporaneous speculation but
> a fully developed theory on which he had been work-
> ing for some time.
>   "Yes, and suppose we were on one of those punts,"
> Newton said, pointing to one of the narrow, flat-
> bottomed boats that idle students used to mess about
> on the Cam. "And suppose that the Bridge was the
> Origin of a system of Cartesian coordinates covering
> Jesus Green and the other land surrounding the river's
> course."

No, no, no, no. Daniel dips his quill and scratches that bit
out. It is an anachronism. Worse, it's a Leibnizism. Natural

Philosophers may talk that way in 1713, but they didn't fifty years ago. He has to translate it back into the sort of language that Descartes would have used.

"And suppose," Newton continued, "that we had a rope with regularly spaced knots, such as mariners use to log their speed, and we anchored one end of it on the Bridge—for the Bridge is a fixed point in absolute space. If that rope were stretched tight it would be akin to one of the numbered lines employed by Monsieur Descartes in his Geometry. By stretching it between the Bridge and the punt, we could measure how far the punt had drifted down-river, and in which direction."

Actually, this is not the way Isaac ever would have said it. But Daniel's writing this for princes and parliamentarians, not Natural Philosophers, and so he has to put long explanations in Isaac's mouth.

"And lastly suppose that the Cam flowed always at the same speed, and that our punt matched it. That is what I call a fluxion—a flowing movement along the curve over time. I think you can see that as we rounded the first limb of the S-curve around Jesus College, where the river bends southward, our fluxion in the north-south direction would be steadily changing. At the moment we passed under the Bridge, we'd be pointed northeast, and so we would have a large northwards fluxion. A minute later, when we reached the point just above Jesus College, we'd be going due east, and so our north-south fluxion would be zero. A minute after that, after we'd curved round and drawn alongside Midsummer Commons, we'd be headed southeast, meaning that we would have developed a large southward fluxion—but even that would reduce and tend

back towards zero as the stream curved round northwards again towards Stourbridge Fair."

He can stop here. For those who know how to read between the lines, this is sufficient to prove Newton had the
calculus—or Fluxions, as he called it—in '65, most likely
'64. No point in beating them over the head with it . . .

Yes, beating someone over the head is the *entire* point.

ॐ

Banks of the River Cam
1665

🜍

Almost five thousand years agone, there were
pilgrims walking to the Celestial City, as these
two honest persons are; and Beelzebub, Apol-
lyon, and Legion, with their companions, per-
ceiving by the path that the pilgrims made that
their way to the City lay through this town of
Vanity, they contrived here to set up a fair; a
fair wherein should be sold all sorts of vanity,
and that it should last all the year long. Therefore at this Fair are all such merchandise sold,
as houses, lands, trades, places, honours,
preferments, titles, countries, kingdoms, lusts,
pleasures, and delights of all sorts, as whores,
bawds, wives, husbands, children, masters, servants, lives, blood, bodies, souls, silver, gold,
pearls, precious stones, and what not.

And moreover, at this Fair there is at all times
to be seen jugglings, cheats, games, plays, fools,
apes, knaves, and rogues, and that of all sorts.
—JOHN BUNYAN, *The Pilgrim's Progress*

IT WAS LESS THAN AN hour's walk to the Fair, strolling along
gently sloped green banks with weeping-willows, beneath
whose canopies were hidden various prostrate students. Black
cattle mowed the grass unevenly and strewed cow-pies along
their way. At first the river was shallow enough to wade across,
and its bottom was carpeted with slender fronds that, near the
top, were bent slightly downstream by the mild current. "Now,
there is a curve whose fluxion in the downstream direction is
nil at the point where it is rooted in the bottom—that is to say,
it rises vertically from the mud—but increases as it rises."

Here Daniel was a bit lost. "Fluxion seems to mean a
flowing over time—so it makes perfect sense when you apply the word to the position of a punt on a river, which is, as
a matter of fact, flowing over time. But now you seem to be
applying it to the shape of a weed, which is not flowing—it's
just standing there sort of bent."

"But Daniel, the virtue of this approach is that it *doesn't
matter* what the actual physical situation *is,* a curve is *ever a
curve,* and whatever you can do to the curve of a *river* you
can do just as rightly to the curve of a *weed*—we are free
from all that old nonsense now." Meaning the Aristotelian
approach, in which such easy mixing of things with obviously different natures would be abhorrent. All that mattered
henceforth, apparently, was what form they adopted when
translated into the language of analysis. "Translating a thing
into the analytical language is akin to what the alchemist
does when he extracts, from some crude ore, a pure spirit, or
virtue, or *pneuma.* The fœces—the gross external forms of
things—which only mislead and confuse us—are cast off to
reveal the underlying spirit. And when this is done we may

learn that some things that are superficially different are, in their real nature, the same."

Very soon, as they left the colleges behind, the Cam became broader and deeper and instantly was crowded with much larger boats. Still, they were not boats for the ocean—they were long, narrow, and flat-bottomed, made for rivers and canals, but with far greater displacement than the little punts. Stourbridge Fair was already audible: the murmur of thousands of haggling buyers and sellers, barking of dogs, wild strains from bagpipes and shawms whipping over their heads like twists of bright ribbon unwinding in the breeze. They looked at the boat-people: Independent traders in black hats and white neck-cloths, waterborne Gypsies, ruddy Irish and Scottish men, and simply Englishmen with complicated personal stories, negotiating with sure-footed boat-dogs, throwing buckets of mysterious fluids overboard, pursuing domestic arguments with unseen persons in the tents or shacks pitched on their decks.

Then they rounded a bend, and there was the Fair, spread out in a vast wedge of land, bigger than Cambridge, even more noisy, much more crowded. It was mostly tents and tent-people, who were not their kind of people—Daniel watched Isaac gain a couple of inches in height as he remembered the erect posture that Puritans used to set a better example. In some secluded parts of the Fair (Daniel knew) serious merchants were trading cattle, timber, iron, barrelled oysters—anything that could be brought upriver this far on a boat, or transported overland in a wagon. But this wholesale trade *wanted* to be invisible, and *was*. What Isaac *saw* was a *retail* fair whose size and gaudiness was all out of proportion to its importance, at least if you went by the amount of money that changed hands. The larger avenues (which meant sluices of mud with planks and logs strewn around for people to step on, or at least push off against) were lined with tents of rope-dancers, jugglers, play-actors, puppet shows, wrestling-champions, dancing-girls, and of course the speciality prostitutes who made the Fair such an important resource for University students. But going up into the smaller byways, they found the tables and stalls and the cleverly fashioned unfolding wagons of traders who'd brought goods from all over Europe, up the Ouse and the Cam to this place to sell them to England.

Daniel and Isaac roamed for the better part of an hour, ignoring the shouts and pleadings of the retailers on all sides, until finally Isaac stopped, alert, and sidestepped over to a small folding display-case-on-legs that a tall slender Jew in a black coat had set up. Daniel eyed this Son of Moses curiously—Cromwell had re-admitted these people to England only ten years previously, after they'd been excluded for centuries, and they were as exotic as giraffes. But Isaac was staring at a constellation of gemlike objects laid out on a square of black velvet. Noting his interest, the Kohan folded back the edges of the cloth to reveal many more: concave and convex lenses, flat disks of good glass for grinding your own, bottles of abrasive powder in several degrees of coarseness, and prisms.

Isaac signalled that he would be willing to open negotiations over two of the prisms. The lens-grinder inhaled, drew himself up, and blinked. Daniel moved round to a supporting position behind and to the side of Isaac. "You have pieces of eight," the circumcised one said—midway between an assertion and a question.

"I know that your folk once lived in a kingdom where that was the coin of the realm, sir," Isaac said, "but . . ."

"You know nothing—my people did not come from Spain. They came from Poland. You have French coins—the louis d'or?"

"The louis d'or is a beautiful coin, befitting the glory of the Sun King," Daniel put in, "and probably much used wherever you came from—Amsterdam?"

"London. You intend to compensate me, then, with what—Joachimsthalers?"

"As you, sir, are English, and so am I, let us use English means."

"You wish to trade cheese? Tin? Broadcloth?"

"How many *shillings* will buy these two prisms?"

The Hebraic one adopted a haggard, suffering look and gazed at a point above their heads. "Let me see the color of your money," he said, in a voice that conveyed gentle regret, as if Isaac *might* have bought some prisms today, and instead would only get a dreary lesson in the unbelievable shabbiness of English coinage. Isaac reached into a pocket and wiggled his fingers to produce a metallic tromping noise that proved many coins were in there. Then he pulled out a handful and let the lens-grinder have a glimpse of a few coins, tarnished black. Daniel, so far, was startled by how good Isaac was at this kind of thing. On the other hand, he had made a business out of lending money to other students— maybe he had talent.

"You must have made a mistake," said the Jew. "Which is perfectly all right—we all make mistakes. You reached into the wrong pocket and you pulled out your black money*— the stuff you throw to beggars."

"Ahem, er, so I did," Isaac said. "Pardon me—where's the money for paying merchants?" Patting a few other pockets. "By the way, assuming I'm not going to offer you black money, how many shillings?"

"When you say shillings, I assume you mean the new ones?"

"The James I?"

"No, no, James I died half a century ago and so one would not normally use the adjective *new* to describe pounds minted during his reign."

"Did you say *pounds*?" Daniel asked. "A pound is rather a lot of money, and so it strikes me as not relevant to this transaction, which has all the appearances of a shilling type of affair *at most*."

"Let us use the word *coins* until I know whether you speak of the new or the old."

---

*Counterfeits made of base metals such as copper and lead.

"*New* meaning the coins minted, say, during our life-times?"

"I mean the Restoration coinage," the Israelite said, "or perhaps your professors have neglected to inform you that Cromwell is dead, and Interregnum coins demonetized these last three years."

"Why, I believe I *have* heard that the King is beginning to mint new coins," Isaac said, looking to Daniel for confirmation.

"My half-brother in London knows someone who *saw* a gold CAROLUS II DEI GRATIA coin once, displayed in a crystal case on a silken pillow," Daniel said. "People have begun to call them Guineas, because they are made of gold that the Duke of York's company is taking out of Africa."

"I say, Daniel, is it true what they say, that those coins are perfectly circular?"

"They are, Isaac—not like the good old English hammered coins that you and I carry in such abundance in our pockets and purses."

"Furthermore," said the Ashkenazi, "the King brought with him a French savant, Monsieur Blondeau, on loan from King Louis, and that fellow built a machine that mills delicate ridges and inscriptions into the edges of the coins."

"Typical French extravagance," Isaac said.

"The King really did spend more time than was good for him in Paris," Daniel said.

"On the contrary," the forelocked one said, "if someone clips or files a bit of metal off the edge of a round coin with a milled edge, it is immediately obvious."

"That must be why everyone is melting those new coins down as fast as they are minted, and shipping the metal to the Orient . . . ?" Daniel began,

". . . making it impossible for the likes of me and my friend to obtain them," Isaac finished.

"Now there is a good idea—if you can show me coins of a bright silver color—not that black stuff—I'll weigh them and accept them as bullion."

"*Bullion!* Sir!"

"Yes."

"I have heard that this is the practice in China," Isaac said sagely. "But here in England, a shilling is a shilling."

"*No matter how little it weighs!?*"

"Yes. In principle, yes."

"So when a lump of metal is coined in the Mint, it takes on a magical power of shillingness, and even after it has been filed and clipped and worn down to a mere featureless nodule, it is still worth a full shilling?"

"You exaggerate," Daniel said. "I have here a fine Queen Elizabeth shilling, for example—which I carry around, mind you, as a souvenir of Gloriana's reign, since it is far too fine a specimen to actually *spend*. But as you can see, it is just as bright and shiny as the day it was minted—"

"Especially where it's recently been clipped there along the side," the lens-grinder said.

"Normal, pleasing irregularity of the hand-hammered currency, nothing more."

Isaac said, "My friend's shilling, though magnificent, and arguably worth two or even three shillings in the market, is no anomaly. Here I have a shilling from the reign of Edward VI, which I obtained after an inebriated son of a Duke, who happened to have borrowed a shilling from me some time earlier, fell unconscious on a floor—the purse in which he carried his finest coins fell open and this rolled out of it—I construed this as repayment of the debt, and the exquisite condition of the coin as interest."

"How could it roll when three of its edges are flat? It is nearly triangular," the lens-grinder said.

"A trick of the light."

"The problem with that Edward VI coinage is that for all I knew it might've been issued during the Great Debasement, when, before Sir Thomas Gresham could get matters in hand, prices doubled."

"The inflation was not because the coins were debased, as some believe," Daniel said, "it was because the wealth confiscated from the Papist monasteries, and cheap silver from the mines of New Spain, were flooding the country."

"If you would allow me to approach within ten feet of these coins, it would help me to appreciate their numismatic excellence," the lens-grinder said. "I could even use some of my magnifying-lenses to . . ."

"I'm afraid I would be offended," Isaac said.

"You could inspect this one as closely as you wanted," Daniel said, "and find no evidence of criminal tampering—I got it from a blind innkeeper who had suffered frostbite in the fingertips—had no idea what he was giving me."

"Didn't he think to bite down on it? Like so?" said the Judaic individual, taking the shilling and crushing it between his rear molars.

"What would he have learned by doing that, sir?"

"That whatever counterfeit-artist stamped it out, had used reasonably good metal—not above fifty percent lead."

"We'll choose to interpret that as a wry jest," Daniel said, "the likes of which you could never direct against *this* shilling, which my half-brother found lying on the ground at the Battle of Naseby, not far from fragments of a Royalist captain who'd been blown to pieces by a bursting cannon—the dead man was, you see, a captain who'd once stood guard at the Tower of London where new coins are minted."

The Jew repeated the biting ceremony, then scratched at the coin in case it was a brass clinker japanned with silver paint. "Worthless. But I owe a shilling to a certain vile man in London, a hater of Jews, and I would drive a shilling's worth of satisfaction from slipping this slug of pig-iron into his hand."

"Very well, then—" said Isaac, reaching for the prisms.

"Avid collectors such as you two must also have pennies—?"

"My father hands out shiny new ones as Christmas presents," Daniel began. "Three years ago—" but he suspended the anecdote when he noticed that the lens-grinder was paying attention, not to him, but to a commotion behind them.

Daniel turned around and saw that it was a man, reasonably well-heeled, having trouble walking even though a friend and a servant were supporting him. He had a powerful desire to lie down, it seemed, which was most awkward, as he happened to be wading through ankle-deep mud. The servant slipped a hand between the man's upper arm and his ribs to bear him up, but the man shrieked like a cat who's been mangled under a cart-wheel and convulsed backwards and landed full-length on his back, hurling up a coffin-shaped wave of mud that spattered things yards away.

"Take your prisms," said the merchant, practically stuffing them into Isaac's pocket. He began folding up his display-case. If he felt the way Daniel did, then it wasn't the sight of a man feeling ill, or falling down, that made him pack up and leave, so much as the sound of that scream.

Isaac was walking toward the sick man with the cautious but direct gait of a tightrope-walker.

"Shall we back to Cambridge, then?" Daniel suggested.

"I have some knowledge of the arts of the apothecary." Isaac said, "Perhaps I could help him."

A circle of people had gathered to observe the sick man, but it was a very broad circle, empty except for Isaac and Daniel. The victim appeared, now, to be trying to get his breeches off. But his arms were rigid, so he was trying to do it by writhing free of his clothes. His servant and his friend were tugging at the cuffs, but the breeches seemed to've shrunk onto his legs. Finally the friend drew his dagger, slashed through the cuffs left and right, and then ripped the pant-legs open from bottom to top—or perhaps the force of the swelling thighs burst them. They came off, anyway. Friend and servant backed away, affording Isaac and Daniel a clear vantage point that would have enabled them to see all the way up to the man's groin, if the view hadn't been blocked by black globes of taut flesh stacked like cannonballs up his inner thighs.

The man had stopped writhing and screaming now because he was dead. Daniel had taken Isaac's arm and was rather firmly pulling him back, but Isaac continued to approach the specimen. Daniel looked round and saw that suddenly there was no one within musket range—horses and tents had been abandoned, back-loads of goods spilled on the ground by porters now halfway to Ely.

"I can *see* the buboes expanding even though the body is dead," Isaac said. "The generative spirit lives on—transmuting dead flesh into something else—just as maggots are generated out of meat, and silver grows beneath mountains—why does it bring death sometimes and life others?"

That they lived was evidence that Daniel eventually pulled Isaac away and got him pointed back up the river toward Cambridge. But Isaac's mind was still on those Satanic miracles that had appeared in the dead man's groin. "I admire Monsieur Descartes' analysis, but there is something missing in his supposition that the world is just bits of matter jostling one another like coins shaken in a bag. How could that account for the ability of matter to organize itself into eyes and leaves and salamanders, to transmute itself into alternate forms? And yet it's not simply that matter comes together in good ways—not some ongoing miraculous Creation—for the same process by which our bodies turn meat and milk into flesh and blood can also cause a man's body to convert itself into a mass of buboes in a few hours' time. It might *seem* aimless, but it *cannot* be. That one man sickens and dies, while another flourishes, are characters in the cryptic message that philosophers seek to decode."

"Unless the message was set down long ago and is there in the Bible for all men to read plainly," Daniel said.

Fifty years later, he hates to remember that he ever talked this way, but he can't stop himself.

"What do you mean by that?"

"The year 1665 is halfway over—you know what year comes next. I must to London, Isaac. Plague has come to England. What we have seen today is a harbinger of the Apocalypse."

Aboard Minerva, off the Coast of New England

NOVEMBER 1713

DANIEL IS ROUSED by a rooster on the forecastledeck* that is growing certain it's not just imagining that light in the eastern sky. Unfortunately, the eastern sky is off to port this morning. Yesterday it was to starboard. *Minerva* has been sailing up and down the New England coast for the better part of a fortnight, trying to catch a wind that will decisively take her out into the deep water, or "off soundings," as they say. They are probably not more than fifty miles away from Boston.

He goes below to the gun deck, a dim slab of sharp-smelling air. When his eyes have adjusted he can see the cannons, all swung around on their low carriages so they are parallel to the hull planking, aimed forwards, lashed in place, and the heavy hatches closed over the gun ports. Now that he cannot see the horizon, he must use the soles of his feet to sense the ship's rolling and pitching—if he waits for his balance-sense to tell him he's falling, it'll be too late. He makes his way aft in very short, carefully planned steps, trailing fingertips along the ceiling, jostling the long ramrods and brushes racked up there for tending the guns. This

---

*The forecastledeck is the short deck that, towards the ship's bow, is built above the upperdeck.

takes him to a door and thence into a cabin at the stern that's as wide as the entire ship and fitted with a sweep of windows, gathering what light they can from the western sky and the setting moon.

Half a dozen men are in here working and talking, all of them relatively old and sophisticated compared to ordinary seamen—this is where great chests full of good tools are stored, and sheets of potent diagrams nested. A tiller the dimensions of a battering-ram runs straight down the middle of the ceiling and out through a hole in the stern to the rudder, which it controls; the forward end of the tiller is pulled to and fro by a couple of cables that pass up through openings in the decks to the wheel. The air smells of coffee, wood-shavings, and pipe-smoke. Grudging hellos are scattered about. Daniel goes back and sits by one of the windows—these are undershot so that he can look straight down and see *Minerva*'s wake being born in a foamy collision down around the rudder. He opens a small hatch below a window and drops out a Fahrenheit thermometer on a string. It is the very latest in temperature measurement technology from Europe—Enoch presented it to him as a sort of party favor. He lets it bounce through the surf for a few minutes, then hauls it in and takes a reading.

He's been trying to perform this ritual every four hours—the objective being to see if there's anything to the rumor that the North Atlantic is striped with currents of warm water. He can present the data to the Royal Society if-God-willing-he-reaches-London. At first he did it from the upperdeck, but he didn't like the way the instrument got battered against the hull, and he was wearied by the looks of incomprehension on the sailors' faces. The old gaffers back here don't necessarily think he's any less crazy but they don't think less of him for it.

So like a sojourner in a foreign city who eventually finds a coffeehouse where he feels at home, Daniel has settled on this place, and been accepted here. The regulars are mostly in their thirties and forties: a Filipino; a Lascar; a half-

African, half-white from the Portuguese city of Goa; a Huguenot; a Cornish man with surprisingly poor English; an Irishman. They're all perfectly at home here, as if *Minerva* were a thousand-year-old ship on which their ancestors had always lived. If she ever sinks, Daniel suspects they'll happily go down with her, for lack of any other place to live. Joined with one another and with *Minerva,* they have the power to travel anywhere on earth, fighting their way past pirates if need be, eating well, sleeping in their own beds. But if *Minerva* were lost, it almost wouldn't make any difference whether it spilled them into the North Atlantic in a January gale, or let them off gently into some port town—either way, it'd be a short, sad life for them after that. Daniel wishes there were a comforting analogy to the Royal Society to be made here, but as that lot are currently trying to throw one of their own number (Baron Gottfried Wilhelm von Leibniz) overboard, it doesn't really work.

A brick-lined cabin is wedged between the upperdeck and the forecastledeck, always full of smoke because fires burn there—food comes out of it from time to time. A full meal is brought to Daniel once a day, and he takes it, usually by himself, sometimes with Captain van Hoek, in the commonroom. He's the only passenger. Here it's evident that *Minerva*'s an old ship, because the crockery and flatware are motley, chipped, and worn. Those parts of the ship that *matter* have been maintained or replaced as part of what Daniel's increasingly certain must be a subtle, understated, but fanatical program of maintenance decreed by van Hoek and ramrodded by one of his mates. The crockery and other clues suggest that the ship's a good three decades old, but unless you go down into the hold and view the keel and the ribs, you don't see any pieces that are older than perhaps five years.

None of the plates match, and so it's always a bit of a game for Daniel to eat his way down through the meal (normally something stewlike with expensive spices) until he can see the pattern on the plate. It is kind of an idiotic game for a Fellow of the Royal Society to indulge in, but he doesn't introspect about it until one evening when he's staring into his plate, watching the gravy slosh with the ship's heaving (a microcosm of the Atlantic?), and all of a sudden it's—

⚔

The Plague Year

SUMMER 1665

⚕

Th'earths face is but thy Table; there are set
Plants, cattell, men, dishes for Death to eate.
In a rude hunger now hee millions drawes
Into his bloody, or plaguy, or sterv'd jawes.
—JOHN DONNE, "Elegie on M Boulstred"

DANIEL WAS EATING POTATOES and herring for the thirty-fifth consecutive day. As he was doing it in his father's house, he was expected loudly to thank God for the privilege before and after the meal. His prayers of gratitude were becoming less sincere by the day.

To one side of the house, cattle voiced their eternal confusion—to the other, men trudged down the street ringing hand-bells (for those who could hear) and carrying long red sticks (for those who could see), peering into court-yards and doorways, and poking their snouts over garden-walls, scanning for bubonic corpses. Everyone else who had enough money to leave London was absent. That included Daniel's half-brothers Raleigh and Sterling and their families, as well as his half-sister Mayflower, who along with her children had gone to ground in Buckinghamshire. Only Mayflower's husband, Thomas Ham, and Drake Water-house, Patriarch, had refused to leave. Mr. Ham *wanted* to leave, but he had a cellar in the City to look after.

The idea of leaving, just because of a spot of the old Black Death, hadn't even *occurred* to Drake yet. Both of his wives had died quite a while ago, his elder children had fled, there was no one left to talk sense into him except Daniel. Cambridge had been shut down for the duration of the Plague. Daniel had ventured down here for what he had en-visioned as a quick, daring raid on an empty house, and had found Drake seated before a virginal playing old hymns from the Civil War. Having spent most of his good coins, first of all helping Newton buy prisms, and secondly bribing a reluctant coachman to bring him down within walking dis-tance of this pest-hole, Daniel was stuck until he could get money out of Dad—a subject he was afraid to even broach. Since God had predestined all events anyway, there was no way for them to avoid the Plague, if that was their doom—and if it *wasn't,* why, no harm in staying there on the edge of the city and setting an example for the fleeing and/or dying populace.

Owing to those modifications that had been made to his head at the behest of Archbishop Laud, Drake Waterhouse made curious percolating and whistling noises when he chewed and swallowed his potatoes and herring.

In 1629, Drake and some friends had been arrested for distributing freshly printed libels in the streets of London. These particular libels inveighed against Ship Money, a new tax imposed by Charles I. But the topic did not matter; if this had happened in 1628, the libels would have been about something else, and no less offensive to the King and the Archbishop.

An indiscreet remark made by one of Drake's comrades after burning sticks had been rammed under his nails led to the discovery of the printing-press that Drake had used to print the libels—he kept it in a wagon hidden under a pile of hay. So as he had now been exposed as the master-mind of the conspiracy, Bishop Laud had him, and a few other supremely annoying Calvinists, pilloried, branded, and mutilated. These were essentially practical techniques more than punishments. The intent was not to reform the criminals, who were clearly un-reformable. The pillory fixed them in one position for a while so that all London could come by and get a good look at their faces and thereafter recognize them. The branding and mutilation marked them permanently so that the rest of the world would know them.

As all of this had happened years before Daniel had even been born, it didn't matter to him—this was just how Dad had always looked—and of course it had *never* mattered to Drake. Within a few weeks, Drake had been back on the highways of England, buying cloth that he'd later smuggle to the Netherlands. In a country inn, on the way to St. Ives, he encountered a saturnine, beetle-browed chap name of Oliver Cromwell who had recently lost his faith, and seen his life ruined—or so he imagined, until he got a look at Drake, and found God. But that was another story.

The goal of all persons who had houses in those days was to possess the smallest number of pieces of furniture needed to sustain life, but to make them as large and heavy and dark as possible. Accordingly, Daniel and Drake ate their potatoes and herring on a table that had the size and weight of a medieval drawbridge. There was no other furniture in the room, although the eight-foot-high grandfather clock in the adjoining hall contributed a sort of immediate presence with the heaving to and fro of its cannonball-sized pendulum, which made the entire house lean from one side to the other like a drunk out for a brisk walk, and the palpable grinding of its gear-train, and the wild clamorous bonging that exploded from it at intervals that seemed suspiciously random, and that caused flocks of migrating waterfowl, thousands of feet overhead, to collide with each other in panic and veer into new courses. The fur of dust beginning to overhang its

Gothick battlements; its internal supply of mouse-turds; the
Roman numerals carven into the back by its maker; and its
complete inability to tell time, all marked it as pre-Huygens
technology. Its bonging would have tried Daniel's patience
even if it had occurred precisely on the hour, half-hour,
quarter-hour, *et cetera,* for it never failed to make him jump
out of his skin. That it conveyed no information whatever as
to what the time actually was, drove Daniel into such trans-
ports of annoyance that he had begun to entertain a phant'sy
of standing at the intersection of two corridors and handing
Drake, every time he passed by, a libel denouncing the ancient Clock, and demanding its wayward pendulum be
stilled, and that it be replaced with a new Huygens model.
But Drake had already told him to shut up about the clock,
and so there was nothing he could do.

Daniel was going for days without hearing any other
sounds but these. All possible subjects of conversation could
be divided into two categories: (1) ones that would cause
Drake to unleash a rant, previously heard so many times that
Daniel could recite it from memory, and (2) ones that might
actually lead to original conversation. Daniel avoided Category 1 topics. All Category 2 topics had already been exhausted. For example, Daniel could not ask, "How is
Praise-God doing in Boston?"* because he had asked this on
the first day, and Drake had answered it, and since then few
letters had arrived because the letter-carriers were dead or
running away from London as fast as they could go. Sometimes private couriers would come with letters, mostly per-
taining to Drake's business matters but sometimes addressed
to Daniel. This would provoke a flurry of conversation

---

*Praise-God W. being the eldest son of Raleigh W., and hence Drake W.'s
first grandchild; he had recently sailed to Boston at the age of sixteen to
study at Harvard, become part of that City on the Hill that was America,
and, if possible, return in glory at some future time to drive Archbishop
Laud's spawn from England and reform the Anglican Church once and for
all.

stretching out as long as half an hour (not counting rants), but mostly what Daniel heard, day after day, was corpse-collectors' bells, and their creaking carts; the frightful Clock; cows; Drake reading the Books of Daniel and of Revelation aloud, or playing the virginal; and the gnawing of Daniel's own quill across the pages of his notebook as he worked his way through Euclid, Copernicus, Galileo, Descartes, Huygens. He actually learned an appalling amount. In fact, he was fairly certain he'd caught up with where Isaac had been several months previously—but Isaac was up at home in Woolsthorpe, a hundred miles away, and no doubt years ahead of him by this point.

He ate down to the bottom of his potatoes and herring with the determination of a prisoner clawing a hole through a wall, finally revealing the plate. The Waterhouse family china had been manufactured by sincere novices in Holland. After James I had outlawed the export of unfinished English cloth to the Netherlands, Drake had begun smuggling it there, which was easily done since the town of Leyden was crowded with English pilgrims. In this way Drake had made the first of several smuggling-related fortunes, and done so in a way pleasing in the sight of the Lord, viz. by boldly defying the King's efforts to meddle in commerce. Not only that but he had met and in 1617 married a pilgrim lass in Leyden, and he had made many donations there to the faithful who were in the market for a ship. The grateful congregation, shortly before embarking on the *Mayflower,* bound for sunny Virginia, had presented Drake and his new wife, Hortense, with this set of Delft pottery. They had obviously made it themselves on the theory that when they sloshed up onto the shores of America, they'd better know how to make stuff out of clay. They were heavy crude plates glazed white, with an inscription in spidery blue letters:

YOU AND I ARE BUT EARTH.

Staring at this through a miasma of the bodily fluids of herring for the thirty-fifth consecutive day, Daniel suddenly announced, "I was thinking that I might go and, God willing, visit John Wilkins."

Wilkins had been exchanging letters with Daniel ever since the debacle of five years ago, when Daniel had arrived at Trinity College a few moments after Wilkins had been kicked out of it forever.

The mention of Wilkins did not trigger a rant, which meant Daniel was as good as there. But there were certain formalities to be gone through: "To what end?" asked Drake, sounding like a pipe-organ with numerous jammed valves as the words emerged partly from his mouth and partly from his nose. He voiced all questions as if they were pat assertions: *To what end* being said in the same tones as *You and I are but earth.*

"My purpose is to learn, Father, but I seem to've learned all I can from the books that are here."

"And what of the Bible." An excellent riposte there from Drake.

"There are Bibles everywhere, praise God, but only one Reverend Wilkins."

"He has been preaching at that Established church in the city, has he not."

"Indeed. St. Lawrence Jewry."

"Then why should it be necessary for you to leave." As the city was a quarter of an hour's walk.

"The Plague, father—I don't believe he has actually set foot in London these last several months."

"And what of his flock."

Daniel almost fired back, *Oh, you mean the Royal Society?* which in most other houses would have been a *bon mot,* but not here. "They've all run away, too, Father, the ones who aren't dead."

"High Church folk," Drake said self-explanatorily. "Where is Wilkins now."

"Epsom."

"He is with Comstock. What can he possibly be thinking."

"It's no secret that you and Wilkins have come down on opposite sides of the fence, Father."

"The golden fence that Laud threw up around the Lord's Table! Yes."

"Wilkins backs Tolerance as fervently as you. He hopes to reform the church from within."

"Yes, and no man—short of an Archbishop—could be more *within* than John Comstock, the Earl of Epsom. But why should you embroil yourself in such matters."

"Wilkins is not pursuing religious controversies at Epsom—he is pursuing natural philosophy."

"Seems a strange place for it."

"The Earl's son, Charles, could not attend Cambridge because of the plague, and so Wilkins and some other members of the Royal Society are there to serve as his tutors."

"Aha! It is all clear, then. It is all an *accommodation*."

"Yes."

"What is it that you hope to learn from the Reverend Wilkins."

"Whatever it is that he wishes to teach me. Through the Royal Society he is in communication with all the foremost natural philosophers of the British Isles, and many on the Continent as well."

Drake took some time considering that. "You are asserting that you require my financial assistance in order to become acquainted with a *hypothetical* body of knowledge which you *assume* has come into existence *out of nowhere*, quite recently."

"Yes, Father."

"A bit of an act of faith then, isn't it."

"Not so much as you might think. My friend Isaac—I've told you of him—has spoken of a 'generative spirit' that pervades all things, and that accounts for the possibility of new things being created from old—and if you don't believe me, then just ask yourself, how can flowers grow up out of manure? Why does meat turn itself into maggots, and ships' planking into worms? Why do images of sea-shells form in rocks far from any sea, and why do new stones grow in farmers' fields after the previous year's crop has been dug out? Clearly some organizing principle is at work, and it pervades all things invisibly, and accounts for the world's ability to have *newness*—to do something other than only decay."

"And yet it decays. Look out the window! Listen to the ringing of the bells. Ten years ago, Cromwell melted down the Crown Jewels and gave all men freedom of religion. Today, a crypto-Papist* and lackey of the Antichrist† rules England, and England's gold goes to making giant punch-bowls for use at the royal orgies, and we of the Gathered Church must worship in secret as if we were early Christians in pagan Rome."

"One of the things about the generative spirit that demands our careful study is that it can go awry," Daniel returned. "In some sense the *pneuma* that causes buboes to grow from the living flesh of plague victims must be akin to the one that causes mushrooms to pop out of the ground after rain, but one has effects we call evil and the other has effects we call good."

"You think Wilkins knows more of this."

"I was actually using it to explain the very *existence* of men like Wilkins, and of this club of his, which he now calls the Royal Society, and of other such groups, such as Monsieur de Montmor's salon in Paris—"

"I see. You suppose that this same spirit is at work *in the minds* of these natural philosophers."

"Yes, Father, and in the very soil of the nations that have produced so many natural philosophers in such a short time—to the great discomfiture of the Papists." Reckoning it could not hurt his chances to get in a dig at Popery. "And just as the farmer can rely on the steady increase of his crops, I can be sure that much new work has been accomplished by such people within the last several months."

---

*King Charles II of England.

†Usually the Pope, but in this context, King Louis XIV of France.

"But with the End of Days drawing so near—"

"Only a few months ago, at one of the last meetings of the Royal Society, Mr. Daniel Coxe said that mercury had been found running like water in a chalk-pit at Line. And Lord Brereton said that at an Inn in St. Alban's, quicksilver was found running in a saw-pit."

"And you suppose this means—what."

"Perhaps this flourishing of so many kinds—natural philosophy, plague, the power of King Louis, orgies at Whitehall, quicksilver welling up from the bowels of the earth—is a necessary preparation for the Apocalypse—the generative spirit rising up like a tide."

"That much is obvious, Daniel. I wonder, though, whether there is any point in furthering your studies when we are so close."

"Would you admire a farmer who let his fields be overrun with weeds, simply because the End was near?"

"No, of course not. Your point is well taken."

"If we have a duty to be alert for the signs of the End Times, then let me go, Father. For if the signs are comets, then the first to know will be the astronomers. If the signs are plague, the first to know—"

"—will be physicians. Yes, I understand. But are you suggesting that those who study natural philosophy can acquire some kind of occult knowledge—special insight into God's Creation, not available to the common Bible-reading man?"

"Er . . . I suppose that's *quite clearly* what I'm suggesting."

Drake nodded. "That is what I thought. Well, God gave us brains for a reason—*not* to use those brains would be a sin." He got up and carried his plate to the kitchen, then went to a small desk of many drawers in the parlor and broke out all of the gear needed to write on paper with a quill. "Haven't much coin just now," he mumbled, moving the quill about in a sequence of furious scribbles separated by long flowing swoops, like a sword-duel. "There you are."

Mr. Ham pray pay to the bearer one pound I say £1—
of that money of myne which you have in your hands
upon sight of this Bill

Drake Waterhouse
London

"What is this instrument, Father?"

"Goldsmith's Note. People started doing this about the
time you left for Cambridge."

"Why does it say 'the bearer'? Why not 'Daniel Waterhouse'?"

"Well, that's the beauty of it. You could, if you chose, use
this to pay a one-pound debt—you'd simply hand it to your
creditor and he could then nip down to Ham's and get a
pound in coin of the realm. Or he could use it to pay one of
his debts."

"I see. But in this case it simply means that if I go into the
City and present this to Uncle Thomas, or one of the other
Hams . . ."

"They'll do what the note orders them to do."

It was, then, a normal example of Drake's innate fiendish-
ness. Daniel was perfectly welcome to flee to Epsom—the
seat of John Comstock, the arch-Anglican—and study Natural Philosophy until, literally, the End of the World. But in
order to obtain the *means*, he would have to demonstrate his
faith by walking all the way across London at the height of
the Plague. Trial by ordeal it was.

The next morning: on with a coat and a down-at-heels pair
of riding-boots, even though it was a warm summer day. A
scarf to breathe through.* A minimal supply of clean shirts

---

*The consensus of the best physicians in the Royal Society was that plague
was not caused by bad air, but had something to do with being crowded together with many other people, especially foreigners (the first victims of the
London plague had been Frenchmen fresh off the boat, who'd died in an inn
about five hundred yards from Drake's house), however, everyone breathed
through scarves anyway.

and drawers (if he was feeling well when he reached Epsom, he'd send for more). A rather small number of books—tiny student octavo volumes of the usual Continental savants, their margins and interlinear spaces now caulked with his notes. A letter he'd received from Wilkins, with an enclosure from one Robert Hooke, during a rare spate of mail last week. All went into a bag, the bag on the end of a staff, and the staff over his shoulder—made him look somewhat Vagabondish, but many people in the city had turned to robbery, as normal sources of employment had been shut down, and there were sound reasons to look impoverished and carry a big stick.

Drake, upon Daniel's departure: "Will you tell old Wilkins that I do not think the less of him for having become an Anglican, as I have the most serene confidence that he has done so in the interest of *reforming* that church, which as you know has been the steady goal of those of us who are scorned by others as Puritans."

And for Daniel: "I want that you should take care that the plague should not infect you—not the Black Plague, but the plague of Skepticism so fashionable among Wilkins's crowd. In some ways your soul might be safer in a brothel than among certain Fellows of the Royal Society."

"It is not skepticism for its own sake, Father. Simply an awareness that we are prone to error, and that it is difficult to view anything impartially."

"That is fine when you are talking about comets."

"I'll not discuss religion, then. Good-bye, Father."

"God be with you, Daniel."

HE OPENED THE DOOR, trying not to flinch when outside air touched his face, and descended the steps to the road called Holborn, a river of pounded dust (it had not rained in a while). Drake's house was a new (post-Cromwell) half-timbered building on the north side of the road, one of a line of mostly wooden houses that formed a sort of fence dividing Holborn from the open fields on its north, which stretched all the way to Scotland. The buildings across the

way, on the south side of Holborn, were the same but two decades older (pre–Civil War). The ground was flat except for
a sort of standing wave of packed dirt that angled across the
fields, indeed across Holborn itself, not far away, off to his
right—as if a comet had landed on London Bridge and sent
up a ripple in the earth, which had spread outwards until it
had gone just past Drake's house and then frozen. These
were the remains of the earth-works that London* had
thrown up early in the Civil War, to defend against the
King's armies. There'd been a gate on Holborn and a star-
shaped earthen fort nearby, but the gate had been torn down
a long time ago and the fort blurred into a grassy hummock
guarded by the younger and more adventurous cattle.

Daniel turned left, towards London. This was utter madness. But the letter from Wilkins, and the enclosure from
Hooke—a Wilkins protégé from his Oxford days, and now
Curator of Experiments of the Royal Society—contained
certain requests. They were phrased politely. Perhaps not so
politely in Hooke's case. They had let Daniel know that he
could be of great service to them by fetching certain items
out of certain buildings in London.

Daniel could have burned the letter and claimed it had
never arrived. He could have gone to Epsom without any of
the items on the list, pleading the Bubonic Plague as his excuse. But he suspected that Wilkins and Hooke did not care
for excuses any more than Drake did.

By going to Trinity at exactly the wrong moment, Daniel
had missed out on the first five years of the Royal Society of
London. Lately he had attended a few meetings, but always
felt as if his nose were pressed up against the glass.

Today he would pay his dues by walking into London. It
was hardly the most dangerous thing anyone had done in the
study of Natural Philosophy.

He put one boot in front of the other, and found that he
had not died yet. He did it again, then again. The place

---

*Which had been pro-Cromwell.

seemed eerily normal for a short while as long as you ignored the continuous ringing of death-knells from about a hundred different parish churches. On a closer look, many people had adorned the walls of their houses with nearly hysterical pleas for God's mercy, perhaps thinking that like the blood of the lambs on Israel's door-posts, these graffiti might keep the Angel of Death from knocking. Wagons came and went on Holborn only occasionally—empty ones going into town, stained and reeking, with vanguards and rear-guards of swooping birds cutting swaths through the banks of flies that surrounded them—these were corpse-wains returning from their midnight runs to the burial-pits and churchyards outside the town. Wagons filled with people, escorted by pedestrians with hand-bells and red sticks, crept out of town. Just near the remains of those earth-works where Holborn terminated at its intersection with the road to Oxford, a pest-house had been established, and when it had filled up with dead people, another, farther away, to the north of the Tyburn gallows, at Marylebone. Some of the people on the wagons appeared normal, others had reached the stage where the least movement caused them hellish buboe-pain, and so even without the bells and red sticks the approach of these wagons would have been obvious from the fusillade of screams and hot prayers touched off at every bump in the road. Daniel and the very few other pedestrians on Holborn backed into doorways and breathed through scarves when these wagons passed by.

Through Newgate and the stumps of the Roman wall, then, past the Prison, which was silent, but not empty. Towards the square-topped tower of Saint Paul's, where an immense bell was being walloped by tired ringers, counting the years of the dead. That old tower leaned to one side, and had for a long time, so that everyone in London had stopped noticing that it did. In these circumstances, though, it seemed to lean more, and made Daniel suddenly nervous that it was about to fall over on him. Just a few weeks ago, Robert Hooke and Sir Robert Moray had been up in its belfry conducting experiments with two-hundred-foot-long pendulums. Now the cathedral was fortified within a rampart of freshly tamped earth, the graves piled up a full yard above ground level.

The old front of the church had become half eaten away by coal-smoke, and a newfangled Classical porch slapped onto it some three or four decades ago. But the new columns were already decaying, and they were marred from where shops had been built between them during Cromwell's time. During those years, Roundhead cavalry had pulled the furniture up from the western half of the church and chopped it up for firewood, then used the empty space as a vast stable for nearly a thousand horses, selling their dung as fuel, to freezing Londoners, for 4d a bushel. Meanwhile, in the eastern half Drake and Bolstrood and others had preached three-hour sermons to diminishing crowds. Now King Charles was supposedly fixing the place up, but Daniel could see no evidence that anything had been done.

Daniel went round the south side of the church even though it was not the most direct way, because he wanted to have a look at the south transept, which had collapsed some years ago. Rumor had it that the bigger and better stones were being carted away and used to build a new wing of John Comstock's house on Piccadilly. Indeed, many of the stones had been removed to somewhere, but of course no one was working there now except for gravediggers.

Into Cheapside, where men on ladders were clambering into upper-story windows of a boarded-up house to remove limp, exhausted children who'd somehow outlived their families. Down in the direction of the river, the only gathering of people Daniel had seen: a long queue before the house of Dr. Nathaniel Hodges, one of the only physicians who hadn't fled. Not far beyond that, on Cheapside, the house of John Wilkins himself. Wilkins had sent Daniel a key, which turned out not to be necessary, as his house had already been broken into. Floorboards pried up, mattresses gutted so that the place looked like a barn for all the loose straw and lumber on the floor. Whole ranks of books pawed from the shelves to see if anything was hidden behind. Daniel went round and re-shelved the books, holding back two or three newish ones that Wilkins had asked him to fetch.

Then to the Church of St. Lawrence Jewry.* "Follow the Drainpipes, find the *Amphib'ns*," Wilkins had written. Daniel walked round the churchyard, which was studded with graves, but had not reached the graves-on-top-of-graves stage—Wilkins's parishioners were mostly prosperous mercers who'd fled to their country houses. At one corner of the roof, a red copper vein descended from the downhill end of a rain-gutter, then ducked into a holed window beneath. Daniel entered the church and traced it down into a cellar where dormant God-gear was cached to expect the steady wheeling of the liturgical calendar (Easter and Christmas stuff, e.g.) or sudden reversals in the prevailing theology (High Church people like the late Bishop Laud wanted a fence round the altar so parish dogs couldn't lift their legs on the Lord's Table, Low Church primitives like Drake didn't; the Rev. Wilkins, more in the Drake mold, had stashed the fence and rail down here). This room hummed, almost shuddered, as if a choir of monks were lurking in the corners intoning one of their chants, but it was actually the buzzing of a whole civilization of flies, so large that many of them seemed to be singing bass—these had grown from the corpses of rats, which carpeted the cellar floor like autumn leaves. It smelled that way, too.

---

*Which had nothing to do with Jews; it was named partly after its location in a part of the city where Jews had lived before they had been kicked out of England in 1290 by Edward I. For Jews to exist in a Catholic or Anglican country was theoretically impossible because the entire country was divided into parishes, and every person who lived in a given parish, by definition, was a member of the parish church, which collected tithes, recorded births and deaths, and enforced regular attendance at services. This general sort of arrangement was called the *Established Church* and was why dissidents like Drake had no logical choice but to espouse the concept of the *Gathered Church,* which drew like-minded persons from an arbitrary geographical territory. In making it legally *possible* for Gathered Churches to exist, Cromwell had, in effect, re-admitted Jews to England.

The drain-pipe came into the cellar from a hole in the floor above, and emptied into a stone baptismal Font—a jumbo, total-baby-immersion style of Font—that had been shoved into a corner, probably around the time that King Henry VIII had kicked out the Papists. Daniel guessed as much from the carvings, which were so thick with symbols of Rome that to remove them all would have destroyed it structurally. When this vessel filled with rain-water from the drain-pipe it would spill excess onto the floor, and it would meander off into a corner and seep into the earth—perhaps this source of drinking-water had attracted the sick rats.

In any case the top of the font was covered with a grille held down by a couple of bricks—from underneath came contented croaking sounds. A gout of pink shot through an interstice and speared a fly out of midair, paused humming-taut for an instant, then snapped back. Daniel removed the bricks and pulled up the grille and looked at, and was looked at by, half a dozen of the healthiest frogs he'd ever seen, frogs the size of terriers, frogs that could tongue sparrows out of the air. Standing there in the City of Death, Daniel laughed. The generative spirit ran amok in the bodies of rats, whose corpses were transmuted into flies, which gave up their spirit to produce happy blinking green frogs.

Faint ticks, by the thousands, merged into a sound like wind-driven sleet against a windowpane. Daniel looked down to see it was just hordes of fleas who had abandoned the rat corpses and converged on him from all across the cellar, and were now ricocheting off his leather boots. He rummaged until he found a bread-basket, packed the frogs into it, imprisoned them loosely under a cloth, and walked out of there.

Though he could not see the river from here, he could infer that the tide was receding from the trickle of Thames-water that was beginning to probe its way down the gutter in the middle of Poultry Lane, running downhill from Leaden-hall. Normally this would be a slurry of paper-scraps discarded by traders at the 'Change, but today it was lumpy with corpses of rats and cats.

He gave that gutter as wide a berth as he could, but proceeded up against the direction of its flow to the edge of the goldsmiths' district, whence Threadneedle and Poultry and Lombard and Cornhill sprayed confusingly. He continued up Cornhill to the highest point in the City of London, where Cornhill came together with Leadenhall (which carried on eastwards, but downhill from here) and Fish Street (downhill straight to London Bridge) and Bishopsgate (downhill towards the city wall, and Bedlam, and the plague-pit they'd dug next to it). In the middle of this intersection a stand-pipe sprouted, with one nozzle for each of those streets, and Thames-water rushed from each nozzle to flush the gutters. It was connected to a buried pipe that ran underneath Fish Street to the northern terminus of London Bridge. During Elizabeth's time some clever Dutchmen had built water-wheels there. Even when the men who tended them were dead or run away to the country, these spun powerfully whenever the tide went out and high water accumulated on the upstream side of the bridge. They were connected to pumps that pressurized the Fish Street pipe and (if you lived on this hill) carried away the accumulated waste, or (if you lived elsewhere) brought a twice-daily onslaught of litter, turds, and dead animals.

He followed said onslaught down Bishopsgate, watching the water get dirtier as he went, but didn't go as far as the wall—he stopped at the great house, or rather compound, that Sir Thomas ("Bad money drives out good") Gresham had built, a hundred years ago, with money he'd made lending to the Crown and reforming the coinage. Like all old half-timbered fabricks it was slowly warping and bending out of true, but Daniel loved it because it was now Gresham's College, home of the Royal Society.

And of Robert Hooke, the R.S.'s Curator of Experiments, who'd moved into it nine months ago—enabling him to do experiments all the time. Hooke had sent Daniel a list of odds and ends that he needed for his work at Epsom. Daniel deposited his frog-basket and other goods on the high table in the room where the Royal Society had its meetings and, using that as a sort of base-camp, made excursions into Hooke's apartment and all of the rooms and attics and cellars that the Royal Society had taken over for storage.

He saw, and rummaged through, and clambered over, slices of numerous tree-trunks that someone had gathered in a bid to demonstrate that the thin parts of the rings tended to point towards true north. A Brazilian compass-fish that Boyle had suspended from a thread to see if (as legend had it) it would do the same (when Daniel came in, it was pointing south by southeast). Jars containing: powder of the lungs and livers of vipers (someone thought you could produce young vipers from it), something called Sympathetic Powder that supposedly healed wounds through a voodoo-like process. Samples of a mysterious red fluid taken from the Bloody Pond at Newington. Betel-nut, camphire-wood, nux vomica, rhino-horn. A ball of hair that Sir William Curtius had found in a cow's belly. Some experiments in progress: a number of pebbles contained in glass jars full of water, the necks of the jars just barely large enough to let the pebbles in; later they would see if the pebbles could be removed, and if not, it would prove that they had grown in the water. Very large amounts of splintered lumber of all types, domestic and foreign—the residue of the Royal Society's endless experiments on the breaking-strength of wooden beams. The Earl of Balcarres's heart, which he had thoughtfully donated to them, but not until he had died of natural causes. A box of stones that various people had coughed up out of their lungs, which the R.S. was saving up to send as a present to the King. Hundreds of wasps' and birds' nests, methodically labeled with the names of the proud patrons who had brought them in. A box of baby vertebrae which had been removed from a large abscess in the side of a woman who'd had a failed pregnancy twelve years earlier. Stored in jars in spirits of wine: various human fœtuses, the head of a colt with a double eye in the center of its forehead, an eel from Japan. Tacked to the wall: the skin of a seven-legged, two-bodied, single-headed lamb. Decomposing in glass boxes: the Royal Society's viper collection, all dead of starvation; some had their heads tied to their tails as part of some sort of Uroburos experiment. More hairballs. The heart of an executed person, superficially no different from that of the Earl of Balcarres. A vial containing seeds that had supposedly been voided in the urine of a maid in Holland. A jar of blue pigment made from tincture of galls, a jar of green made from Hungarian vitriol. A sketch of one of the Dwarves who supposedly inhabited the Canary Islands. Hundreds of lodestones of various sizes and shapes. A model of a giant crossbow that Hooke had designed for flinging harpoons at whales. A U-shaped glass tube that Boyle had filled with quicksilver to prove that its undulations were akin to those of a pendulum.

Hooke wanted Daniel to bring various parts and tools and materials used in the making of watches and other fine mechanisms; some of the stones that had been found in the Earl's heart; a cylinder of quicksilver; a hygroscope made from the beard of a wild oat; a burning-glass in a wooden frame; a pair of deep convex spectacles for seeing underwater; his dew-collecting glass,* and selections from his large collection of preserved bladders: carp, pig, cow, and so on. He also wanted enormous, completely impractical numbers of different-sized spheres of different materials such as lead, amber, wood, silver, and so forth, which were useful in all manner of rolling and dropping experiments. Also, various spare parts for his air-compressing engine, and his Artificial Eye. Finally, Hooke asked him to collect "any puppies, kit-

---

*A conical glass, wide at the top and pointed on the bottom, which when filled with cold water or (preferably) snow and left outside overnight, would condense dew on its outside; the dew would run down and drip into a receptacle underneath.

tens, chicks, or mice you might come across, as the supply hereabouts is considerably diminished."

Some mail had piled up here, despite the recent difficulties, much of it addressed simply "GRUBENDOL London." Following Wilkins's instructions, Daniel gathered it all up and added it to the pile. But the GRUBENDOL stuff he culled out, and tied up into a packet with string.

Now he was ready to leave London, and wanted only money, and some way to carry all of this stuff. Back down Bishopsgate he went (leaving everything behind at Gresham College, except for the frogs, who demanded close watching) and turned on Threadneedle, which he followed westwards as it converged on Cornhill. Close to their intersection stood a series of row-houses that fronted on both of these streets. As even the illiterate might guess from the men with muskets smoking pipes on the rooftops, all were goldsmiths. Daniel went to the one called HAM BROS. A few trinkets and a couple of gold plates were displayed in a window by the door, as if to suggest that the Hams were still literally in the business of fabricating things out of gold.

A face in a grate. "Daniel!" The grate slammed and latched, the door growled and clanged as might works of ironmongery were slid and shot on the inside. Finally it was open. "Welcome!"

"Good day, Uncle Thomas."

"Half-brother-in-law actually," said Thomas Ham, out of a stubborn belief that pedantry and repetitiveness could through some alchemy be forged into wit. Pedantry because he was technically correct (he'd married Daniel's half-sister) and repetitive because he'd been making the same joke for as long as Daniel had been alive. Ham was more than sixty years old now, and he was one of those who is fat and skinny at the same time—a startling pot-belly suspended from a lanky armature, waggling jowls draped over a face like an edged weapon. He had been lucky to capture the fair Mayflower Waterhouse, or so he was encouraged to believe.

"I was affrighted when I came up the street—thought you were burying people," Daniel said, gesturing at several mounds of earth around the house's foundations.

Ham looked carefully up and down Threadneedle—as if what he was doing could possibly be a secret from anyone. "We are making a Crypt of a different sort," he said. "Come, enter. Why is that basket croaking?"

"I have taken a job as a porter," Daniel said. "Do you have a hand-cart or wheelbarrow I could borrow for a few days?"

"Yes, a very heavy and strong one—we use it to carry lock-boxes back and forth to the Mint. Hasn't moved since the Plague started. By all means take it!"

The parlor held a few more pathetic vestiges of a retail jewelry business, but it was really just a large writing-desk and some books. Stairs led to the Ham residence on the upper floors—dark and silent. "Mayflower and the children are well in Buckinghamshire?" Daniel asked.

"God willing, yes, her last letter quite put me to sleep. Come downstairs!" Uncle Thomas led him through another fortress-door that had been left wedged open, and down a narrow stair into the earth—for the first time since leaving his father's house, Daniel smelled nothing bad, only the calm scent of earth being disturbed.

He'd never been invited into the cellar, but he'd always known about it—from the solemn way it was talked about, or, to be precise, talked *around,* he'd always known it must be full of either ghosts or a large quantity of gold. Now he found it to be absurdly small and homely compared to its awesome reputation, in a way that was heartwarmingly English—but it *was* full of gold, and it was getting larger and less ditch-like by the minute. At the end nearest the base of the stairway, piled simply on the dirt floor, were platters, punch-bowls, pitchers, knives, forks, spoons, goblets, ladles, candlesticks, and gravy-boats of gold—also sacks of coins, boxed medallions stamped with visages of Continental nobles commemorating this or that battle, actual gold bars, and irregular sticks of gold called pigs. Each item was somehow tagged: *367-11/32 troy oz. depos. by my Lord Rochester on 29 Sept. 1662* and so on. The stuff was piled up like a dry-stone wall, which is to say that bits were packed into spaces between other bits in a way calculated to keep the whole formation from collapsing. All of it was spattered with dirt and brick-fragments and mortar-splats from the work proceeding at the other end of the cellar: a laborer with pick and shovel, and another with a back-basket to carry the dirt upstairs; a carpenter working with heavy timbers, doing something Daniel assumed was to keep the House of Ham from collapsing; and a bricklayer and his assistant, giving the new space a foundation and walls. It was a tidy cellar now; no rats in here.

"Your late mother's candlesticks are, I'm afraid, not on view just now—rather far back in the, er, Arrangement—" said Thomas Ham.

"I'm not here to disturb the Arrangement," Daniel said, producing the Note from his father.

"Oh! Easily done! Easily and cheerfully done!" announced Mr. Ham after donning spectacles and shaking his jowls at the Note for a while, a hound casting after a scent. "Pocket money for the young scholar—the young divine—is it?"

"Cambridge is very far from re-opening, they say—need to be applying myself elsewhere," Daniel said, merely dribbling small talk behind him as he went to look at a small pile of dirty stuff that was not gold. "What are these?"

"Remains of the house of some Roman that once stood here," Mr. Ham said. "Those who follow these things—and I'm sorry to say I *don't*—assure me that something called Walbrook Stream flowed just through here, and spilled into the Thames at the Provincial Governor's Palace, twelve hundred odd years ago—the Roman mercers had their houses along its banks, so that they could ferry goods up and down from the River."

Daniel was using the sole of one boot to sweep loose dirt

away from a hard surface he'd sensed underneath. Wee polygons—terra-cotta, indigo, bone-white, beige—appeared. He
was looking at a snatch of a mosaic floor. He swept away
more dirt and recognized it as a rendering of a naked leg,
knee flexed and toe pointed as if its owner were on the run. A
pair of wings sprouted from the ankle. "Yes, the Roman
floor we'll keep," said Mr. Ham, "as we need a barrier—to
discourage clever men with shovels. Jonas, where are the
loose bits?"

The digger kicked a wooden box across the floor towards
them. It was half-full of small bits of dirty junk: a couple of
combs carved out of bone or ivory; a clay lantern; the skeleton of a brooch, jewels long since missing from their sockets; fragments of glazed pottery; and something long and
slender: a hairpin, Daniel reckoned, rubbing the dirt away. It
was probably silver, though badly tarnished. "Take it, my
lad," said Mr. Ham, referring not only to the hairpin but also
to a rather nice silver one-pound coin that he had just quarried from his pocket. "Perhaps the future Mrs. Waterhouse
will enjoy fixing her coif with a bauble that once adorned the
head of some Roman trader's wife."

"Trinity College does not allow us to have wives," Daniel
reminded him, "but I'll take it anyway—perhaps I'll have a
niece or something who has pretty hair, and who isn't
squeamish about a bit of paganism." For it was clear now
that the hairpin was fashioned in the shape of a caduceus.

"Paganism? Then we are all pagans! It is a symbol of
Mercury—patron of commerce—who has been worshipped
in this cellar—and in this city—for a thousand years, by
Bishops as well as business-men. It is a cult that adapts itself
to any religion, just as easily as quicksilver adopts the shape
of any container—and someday, Daniel, you'll meet a young
lady who is just as adaptable. Take it." Putting the silver coin
next to the caduceus in Daniel's palm, he folded Daniel's
fingers over the top and then clasped the fist—chilled by the
touch of the metal—between his two warm hands in bene-
diction.

*   *   *

DANIEL PUSHED HIS HAND-CART westwards down Cheapside. He held his breath as he hurried around the reeking tumulus that surrounded St. Paul's, and did not breathe easy again until he'd passed out of Ludgate. The passage over Fleet Ditch was even worse, because it was strewn with bodies of rats, cats, and dogs, as well as quite a few plague-corpses that had simply been rolled out of wagons, and not even dignified with a bit of dirt. He kept a rag clamped over his face, and did not take it off until he had passed out through Temple Bar and gone by the little Watch-house that stood in the middle of the Strand in front of Somerset House. From there he could glimpse green fields and open country between certain of the buildings, and smell whiffs of manure on the breeze, which smelled delightful compared to London.

He had worried that the wheels of his cart would bog down in Charing Cross, which was a perpetual morass, but summer heat, and want of traffic, had quite dried the place up. A pack of five stray dogs watched him make his way across the expanse of rutted and baked dirt. He was worried that they would come after him until he noticed that they were uncommonly fat, for stray dogs.

Oldenburg lived in a town-house on Pall Mall. Except for a heroic physician or two, he was the only member of the R.S. who'd stayed in town during the Plague. Daniel took out the GRUBENDOL packet and put it on the doorstep—letters from Vienna, Florence, Paris, Amsterdam, Berlin, Moscow.

He knocked thrice on the door, and backed away to see a round face peering down at him through obscuring layers of green window-glass, like a curtain of tears. Oldenburg's wife had lately died—not of Plague—and some supposed that he stayed in London hoping that the Black Death would carry him off to wherever she was.

On his long walk out of town, Daniel had plenty of time to work out that GRUBENDOL was an anagram for Oldenburg.

Epsom
1665–1666

> By this it appears how necessary it is for any man
> that aspires to true knowledge, to examine the
> definitions of former authors; and either to cor-
> rect them, where they are negligently set down,
> or to make them himself. For the errors of defi-
> nitions multiply themselves according as the
> reckoning proceeds, and lead men into absurd-
> ities, which at last they see, but cannot avoid,
> without reckoning anew from the beginning.
> —HOBBES, *Leviathan*

JOHN COMSTOCK'S SEAT was at Epsom, a short journey from
London. It was large. That largeness came in handy during the
Plague, because it enabled his Lordship to stable a few Fellows of the Royal Society (which would enhance his already
tremendous prestige) without having to be very close to them
(which would disturb his household, and place his domestic
animals in extreme peril). All of this was obvious enough to
Daniel as one of Comstock's servants met him at the gate and
steered him well clear of the manor house and across a sort of
defensive buffer zone of gardens and pastures to a remote cottage with an oddly dingy and crowded look to it.

To one side lay a spacious bone-yard, chalky with skulls
of dogs, cats, rats, pigs, and horses. To the other, a pond clut-

tered with the wrecks of model ships, curiously rigged. Above the well, some sort of pulley arrangement, and a rope extending from the pulley, across a pasture, to a half-assembled chariot. On the roof of the cottage, diverse small windmills of outlandish design—one of them mounted over the mouth of the cottage's chimney and turned by the rising of its smoke. Every high tree-limb in the vicinity had been exploited as a support for pendulums, and the pendulum-strings had all gotten twisted round each other by winds, and merged into a tattered philosophickal cobweb. The green space in front was a mechanical phant'sy of wheels and gears, broken or never finished. There was a giant wheel, apparently built so that a man could roll across the countryside by climbing inside it and driving it forward with his feet.

Ladders had been leaned against any wall or tree with the least ability to push back. Halfway up one of the ladders was a stout, fair-haired man who was not far from the end of his natural life span—though he apparently did not entertain any ambitions of actually reaching it. He was climbing the ladder one-handed in hard-soled leather shoes that were perfectly frictionless on the rungs, and as he swayed back and forth, planting one foot and then the next, the ladder's feet, down below him, tiptoed backwards. Daniel rushed over and braced the ladder, then forced himself to look upwards at the shuddering battle-gammoned form of the Rev. Wilkins. The Rev. was carrying, in his free hand, some sort of winged object.

And speaking of winged objects, Daniel now felt himself being tickled, and glanced down to find half a dozen honey-bees had alighted on each one of his hands. As Daniel watched in empirical horror, one of them drove its stinger into the fleshy place between his thumb and index finger. He bit his lip and looked up to see whether letting go the ladder would lead to the immediate death of Wilkins. The answer: yes. Bees were now swarming all round—nuzzling the fringes of Daniel's hair, playing crack-the-whip through the ladder's rungs, and orbiting round Wilkins's body in a humming cloud.

Reaching the highest possible altitude—flagrantly tempting the LORD to strike him dead—Wilkins released the toy in his hand. Whirring and clicking noises indicated that some sort of spring-driven clockwork had gone into action—there was fluttering, and skidding through the air—some sort of interaction with the atmosphere, anyway, that went beyond mere falling—but fall it did, veering into the cottage's stone wall and spraying parts over the yard.

"Never going to fly to the moon *that* way," Wilkins grumbled.

"I thought you wanted to be *shot out of a cannon* to the Moon."

Wilkins whacked himself on the stomach. "As you can see, I have far too much *vis inertiae* to be shot out of *anything* to *anywhere*. Before I come down there, are you feeling well, young man? No sweats, chills, swellings?"

"I anticipated your curiosity on that subject, Dr. Wilkins, and so the frogs and I lodged at an inn in Epsom for two nights. I have never felt healthier."

"Splendid! Mr. Hooke has denuded the countryside of small animals—if you hadn't brought him anything, he'd have cut *you* up." Wilkins was coming down the ladder, the sureness of each footfall very much in doubt, massy buttocks approaching Daniel as a spectre of doom. Finally on terra firma, he waved a hundred bees off with an intrepid sweep of the arm. They wiped bees away from their palms, then exchanged a long, warm handshake. The bees were collectively losing interest and seeping away in the direction of a large glinting glass box. "It is Wren's design, come and see!" Wilkins said, bumbling after them.

The glass structure was a model of a building, complete with a blown dome, and pillars carved of crystal. It was of a Gothickal design, and had the general look of some Government office in London, or a University college. The doors and windows were open to let bees fly in and out. They had built a hive inside—a cathedral of honeycombs.

"With all respect to Mr. Wren, I see a clash of architectural styles here—"

"What! Where?" Wilkins exclaimed, searching the roofline for aesthetic contaminants. "I shall cane the boy!"

"It's not the builder, but the tenants who're responsible. All those little waxy hexagons—doesn't fit with Mr. Wren's scheme, does it?"

"Which style do you prefer?" Wilkins asked, wickedly.

"Err—"

"Before you answer, know that Mr. Hooke approaches," the Rev. whispered, glancing sidelong. Daniel looked over toward the house to see Hooke coming their way, bent and gray and transparent, like one of those curious figments that occasionally floats across one's eyeball.

"Is he all right?" Daniel asked.

"The usual bouts of melancholy—a certain peevishness over the scarcity of adventuresome females—"

"I meant is he sick."

Hooke had stopped near Daniel's luggage, attracted by the croaking of frogs. He stepped in and seized the basket.

"Oh, he ever looks as if he's been bleeding to death for several hours—fear for the frogs, not for Hooke!" Wilkins said. He had a perpetual knowing, amused look that enabled him to get away with saying almost anything. This, combined with the occasional tactical master-stroke (e.g., marrying Cromwell's sister during the Interregnum), probably accounted for his ability to ride out civil wars and revolutions as if they were mere theatrical performances. He bent down in front of the glass apiary, pantomiming a bad back; reached underneath; and, after some dramatic rummaging, drew out a glass jar with an inch or so of cloudy brown honey in the bottom. "Mr. Wren provided sewerage, as you can see," he said, giving the jar to Daniel. It was bloodwarm. The Rev. now headed in the direction of the house, and Daniel followed.

"You say you quarantined yourself at Epsom town—you must have paid for lodgings there—that means you have pocket-money. Drake must've given it you. What on earth did you tell him you were coming here to do? I need to know," Wilkins added apologetically, "only so that I can write him the occasional letter claiming that you are doing it."

"Keeping abreast of the very latest, from the Continent or whatever. I'm to provide him with advance warning of any events that are plainly part of the Apocalypse."

Wilkins stroked an invisible beard and nodded profoundly, standing back so that Daniel could dart forward and haul open the cottage door. They went into the front room, where a fire was decaying in a vast hearth. Two or three rooms away, Hooke was crucifying a frog on a plank, occasionally swearing as he struck his thumb. "Perhaps you can help me with my book . . ."

"A new edition of the *Cryptonomicon*?"

"Perish the thought! Damn me, I'd almost forgotten about *that* old thing. Wrote it a quarter-century ago. Consider the times! The King was losing his mind—his Ministers being lynched in Parliament—his own drawbridge-keepers locking him out of his own arsenals. His foes intercepting letters abroad, written by that French Papist wife of his, *begging* foreign powers to invade us. Hugh Peters had come back from Salem to whip those Puritans into a frenzy—no great difficulty, given that the King, simply out—*out*—of money, had seized all of the merchants' gold in the Tower. Scottish Covenanters down as far as Newcastle, Catholics rebelling in Ulster, sudden panics in London—gentlemen on the street whipping out their rapiers for little or no reason. Things no better elsewhere—Europe twenty-five years into the Thirty Years' War, wolves eating children along the road in Besançon, for Christ's sake—Spain and Portugal dividing into two separate kingdoms, the Dutch taking advantage of it to steal Malacca from the Portuguese—of *course* I wrote the *Cryptonomicon*! And of course people bought it! But if it was the Omega—a way of hiding information, of making the light into darkness—then the Universal Character is the Alpha—an opening. A dawn. A candle in the darkness. Am I being disgusting?"

"Is this anything like Comenius's project?"

Wilkins leaned across and made as if to box Daniel's ears. "It *is* his project! This was what he and I, and that whole gang of odd Germans—Hartlib, Haak, Kinner, Oldenburg— wanted to do when we conceived the Invisible College* back in the Dark Ages. But Mr. Comenius's work was burned up in a fire, back in Moravia, you know."

"Accidental, or—"

"*Excellent* question, young man—in Moravia, one never knows. Now, if Comenius had listened to my advice and accepted the invitation to be Master of Harvard College back in '41, it might've been different—"

"The colonists would be twenty-five years ahead of us!"

"Just so. Instead, Natural Philosophy flourishes at Oxford—less so at Cambridge—and Harvard is a pitiable backwater."

"Why didn't he take your advice, I wonder—?"

"The tragedy of these middle-European savants is that they are always trying to apply their *philosophick* acumen in the *political* realm."

"Whereas the Royal Society is—?"

"*Ever so strictly* apolitical," Wilkins said, and then favored Daniel with a stage-actor's hugely exaggerated wink. "If we stayed away from politics, we could be flying winged chariots to the Moon within a few generations. All that's needed is to pull down certain barriers to progress—"

"Such as?"

"Latin."

"*Latin!?* But Latin is—"

"I know, the universal language of scholars and divines, *et cetera, et cetera.* And it *sounds* so lovely, doesn't it. You can say any sort of nonsense in Latin and our feeble University

---

*Forerunner of the Royal Society.

men will be stunned, or at least profoundly confused. That's how the Popes have gotten away with peddling bad religion for so long—they simply say it in Latin. But if we were to unfold their convoluted phrases and translate them into a *philosophical* language, all of their contradictions and vagueness would become manifest."

"Mmm . . . I'd go so far as to say that if a proper philosophical language existed, it would be impossible to express any false concept in it without violating its rules of grammar," Daniel hazarded.

"You have just uttered the most succinct possible definition of it—I say, you're not *competing* with me, are you?" Wilkins said jovially.

"No," Daniel said, too intimidated to catch the humor. "I was merely reasoning by analogy to Cartesian analysis, where false statements cannot legally be written down, as long as the terms are understood."

"The terms! That's the difficult part," Wilkins said. "As a way to write down the terms, I am developing the Philosophical Language and the Universal Character—which learned men of all races and nations will use to signify ideas."

"I am at your service, sir," Daniel said. "When may I begin?"

"Immediately! Before Hooke's done with those frogs—if he comes in here and finds you idle, he'll *enslave* you—you'll be shovelling guts or, worse, trying the precision of his clocks by standing before a pendulum and counting . . . its . . . alternations . . . all . . . day . . . long."

Hooke came in. His spine was all awry: not only stooped, but bent to one side. His long brown hair hung unkempt around his face. He straightened up a bit and tilted his head back so that the hair fell away to either side, like a curtain opening up to reveal a pale face. Stubble on the cheeks made him look even gaunter than he actually was, and made his gray eyes look even more huge. He said: "Frogs, too."

"Nothing surprises me *now*, Mr. Hooke."

"I put it to you that all living creatures are made out of them."

"Have you considered writing any of this down? Mr. Hooke? Mr. Hooke?" But Hooke was already gone out into the stable-yard, off on some other experiment.

"Made out of *what*??" Daniel asked.

"Lately, every time Mr. Hooke peers at something with his Microscope he finds that it is divided up into small compartments, each one just like its neighbors, like bricks in a wall," Wilkins confided.

"What do these bricks look like?"

"He doesn't call them bricks. Remember, they are hollow. He has taken to calling them 'cells' . . . but you don't want to get caught up in all *that* nonsense. Follow me, my dear Daniel. Put thoughts of cells out of your mind. To understand the Philosophical Language you must know that all things in Earth and Heaven can be classified into forty different genera . . . within each of those, there are, of course, further subclasses."

Wilkins showed him into a servant's room where a writing desk had been set up, and papers and books mounded up with as little concern for order as the bees had shown in building their honeycomb. Wilkins moved a lot of air, and so leaves of paper flew off of stacks as he passed through the room. Daniel picked one up and read it: "Mule fern, panic-grass, hartstongue, adderstongue, moonwort, sea novelwort, wrack, Job's-tears, broomrope, toothwort, scurvy-grass, sowbread, golden saxifrage, lily of the valley, bastard madder, stinking ground-pine, endive, dandelion, sowthistle, Spanish picktooth, purple loose-strife, bitter vetch."

Wilkins was nodding impatiently. "The capsulate herbs, not campanulate, and the bacciferous sempervirent shrubs," he said. "Somehow it must have gotten mixed up with the glandiferous and the nuciferous trees."

"So, the Philosophical Language is some sort of botanical—"

"Look at me, I'm shuddering. Shuddering at the *thought*.

Botany! Please, Daniel, try to collect your wits. In this stack we have all of the animals, from the belly-worm to the tyger. Here, the terms of Euclidean geometry, relating to time, space, and juxtaposition. There, a classification of diseases: pustules, boils, wens, and scabs on up to splenetic hypochondriacal vapours, iliac passion, and suffocation."

"Is suffocation a disease?"

"Excellent question—get to work and answer it!" Wilkins thundered.

Daniel, meanwhile, had rescued another sheet from the floor: "Yard, Johnson, dick . . ."

"Synonyms for 'penis,'" Wilkins said impatiently.

"Rogue, mendicant, shake-rag . . ."

"Synonyms for 'beggar.' In the Philosophical Language there will only be one word for penises, one for beggars. Quick, Daniel, is there a distinction between groaning and grumbling?"

"I should say so, but—"

"On the other hand—may we lump genuflection together with curtseying, and give them one name?"

"I—I cannot say, Doctor!"

"Then, I say, there is work to be done! At the moment, I am bogged down in an *endless* digression on the Ark."

"Of the Covenant? Or—"

"The other one."

"How does that enter into the Philosophical Language?"

"Obviously the P.L. must contain one and only one word for every type of animal. Each animal's word must reflect its classification—that is, the words for *perch* and *bream* should be noticeably similar, as should the words for *robin* and *thrush*. But bird-words should be quite different from fish-words."

"It strikes me as, er, *ambitious* . . ."

"Half of Oxford is sending me tedious lists. My—*our*—task is to organize them—to draw up a table of every type of bird and beast in the world. I have entabulated the animals troublesome to other animals—the louse, the flea. Those designed for further transmutation—the caterpillar, the maggot. One-horned sheathed winged insects. Testaceous turbinated exanguious animals—and before you ask, I have subdivided them into those with, and without, spiral convolutions. Squamous river fish, phytivorous birds of long wings, rapacious beasts of the cat-kind—anyway, as I drew up all of these lists and tables, it occurred to me that (going back to Genesis, sixth chapter, verses fifteen through twenty-two) Noah must have found a way to fit all of these creatures into one gopher-wood tub three hundred cubits long! I became concerned that certain *Continental* savants, of an *atheistical* bent, might *misuse* my list to suggest that the events related in Genesis could not have happened—"

"One could also imagine certain Jesuits turning it against you—holding it up as proof that you harbored atheistical notions of your own, Dr. Wilkins."

"Just so! Daniel! Which makes it imperative that I include, in a separate chapter, a complete plan of Noah's Ark—demonstrating not only where each of the beasts was berthed, but also the fodder for the herbivorous beasts, and live cattle for the carnivorous ones, and *more* fodder yet to keep the cattle alive, long enough to be eaten by the carnivores—where, I say, 'twas all stowed."

"Fresh water must have been wanted, too," Daniel reflected.

Wilkins—who tended to draw closer and closer to people when he was talking to them, until they had to edge backwards—grabbed a sheaf of paper off a stack and bopped Daniel on the head with it. "Tend to your Bible, foolish young man! It rained the entire time!"

"Of course, of course—they could've drunk rainwater," Daniel said, profoundly mortified.

"I have had to take some liberties with the definition of 'cubit,'" Wilkins said, as if betraying a secret, "but I think he could have done it with eighteen hundred and twenty-five sheep. To feed the carnivores, I mean."

"The sheep must've taken up a whole deck!?"

"It's not the space they take up, it's all the manure, and the

labor of throwing it overboard," Wilkins said. "At any rate—
as you can well imagine—this Ark business has stopped all
progress cold on the P.L. front. I need you to get on with the
Terms of Abuse."

"Sir!"

"Have you felt, Daniel, a certain annoyance, when one of
your semi-educated Londoners speaks of 'a vile rascal' or 'a
miserable caitiff' or 'crafty knave,' 'idle truant,' or 'flattering
parasite'?"

"Depends upon who is calling whom what . . ."

"No, no, no! Let's try an easy one: 'fornicating whore.' "

"It is redundant. Hence, annoying to the cultivated listener."

" 'Senseless fop.' "

"Again, redundant—as are 'flattering parasite' and the
others."

"So, clearly, in the Philosophical Language, we needn't
have separate adjectives and nouns in such cases."

"How about 'filthy sloven?"

"Excellent! Write it down, Daniel!"

" 'Licentious blade' . . . 'facetious wag' . . . 'perfidious
traitor' . . ." As Daniel continued in this vein, Wilkins bustled over to the writing-desk, withdrew a quill from an
inkwell, shook off redundant ink, and then came over to
Daniel; wrapped his fingers around the pen; and guided him
over to the desk.

And so to work. Daniel exhausted the Terms of Abuse in a
few short hours, then moved on to Virtues (intellectual,
moral, and homiletical), Colors, Sounds, Tastes and Smells,
Professions, Operations (viz. carpentry, sewing, alchemy),
and so on. Days began passing. Wilkins became fretful if
Daniel, or anyone, worked too hard, and so there were fre-
quent "seminars" and "symposia" in the kitchen—they used
honey from Christopher Wren's Gothic apiary to make flip.
Frequently Charles Comstock, the fifteen-year-old son of
their noble host, came to visit, and to hear Wilkins or Hooke
talk. Charles tended to bring with him letters addressed to
the Royal Society from Huygens, Leeuwenhoek, Swammer-

dam, Spinoza. Frequently these turned out to contain new concepts that Daniel had to fit into the Philosophical Language's tables.

Daniel was hard at work compiling a list of all the things in the world that a person could own (aquæducts, axle-trees, palaces, hinges) when Wilkins called him down urgently. Daniel came down to find the Rev. holding a grand-looking Letter, and Charles Comstock clearing the decks for action: rolling up large diagrams of the Ark, and feeding-schedules for the eighteen hundred and twenty-five sheep, and stowing them out of the way to make room for more important affairs. Charles II, by the Grace of God of England King, had sent them this letter: His Majesty had noticed that ant eggs were bigger than ants, and demanded to know how *that* was possible.

Daniel ran out and sacked an ant-nest. He returned in triumph carrying the nucleus of an anthill on the flat of a shovel. In the front room Wilkins had begun dictating, and Charles Comstock scribbling, a letter back to the King—not the substantive part (as they didn't have an answer yet), but the lengthy paragraphs of apologies and profuse flattery that had to open it: "With your brilliance you illuminate the places that have long, er, languished in, er—"

"Sounds more like a Sun King allusion, Reverend," Charles warned him.

"Strike it, then! Sharp lad. Read the entire mess back to me."

Daniel slowed before the door to Hooke's laboratory, gathering his courage to knock. But Hooke had heard him approaching, and opened it for him. With an outstretched hand he beckoned Daniel in, and aimed him at a profoundly stained table, cleared for action. Daniel entered the room, upended the ant-nest, set the shovel down, and only then worked up the courage to inhale. Hooke's laboratory didn't smell as bad as he'd always assumed it would.

Hooke ran his hands back through his hair, pulling it away from his face, and tied it back behind his neck with a wisp of twine. Daniel was perpetually surprised that Hooke was only ten years older than he. Hooke just turned thirty a few weeks ago, in June, at about the same time that Daniel and Isaac had fled plaguey Cambridge for their respective homes.

Hooke was now staring at the mound of living dirt on his tabletop. His eyes were always focused on a narrow target, as if he peered out at the world through a hollow reed. When he was out in the broad world, or even in the house's front room, that seemed strange, but it made sense when he was looking at a small world on a tabletop—ants scurrying this way and that, carrying egg-cases out of the wreckage, establishing a defensive perimeter. Daniel stood opposite and *looked at,* but apparently did not *see,* the same things.

Within a few minutes Daniel had seen most of what he was going to see among the ants, within five minutes he was bored, within ten he had given up all pretenses and begun wandering round Hooke's laboratory, looking at the remnants of everything that had passed beneath the microscope: shards of porous stone, bits of moldy shoe-leather, a small glass jar labelled WILKINS URINE, splinters of petrified wood, countless tiny envelopes of seeds, insects in jars, scraps of various fabrics, tiny pots labelled SNAILS TEETH and VIPERS FANGS. Shoved back into a corner, a heap of dusty, rusty sharp things: knife-blades, needles, razors. There was probably a cruel witticism to be made here: given a razor, Hooke would sooner put it under his microscope than shave with it.

As the wait went on, and on, and on, Daniel decided that he might as well be improving himself. So with care he reached into the sharp-things pile, drew out a needle, and carried it over to a table where sun was pouring in (Hooke had grabbed all of the south-facing rooms in the cottage, to own the light). There, mounted to a little stand, was a tube, about the dimensions of a piece of writing-paper rolled up, with a lens at the top for looking through, and a much smaller one—hardly bigger than a chick's eye—at the bottom, aimed at a little stand that was strongly illuminated by the sunlight. Daniel put the needle on the stand and peered through the Microscope.

He expected to see a gleaming, mirrorlike shaft, but it was a gnawed stick instead. The needle's sharp point turned out to be a rounded and pitted slag-heap.

"Mr. Waterhouse," Hooke said, "when you are finished with whatever you are doing, I will consult my faithful Mercury."

Daniel stood up and turned around. He thought for a moment that Hooke was asking him to fetch some quicksilver (Hooke drank it from time to time, as a remedy for headaches, vertigo, and other complaints). But Hooke's giant eyes were focused on the Microscope instead.

"Of course!" Daniel said. Mercury, the Messenger of the Gods—bringer of information.

"What think you now of needles?" Hooke asked.

Daniel plucked the needle away and held it up before the window, viewing it in a new light. "Its appearance is almost physically disgusting," he said.

"A razor looks worse. It is all kinds of shapes, except what it should be," Hooke said. "That is why I never use the Microscope any more to look at things that were made by men—the rudeness and bungling of Art is painful to view. And yet things that one would *expect* to look disgusting become beautiful when magnified—you may look at my drawings while I satisfy the King's curiosity." Hooke gestured to a stack of papers, then carried a sample ant-egg over to the microscope as Daniel began to page through them.

"Sir. I did not know that you were an artist," Daniel said.

"When my father died, I was apprenticed to a portrait-painter," Hooke said.

"Your master taught you well—"

"The ass taught me *nothing*," Hooke said. "Anyone who is not a half-wit can learn all there is to know of painting, by standing in front of paintings and *looking* at them. What was the use, then, of being an apprentice?"

"This flea is a magnificent piece of—"

"It is not *art* but a higher form of *bungling*," Hooke demurred. "When I viewed that flea under the microscope, I could see, in its eye, a complete and perfect reflection of

John Comstock's gardens and manor-house—the blossoms on his flowers, the curtains billowing in his windows."

"It's magnificent to me," Daniel said. He was sincere—not trying to be a Flattering Parasite or Crafty Knave.

But Hooke only became irritated. "I tell you again. True beauty is to be found in natural forms. The more we magnify, and the closer we examine, the works of Artifice, the grosser and stupider they seem. But if we magnify the natural world it only becomes more intricate and excellent."

Wilkins had asked Daniel which he preferred: Wren's glass apiary, or the bees' honeycomb inside of it. Then he had warned Daniel that Hooke was coming into earshot. Now Daniel understood why: for Hooke there could only be one answer.

"I defer to you, sir."

"Thank you, sir."

"But without seeming to be a Cavilling Jesuit, I should like to know whether Wilkins's urine is a product of Art or Nature."

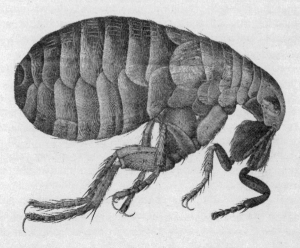

"You saw the jar."

"Yes."

"If you take the Rev.'s urine and pour off the fluid and ex-amine what remains under the Microscope, you will see a hoard of jewels that would make the Great Mogul swoon. At lower magnification it seems nothing more than a heap of gravel, but with a better lens, and brighter light, it is revealed as a mountain of crystals—plates, rhomboids, rectangles, squares—white and yellow and red ones, gleaming like the diamonds in a courtier's ring."

"Is that true of everyone's urine?"

"It is more true of his than of most people's," Hooke said. "Wilkins has the stone."

"Oh, God!"

"It is not so bad now, but it grows within him, and will certainly kill him in a few years," Hooke said.

"And the stone in his bladder is made of the same stuff as these crystals that you see in his urine?"

"I believe so."

"Is there some way to—"

"To dissolve it? Oil of vitriol works—but I don't suppose that our Reverend wants to have that introduced into his bladder. You are welcome to make investigations of your own. I have tried all of the *obvious* things."

WORD ARRIVED THAT FERMAT had died, leaving behind a theorem or two that still needed proving. King Philip of Spain died, too, and his son succeeded him; but the new King Carlos II was sickly, and not expected to live to the end of the year. Portugal was independent. Someone named Lubomirski was staging a rebellion in Poland.

John Wilkins was trying to make horse-drawn vehicles more efficient; to test them, he had rigged up a weight on a rope, above a well, so that when the weight fell down into the well, it would drag his chariots across the ground. Their progress could then be timed using one of Hooke's watches.

That duty fell to Charles Comstock, who spent many days standing out in the field making trials or fixing broken wheels. His father's servants needed the well to draw water for livestock, and so Charles was frequently called out to move the contraption out of the way. Daniel enjoyed watching all of this, out the window, while he worked on Punishments:

PUNISHMENTS CAPITAL

ARE THE VARIOUS MANNERS OF PUTTING MEN
TO DEATH IN A JUDICIAL WAY, WHICH IN SEVERAL
NATIONS ARE, OR HAVE BEEN, EITHER *SIMPLE*; BY

Separation of the parts;
  Head from Body: BEHEADING, strike of one's head
  Member from Member: QUARTERING, Dissecting.
Wound
  At distance, whether
    from hand: STONING, Pelting
    from Instrument, as Gun, Bow, &c.: SHOOTING.
  At hand, either by
    Weight;
      of something else: PRESSING.
      of one's own: PRECIPITATING, Defenestration,
      casting headlong.
    Weapon;
      any way: STABBING
      direct upwards: EMPALING
Taking away necessary Diet: or giving that which is noxious
  STARVING, famishing
  POISONING, Venom, envenom, virulent
Interception of the air
  at the Mouth
    in the air: stifling, smother, suffocate.
    in the Earth: BURYING ALIVE
    in water: DROWNING
    in fire: BURNING ALIVE

at the Throat
  by weight of a man's own body: HANGING
  by the strength of others: STRANGLING, *throttle,*
  choke, suffocate

MIXED OF WOUNDING AND STARVING; THE BODY BEING
  Erect: *CRUCIFYING*
  Lying on a Wheel: *BREAKING ON THE WHEEL*

PUNISHMENTS NOT CAPITAL

ARE DISTINGUISHED BY THE THINGS OR
SUBJECTS RECEIVING DETRIMENT BY THEM,
AS BEING EITHER OF THE *BODY;*
according to the General *name; signifying great pain:*
TORTURE *according to special kinds:*
  by Striking;
    with a limber instrument: WHIPPING, *lashing,*
    scourging, leashing, rod, slash, switch, stripe, Beadle
    with a stiff instrument: CUDGELLING, *bastinado,*
    baste, swinge, swaddle, shrubb, slapp, thwack;
  by Stretching *of the limbs violently;*
    the body being laid along: RACK
    the body lifted up into the Air: STRAPPADO
LIBERTY; OF WHICH ONE IS DEPRIVED, BY
RESTRAINT
into
  a place: IMPRISONMENT, *Incarceration, Durance,*
  Custody, Ward, clap up, commit, confine, mure, Pound,
  Pinfold, Gaol, Cage, Set fast
  an Instrument: BONDS, *fetters, gyves, shackles,*
  manicles, pinion, chains.
Out of *a place or country, whether*
    with allowance of any other: EXILE, *banishment*
    confinement to one other: RELEGATION
REPUTE, WHETHER
  more gently: *INFAMIZATION, Ignominy, Pillory*

more severely by burning marks in one's flesh:
STIGMATIZATION, Branding, Cauterizing

ESTATE; WHETHER
in part: *MULCT, fine, sconce*
in whole: *CONFISCATION, forfeiture*

DIGNITY AND POWER; BY DEPRIVING ONE OF
his degree: *DEGRADING, deposing, depriving*
his capacity to bear office: *INCAPACITATING,
cashier, disable, discard, depose, disfranchize.*

As Daniel scourged, bastinadoed, racked, and strappadoed his mind, trying to think of punishments that he and Wilkins had missed, he heard Hooke striking sparks with flint and steel, and went down to investigate.

Hooke was aiming the sparks at a blank sheet of paper. "Mark where they strike," he said to Daniel. Daniel hovered with a pen, and whenever an especially large spark hit the paper, he drew a tight circle around it. They examined the paper under the Microscope, and found, in the center of each circle, a remnant: a more or less complete hollow sphere of what was obviously steel. "You see that the Alchemists' conception of heat is ludicrous," Hooke said. "There is no Element of Fire. Heat is really nothing more than a brisk agitation of the parts of a body—hit a piece of steel with a rock hard enough, and a bit of steel is torn away—"

"And that is the spark?"

"That is the spark."

"But why does the spark emit light?"

"The force of the impact agitates its parts so vehemently that it becomes hot enough to melt."

"Yes, but if your hypothesis is correct—if there is no Element of Fire, only a jostling of internal parts—then why should hot things emit light?"

"I believe that light consists of vibrations. If the parts move violently enough, they emit light—just as a struck bell vibrates to produce sound."

Daniel supposed that was all there was to that, until he went with Hooke to collect samples of river insects one day, and they squatted in a place where a brook tumbled over the brink of a rock into a little pool. Bubbles of water, forced beneath the pool by the falling water, rose to the surface: millions of tiny spheres. Hooke noticed it, pondered for a few moments, and said: "Planets and stars are spheres, for the same reason that bubbles and sparks are."

"What!?"

"A body of fluid, surrounded by some different fluid, forms into a sphere. Thus: air surrounded by water makes a sphere, which we call a bubble. A tiny bit of molten steel surrounded by air makes a sphere, which we call a spark. Molten earth surrounded by the Cœlestial Æther makes a sphere, which we call a planet."

And on the way back, as they were watching a crescent moon chase the sun below the horizon, Hooke said, "If we could make sparks, or flashes of light, bright enough, we could see their light reflected off the shadowed part of that moon later, and reckon the speed of light."

"If we did it with gunpowder," Daniel reflected, "John Comstock would be happy to underwrite the experiment."

Hooke turned and regarded him for a few moments with a cold eye, as if trying to establish whether Daniel, too, was made up out of cells. "You are thinking like a courtier," he said. There was no emotion in his voice; he was stating, not an opinion, but a fact.

> The chief Design of the aforementioned Club, was to propagate new Whims, advance mechanic Exercises, and to promote useless, as well as useful Experiments. In order to carry on this commendable Undertaking, any frantic Artist, chemical Operator, or whimsical Projector, that had but a Crotchet in their Heads, or

but dream'd themselves into some strange fanciful Discovery, might be kindly admitted, as welcome Brethren, into this teeming Society, where each Member was respected, not according to his Quality, but the searches he had made into the Mysteries of Nature, and the Novelties, though Trifles, that were owing to his Invention: So that a Mad-man, who had beggar'd himself by his Bellows and his Furnaces, in a vain pursuit of the Philosopher's Stone; or the crazy Physician who had wasted his Patrimony, by endeavouring to recover that infallible Nostrum, *Sal Graminis*, from the dust and ashes of a burnt Hay-cock, were as much reverenc'd here, as those mechanic Quality, who, to shew themselves *Vertuoso's*, would sit turning of Ivory above in their Garrets, whilst their Ladies below Stairs, by the help of their He-Cousins, were providing Horns for their Families.

—NED WARD, *The Vertuoso's Club*

THE LEAVES WERE TURNING, the Plague in London was worse. Eight thousand people died in a week. A few miles away in Epsom, Wilkins had finished the Ark digression and begun to draw up a grammar, and a system of writing, for his Philosophical Language. Daniel was finishing some odds and ends, viz. Nautical Objects: Seams and Spurkets, Parrels and Jears, Brales and Bunt-Lines. His mind wandered.

Below him, a strange plucking sound, like a man endlessly tuning a lute. He went down stairs and found Hooke sitting there with a few inches of quill sticking out of his ear, plucking a string stretched over a wooden box. It was far from the strangest thing Hooke had ever done, so Daniel went to work for a time, trying to dissolve Wilkins's bladder-gravel in various potions. Hooke continued plucking and humming. Finally Daniel went over to investigate.

A housefly was perched on the end of the quill that was stuck in Hooke's ear. Daniel tried to shoo it away. Its wings blurred, but it didn't move. Looking more closely Daniel saw that it had been glued down.

"Do that again, it gives me a different pitch," Hooke demanded.

"You can hear the fly's wings?"

"They drone at a certain fixed pitch. If I tune this string"—*pluck, pluck*—"to the same pitch, I know that the string, and the fly's wings, are vibrating at the same frequency. I already know how to reckon the frequency of a string's vibration—hence, I know how many times in a second a fly's wings beat. Useful *data* if we are ever to build a flying-machine."

Autumn rain made the field turn mucky, and ended the chariot experiments. Charles Comstock had to find other things to do. He had matriculated at Cambridge this year, but Cambridge was closed for the duration of the Plague. Daniel reckoned that as a *quid pro quo* for staying here at Epsom, Wilkins was obliged to tutor Charles in Natural Philosophy. But most of the tutoring was indistinguishable from drudge work on Wilkins's diverse experiments, many of which (now that the weather had turned) were being conducted in the cottage's cellar. Wilkins was starving a toad in a jar to see if new toads would grow out of it. There was a carp living out of water, being fed on moistened bread; Charles's job was to wet its gills several times a day. The King's ant question had gotten Wilkins going on an experiment he'd wanted to try for a long time: before long, down in the cellar, between the starving toad and the carp, they had a maggot the size of a man's thigh, which had to be fed rotten meat, and weighed once a day. This began to smell and so they moved it outside, to a shack downwind, where Wilkins had also embarked on a whole range of experiments concerning the generation of flies and worms out of decomposing meat, cheese, and other substances. Everyone knew, or thought they knew, that this happened spontaneously. But Hooke with his microscope had found tiny motes on the undersides of certain leaves, which grew up into insects, and in water he had found tiny eggs that grew up into gnats, and this had given him the idea that perhaps all things that were believed to be bred from putrefaction might have like origins: that the air and the water were filled with an invisible dust of tiny eggs and seeds that, in order to germinate, need only be planted in something moist and rotten.

From time to time, a carriage or wagon from the outside world was suffered to pass into the gate of the manor and approach the big house. On the one hand, this was welcome evidence that some people were still alive out there in England. On the other—

"Who is that madman, coming and going in the midst of the Plague," Daniel asked, "and why does John Comstock let him into his house? The poxy bastard'll infect us all."

"John Comstock could not exclude that fellow any more than he could ban air from his lungs," Wilkins said. He had been tracking the carriage's progress, at a safe distance, through a prospective glass. "That is his money-scrivener."

Daniel had never heard the term before. "I have not yet reached that point in the Tables where 'money-scrivener' is defined. Does he do what a goldsmith does?"

"Smite gold? No."

"Of course not. I was referring to this new line of work that goldsmiths have got into—handling notes that serve as money."

"A man such as the Earl of Epsom would not suffer a money-goldsmith to draw within a mile of his house!" Wilkins said indignantly. "A money-scrivener is different altogether! And yet he does something very much the same."

"Could you explain that, please?" Daniel said, but they were interrupted by Hooke, shouting from another room:

"Daniel! Fetch a cannon."

In other circumstances this demand would have posed severe difficulties. However, they were living on the estate of the man who had introduced the manufacture of gunpowder to Britain, and provided King Charles II with many of his armaments. So Daniel went out and enlisted that man's son, young Charles Comstock, who in turn drafted a corps of servants and a few horses. They procured a field-piece from John Comstock's personal armoury and towed it out into the middle of a pasture. Meanwhile, Mr. Hooke had caused a certain servant, who had long been afflicted with deafness, to be brought out from the town. Hooke bade the servant stand in the same pasture, only a fathom away from the muzzle of the cannon (but off to one side!). Charles Comstock (who knew how to do such things) charged the cannon with some of his father's finest powder, shoved a longish fuse down the touch-hole, lit it, and ran away. The result was a sudden immense compression of the air, which Hooke had hoped would penetrate the servant's skull and knock away whatever hidden obstructions had caused him to become deaf. Quite a few window-panes in John Comstock's manor house were blown out of their frames, amply demonstrating the soundness of the underlying idea. But it didn't cure the servant's deafness.

"As you may know, my dwelling is a-throng, just now, with persons from the city," said John Comstock, Earl of Epsom and Lord Chancellor of England.

He had appeared, suddenly and unannounced, in the door of the cottage. Hooke and Wilkins were busy hollering at the deaf servant, trying to see if he could hear anything at all. Daniel noticed the visitor first, and joined in the shouting: "Excuse me! Gentlemen! REVEREND WILKINS!"

After several minutes' confusion, embarrassment, and makeshift stabs at protocol, Wilkins and Comstock ended up sitting across the table from each other with glasses of claret while Hooke and Waterhouse and the deaf servant held up a nearby wall with their arses.

Comstock was pushing sixty. Here on his own country estate, he had no patience with wigs or other Court foppery, and so his silver hair was simply queued, and he was dressed in plain simple riding-and-hunting togs. "In the year of my birth, Jamestown was founded, the pilgrims scurried off to Leyden, and work commenced on the King James version of the Bible. I have lived through London's diverse riots and panics, plagues and Gunpowder Plots. I have escaped from burning buildings. I was wounded at the Battle of Newark and made my way, in some discomfort, to safety in Paris. It was not my last battle, on land or at sea. I was there when His Majesty was crowned in exile at Scone, and I was there when he returned in triumph to London. I have killed men. You know all of these things, Dr. Wilkins, and so I mention them, not to boast, but to emphasize that *if I were living a solitary life* in that large House over yonder, you could set off cannonades, and larger detonations, at all hours of day and night, without warning, and for that matter you could make a pile of meat five fathoms high and let it fester away beneath my bed-chamber's window—*and none of it would matter to me.* But as it is, my house is crowded, just now, with Persons of Quality. Some of them are of *royal* degree. Many of them are *female*, and some are of *tender years*. Two of them are *all three.*"

"My lord!" Wilkins exclaimed. Daniel had been carefully watching him, as who wouldn't—the opportunity to watch a man like Wilkins being called on the carpet by a man like Comstock was far more precious than any Southwark bear-baiting. Until just now, Wilkins had *pretended* to be mortified—though he'd done a very good job of it. But now, suddenly, he really *was.*

Two of them are all three—what could *that* possibly mean? Who was royal, female, and of tender years? King Charles II didn't have any daughters, at least *legitimate* ones. Elizabeth, the Winter Queen, had *littered* Europe with princes and princesses until she'd passed away a couple of years ago—but it seemed unlikely that any Continental royalty would be visiting England during the Plague.

Comstock continued: "These persons have come here seeking refuge, as they are terrified *to begin with,* of the Plague and other horrors—including, but hardly limited to, a possible *Dutch* invasion. The violent compression of the air, which you and I might think of as a possible cure for deafness, is construed, by such people, entirely differently . . ."

Wilkins said something fiendishly clever and appropriate and then devoted the next couple of days to abjectly humbling himself and apologizing to every noble person within ear- and nose-shot of the late Experiments. Hooke was put to work making little wind-up toys for the two little royal girls. Meanwhile Daniel and Charles had to dismantle all of the bad-smelling experiments, and oversee their decent burials, and generally tidy things up.

It took days' peering at Fops through hedges, deconstructing carriage-door scutcheons, and shinnying out onto the branches of diverse noble and royal family trees for Daniel to understand what Wilkins had inferred from a few of John Comstock's pithy words and eyebrow-raisings. Comstock had formal gardens to one side of his house, which for many excellent reasons were off-limits to Natural Philosophers. Persons in French clothes strolled in them. That was not remarkable. To dally in gardens was some people's life-work, as to shovel manure was a stable-hand's. At a distance they all looked the same, at least to Daniel. Wilkins, much more conversant with the Court, spied on them from time to time through a prospective-glass. As a mariner, seeking to establish his bearings at night, will first look for Ursa Major, that being a constellation of exceptional size and brightness, so Wilkins would always commence his obs'v'ns. by zeroing his sights, as it were, on a particular woman who was easy to find because she was twice the size of everyone else. Many furlongs of gaily dyed fabrics went into her skirts, which shewed bravely from a distance, like French regimental standards. From time to time a man with blond hair would come out and stroll about the garden with her, moon orbiting planet. He reminded Daniel, from a distance, of Isaac.

Daniel did not reck who that fellow was, and was too abashed to discover his ignorance by asking, until one day a carriage arrived from London and several men in admirals' hats climbed out of it and went to talk to the same man in the garden. Though first they all doffed those hats and bowed low.

"That blond man who walks in the garden, betimes, on the arm of the Big Dipper—would that be the Duke of York?"

"Yes," said Wilkins—not wishing to say more, as he was breathing shallowly, his eye peeled wide open and bathed in a greenish light from the eyepiece of his prospective-glass.

"And Lord High Admiral," Daniel continued.

"He has many titles," Wilkins observed in a level and patient tone.

"So those chaps in the hats would be—obviously—"

"The Admiralty," Wilkins said curtly, "or some moiety or faction thereof." He recoiled from the scope. Daniel phant'sied he was being proffered a look-see, but only for a moment— Wilkins lifted the instrument out of the tree-crook and collapsed it. Daniel collected that he had seen something Wilkins wished he hadn't.

The Dutch and the English were at war. Because of the Plague, this had been a desultory struggle thus far, and Daniel had forgotten about it. It was midwinter. Cold had brought the Plague to a stand. Months would pass before the weather permitted resumption of the sea-campaign. But the time to lay plans for such campaigns was now. It ought to surprise no one if the Admiralty met with the Lord High Admiral now. It would be surprising if they *didn't*. What struck Daniel was that Wilkins *cared* that he, Daniel, had seen something. The Restoration, and Daniel's Babylonian exile and subjugation at Cambridge, had led him to think of himself as a perfect nobody, except perhaps when it came to Natural Philosophy—and it was more obvious every day that even within the Royal Society he was nothing compared to Wren and Hooke. So why should John Wilkins give a fig

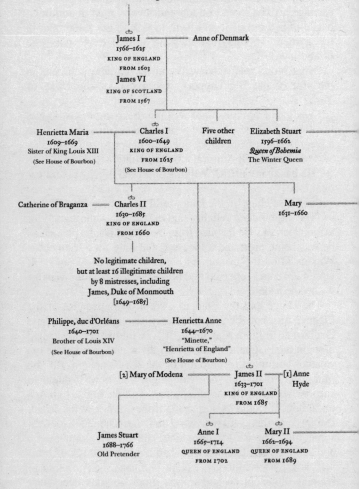

House of Stuart

James I
1566–1625
KING OF ENGLAND
FROM 1603

James VI
KING OF SCOTLAND
FROM 1567

Anne of Denmark

Henrietta Maria
1609–1669
Sister of King Louis XIII
(See House of Bourbon)

Charles I
1600–1649
KING OF ENGLAND
FROM 1625
(See House of Bourbon)

Five other
children

Elizabeth Stuart
1596–1662
Queen of Bohemia
The Winter Queen

Catherine of Braganza

Charles II
1630–1685
KING OF ENGLAND
FROM 1660

Mary
1631–1660

No legitimate children,
but at least 16 illegitimate children
by 8 mistresses, including
James, Duke of Monmouth
[1649–1685]

Philippe, duc d'Orléans
1640–1701
Brother of Louis XIV
(See House of Bourbon)

Henrietta Anne
1644–1670
"Minette,"
"Henrietta of England"
(See House of Bourbon)

[2] Mary of Modena

James II
1633–1701
KING OF ENGLAND
FROM 1685

[1] Anne
Hyde

James Stuart
1688–1766
Old Pretender

Anne I
1665–1714
QUEEN OF ENGLAND
FROM 1702

Mary II
1662–1694
QUEEN OF ENGLAND
FROM 1689

House of Orange-Nassau

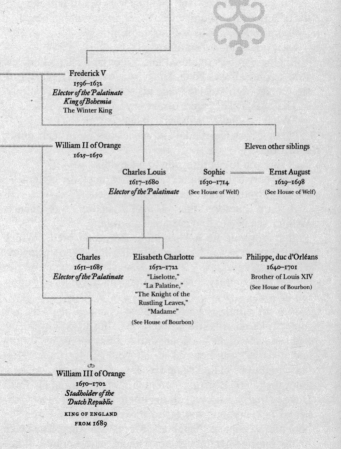

Frederick V
1596–1632
Elector of the Palatinate
King of Bohemia
The Winter King

William II of Orange
1625–1650

Eleven other siblings

Charles Louis
1617–1680
Elector of the Palatinate

Sophie
1630–1714
(See House of Welf)

Ernst August
1629–1698
(See House of Welf)

Charles
1651–1685
Elector of the Palatinate

Elisabeth Charlotte
1652–1722
"Liselotte,"
"La Palatine,"
"The Knight of the
Rustling Leaves,"
"Madame"
(See House of Bourbon)

Philippe, duc d'Orléans
1640–1701
Brother of Louis XIV
(See House of Bourbon)

William III of Orange
1650–1701
Stadholder of the
Dutch Republic
KING OF ENGLAND
FROM 1689

whether Daniel spied a flotilla of admirals and collected, from that, that John Comstock was hosting James, Duke of York, brother of Charles II and next in line to the throne?

It must be (as Daniel realized, walking back through a de-foliated orchard alongside the brooding Wilkins) because he was the son of Drake. And though Drake was a retired agita-tor of a defeated and downcast sect, at bay in his house on Holborn, *someone* was still afraid of him.

Or if not of him, then of his sect.

But the sect was shattered into a thousand claques and ca-bals. Cromwell was gone, Drake was too old, Gregory Bol-strood had been executed, and his son Knott was in exile—

That was it. They were afraid of *Daniel.*

"What is funny?" Wilkins demanded.

"People," Daniel said, "and what goes on in their minds sometimes."

"I say, you're not referring to *me* by that—?—!"

"Oh, perish the thought. I would not mock my betters."

"Pray, who on this estate is *not* your better?"

A hard question that. Daniel's answer was silence. Wilkins seemed to find even that alarming.

"I forget you are a Phanatique born and bred." Which was the same as saying, *You recognize no man as your bet-ter, do you?*

"On the contrary, I see now that you have *never* forgot-ten it."

But something seemed to have changed in Wilkins's mind. Like an Admiral working his ship to windward, he had suddenly come about and, after a few moments' luffing and disarray, was now on an altogether novel tack: "The lady used to be called Anne Hyde—a close relation of John Comstock. So, far from common. Yet too common for a Duke to marry. And yet still too noble to send off to a Conti-nental nunnery, and too fat to move far, in any case. She bore him a couple of daughters: Mary, then Anne. The Duke finally married her, though not without many complications.

Since Mary or Anne could conceivably inherit the throne one day, it became a State matter. Various courtiers were talked, bribed, or threatened into coming forward and swearing on stacks of Bibles that they'd fucked Anne Hyde up and down, fucked her in the British Isles and in France, in the Low Countries and the Highlands, in the city and in the country, in ships and palaces, beds and hammocks, bushes, flower-beds, water-closets, and garrets, that they had fucked her drunk and fucked her sober, from behind and in front, from above, below, and both the right and left sides, singly and in groups, in the day and in the night and during all phases of the moon and signs of the Zodiac, whilst also intimating that any number of blacksmiths, Vagabonds, French gigolos, Jesuit provocateurs, comedians, barbers, and apprentice saddlers had been doing the same whensoever they weren't. But despite all of this the Duke of York married her, and socked her away in St. James's Palace, where she's grown like one of our *entomologickal* prodigies in the cellar."

Daniel had heard a good bit of this before, of course, from men who came to the house on Holborn to pay court to Drake—which gave him the odd sense that Wilkins was paying court to *him*. Which could not be, for Daniel had no real power or significance at all, and no prospects of getting any.

It seemed more plausible that Wilkins felt sorry for Daniel, than afraid of him; and as such was trying to shield him from those dangers that were avoidable while tutoring him in how to cope with the rest.

Which meant, if true, that Daniel ought at least to attend to the lesson that Wilkins was trying to give him. The two Princesses, Mary and Anne, would, respectively, be three and one years old now. And as their mother was related to John Comstock, it was entirely plausible that they might be visitors in the house. Which explained Comstock's remark to Wilkins: "Two of them are *all three*." Female, of tender years, and royal.

The burdensome restrictions imposed on their Natural-Philosophic researches by the host made it necessary to convene a very long Symposium in the Kitchen, where Hooke and Wilkins dictated a list (written by Daniel in a loosening hand) of experiments that were neither noisy nor smelly, but (as the evening wore on) increasingly fanciful. Hooke put Daniel to work mending his Condensing Engine, which was a piston-and-cylinder arrangement for compressing or rarefying air. He was convinced that air contained some kind of spirit that sustained both fire and life, which, when it was used up, caused both to be extinguished. So there was a whole range of experiments along the lines of: sealing up a candle and a mouse in a glass vessel, and watching to see what happened (mouse died before candle). They fixed up a huge bladder so that it was leakproof, and put it to their mouths, and took turns breathing the same air over and over again, to see what would happen. Hooke used his engine to produce a vacuum in a large glass jar, then set a pendulum swinging in the vacuum, and set Charles there to count its swings. On the first really clear night at the onset of winter, Hooke had gone outside with a telescope and peered at Mars: he had found some light and dark patches on its surface, and ever since had been tracking their movements so that he could figure out how long it took that planet to rotate on its axis. He put Charles and Daniel to work grinding better and better lenses, or else bought them from Spinoza in Amsterdam, and they took turns looking at smaller and smaller structures on the moon. But here again, Hooke saw things Daniel didn't. "The moon must have gravity, like the earth," he said.

"What makes you say so?"

"The mountains and valleys have a settled shape to them—no matter how rugged the landforms, there is nothing to be seen, on that whole orb, that would fall over under gravitation. With better lenses I could measure the Angle of Repose and calculate the force of her gravity."

"If the moon gravitates, so must everything else in the heavens," Daniel observed.*

A long skinny package arrived from Amsterdam. Daniel opened it up, expecting to find another telescope—instead it was a straight, skinny horn, about five feet long, with helical ridges and grooves. "What is it?" he asked Wilkins.

Wilkins peered at it over his glasses and said (sounding mildly annoyed), "The horn of a unicorn."

"But I thought that the unicorn was a mythical beast."

"*I've* never seen one."

"Then where do you suppose this came from?"

"How the devil should I know?" Wilkins returned. "All I know is, you can buy them in Amsterdam."

> Kings most commonly, though strong in legions, are but weak in Arguments; as they who have ever accustom'd from the Cradle to use thir will onely as thir right hand, thir reason alwayes as thir left. Whence unexpectedly constrain'd to that kind of combat, they prove but weak and puny Adversaries.
>
> —MILTON, PREFACE TO *Eikonoklastes*

DANIEL GOT USED TO SEEING the Duke of York out riding and hunting with his princely friends—as much as the son of Drake *could* get used to such a sight. Once the hunters rode past within a bowshot of him, near enough that he could hear the Duke talking to his companion—*in French.* Which gave Daniel an impulse to rush up to this French Catholic man in his French clothes, who claimed to be England's next king, and put an end to him. He mastered it by recalling to mind the way that the Duke's father's head had plopped into the basket on the scaffold at the Banqueting House. Then he thought to himself: *What an odd family!*

---

*He was not the first person to observe it.

Too, he could no longer muster quite the same malice towards these people. Drake had raised his sons to hate the nobility by wasting no opportunity to point out their privileges, and the way they profited from those privileges without really being aware of them. This sort of discourse had wrought extraordinarily, not only in Drake's sons but in every Dissident meeting-house in the land, and led to Cromwell and much else; but Cromwell had made Puritans powerful, and as Daniel was now seeing, that power—as if it were a living thing with a mind of its own—was trying to pass itself on to *him,* which would mean that Daniel was a child of privilege too.

The tables of the Philosophical Language were finished: a vast fine-meshed net drawn through the Cosmos so that everything known, in Heaven and Earth, was trapped in one of its myriad cells. All that was needed to identify a particular thing was to give its location in the tables, which could be expressed as a series of numbers. Wilkins came up with a system for assigning names to things, so that by breaking a name up into its component syllables, one could know its location in the Tables, and hence what thing it referred to.

Wilkins drained all the blood out of a large dog and put it into a smaller dog; minutes later the smaller dog was out chasing sticks. Hooke built a new kind of clock, using the Microscope to examine some of its tiny parts. In so doing he discovered a new kind of mite living in the rags in which these parts had been wrapped. He drew pictures of them, and then performed an exhaustive three-day series of experiments to learn what would and wouldn't kill them: the most effective killer being a Florentine poison he'd been brewing out of tobacco leaves.

Sir Robert Moray came to visit, and ground up a bit of the unicorn's horn to make a powder, which he sprinkled in a ring, and placed a spider in the center of the ring. But the spider kept escaping. Moray pronounced the horn to be a fraud.

Wilkins hustled Daniel out of bed one night in the wee

hours and took him on a dangerous nighttime hay-wain ride to the gaol in Epsom town. "Fortune has smiled on our endeavours," Wilkins said. "The man we are going to interview was condemned to hang. But hanging crushes the parts that are of interest to us—certain delicate structures in the neck. Fortunately for us, before the hangman could get to him, he died of a bloody flux."

"Is this going to be a new addition to the Tables, then?" Daniel asked wearily.

"Don't be foolish—the anatomical structures in question have been known for centuries. This dead man is going to help us with the Real Character."

"That's the alphabet for writing down the Philosophical Language?"

"You know that perfectly well. Wake up, Daniel!"

"I ask only because it seems to me you've already come up with *several* Real Characters."

"All more or less arbitrary. A natural philosopher on some other world, viewing a document written in those characters, would think that he were reading, not the Philosophical Language, but the *Cryptonomicon!* What we need is a *systematic* alphabet—made so that the shapes of the characters themselves provide full information as to how they are pronounced."

These words filled Daniel with a foreboding that turned out to be fully justified: by the time the sun rose, they had fetched the dead man from the gaol, brought him back out to the cottage, and carefully cut his head off. Charles Comstock was rousted from bed and ordered to dissect the corpse, as a lesson in anatomy (and as a way of getting rid of it). Meanwhile, Hooke and Wilkins connected the head's wind-pipe to a large set of fireplace-bellows, so that they could blow air through his voice-box. Daniel was detailed to saw off the top of the skull and get rid of the brains so that he could reach in through the back and get hold of the soft palate, tongue, and other meaty bits responsible for making sounds. With Daniel thus acting as a sort of meat puppeteer, and Hooke manipulating the lips and nostrils, and Wilkins plying the bellows, they were able to make the head speak. When his speaking-parts were squished into one configuration he made a very clear "O" sound, which Daniel (very tired now) found just a bit unsettling. Wilkins wrote down an *O*-shaped character, reflecting the shape of the man's lips. This experiment went on *all day,* Wilkins reminding the others, when they showed signs of tiredness, that this rare head wouldn't keep forever—as if that weren't already obvious. They made the head utter thirty-four different sounds. For each one of them, Wilkins drew out a letter that was a sort of quick freehand sketch of the positions of lips, tongue, and other bits responsible for making that noise. Finally they turned the head over to Charles Comstock, to continue his anatomy-lesson, and Daniel went to bed for a series of rich nightmares.

Looking at Mars had put Hooke in mind of cœlestial affairs; for that reason he set out with Daniel one morning in a wagon, with a chest of equipment. This must have been important, because Hooke packed it himself, and wouldn't let anyone else near it. Wilkins kept trying to persuade them to use the giant wheel, instead of borrowing one of John Comstock's wagons (and further wearing out their welcome). Wilkins claimed that the giant wheel, propelled by the youthful and vigorous Daniel Waterhouse, could (in theory) traverse fields, bogs, and reasonably shallow bodies of water with equal ease, so they could simply travel in a perfectly straight line to their destination, instead of having to follow roads. Hooke declined, and chose the wagon.

They traveled for several hours to a certain well, said to be more than three hundred feet deep, bored down through solid chalk. Hooke's mere appearance was enough to chase away the local farmers, who were only loitering and drinking anyway. He got Daniel busy constructing a solid, level platform over the mouth of the well. Hooke meanwhile took out his best scale and began to clean and calibrate it. He explained, "For the sake of argument, suppose it really is true that planets are kept in their orbits, not by vortices in the æther, but by the force of gravity."

"Yes?"

"Then, if you do some mathematicks, you can see that it simply would not work unless the force of gravity got weaker, as the distance from the center of attraction increased."

"So the weight of an object should diminish as it rises?"

"And increase as it descends," Hooke said, nodding significantly at the well.

"Aha! So the experiment is to weigh something here at the surface, and then to . . ." and here Daniel stopped, horror-stricken.

Hooke twisted his bent neck around and peered at him curiously. Then, for the first time since Daniel had met him, he laughed out loud. "You're afraid that I'm proposing to lower you, Daniel Waterhouse, three hundred feet down into the bottom of this well, with a scale in your lap, to weigh something? And that once down there the rope will break?" More laughing. "You need to think more carefully about what I said."

"Of course—it wouldn't work that way," Daniel said, deeply embarrassed on more than one level.

"And why not?" Hooke asked, Socratically.

"Because the scale works by balancing weights on one pan against the object to be weighed, on the other . . . and if it's true that all objects are heavier at the bottom of the well, then both the object, and the weights, will be heavier by the same amount . . . and so the result will be the same, and will teach us nothing."

"Help me measure out three hundred feet of thread," Hooke said, no longer amused.

They did it by pulling the thread off a reel, and stretching it alongside a one-fathom-long rod, and counting off fifty fathoms. One end of the thread Hooke tied to a heavy brass slug. He set the scale up on the platform that Daniel had improvised over the mouth of the well, and put the slug, along with its long bundle of thread, on the pan. He weighed the slug and thread carefully—a seemingly endless procedure disturbed over and over by light gusts of wind. To get a reliable measurement, they had to devote a couple of hours to setting up a canvas wind-screen. Then Hooke spent another half hour peering at the scale's needle through a magnifying lens while adding or subtracting bits of gold foil, no heavier than snowflakes. Every change caused the scale to teeter back and forth for several minutes before settling into a new position. Finally, Hooke called out a weight in pounds, ounces, grains, and fractions of grains, and Daniel noted it down. Then Hooke tied the free end of the thread to a little eye he had screwed to the bottom of the pan, and he and Daniel took turns lowering the weight into the well, letting it drop a few inches at a time—if it got to swinging, and scraped against the chalky sides of the hole, it would pick up a bit of extra weight, and ruin the experiment. When all three hundred feet had been let out, Hooke went for a stroll, because the weight was swinging a little bit, and its movements would disturb the scale. Finally it settled down enough that he could go back to work with his magnifying glass and his tweezers.

Daniel, in other words, had a lot of time to think that day. Cells, spiders' eyes, unicorns' horns, compressed and rarefied air, dramatic cures for deafness, philosophical languages, and flying chariots were all perfectly fine subjects, but lately Hooke's interest had been straying into matters cœlestial, and that made Daniel think about his roommate. Just as certain self-styled philosophers in minor European courts were frantic to know what Hooke and Wilkins were up to at Epsom, so Daniel wanted only to know what Isaac was doing up at Woolsthorpe.

"It weighs the same," Hooke finally pronounced, "three hundred feet of altitude makes no *measurable* difference." That was the signal to pack up all the apparatus and let the farmers draw their water again.

"This proves nothing," Hooke said as they rode home through the dark. "The scale is not precise enough. But if one were to construct a clock, driven by a pendulum, in a sealed glass vessel, so that changes in moisture and baroscopic pressure would not affect its speed . . . and if one were to run that clock in the bottom of a well for a long period of time . . . any difference in the pendulum's weight would be manifest as a slowing, or quickening, of the clock."

"But how would you know that it was running slow or fast?" Daniel asked. "You'd have to compare it against another clock."

"Or against the rotation of the earth," Hooke said. But it seemed that Daniel's question had thrown him into a dark mood, and he said nothing more until they had reached Epsom, after midnight.

THE TEMPERATURE AT NIGHT began to fall below freezing, and so it was time to calibrate thermometers. Daniel and Charles and Hooke had been making them for some weeks out of yard-long glass tubes, filled with spirits of wine, dyed with cochineal. But they had no markings on them. On cold nights they would bundle themselves up and immerse those thermometers in tubs of distilled water and then sit there for hours, giving the tubs an occasional stir, and waiting. When the water froze, if they listened carefully enough, they could hear a faint searing, splintering noise come out of the tub as flakes of ice shot across the surface—then they'd rouse themselves into action, using diamonds to make a neat scratch on each tube, marking the position of the red fluid inside.

Hooke kept a square of black velvet outside so that it would stay cold. When it snowed during the daytime, he would take his microscope outside and spread the velvet out on the stage and peer at any snowflakes that happened to fall on it. Daniel saw, as Hooke did, that each one was unique. But again Hooke saw something Daniel missed: "in any particular snowflake, all six arms are the same—why does this happen? Why shouldn't each of the six arms develop in a different and unique shape?"

"Some central organizing principle must be at work, but—?" Daniel said.

"That is too obvious to even *bother* pointing out," Hooke said. "With better lenses, we could peer into the core of a snowflake and discover that principle at work."

A week later, Hooke opened up the thorax of a live dog and removed all of its ribs to expose the beating heart. But the lungs had gone flaccid and did not seem to be doing their job.

The screaming sounded almost human. A man with an expensive voice came down from John Comstock's house to enquire about it. Daniel, too bleary-eyed to see clearly and too weary to think, took him for a head butler or something. "I shall write an explanation, and a note of apology to him," Daniel mumbled, looking about for a quill, rubbing his blood-sticky hand on his breeches.

"To *whom*, prithee? asked the butler, amused. Though he seemed young for a head-butler. In his early thirties. He was in a linen night-dress. His scalp glistered with a fine carpet of blond stubble, the mark of a man who always wore a periwig.

"The Earl of Epsom."

"Why not write it to the Duke of York?"

"Very well then, I'll write it to him."

"Then why not dispense with writing altogether and simply tell me what the hell you are doing?"

Daniel took this for insolence until he looked the visitor in the face and realized it was the Duke of York in person.

He really ought to bow, or something. Instead of which he jerked. The Duke made a gesture with his hand that seemed to mean that the jerk was accepted as due obeisance and could they please get on with the conversation now.

"The Royal Society—" Daniel began, thrusting that word *Royal* out in front of him like a shield, "has brought a dead dog to life with another's blood, and has now embarked on a study of artificial *breath*."

"My brother is fond of your Society," said James, "or *his* Society I should say, for he made it Royal." This, Daniel suspected, was to explain why he was not going to have them all horsewhipped. "I do wonder at the noise. Is it expected to continue all night?"

"On the contrary, it has already ceased," Daniel pointed out.

The Lord High Admiral preceded him into the kitchen, where Hooke and Wilkins had thrust a brass pipe down the dog's windpipe and connected it to the same trusty pair of bellows they'd used to make the dead man's head speak. "By pumping the bellows they were able to inflate and deflate the lungs, and prevent the dog from asphyxiating," explained Charles Comstock, after the experimenters had bowed to the Duke. "Now it only remains to be seen how long the animal can be kept alive in this way. Mr. Waterhouse and I shall spell each other at the bellows until Mr. Hooke pronounces an end to the experiment."

At the mention of Daniel's family name, the Duke flicked his eyes towards him for a moment.

"If it must suffer in the name of your inquiry, thank Heaven it does so quietly," the Duke remarked, and turned to leave. The others would follow; but the Duke stopped them with a "Do carry on, as you were." But to Daniel he said, "A word, if you please, Mr. Waterhouse," and so Daniel escorted him out onto the lawn half wondering whether he was about to be carved up worse than the dog.

A few moments previously, he'd mastered a daft impulse to tackle his royal highness before his royal highness reached the kitchen, for fear that his royal highness would be disgusted by what was going on in there. But he'd not reckoned on the fact that the Duke, young though he was, had fought in a lot of battles, both at sea and on land. Which was to say that as bad as this business with the dog was, the Duke of York had seen much worse done to *humans*. The R.S., far from seeming like a band of mad ruthless butchers, were dilettantes by his standards. Further grounds (as if any were wanted!) for Daniel to feel queasy.

Daniel really knew of no way to regulate his actions other than to be rational. Princes were taught a thing or two about being rational, as they were taught to play a little lute and dance a passable ricercar. But what drove their actions was their own force of will; in the end they did as they pleased, rational or not. Daniel had liked to tell himself that rational thought led to better actions than brute force of will; yet here was the Duke of York all but rolling his eyes at them and their experiment, seeing naught that was new.

"A friend of mine brought back something nasty from France," his royal highness announced.

It took Daniel a long time to decrypt this. He tried to understand it in any number of different ways, but suddenly the knowledge rumbled through his mind like a peal of thunder through a coppice. The Duke had said: *I have syphilis.*

"Shame, that," Daniel said. For he was not sure, yet, that he had translated it correctly. He must be ever so careful and vague lest this conversation degenerate into a comedy of errors ending with his death by rapier-thrust.

"Some are of the opinion that mercury cures it."

"It is also a poison, though," Daniel said.

Which was common knowledge; but it seemed to confirm, in the mind of James Stuart, Duke of York and Lord High Admiral, that he was talking to just the right chap. "Surely with so many clever Doctors in the Royal Society, working on artificial breath and such, there must be some thought of how to cure a man such as my friend."

And his wife and his children, Daniel thought, for James must have either gotten it from, or passed it on to, Anne Hyde, who had therefore probably given it to the daughters, Mary and Anne. To date, James's older brother the King had not been able to produce any legitimate children. There were plenty of bastards like Monmouth. But none eligible to inherit the throne. And so this nasty thing that James had brought back from France was really a matter of whether the Stuart dynasty was to survive.

This raised a fascinating side question. With a whole cottage full of Royal Society Fellows to choose from, why had James carefully chosen to speak with the one who happened to be the son of a Phanatique?

"It is a sensitive matter," the Duke remarked, "the sort of thing that stains a man's honor, if it is bandied about."

Daniel readily translated this as follows: *If you tell anyone, I'll send someone round to engage you in a duel.* Not that anyone would pay any notice, anyway, if the son of Drake were to level an accusation of moral turpitude against the Duke of York. Drake had been doing such things without letup for fifty years. And so the Duke's strategy was now plain to Daniel: he had chosen Daniel to hear about his syphilis because if Daniel were so foolish as to spread rumors, no one would hear them above the roar of obloquy produced at all times by Drake. In any case, Daniel would not be able to keep it up for very long before he was found in a field outside of London with a lot of rapier wounds in his body.

"You will let me know, won't you, if the Royal Society learns anything on this front?" said James, making to leave.

"So that you can pass the information on to your friend? Of course," Daniel said. Which was the end of that conversation. He returned to the kitchen to get an idea of how much longer the experiment was going to go on.

The answer: longer than any of them really wanted. By the time they were finished, dawn-light was beginning to come in the windows, giving them a premonition of just how ghastly the kitchen was going to look when the sun actually rose. Hooke was sitting crookedly in a chair, shocked and morose, appalled by himself, and Wilkins was hunched forward supporting his head on a smeared fist.

They'd come here supposedly as refugees from the Black Death, but really they were fleeing their own ignorance—they hungered for understanding, and were like starving wretches who had broken into a lord's house and gone on an orgy of gluttonous feasting, wolfing down new meals before they could digest, or even chew, the old ones. It had lasted for the better part of a year, but now, as the sun rose over the aftermath of the artificial breath experiment, they were scattered around, blinking stupidly at the devastated kitchen, with its dog-ribs strewn all over the floor, and huge jars of preserved spleens and gall-bladders, specimens of exotic parasites nailed to planks or glued to panes of glass, vile poisons bubbling over on the fire, and suddenly they felt completely disgusted with themselves.

Daniel gathered the dog's remains up in his arms—messy, but it scarcely mattered—all their clothes would have to be burned anyway—and walked out to the bone-yard on the east side of the cottage, where the remains of all Hooke's and Wilkins's investigations were burned, buried, or used to study the spontaneous generation of flies. Notwithstanding which, the air was relatively clean and fresh out here. Having set the remains down, Daniel found that he was walking directly towards a blazing planet, a few degrees above the western horizon, which could only be Venus. He walked and walked, letting the dew on the grass cleanse the blood from his shoes. The dawn was making the fields shimmer pink and green.

Isaac had sent him a letter: "Require asst. w/obs. of Venus pls. come if you can." He had wondered at the time if this might be something veiled. But standing there in that dew-silvered field with his back to the house of carnage and nothing before him but the Dawn Star, Daniel remembered what Isaac had said years ago about the natural harmony between the heavenly orbs and the orbs we view them with. Four hours later he was riding north on a borrowed horse.

Aboard Minerva,
Plymouth Bay, Massachusetts
NOVEMBER 1713

DANIEL WAKES UP WORRIED. The stiffness in his *masseter* muscles, the aching in his *frontalis* and *temporalis,* tells him he's been worrying about something in his sleep. Still, being worried is preferable to being terrified, which he was until yesterday, when Captain van Hoek finally gave up on the idea of trying to sail *Minerva* into the throat of a gale and turned back to calmer waters along the Massachusetts coast.

Captain van Hoek would probably have called it "a bit of chop" or some other nautical euphemism, but Daniel had gone to his cabin with a pail to catch his vomit, and an empty bottle to receive the notes he'd been scratching out in the last few days. If the weather had gotten any worse, he'd have tossed these down the head. Perhaps some Moor or Hottentot would have found them in a century or two and read about Dr. Waterhouse's early memories of Newton and Leibniz.

The planks of the poop deck are only a few inches above Daniel's face as he lies on his sack of straw. He's learned to recognize the tread of van Hoek's boots on those boards. On a ship it is bad manners to approach within a fathom of the captain, so even when the poop deck is crowded, van Hoek's footsteps are always surrounded by a large empty space. As *Minerva*'s quest for a steady west wind has stretched out to a

week and then two, Daniel has learned to read the state of
the captain's mind from the figure and rhythm of his movements—each pattern like the steps of a courtly dance. A
steady long stride means that all is well, and van Hoek is
merely touring the precincts. When he's watching the
weather he walks about in small eddies, and when he's
shooting the sun with his back-staff he stands still, grinding
the balls of his feet against the planks to keep his balance.
But this morning (Daniel supposes it is early in the morning,
though the sun hasn't come up yet) van Hoek is doing something Daniel's never observed before: flitting back and forth
across the poop deck with brisk angry steps, pausing at one
rail or another for a few seconds at a time. The sailors, he
senses, are mostly awake, but they are all belowdecks shush-
ing one another and tending to small, intense, quiet jobs.

Yesterday they had sailed into Cape Cod Bay—the shallow lake held in the crook of Cape Cod's arm—to ride out
the tail end of that northeast gale, and to make certain re-
pairs, and get the ship more winter-ready than it had been.
But then the wind shifted round to the north and threatened
to drive them against the sand-banks at the southern fringe
of said Bay, and so they sailed toward the sunset, and maneuvered the big ship with exquisite care between rocks to
starboard and sunken islands to port, and thus entered Plymouth Bay. As night fell they dropped anchor in an inlet,
well sheltered from the weather, and (as Daniel supposed)
prepared to tarry there for a few days and await more auspi-
cious weather. But van Hoek was obviously nervous—he
doubled the watch, and put men to work cleaning and oiling
the ship's surprisingly comprehensive arsenal of small
firearms.

A distant boom rattles the panes in Daniel's cabin window. He rolls out of bed like a fourteen-year-old and scurries
to the exit, flailing one hand over his head in the dark so he
won't brain himself on the overhead beam. When he
emerges onto the quarter-deck he seems to hear answering

fire from all the isles and hillside around them—then he understands that they are merely echoes of the first explosion. With a good pocket-watch he could map their surroundings by the timing of those echoes—

Dappa, the first mate, sits crosslegged on the deck near the wheel, reviewing charts by candle-light. This is an odd place for such work. Diverse feathers and colored ribbons dangle from a string above his head—Daniel supposes it to be a tribal fetish (Dappa is an African) until a fleck of goose-down crawls in a breath of cold air, and he understands that Dappa is trying to guess what the wind will do as the sun rises. He holds up one hand to silence Daniel before Daniel's had a chance to speak. There is shouting on the water, but it is all distant—*Minerva* is silent as a ghost ship. Stepping farther out onto the quarter-deck, Daniel can see yellow stars widely scattered across the water, blinking as they are eclipsed by rolling seas.

"You didn't know what you were getting yourself into," Dappa observes.

"I'll rise to that bait—what have I gotten myself into?"

"You're on a ship whose captain refuses to have anything to do with pirates," Dappa says. "Hates 'em. He nailed his colors to the mast twenty years ago, van Hoek did—he would burn this ship to the waterline before handing over a single penny."

"Those lights on the water—"

"Whaleboats mostly," Dappa says. "Possibly a barge or two. When the sun comes up we may expect to see sails—but before we concern ourselves with those, we shall have to contend with the whaleboats. Did you hear the shouting, an hour ago?"

"I must have slept through it."

"A whaleboat stole up towards us with muffled oars. We let her suppose that we were asleep—waited until she was alongside, then dropped a comet into her."

"Comet?"

"A small cannonball, wrapped in oil-soaked rags and set aflame. Once it lands in such a boat, it's difficult to throw overboard. Gave us a good look, while it lasted: there were a dozen Englishmen in that boat, and one of 'em was already swinging a grappling-hook."

"Do you mean that they were English colonists, or—"

"That's one of the things we aim to find out. After we chased that lot off, we sent some men out in our own whaler."

"The explosion—?"

"'Twas a grenade. We have a few retired grenadiers in our number—"

"You threw a *bomb* into someone else's boat?"

"Aye, and then—if all went according to plan—our Filipinos—former pearl divers, excellent swimmers—climbed over the gunwales with daggers in their teeth and cut a few throats—"

"But that's *mad*! This is *Massachusetts*!"

Dappa chuckles. "Aye. That it is."

An hour later the sun rises gorgeously over Cape Cod Bay. Daniel is pacing around the ship, trying to find a place where he won't have to listen to the screams of the pirates. Two open boats are now thudding against *Minerva*'s hull: the ship's own longboat, freshly caulked and painted, and the pirate whaler, which was evidently in poor condition even before this morning's action. Splinters of fresh blond wood show where a bench was snapped by the grenade, and an inch or two of blood sloshes back and forth in the bottom as the empty boat is tossed around by a rising wind. Five pirates survived, and were towed back to *Minerva* by the raiding party. Now (judging from the sounds) they are all down in the bilge, where two of *Minerva*'s largest sailors are holding their heads beneath the filthy water. When they are hauled out, they scream for air, and Daniel thinks about Hooke and Wilkins with their poor dogs.

Woolsthorpe, Lincolnshire
SPRING 1666

⚱

He discovereth the depe & secret things: he
knoweth what is in the darkenes, and the light
dwelleth with him.

—DANIEL 2:22

FROM ISAAC'S INSTRUCTIONS ("Turn left at Grimethorpe
Ruin") he'd been expecting a few hovels gripping the rim of
a windburned scarp, but Woolsthorpe was as pleasant a specimen of English countryside as he'd ever seen. North of
Cambridge it was appallingly flat, a plain scratched with
drainage ditches. But beyond Peterborough the coastal fens
fell away and were replaced by pastures of radiant greenness,
like stained-glass windows infested with sheep. There were a
few tall pine trees that made the place seem farther north
than it really was. Another day north, the country began to
roll, and the earth turned brown as coffee, with cream-
colored stone rising out of the soil here and there: once-
irregular croppings rationalized to squared-off block-heaps
by the efforts of quarrymen. Woolsthorpe gave an impression of being high up in the world, close to the sky, and the
trees that lined the lane from the village all had the same telltale skewage, suggesting that the place might not be as pleasant all year round as it was on the morning Daniel arrived.

Woolsthorpe Manor was a very simple house, shaped like

a fat *T* with its crossbar fronting on the lane, made of the soft pale stone that was used for everything around here—its roof a solid mass of lichens. It was built sideways to a long slope that rose as it went northwards, and so, on its southern end, the land fell away from it, giving it a clear sunny exposure. But this opportunity had been wasted by the builders, who had put almost no windows there—just a couple of them, scarcely larger than gun-slits, and one tiny portal up in the attic that made no sense to Daniel at first. As Daniel noted while his horse toiled up the hill through the grasping spring mud, Isaac had already taken advantage of this south-facing wall by carving diverse sundials into it. Sprawling away from there, down the hill and away from the lane, were long stables and barns that marked the place as an active farmstead, and that Daniel didn't have to concern himself with.

He turned off the lane. The house was set back from it not more than twenty feet. Set above the door was a coat of arms carved into the stone: on a blank shield, a pair of human thigh-bones crossed. A Jolly Roger, minus skull. Daniel sat on his horse and contemplated its sheer awfulness for a while and savored the dull, throbbing embarrassment of being English. He was waiting for a servant to notice his arrival.

Isaac had mentioned in his letter that his mother was away for a few weeks, and this was perfectly acceptable to Daniel—all he knew of the mother was that she had abandoned Isaac when he'd been three years old, and gone to live with a rich new husband several miles away, leaving the toddler to be raised in this house by his grandmother. Daniel had noticed that there were some families (like the Waterhouses) skilled at presenting a handsome façade to the world, no matter what was *really* going on; it was all lies, of course, but at least it was a convenience to visitors. But there were other families where the emotional wounds of the participants never healed, never even closed up and scabbed over, and no one even bothered to cover them up—like certain ghastly ef-

figies in Papist churches, with exposed bleeding hearts and
gushing stigmata. Having dinner or even polite conversation
with them was like sitting around the table participating in
Hooke's dog experiment—everything you did or said was another squeeze of the bellows, and you could stare right in
through the vacancies in the rib cage and see the organs helplessly responding, the heart twitching with its own macabre
internal power of perpetual motion. Daniel suspected that the
Newtons were one of *those* families, and he was glad Mother
was absent. Their coat of arms was a proof, of Euclidean cer-
tainty, that he was right about this.

"Is that you, Daniel?" said the voice of Isaac Newton, not
very loud. A little bubble of euphoria percolated into
Daniel's bloodstream: to re-encounter *anyone,* after so long,
during the Plague Years, and find them still alive, was a miracle. He looked uphill. The northern end of the house looked
into, and was sheltered by, rising terrain. A small orchard of
apple trees had been established on that side. Seated on a
bench, with his back to Daniel and to the sun, was a man or
woman with long colorless hair spilling down over a blanket
that had been drawn round the shoulders like a shawl.

"Isaac?"

The head turned slightly. "It is I."

Daniel rode up out of the mud and into the apple-garden,
then dismounted and tethered the horse to the low branch of
an apple tree—a garland of white flowers. The petals were
coming down from the apple-blossoms like snow. Daniel
swung round Isaac in a wide Copernican arc, peering at him
through the fragrant blizzard. Isaac's hair had always been
pale, and prematurely streaked with gray, but in the year
since Daniel had seen him, he'd gone almost entirely silver.
The hair fell about him like a hood—as Daniel came around
to the front, he was expecting to see Isaac's protruding eyes,
but instead he saw two disks of gold looking back at him, as
if Isaac's eyes had been replaced by five-guinea coins.
Daniel must have shouted, because Isaac said, "Don't be

alarmed. I fashioned these spectacles myself. I'm sure you know that gold is almost infinitely malleable—but did you know that if you pound it thin enough, you can see through it? Try them." He took the spectacles off with one hand while clamping the other over his eyes. Daniel bobbled them because they were lighter than he'd expected—they had no lenses, just membranes of gold stretched like drum-heads over wire frames. As he raised them towards his face, their color changed.

"They are blue!"

"It is another clue about the nature of light," Isaac said. "Gold is yellow—it reflects the part of light that is yellow, that is, but allows the remnant to pass through—which being deprived of its yellow part, appears blue."

Daniel was peering out at a dim vision of blue-blossomed apple trees before a blue stone house—a blue Isaac Newton sitting with his back to a blue sun, one blue hand covering his eyes.

"Forgive me their rude construction—I made them in the dark."

"Is there something the matter with your eyes, Isaac?"

"Nothing that cannot heal, God willing. I have been staring into the sun too much."

"Oh." Daniel was semi-dumbstruck by Puritan guilt for having left Isaac alone for so long. It was fortunate he hadn't killed himself.

"I can still work in a dark room, with the spectra that are cast through the prism by the Sun. But the spectra of Venus are too faint."

"Of *Venus*?!"

"I have made observations concerning the nature of Light that contradict the theories of Descartes, Boyle, and Huygens," Isaac said. "I have divided the white light of the Sun into colors, and then recombined these rays to make white light again. I have done the experiment many times, changing the apparatus to rule out possible sources of error. But there is one I have yet to eliminate: the Sun is not a point source of light. Its face subtends a considerable arc in the heavens. Those who will seek to find fault with my work, and to attack me, will claim that this—the fact that the light entering my prism, from different parts of the Sun's disk, strikes it from slightly different angles—renders my conclusions suspect, and therefore worthless. In order to defeat these objections I must repeat the experiments using light, not from the Sun, but from Venus—an almost infinitely narrow point of light. But the light from Venus is so faint that my burned eyes cannot see it. I need you to make the observations with your good eyes, Daniel. We begin tonight. Perhaps you'd care to take a nap?"

The house was divided in half, north/south: the northern part, which had windows but no sunlight, was the domain of Newton's mother—a parlor on the ground floor and a bedchamber above it, both furnished in the few-but-enormous style then mandatory. The southern half—with just a few tiny apertures to admit the plentiful sunlight—was Isaac's: on the ground floor, a kitchen with a vast walk-in fireplace, suitable for alchemical work, and above it a bedchamber.

Isaac persuaded Daniel to lie down in, or at least *on,* his mother's bed for a bit of a nap—then made the mistake of mentioning that it was the same bed in which Isaac had been born, several weeks premature, twenty-four years earlier. So after half an hour of lying in that bed, as rigid as a tetanus victim, looking out between his feet at the first thing Isaac had ever laid eyes on (the window and the orchard), Daniel got up and went outside again. Isaac was still sitting on the bench with a book in his lap, but his gold spectacles were aimed at the horizon. "Defeated them soundly, I should say."

"I beg your pardon?"

"When it started it was close to shore—but it has steadily moved away."

"What on earth can you be talking about, Isaac?"

"The naval battle—we are fighting the Dutch in the Narrow Seas. Can you not hear the sound of the cannons?"

"I've been lying quietly in bed and heard nothing."

"Out here, it is very distinct." Isaac reached out and caught a fluttering petal. "The winds favor our Navy. The Dutch chose the wrong time to attack."

A fit of dizziness came over Daniel just then. Partly it was the thought that James, Duke of York, who a couple of weeks ago had been standing arm's length from Daniel discoursing of syphilis, at this moment stood on the deck of a flagship, firing on, and taking fire from, the Dutch fleet; and the booms rolled across the sea and were gathered in by the great auricle of the Wash, the Boston and the Lynn Deeps, the Long Sand and the Brancaster Roads perhaps serving as the greased convolutions of an ear, and propagated up the channel of the Welland, fanned out along its tributary rivers and rills into the swales and hills of Lincolnshire and into the ears of Isaac. It was partly that, and partly the vision that filled his eyes: thousands of white petals were coming off the apple trees and following the same diagonal path to the ground, their descent skewed by a breeze that was blowing out toward the sea.

"Do you remember when Cromwell died, and Satan's Wind came along to carry his soul to Hell?" Isaac asked.

"Yes. I was marching in his funeral procession, watching old Puritans getting blown flat."

"I was in the schoolyard. We happened to be having a broad-jumping competition. I won the prize, even though I was small and frail. In fact, perhaps I won *because* I was so—I knew that I should have to use my brains. I situated myself so that Satan's Wind was at my back, and then timed my leap so that I left the ground during an especially powerful gust. The wind carried my little body through space like one of these petals. For a moment I was gripped by an emotion—part thrill and part terror—as I imagined that the wind might carry me away—that my feet might never touch the earth again—that I would continue to skim along, just above the ground, until I had circumnavigated the globe. Of course I was just a boy. I didn't know that projectiles rise and fall in parabolic curves. Be those curves ever so flat, they always tend to earth again. But suppose a cannonball, or a boy caught up in a supernatural wind, flew so fast that the centrifugal force (as Huygens has named it) of his motion around the earth just counteracted his tendency to fall?"

"Er—depends on what you assume about the nature of falling," Daniel said. "Why do we fall? In what direction?"

"We fall towards the center of the earth. The same center on which the centrifugal force pivots—like a rock whirled on the end of a string."

"I suppose that if, somehow, you could get the forces to balance just so, you'd keep going round and round, and never fall or fly away. But it seems terrifically improbable—God would have to set it up just so—as He set the planets in their orbits."

"If you make certain assumptions about the force of gravity, and how the weight of an object diminishes as it gets farther away, it's not improbable at all," Isaac said. "It just *happens*. You would keep going round and round forever."

"In a circle?"

"An ellipse."

"An ellipse . . ." and here the bomb finally went off in his head, and Daniel had to sit down on the ground, the moisture of last year's fallen apples soaking through his breeches. "Like a planet."

"Just so—if only we could jump fast enough, or had a strong enough wind at our backs, we could *all* be planets."

It was so pure and obviously Right that it did not occur to Daniel to question Isaac about the details for several hours, as the Sun was going down, and they were preparing for Venus to wheel round into the southern sky. "I have developed a method of fluxions that renders it all perfectly obvious," Isaac said.

Daniel's first thought had been *I have to tell Wilkins* because Wilkins, who had written a novel in which men flew to the moon, would be delighted with Isaac's phrase: *We could all be planets*. But that put him in mind of Hooke, and the experiment at the deep well. Some premonition told him that he had best keep Newton and Hooke in separate cells for now.

Isaac's bedroom might have been designed specifically

for doing prism experiments, because one wanted an opening just big enough to admit a ray of light in which to center
the prism, but otherwise the room needed to be dark so that
the spectrum could be clearly viewed where it struck the
wall. The only drawback for Daniel was stumbling over debris. This was the room where Isaac had lived in the years
before going to Cambridge. Daniel inferred that they had
been lonely years. The floor was cluttered with stuff Isaac
had made but been too busy to throw away, and the white
plaster walls were covered with graffiti he had sketched with
charcoal or scratched with nails: designs for windmills, depictions of birds, geometrickal proofs. Daniel shuffled
through the darkness, never lifting a foot off the floor lest it
come down on an old piece of doll-furniture or jagged remains of a lens-grinding experiment, the delicate works of a
water-clock or the papery skull of a small animal, or a foamy
crucible crowned with frozen drips of metal.

Isaac had worked out during which hours of the night
Venus would be shining her perfectly unidirectional light on
Woolsthorpe Manor's south wall, and he'd done it not only
for tonight but for every night in the next several weeks. All
of those hours were spoken for: he had planned out a whole
program of experiments. It was clear to Daniel that Isaac
had been arguing his case against a whole court full of imaginary Jesuits hurling Latin barbs at him from every quarter,
objecting to his methods in ways that were often ridicu-
lous—that Isaac fancied himself as a combination of Galileo
and St. Anne, but that unlike Galileo he had no intention of
knuckling under, and unlike St. Anne he would not end up
riddled with his tormentors' arrows—he was getting ready to
catch the arrows, and fling them back.

It was the sort of thing that Hooke never bothered with—
because for Hooke being right was enough, and he didn't
care what anyone else thought of him or his ideas.

When Isaac had got his prisms situated in the window and
blown out the candle, Daniel was blind, and painfully embarrassed, for several minutes—he was anxious that, lacking

Isaac's acute senses, he would not be able to see the spectrum cast against the wall by the light shining from Venus. "Have due patience," Isaac said with a tenderness Daniel hadn't heard from him in years. The thought stole upon Daniel, as he sat there in the dark with Isaac, that Isaac might have more than one reason for wearing those golden spectacles all the time. They shielded his burnt eyes from the light, yes. But as well, might they hide his burnt heart from the sight of Daniel?

Then Daniel noticed a multicolored blur on the wall—a sliver, red on one end and violet on the other. He said, "I have it."

He was startled by a heavy rustling directly above them, in the attic, a scrabbling of claws.

"What was that?"

"There is a tiny window up there—an invitation for owls to build nests in the attic," Isaac said. "So vermin don't eat the grain stored up there."

Daniel laughed at it. For a moment he and Isaac were boys up past bedtime playing with their toys, the complications of their past forgotten and the perils of the future unthought of.

A deep hooing noise, like the resonant tone of an organ pipe. Then the rustle of feathers as the bird squeezed through the opening, and the rhythm of powerful wings, like the beating of a heart, receding into the sky. The spectrum of Venus flashed off, then on, as the owl momentarily eclipsed the planet. When Daniel looked, he realized that he could now see not only the spectrum from Venus, but tiny, ghostly streaks of color all over the wall: the spectra cast by the stars that surrounded Venus in the southern sky. But spectra were *all* he could see. The earth spun and the ribbons of color migrated across the invisible wall, an inch a minute, pouring across the rough plaster like shining puddles of quicksilver driven before a steady wind, revealing, in gorgeous colors, tiny strips of the pictures that Isaac had drawn and scratched on those walls. Each of the little rainbows showed only a fragment of a picture, and each picture in turn was only part

of Isaac's tapestry of sketchings and scratchings, but Daniel
supposed that if he stood there through a sufficient number
of long cold nights and concentrated very hard, he might be
able to assemble, in his mind, a rough conception of the entire thing. Which was the way he had to address Isaac Newton in any case.

> But I did believe, and do still, that the end of
> our City will be with fire and brimstone from
> above, and therefore I have made mine escape.
> —JOHN BUNYAN, *The Pilgrim's Progress*

CAMBRIDGE TRIED TO RESUME that spring, but Daniel and
Isaac had only just settled back into their chamber when
someone died of the Plague and they had to move out
again—Isaac back to Woolsthorpe, Daniel back to a wandering life. He spent some weeks with Isaac working on the colors experiment, others with Wilkins (now back in London,
running regular meetings of the Royal Society again) working on the Universal Character manuscript, others with
Drake or with his older half-siblings, who'd returned to
London at Drake's command, to await the Apocalypse. The
Year of the Beast, 1666, was halfway through, then two-
thirds. Plague had gone away. War continued, and it was
more than just an Anglo-Dutch war now, for the French had
made a league with the Dutch against the English. But whatever plans the Duke of York had hatched with his Admirals
on that chilly day at Epsom must not have been altogether
worthless, because it was going well for them. Drake must
be torn between patriotic ardor, and a feeling of disappointment that it showed no sign whatever of developing into an
Armageddon sort of war. It was merely a string of naval engagements, and the gist of it was that the English fleet was
driving the Dutch and French from the Channel. All in all,
there was a failure of events to match up with the program
laid out in the Books of Daniel and of Revelation, which

forced Drake to re-read them almost every day, working out interpretations new and ever more strained. For Daniel's part, he sometimes went for days without thinking about the End of the World at all.

One evening early in September he was riding back toward London from the north. He'd been up in Woolsthorpe helping Isaac run the numbers on his planetary orbit theory, but with inconclusive results, because they did not know exactly how far from the center of the Earth they were when they stood on the ground and weighed things. He had stopped in at that plague-ridden town of Cambridge to fetch a new book that claimed to specify the crucial figure: how big around was the Earth? and now he was going down to visit his father, who'd sent him an alarming letter, claiming that he had just calculated a different crucial figure: the exact date (early in September, as it happened) that the world would end.

Daniel was still twenty miles outside of the city, riding along in the late afternoon, when a messenger came galloping up the road toward him and shouted, "London has been burning for a day and is burning still!" as he hurtled past.

Daniel knew this, in a way, but he had been denying it. The air had had a burnt smell about it all day long, and a haze of smoke had clung about the trees and the sheltered hollows in the fields. The sun had been a glaring patch that seemed to fill half the southern sky. Now, as the day went on and it sank toward the horizon, it turned orange and then red, and began to limn vast billows and towers of smoke—portents and omens that seemed incomparably vaster than the (still unknown) radius of the Earth. Daniel rode into the night, but not into darkness. A vault of orange light had been thrown about a mile high up into the sky above London. Thuds propagated through the earth—at first he supposed they must be the impacts of buildings falling down, but then they began coming in slow premeditated onslaughts and he reckoned that they must be blowing up whole buildings with powder-kegs, trying to gouge fire-breaks through the city.

At first he'd thought it was impossible for any fire to reach as far as Drake's house outside of town on Holborn, but the number of explosions, the diameter of the arch of light, told him nothing was safe. He was working upstream against a heavy traffic of soot-faced wretches now. It made for slow going, but there was nothing to do about it. The folds of his clothing, and even the porches of his ears, were collecting black grit, nodules and splinters and flakes of charcoal that rained down tickingly on everything.

"Cor, look, it's snowing!" exclaimed a boy with his face turned upwards to catch reflected light. Daniel—not wanting to see it, really—raised his eyes slowly, and found the sky filled with some kind of loose chaff, swirling in slow vortices here and there but heading generally downwards. He grabbed a piece of it from the air: it was page 798 of a Bible, all charred round the margins. He reached again and snared a hand-written leaf from a goldsmith's account-book, still glowing at one corner. Then a handbill—a libel attacking Free Coinage. A personal letter from one Lady to another. They accumulated on his shoulders like falling leaves and he stopped reading them after a while.

It took so long to get there that when he actually saw a house burning by the roadside, he was shocked. Solid beams of flame protruded from the windows, silhouetting people with leather buckets, jewels of water spinning off their rims. Refugees had flooded the fields along Gray's Inn Road and, tired of watching the fire, had begun throwing up shelters out of whatever stuff they could find.

Not far from Holborn, the road was nearly blocked by a rampart of shattered masonry that had spilled across it when buildings to either side had been blown up—even above the smell of burning London, Daniel could detect the brimstone-tang of the gunpowder. Then a building just to his right exploded—to Daniel, an instant's warning, a yellow flare in the corner of his eye, and then gravel embedded in one side of his face (but it felt like that side of his head had simply been sheared off) and deafness. His horse bolted and instantly broke a leg in the rubble-pile, then threw Daniel off—he came down hard on stones and splinters, and got up after lying there for he had no idea how long. There had been more explosions, coming faster now as the main front of the fire drew closer, its heat drawing curtains of steam and smoke out of walls, rooves, and the clothing on the living and dead persons in the street. Daniel took advantage of the fire's light to stumble over the rubble-wall and into a stretch of the road that was still clear, but doomed to burn.

Reaching Holborn, he turned his back to the fire and ran toward the sound of the explosions. Some part of his mind had been doing geometry through all of this, plotting the points of the explosions and extrapolating them, and he was more and more certain that the curve was destined to pass near Drake's house.

There was another rubble-heap on Holborn, so fresh that it was still sledding toward its angle of repose. Daniel charged up it, almost afraid to look down lest he should discover Drake's furniture beneath his feet. But from the top of the heap he obtained a perfect view of Drake's house, still standing, but standing alone now, in a sag-shouldered posture, as the houses to either side of it had been blown up. The walls had begun to smoke, and fire-brands were raining down around it like meteors, and Drake Waterhouse was up on the roof holding a Bible above his head with both hands. He was bellowing something that could not be heard, and did not need to be.

The street below was crowded with an uncommon number of Gentlemen, and better, brandishing swords—their gay courtiers' clothing burnt and blackened—and musketeers, too, looking somewhat unhappy to be standing in such a place with containers of gunpowder strapped to their midsections. Very wealthy and prominent men were looking up at Drake, shouting and pointing at the street, insisting he come down. But Drake had eyes only for the fire.

Daniel turned round to see what his father was seeing, and was nearly slapped to the ground by the heat and the spectacle of it—the Fire. Everything between East and South was flame, and everything below the stars. It fountained and throbbed, jetted and pulsed, and buildings went down beneath it as blades of grass beneath John Wilkins's giant Wheel.

And it was approaching, so fast that it overtook some persons who were trying to run away from it—they were blurring into ghosts of smoke and bursting into flames, their sprinting forms dissolving into light: the Rapture. This had not escaped Drake's notice—he was pointing at it—but the crowd of Court fops below were not interested. To Drake, these particular men had been demons from Hell even *before* London had caught fire, because they were the personal bootlicks of King Charles II, an arch-daemon of King Louis XIV himself. Now, here they were, perversely convened in front of his house.

Daniel had been waving his arms over his head trying to get Drake's attention, but he understood now that he must be an indistinct black shape against a vast glare, the least interesting thing in Drake's panorama.

All of the courtiers had turned inward, attent on the same man—even Drake was looking at him. Daniel caught sight of the Lord Mayor, and thought perhaps *he* was the center of attention—but the Lord Mayor had eyes only to look at another. Sidestepping to a new position on the heap, Daniel finally saw a tall dark man in impossibly glorious clothing and a vast wig, which was shaking from side to side in exasperation. This man suddenly moved forward, seized a torch from a toady, looked up one last time at Drake, then bent down and touched the fire to the street. A bright smoking star rolled across the pavement toward Drake's front door, which had been smashed open.

The man with the torch turned around, and Daniel recognized him as England.

There was a kind of preliminary explosion of humanity away from the house. Courtiers and musketeers formed a crowd behind the King to shield his back from flying harpsichords. Up on the roof, Drake aimed a finger at His Majesty and raised his Bible on high to call down some fresh damnation. From the burning timbers that were now coming down from Heaven like flaming spears hurled by avenging angels, he might have thought, in these moments, that he'd played an important part in Judgment Day. But nothing hit the King.

The spark was climbing the front steps. Daniel plunged forward down the piled house-guts, because he was fairly certain that he could outrun the spark, reach the fuse, and jerk it loose before it touched whatever powder-kegs had been rolled into Drake's parlor. His path was blocked by members of the King's personal bodyguard who were running the other way. They looked at Daniel curiously while Daniel changed course to swing round them. In the corner of his eye he saw one of them understand what Daniel was doing—that slackening of the face, the opening of the features, that came over the faces of students when, suddenly, they knew. This man stepped clear from the group and raised a yawning tube to his shoulder. Daniel looked at his father's house and saw the star snaking down the dark hallway. He was tense for the explosion, but it came from behind him— at the same moment he was bitten in a hundred places and slammed face-down into the street.

He rolled over on his back, trying to snuff the fires of pain burning all over him, and saw his father ascending into heaven, his black clothes changing into a robe of fire. His table, books, and grandfather clock were not far behind.

"Father?" he said.

Which was senseless, if the only kind of sense you heeded was that of Natural Philosophy. Even supposing Drake was alive at the moment Daniel spoke to him—a daring supposition indeed, and not the sort of thing that contributed to a young man's reputation in the Royal Society—he was far away, and getting farther, washed in apocalyptic roar and tumult, beset by many distractions, and probably deaf from the blast. But Daniel had just seen his house exploded and been shot with a blunderbuss in the same instant, and all sense of the Natural-Philosophic kind had fled from him. All that remained to shape his actions was the sentimental logic of a five-year-old bewildered that his father seemed to be leaving him: which was hardly the natural and correct order of things. Moreover, Daniel had another twenty years' important things to say to his father. He had sinned against Drake and would make confession and be absolved, and Drake had sinned against him and must needs be brought to account. Determined to put a stop to this heinous, unnatural leaving, he used the only means of self-preservation that God had granted to five-year-olds: the voice. Which by itself did naught but wiggle air. In a loving home, that could raise alarms and summon help. "Father?" he tried again. But his home was a storm of bricks and a spray of timbers, each tracing its own arc to the smoking and steaming earth, and his father was a glowing cloud. Like a theophany of the Old Testament. But whereas fiery clouds were for YHWH a manifestation, a means of revealing Himself to His children below, this one swallowed Drake up and did not spit him out but made him one with the *Mysterium Tremendum.* He was hidden from Daniel now forever.

ↄ⅛ↄ

Aboard Minerva,
Plymouth Bay, Massachusetts
NOVEMBER 1713

HIS MIND HAS QUITE RUN ahead of his quill; his pen has gone dry, but his face is damp. Alone in his cabin, Daniel indulges himself for a minute in another favorite pastime of five-year-olds. Some say that crying is childish. Daniel—

who since the birth of Godfrey has had more opportunities than he should have liked to observe crying—takes a contrary view. Crying *loudly* is childish, in that it reflects a belief, on the cryer's part, that someone is around to hear the noise, and come a-running to make it all better. Crying in absolute silence, as Daniel does this morning, is the mark of the mature sufferer who no longer nurses, nor is nursed by, any such comfortable delusions.

There's a rhythmical chant down on the gundeck that slowly builds and then explodes into a drumming of many feet on mahogany stair-steps, and suddenly *Minerva*'s deck is crowded with sailors, running about and colliding with each other, like a living demonstration of Hooke's ideas about heat. Daniel wonders if perhaps a fire has been noticed down in the powder-magazine, and the sailors have all come up to abandon ship. But this is a highly organized sort of panic.

Daniel pats his face dry, stoppers his ink-well, and goes out onto the quarter-deck, chucking his ink-caked quill overboard. Most of the sailors have already ascended into the rigging, and begun to drop vast white curtains as if to shield landlubber Daniel's eyes from the fleet of sloops and whaleboats that seems now to be converging on them from every cove and inlet on Plymouth Bay. Rocks and trees ashore are moving, with respect to fixed objects on *Minerva,* in a way that they shouldn't. "We're moving—we are adrift!" he protests. Weighing anchor on a ship of *Minerva*'s bulk is a ludicrously complicated and lengthy procedure—a small army of chanting sailors pursuing one another round the giant capstan on the upperdeck, boys scrubbing slime off, and sprinkling sand onto, the wet anchor cable to afford a better purchase for the messenger cable—an infinite loop, passed three times round the capstan, that nimble-fingered riggers are continually lashing alongside the anchor cable in one place and unlashing in another. None of this has even begun to happen in the hour since the sun rose.

"We are adrift!" Daniel insists to Dappa, who's just

vaulted smartly off the edge of the poop deck and nearly landed on Daniel's shoulders.

"But naturally, Cap'n—we're all in a panic, don't you see?"

"You are being unduly harsh on yourself and your crew, Dappa—and why are you addressing me as Captain? And how can we be adrift, when we haven't weighed anchor?"

"You're wanted on the poop deck, Cap'n—that's right, just step forward—"

"Let me fetch my hat."

"None of it, Cap'n, we want every pirate in New England—for they're *all* out there, at the moment—to see your white hair shining in the sun, your bald pate, pale and pink, like that of a Cap'n who ain't been abovedecks in years—this way, mind the wheel, sir—that's right—could you dodder just a bit more? Squint into the unaccustomed sunlight—well played, Cap'n!"

"May the Good Lord save us, Mr. Dappa, we've lost our anchors! Some madman has cut the anchor cables!"

"I told you we were in a panic—steady up the stairs, there, Cap'n!"

"Let go my arm! I'm perfectly capable of—"

"Happy to be of service, Cap'n—as is that lopsided Dutchman at the top o' the stairs—"

"Captain van Hoek! Why are you dressed as an ordinary seaman!? And what has become of our anchors!?"

"Dead weight," van Hoek says, and then goes on to mutter something in Dutch.

"He said, you are showing just the sort of impotent choler that we need. Here, take a spyglass! I've an idea—why don't you peer into the wrong end of it first—then look befuddled, and angry, as if some subordinate had stupidly reversed the lenses."

"I'll have you know, Mr. Dappa, that at one time I knew as much of opticks as any man alive, save one—possibly two, if you count Spinoza—but he was only a *practical* lens-grinder, and generally more concerned with *atheistical* ru-minations—"

"Do it!" grunts the one-armed Dutchman. He is still the captain, so Daniel steps to the railing of the poop deck, raises the spyglass, and peers through the objective lens. He can actually *hear* pirates on distant whaleboats laughing at him. Van Hoek plucks the glass from Daniel, spins it around on the knuckles of his only hand, and thrusts it at him. Daniel accepts it and tries to hold it steady on an approaching whaler. But the forward end of that boat is fogged in a bank of smoke, rapidly dispersing in the freshening breeze. For the last few minutes, *Minerva*'s sails have been inflating, frequently with brisk snapping noises, almost like gunshots—but—

"Damn me," he says, "they *fired* on us!" He can see, now, the swivel-gun mounted in the whaleboat's prow, an unsavory-looking fellow feeding a neatly bound cluster of lead balls into its small muzzle.

"Just a shot across the bow," Dappa says. "That panicky look on your face—the gesticulating—perfect!"

"The number of boats is *incredible*—are these all pirating *together*?"

"Plenty of time for explanations later—now's the moment to look stricken—perhaps get wobbly in the knees and clutch your chest like an apoplectic—we'll assist you to your cabin on the upperdeck."

"But my cabin, as you know, is on the quarter-deck . . ."

"Today only, you're being given a complimentary upgrade—Cap'n. Come on, you've been in the sun too long—best retire and break open a bottle of rum."

"DON'T BE MISLED BY THESE exchanges of cannon-fire," Dappa reassures him, thrusting his woolly and somewhat grizzled head into the Captain's cabin. "If this were a true fight, sloops and whaleboats'd be simply exploding all round us."

"Well, if it's *not* a fight, what would you call it when men on ships shoot balls of lead at each other?"

"A game—a dance. A theatrickal performance. Speaking of which—have you practiced your role recently?"

"Didn't seem safe, when grapeshot was flying—but—as it's only an *entertainment*—well . . ." Daniel gets up from his squatting position underneath the Captain's chart-table and sidles over toward the windows, moving in a sort of Zeno's Paradox mode—each step only half as long as the previous. Van Hoek's cabin is as broad as the entire stern of the ship— two men could play at shuttlecocks in here. The entire aft bulkhead is one gently curved window commanding (now that Daniel's in position to see through it) a view of Plymouth Bay: wee cabins and wigwams on the hills, and, on the waves, numerous scuttling boats all flocked with gunpowder-smoke, occasionally thrusting truncated bolts of yellow fire in their general direction. "The critical reaction seems hostile," Daniel observes. Off to his left, a small pane gets smashed out of its frame by what he takes to have been a musket-ball.

"Excellent cringing! The way you raise your hands as if to clap them over your ears, then arrest them in midair, as if already seized in *rigor mortis*—thank God you were delivered into our hands."

"I am meant to believe that all of these goings-on are nothing more than an elaborate manipulation of the pirates' mental state?"

"No need to be haughty—*they* do it to *us*, too. Half of the cannon on those boats are carved out of logs, painted to look real."

A large meteor-like something blows the head door off its hinges and buries itself in an oaken knee-brace, knocking it askew and bending the entire cabin slightly out of shape— wreaking some sort of parallelogram effect on Daniel's Frame o' Reference, so it appears that Dappa's now standing up at an angle—or perhaps the ship's beginning to heel over. "Some of the cannon are, of course, real," Dappa admits before Daniel can score any points there.

"If we are playing with the pirates' minds, what is the advantage in making the ship's captain out as a senile poltroon—which, if I may read 'tween the lines, would appear to be *my* role? Why not fling open every gunport, run out every cannon, make the hills ring with broadsides, set van Hoek up on the poop waving his hook in the air?"

"We'll get round to all that later, in all likelihood. For now we must pursue a multilayered bluffing strategy."

"*Why?*"

"Because we have more than one group of pirates to contend with."

"*What!?*"

"This is why we captured and questioned—"

"*Some* would say tortured—"

"—several pirates before dawn. There are simply too many pirates in this Bay to make sense. Some of them would appear to be mutually hostile. Indeed, we've learned that the traditional, honest, hardworking Plymouth Bay pirates—the ones in the small boats—get over, Cap'n, I say! Two paces over to larboard, if you please!"

Dappa's adverting on something outside the window. Daniel turns round to see a taut manila line dangling vertically just outside—not an unusual sight in and of itself, but it wasn't there a few seconds ago. The stretched line shudders, tattooing a beat on the window-pane. A pair of blistered hands appears, then a broad-brimmed hat, then a head with a dagger clenched in its teeth. Then behind Daniel a tremendous *FOOM* while something unsightly happens to the climber's face—clearly visible through a suddenly absent pane. A gout of smoke roils and rebounds against the panes that are still there, and by the time it's cleared away the pirate is gone. Dappa's in the middle of the cabin holding a hot smoky shooting-iron.

He rummages in van Hoek's chest and pulls out a hook with various straps and stump-cups all a-dangle. "That was one of the sort I was speaking of. Never would've tried anything so foolhardy if the newer breed hadn't brought such hard times down on 'em."

"What newer breed?"

Dappa, wearing a fastidious and disgusted look, threads the hook out through the missing window-pane and catches the dangling pirate-rope, then draws it inside the cabin and severs it with a smart swing of his cutlass. "Lift your head toward the horizon, Cap'n, and behold the flotilla of coasting craft—sloops and topsail schooners, and a ketch—that is forming up there in Plymouth Bay. Half a dozen or more vessels. Strange information glancing from one to the next embodied in pennants, guns, and flashes of sunlight."

"It is because of *them* that the riffraff in the small craft cannot make a living?"

"Just so, Cap'n. Now, if we'd put up a brave front, as you suggested, they'd've known their cause was hopeless, and might've been tempted to make common cause with Teach."

"Teach?"

"Cap'n Edward Teach, the Admiral of yonder pirate-fleet. But as it is, these small-timers have spent themselves in a futile try at seizing *Minerva* before Teach could make sail and form up. Now we can address the Teach matter separately."

"There was a Teach in the Royal Navy—"

"He is the same fellow. He and his men fought on the Queen's side in the War, helping themselves to Spanish shipping. Now that the treaty is signed and we are friendly with Spain, these fellows are at loose ends, and have crossed the Atlantic to seek a home port for American piracy."

"So I ween it's not our cargo that Teach wants, so much as—"

"If we threw every last bale overboard, still he would come after us. He wants *Minerva* for his flagship. And a mighty raider she would be."

There's been no gunfire recently, so Daniel crosses over to the window and watches sail after sail unfurling, Teach's fleet developing into a steady cloud on the bay. "They look like fast ships," he says. "We'll be seeing Teach soon."

"He's easily recognized—according to them we questioned, he's a master of piratical performances. Wears smoking punks twined about his head, like burning dreadlocks, and, at night, burning tapers in his thick black beard. He's got half the people in Plymouth convinced he's the Devil incarnate."

"What think you, Dappa?"

"I think there never was a Devil so fierce as Cap'n van Hoek, when pirates are after his Lady."

⚜

Charing Cross
1670

⚕

Sir ROBERT MORAY produced a discourse concerning coffee, written by Dr. GODDARD at the King's command; which was read, and the author desired to leave a copy of it with the society.

Mr. BOYLE mentioned, that he had been informed, that the much drinking of coffee produced the palsy.

The bishop of Exeter seconded him, and said, that himself had found it dispose to paralytical effects; which however he thought were caused only in hot constitutions, by binding.

Mr. GRAUNT affirmed, that he knew two gentlemen, great drinkers of coffee, very paralytical.

Dr. WHISTLER suggested, that it might be

inquired, whether the same persons took
much tobacco.

> —THE HISTORY OF THE ROYAL SOCIETY
> OF LONDON FOR IMPROVING OF
> NATURAL KNOWLEDGE,
> JAN. 18, 1664/5*

HAVING NO DESIRE to be either palsied, *or* paralytical,
Daniel avoided the stuff until 1670, when he got his first
taste of it at Mrs. Green's Coffee-House, cunningly sited in
the place where the western end of the Strand yawned into
Charing Cross. The Church of St. Martin-in-the-Fields lay
to the west.[†] To the east was the New Exchange—this was
the nucleus of a whole block of shops. North was Covent
Garden, and South, according to rumor and tradition, was
the River Thames, a few hundred yards distant—but you
couldn't see it because noble Houses and Palaces formed a
solid levee running from the King's residence (Whitehall
Palace) all the way round the river-bend to Fleet Ditch,
where the wharves began.

Daniel Waterhouse walked past Mrs. Green's one summer
morning in 1670, a minute after Isaac Newton had done so. It
had a little garden in the front, with several tables. Daniel
went into it and stood for a moment, checking out his lines of
sight. Isaac had risen early, sneaked out of his bedchamber,
and taken to the streets without eating any breakfast—not unusual for Isaac. Daniel had followed him out the front door of
the (rebuilt, and dramatically enlarged) Waterhouse residence; across Lincoln's Inn Fields, where a few fashionable

---

*I.e., it was already 1665 everywhere except England, where the new year
was held to begin on March 25th.

†Though the fields were becoming city streets, so at this point it was more
like St. Martin-at-the-edge-of-*a*-field, and soon to be St. Martin-within-
visual-range-of-a-very-expensive-field-or-two.

early risers were walking dogs, or huddling in mysterious conferences; and (coincidentally) right past the very place at Drury Lane and Long Acre where those two Frenchmen had died of the Black Death six years earlier, inaugurating the memorable Plague Years. Thence into the dangerous chasm of flying earth and loose paving-stones that was St. Martin's Lane—for John Comstock, Earl of Epsom, acting in his capacity as Commissioner of Sewers, had decreed that this meandering country cow-path must be paved, and made over into a city street—the axis of a whole new London.

Daniel had been keeping his distance so that Isaac wouldn't notice him if he turned around—though you never knew with Isaac, who had better senses than most wild animals. St. Martin's Lane was crowded with heavy stone-carts drawn by teams of mighty horses, just barely under the control of their teamsters, and Daniel was forced to dodge wagons, and to scurry around and over piles of dirt and cobbles, in order to keep sight of Isaac.

Once they had reached the open spaces of Charing Cross, and the adjoining Yard where Kings of Scotland had once come to humble themselves before their liege-lord in Whitehall, Daniel could afford to maintain more distance—Isaac's silver hair was easy to pick out in a crowd. And if Isaac's destination was one of the shops, coffee-houses, livery stables, gardens, markets, or noblemen's houses lining the great Intersection, why, Daniel could sit down right about here and spy on him at leisure.

Why he was doing so, Daniel had no idea. It was just that by getting up and leaving so mysteriously, Isaac begged to be followed. Not that he was doing a good job of being sneaky. Isaac was accustomed to being so much brighter than everyone else that he really had no idea of what others were or weren't capable of. So when he got it into his head to be tricky, he came up with tricks that would not deceive a dog. It was hard not to be insulted—but being around Isaac was never for the thin-skinned.

They continued to live together at Trinity, though now they

shared a cottage without the Great Gate. They performed experiments with lenses and prisms, and Isaac went to a hall twice a week and lectured to an empty room on mathematical topics so advanced that no one else could understand them. So in *that* sense nothing was different. But lately Isaac had obviously lost interest in optics (probably because he knew everything about the subject now) and become mysterious. Then three days ago he had announced, with studied nonchalance, that he was going to nip down to London for a few days. When Daniel had announced that he was planning to do the same—to pay a visit to poor Oldenburg, and attend a Royal Society meeting—Isaac had done a poor job of hiding his annoyance. But he had at least *tried* to hide it, which was touching.

Then, halfway to London, Daniel (as a sort of experiment) had professed to be shocked that Isaac intended to lodge in an inn. Daniel would not hear of it—not when Raleigh had put so many Waterhouse assets into constructing a large new house on Holborn. At this point Isaac's eyes had bulged even more than usual and he had adopted his suffering-martyr look, and relented only when Daniel mentioned that Raleigh's house was so large, and had so many empty rooms, that Daniel wasn't sure if they would ever *see* each other.

Daniel's hypothesis, based on these observations, was that Isaac was committing Sins Against Nature with someone, but then certain clues (such as that Isaac *never* received any mail) argued against this.

As he stood there in front of the coffee-house, a gentleman* rode out of St. Martin's Lane, reined in his horse, stood up in the stirrups, and surveyed the ongoing low-intensity riot that was Charing Cross, looking anxious until he caught sight of whatever he was looking for. Then he relaxed, sat down, and rode slowly in the general direction of—Isaac Newton. Daniel sat down in that wee garden in front of Mrs. Green's, and ordered coffee and a newspaper.

King Carlos II of Spain was *both* feeble *and* sick, and not

---

*I.e., he had a sword.

expected to live out the year. Comenius was dying, too. Anne Hyde, the Duke of York's wife, was very ill with what everyone assumed to be syphilis. John Locke was writing a constitution for Carolina, Stenka Razin's Cossack rebellion was being crushed in the Ukraine, the Grand Turk was taking Crete away from Venice with his left hand and declaring war on Poland with his right. In London, the fall of pepper prices was sending many City merchants into bankruptcy—while a short distance across the Narrow Seas, the V.O.C.—the Dutch East India Company—was paying out a dividend of 40 percent.

But the *news* was of the doings of the CABAL* and the *courtiers*. John Churchill was one of the few courtiers who actually did things like go to Barbary and go *mano a mano* with heathen corsairs, and so there was plenty concerning him. He and most of the rest of the English Navy were blockading Algiers, trying to do something, at long last, about the Barbary Pirates.

The gentleman on horseback had a courtier look about him, though unfashionably battered and frayed. He had nearly ridden Daniel down a few minutes previously when Daniel had emerged from Raleigh's house and foolishly planted himself in the middle of the road trying to catch sight of Isaac. He had the general look of a poor baron from some slaty place in the high latitudes who wanted to make a name for himself in London but lacked the means. He was dressed practically enough in actual boots, rather than the witty allusions to boots worn by young men about town. He wore a dark cassock—a riding garment loosely modeled after a priest's tent-like garment—with numerous silver but-

---

*The five men King Charles II had chosen to run England: John Comstock, the Earl of Epsom, Lord Chancellor; Thomas More Anglesey, Duke of Gunfleet, Chancellor of the Exchequer; Knott Bolstrood, who'd been coaxed back from Dutch self-exile to serve as His Majesty's Secretary of State; Sir Richard Apthorp, a banker, and a founder of the East India Company; and General Hugh Lewis, the Duke of Tweed.

tons. He had an expensive saddle on a mediocre horse. The horse thus looked something like a fishwife dressed up in a colonel's uniform. If Isaac was looking for a mistress (or a master or whatever the sodomitical equivalent of a mistress was), he could've done worse and he could've done better.

Daniel had brought a Valuable Object with him—not because he'd expected to use it, but out of fear that one of Raleigh's servants would wreck or steal it. It was in a wooden case buckled shut, which he had set on the table. He undid the buckles, raised the lid, and peeled back red velvet to divulge a tubular device about a foot long, fat enough that you could insert a fist, closed at one end. It was mounted on a wooden sphere the size of a large apple, and the sphere was held in a sort of clamp that gave it freedom to rotate around all axes—i.e., you could set it down on a tabletop and then point the open end of the tube in any direction, which was how Daniel used it. Bored through the tube's wall near the open end was a finger-sized hole, and mounted below this, in the center of the tube, was a small mirror, angled backwards at a concave dish of silvered glass that sealed the butt of the tube. The design was Isaac's, certain refinements and much of the construction were Daniel's. Putting an eye to the little hole, he saw a colored blur. Adjusting a thumbscrew at the mirror end, and thereby collapsing the tube together a bit, he resolved the blur into a chunk of ornamented window-frame with a lace curtain being sucked out of it, down at the other end of Charing Cross. Daniel was startled to realize that he was looking all the way across the Great Court that lay before Whitehall Palace, and peering in through someone's windows—unless he was mistaken, these were the apartments of Lady Castlemaine, the King of England's favorite mistress.

Nudging it round to a slightly different bearing, he saw the end of the Banqueting House, where King Charles I had been beheaded, back when Daniel had been small—Divine Right of Kings demolished, the Commonwealth founded, Free Enterprise introduced, Drake happy for once, and

Daniel sitting on his shoulders, watching the King's head rock. In those days, all of Whitehall's windows that faced the outside had been bricked up to keep musket-balls out, and many superstitious fopperies, e.g., paintings and sculptures, had been crated up and sold to Dutchmen. But now the windows were windows again, and the artworks had been bought back, and there wasn't a decapitated King in sight.

So it was not a good time to reminisce about Drake. Daniel swiveled the Reflecting Telescope around until the ragged plume in the horseman's hat showed up as a bobbing white blur, like the tail of a hustling rabbit. Once he'd focused on that, a couple of tiny adjustments brought Isaac's waterfall of argent hair into view—just in time, for he was ascending a few steps into a building across from the Haymarket, along the convergence of traffic that eventually became Pall Mall. Daniel played the telescope around the front of the building, expecting it to be a coffee-house or pub or inn where Isaac would await his gentleman friend. But he was completely wrong. To begin with, this place was apparently nothing more than a town-house. And yet well-dressed men came and went occasionally, and when they emerged, they (or their servants) were carrying packages. Daniel reckoned it must be some sort of shop too discreet to announce itself—hardly unusual in this part of London, but not Isaac's sort of place.

The horseman did not go inside. He rode past the shop once, twice, thrice, looking at it sidelong—just as baffled as Daniel was. Then he seemed to be talking to a pedestrian. Daniel recalled, now, that this rider had been pursued by a couple of servants on foot. One of these pages, or whatever they were, now took off at a run, and weaved between hawkers and hay-wains all the way across Charing Cross and finally vanished into the Strand.

The horseman dismounted, handed the reins to another page, and made a vast ceremony of unbuttoning his sleeves so that the cassock devolved into a cloak. He peeled off spatterdashes to reveal breeches and stockings that were only

out-moded by six months to a year, and then found a coffee-
house of his own, just across Pall Mall from the mysterious
shop, along (therefore) the southern limit of St. James's
Fields—one of those Fields that the Church of St. Martin
had formerly been in the middle of. But now houses were being built all around it, enclosing a little rectangle of farm-
land rapidly being gardenized.

Daniel could do nothing but sit. As a way of paying rent
on this chair, he kept having more coffee brought out. The
first sip had been tooth-looseningly unpleasant, like one of
those exotic poisons that certain Royal Society members
liked to brew. But he was startled to notice after a while that
the cup was empty.

This whole exercise had begun rather early in the day
when no one of quality was awake, and when it was too cold
and dewy to sit at the outdoor tables anyway. But as Daniel
sat and pretended to read his newspaper, the sun swung up
over York House and then Scotland Yard, the place became
comfortable, and Personages began to occupy seats nearby,
and to pretend to read *their* newspapers. He even sensed that
in this very coffee-house were some members of the cast of
characters he had heard about while listening to his siblings
talk over the dinner table. Actually being here and mingling
with them made him feel like a theatregoer relaxing after a
performance with the actors—and in these racy times, actresses.

Daniel spent a while trying to spy into the upper windows
of the mystery-shop with his telescope, because he thought
he'd glimpsed silver hair in one of them, and so for a while
he was only aware of other customers' comings and goings
by their bow-waves of perfume, the rustling of ladies' crino-
lines, the ominous creaking of their whalebone corset-stays,
the whacking of gentlemen's swords against table-legs as
they misjudged distances between furniture, the clacking of
their slap-soled booties.

The perfumes smelled familiar, and he had heard all of
the jokes before, while dining at Raleigh's house. Raleigh,

who at this point was fifty-two years old, knew a startling number of dull persons who evidently had nothing else to do but roam around to one another's houses, like mobs of Vagabonds poaching on country estates, and share their dullness with each other. Daniel was always startled when he learned that these people were Knights or Barons or merchant-princes.

"Why, if it isn't Daniel Waterhouse! God save the King!"

"God save the King!" Daniel murmured reflexively, looking up into a vast bursting confusion of clothing and bought hair, within which, after a brief search, he was able to identify the face of Sir Winston Churchill—Fellow of the Royal Society, and father of that John Churchill who was making such a name for himself in the fighting before Algiers.

There was a moment of exquisite discomfort. Churchill had remembered, a heartbeat too late, that the aforementioned King had personally blown up Daniel's father. Churchill himself had many anti-Royalists in his family, and so he prided himself on being a little defter than *that*.

Now Drake's pieces had never been found. Daniel's vague recollection (vague because he'd just been shot with a blunderbuss, at the time) was that the explosion had flung him in the general direction of the Great Fire of London, so it was unlikely that anything was left of him except for a stubborn film of greasy ash deposited on the linens and windowsills of downwind neighbors. Discovery of shattered YOU AND I ARE BUT EARTH crockery in remains of burnt houses confirmed it. John Wilkins (still distraught over the burning of his Universal Character books in the Fire) had been good enough to preside over the funeral, and only a bridge-builder of his charm and ingenuity could have prevented it from becoming a brawl complete with phalanxes of enraged Phanatiques marching on Whitehall Palace to commit regicide.

Since then—and since most of Drake's fortune had passed to Raleigh—Daniel hadn't seen very much of the family. He'd been working on optics with Newton and was always startled, somehow, to find that the other Waterhouses were doing things when he wasn't watching. Praise-God, Raleigh's eldest son, who had gone to Boston before the Plague, had finally gotten his Harvard degree and married someone, and so everyone (Waterhouses and their visitors alike) had been talking about him—but they always did so mischievously, like naughty children getting away with something, and with occasional furtive glances at Daniel. He had to conclude that he and Praise-God were now the last vestiges of Puritanism in the family and that Raleigh was discreetly admired, among the coffee-house set, for having stashed one of them away at Cambridge and the other at Harvard where they could not interfere in whatever it was that the other Waterhouses were up to.

In this vein: he had gotten the impression, from various tremendously significant looks exchanged across tables at odd times by his half-siblings, their extended families, and their overdressed visitors, that the Waterhouses and the Hams and perhaps a few others had joined together in some kind of vast conspiracy the exact nature of which wasn't clear—but to them it was as huge and complicated as, say, toppling the Holy Roman Empire.

Thomas Ham was now called Viscount Walbrook. All of his gold had melted in the Fire, but none had leaked out of his newly refurbished cellar—when they came back days later they found a slab of congealed gold weighing tons, the World's Largest Gold Bar. None of his depositors lost a penny. Others hastened to deposit their gold with the incredibly reliable Mr. Ham. He began lending it to the King to finance the rebuilding of London. Partly in recognition of that, and partly to apologize for having blown up his father-in-law, the King had bestowed an Earldom on him.

All of which was Context for Daniel as he sat there gazing upon the embarrassed face of Sir Winston Churchill. Now if Churchill had only *asked,* Daniel might have told him that blowing up Drake was probably the correct action for the King to have taken under the circumstances. But Churchill didn't ask, he *assumed.* Which was why he'd never make a real Natural Philosopher. Though the Royal Society would tolerate him as long as he continued paying his dues.

Daniel for his part was aware, now, that he was surrounded by the Quality, and that they were all peering at him. He had gotten himself into a Complicated Situation, and he did not like those. The Reflecting Telescope was resting on the table right in front of him, as obvious as a severed head. Sir Winston was too embarrassed to've noticed it yet, but he *would*, and given that he'd been a member of the Royal Society since before the Plague, he would probably be able to guess what it was—and even if Daniel lied to him about it, the lie would be discovered this very evening when Daniel presented it, on Isaac's behalf, to the Royal Society. He felt an urge to snatch it away and hide it, but this would only make it more conspicuous.

And Sir Winston was only *one* of the people Daniel recognized here. Daniel seemed to have inadvertently sat down along a major game trail: persons coming up from Whitehall Palace and Westminster to buy their stockings, gloves, hats, syphilis-cures, *et cetera* at the New Exchange, just a stone's throw up the Strand, all passed by this coffee-house to get a last fix on what was or wasn't in fashion.

Daniel hadn't moved or spoken in what seemed like ten minutes . . . he was (glancing at the telltale coffee cup here) paralyzed, in fact! Then he solved Sir Winston's etiquette jam by blurting something like "I *say*!" and attempting to stand up, which came out as a palsied spasm of the entire body—he got into a shin-kicking match with his own table and produced a disturbance that sheared cups off their saucers. Everyone looked.

"Ever the diligent Natural Philosopher, Mr. Waterhouse pursues an experiment in Intoxication by Coffee!" Sir Winston announced roundly. Simply *tremendous* laughter and light applause.

Sir Winston was of Raleigh's generation and had fought in the Civil War as a Cavalier—he was a serious man and so was dressed in a way that passed for dignified and understated here, in a black velvet coat, flaring out to just above the knee, with lace handkerchiefs trailing from various openings like wisps of steam, and a yellow waistcoat under that, and God only knew what else beneath the waistcoat—the sleeves of all these garments terminated near the elbows in huge wreaths of lace, ruffles, *et cetera,* and that was to show off his tan kid gloves. He had a broad-brimmed Cavalier-hat fringed with fluffy white stuff probably harvested from the buttocks of some bird that spent a lot of time sitting on ice floes, and a very thin mustache, and a wig of yellow hair, expensively disheveled and formed into bobbling ringlets. He had black stockings fashionably wrinkled up his calves, and high-heeled shoes with bows of a wingspan of eight inches. The stocking/breech interface was presumably somewhere around his knees and was some sort of fantastically complex spraying phenomenon of ribbons and gathers and skirtlets designed to peek out under the hems of his coat, waistcoat, and allied garments.

Mrs. Churchill, for her part, was up to something mordant involving a Hat. It had the general outlines of a Puritan-hat, a Pilgrimish number consisting of a truncated cone mounted on a broad flat brim, but enlivened with colorful bands, trailing ribbons, jeweled badges, curious feathers, and other merchandise—a parody, then, a tart assertion of non-pilgrimhood. Everything from the brim of this hat to the hem of her dress was too complex for Daniel's eye to comprehend—he was like an illiterate savage staring at the first page of an illuminated Bible—but he did notice that the little boy carrying her train was dressed as a Leprechaun (Sir Winston did a lot of business for the King in Ireland).

It was a lot to put on, just to nip out for a cup of coffee, but the Churchills must have known that everyone was going to be fawning over them today because of their gallant son, and decided they ought to dress for it.

Mrs. Churchill was looking over Daniel's shoulder, toward the street. This left Daniel free to stare at her face, to which she had glued several spots of black velvet—which,

since the underlying skin had been whitened with some kind
of powerful cosmetic, gave her a sort of Dalmatian appearance. "He's here," she said to whomever she was looking at.
Then, confused: "Were you expecting your half-brother?"

Daniel turned around and recognized Sterling Waterhouse, now about forty, and his wife of three years, Beatrice,
and a whole crowd of persons who'd apparently just staged
some type of pillaging-raid on the New Exchange. Sterling
and Beatrice were shocked to see him. But they had no
choice but to come over, now that Mrs. Churchill had done
what she'd done. So they did, cheerfully enough, and then
there was a series of greetings and introductions and other
formalities (including that all parties congratulated the
Churchills on the dazzling qualities of their son John, and
promised to say prayers for his safe return from the shores
of Tripoli) extending to something like half an hour. Daniel
wanted to slash his own throat. These people were doing
what they did for a *living*. Daniel *wasn't*.

But he did achieve one insight that would prove useful in
later dealings with his own family. Because Raleigh was involved in the mysterious Conspiracy of which Daniel had,
lately, become vaguely aware, it probably had something to
do with land. Because Uncle Thomas ("Viscount Walbrook") Ham was mixed up in it, it must have something to
do with putting rich people's money to clever uses. And because Sterling was involved, it probably had something to
do with shops, because ever since Drake had ascended into
the flames over London, Sterling had been moving away
from Drake's style of business (smuggling, and traveling
around cutting private deals away from markets) and towards the newfangled procedure of putting all the merchandise in a fixed building and waiting for customers to
transport themselves to it. The whole thing came together
complete in Daniel's head when he sat in that coffeehouse in
Charing Cross and looked at the courtiers, macaronis,
swells, and fops streaming in from the new town-houses going up on land that had been incinerated, or that had been

open pastures, four years earlier. They were planning some sort of real estate development on the edge of the city—probably on that few acres of pasture out back of the Waterhouse residence. They would put up town-houses around the edges, make the center into a square, and along the square Sterling would put up shops. Rich people would move in, and the Waterhouses and their confederates would control a patch of land that would probably generate more rent than any thousand square miles of Ireland—basically, they would become farmers of rich people.

And what made it extraordinarily clever—as only Sterling could be—was that this project would not even be a *struggle* as such. They would not have to defeat any adversary or overcome any obstacle—merely ride along with certain inexorable trends. All they—all Sterling—had to do was *notice* these trends. He'd always had a talent for noticing—which was why his shops were so highly thought of—so all he needed was to be in the right place to do the necessary noticing, and the right place was obviously Mrs. Green's coffee-house.

But it was the wrong place for Daniel, who only wanted to notice what Isaac was up to. A lively conversation was underway all round him, but it might as well've been in a foreign language—in fact, frequently it was. Daniel divided his time between looking at the telescope and wondering when he could snatch it off the table without attracting attention; staring at the mystery-shop and at the gentleman-rider; fraternal staredowns with Sterling (who was in his red silk suit with silver buttons today, and had numerous scraps of black glued to his face, though not as many as Beatrice); and watching Sir Winston Churchill, who looked equally bored, distracted, and miserable.

At one point he caught Sir Winston gazing fixedly at the telescope, his eyes making tiny movements and focusings as he figured out how it worked. Daniel waited until Sir Winston looked up at him, ready with a question—then Daniel winked and shook his head minutely. Sir Winston raised his eyebrows and looked *thrilled* that he and Daniel now had a small Intrigue of their own—it was like having a pretty seventeen-year-old girl unexpectedly sit on his lap. But this exchange was fully noticed by someone of Sterling's crowd—one of Beatrice's young lady friends—who demanded to know what the Tubular Object was.

"Thank you for reminding me," Daniel said, "I'd best put it away."

"What is it?" the lady demanded.

"A Naval Device," Sir Winston said, "or a model of one—pity the Dutch Fleet when Mr. Waterhouse's invention is realized at full scale!"

"How's it work?"

"This is not the place," said Sir Winston significantly, eyes rattling back and forth in a perfunctory scan for Dutch spies. This caused all of the *other* heads to turn, which led to an important Sighting: an entourage was migrating out of the Strand and into Charing Cross, and someone frightfully significant must be in the middle of it. While they were all trying to figure out *who,* Daniel put the telescope away and closed the box.

"It's the Earl of Upnor," someone whispered, and then Daniel had to look, and see what had become of his former roommate.

The answer: now that Louis Anglesey, Earl of Upnor, was in London, freed from the monastic constraints of Cambridge, and a full twenty-two years of age, he was able to live, and dress, as he pleased. Today, walking across Charing Cross, he was wearing a suit that appeared to've been constructed by (1) dressing him in a blouse with twenty-foot-long sleeves of the most expensive linen; (2) bunching the sleeves up in numerous overlapping gathers on his arms; (3) painting most of him in glue; (4) shaking and rolling him in a bin containing thousands of black silk doilies; and (5) (because King Charles II, who'd mandated, a few years earlier, that all courtiers wear black and white, was getting bored with it, but had not formally rescinded the order) adding dashes of color here and there, primarily in the form of clusters of elaborately gathered and knotted ribbons—enough ribbon, all told, to stretch all the way to whatever shop in Paris where the Earl had bought all of this stuff. The Earl also had a white silk scarf tied round his throat in such a way as to show off its lacy ends. Louis XIV's Croatian mercenaries, *les Cravates,* had made a practice of tying their giant, flapping lace collars down so that gusts of wind would not blow them up over their faces in the middle of a battle or duel, and this had become a fashion in Paris, and the Earl of Upnor, always pushing the envelope, was now doing the *cravate* thing with a scarf instead of an (as of ten minutes ago) outmoded collar. He had a wig that was actually wider than his shoulders, and a pair of boots that contained enough really good snow-white leather that, if pulled on straight, they would have reached all the way to his groin, at which point each one of them would have been larger in circumference than his waist; but he had of course folded the tops down and then (since they were so long) folded them back up again to keep them from dragging on the ground, so that around each knee was a complex of white leather folds about as wide as a bushel-basket, filled with a froth of lace. Gold spurs, beset with jewels, curved back from each heel to a distance of perhaps eight inches. The heels themselves were cherry-red, four inches high, and protected from the muck of Charing Cross by loose slippers whose flat soles dragged on the ground and made clacking noises with each step. Because of the width of his boot-tops, the Earl had to swing his legs around each other with each step, toes pointed, rolling so violently from side to side that he could only maintain balance with a long, encrusted, beribboned walking-stick.

For all that, he made excellent headway, and his admirers in the garden of the coffee-house had only a few moments in which to memorize the details. Daniel secured the Reflecting Telescope and then looked across the square, wanting to regain sight of the strange gentleman who'd been following Isaac.

But that fellow was no longer sitting in the coffee-house opposite. Daniel feared that he'd lost the man's trail—until he happened to glance back at the Earl of Upnor, and noticed that his entourage was parting to admit, and swallow up, none other than the same gentleman rider.

Daniel, unencumbered by sword, giant flaring boots, or clacking boot-protectors, very quickly rose and stepped out of Mrs. Green's without bothering to excuse himself. He did not walk directly towards Upnor, but plotted a course to swing wide around his group, as if going to an errand on the other side of Charing Cross.

As he drew close, he observed the following: the gentleman dismounted and approached the Earl, smiling confidently. Proud of himself, showing big mossy teeth.

While the rider bowed, Upnor glanced, and nodded, at one of his hangers-on. This man stepped in from the side, bending low, and made a sweeping gesture aimed at one of Upnor's boots. Something flew from his hand and struck the top of the boot. In the same moment, this fellow extended his index finger and pointed to it: a neat dollop of brown stuff the size of a guinea coin. Everyone except the Earl of Upnor and the gentleman rider gasped in horror. "What is it?" the Earl inquired.

"Your boot!" someone exclaimed.

"I cannot see it," the Earl said, "the boot-tops obstruct my view." Supporting himself with the walking-stick, he extended one leg out in front of himself and pointed the toe. Everyone in Charing Cross could see it now, including the Earl. "You have got shit on my boot!" he announced. "Shall I have to kill you?"

The rider was nonplussed; he hadn't come close enough to get shit on anyone—but the only other people who could testify to that were the Earl's friends. Looking around, all he could see were the rouged and black-patched faces of the Earl's crowd glowering at him.

"Whyever would you say such a thing, my lord?"

"*Fight a duel with you,* I should say—which would *presumably* mean killing you. Everyone I fight a duel with seems to die—why should you be any exception?"

"Why a . . . duel, my lord?"

"Because to extract an apology from you seems *impossible.* Even my *dog* is apologetic. But you! Why can you not show that you are ashamed of your actions?"

"My actions . . ."

"You have got shit on my boot!"

"My lord, I fear you have been misinformed."

Very ugly noises now from the entourage.

"Meet me tomorrow morning at Tyburn. Bring a second—someone strong enough to carry you away when I'm finished."

The rider finally understood that claiming innocence was getting him nowhere. "But I *can* show that I am ashamed, my lord."

"Really? E'en like a dog?"

"Yes, my lord."

"When my dog gets shit in the wrong place, I rub his nose in it," said the Earl, extending his pointed toe again, so it was nearly in the rider's face.

Daniel was now walking nearly behind the rider, no more than twelve feet distant, and could clearly see a stream of urine form in the crotch of his breeches and pizzle out onto the road. "Please, my lord. I did as you asked. I followed the white-haired man—I sent the message. Why are you doing this to me?"

But the Earl of Upnor fixed his stare on the rider, and raised his boot an inch. The rider bowed his head—lowered his nose toward it—but then the Earl slowly lowered his boot until it was on the ground, forcing the other to bend low, then clamber down onto his knees, and finally to put his elbows into the dirt, in order to put his nose exactly where the Earl wanted it.

Then it was over, and the gentleman rider was running out of Charing Cross with his face buried in his hands, presumably never to be seen in London again—which must have been exactly what the Earl wanted.

The Earl, for his part, shed his entourage at a tavern, and went alone into the same shop as Isaac Newton. Daniel, by that point, wasn't even certain that Isaac was still *in* there. He walked by the front of it once and finally saw a tiny sign in the window: MONSIEUR LEFEBURE—CHYMIST.

Daniel roamed around Charing Cross for the next half an hour, glancing into M. LeFebure's windows from time to time, until he finally caught sight of silver-haired Isaac framed in a window, deep in conversation with Louis Anglesey, the Earl of Upnor, who only nodded, and nodded, and (for good measure) nodded again, rapt.

Much as the sun had burnt its face into Isaac's retinas at Woolsthorpe, this image remained before Daniel long after he had turned his back upon Charing Cross and stalked away. He walked for a long time through the streets, shifting the burden of the telescope from one shoulder to the other from time to time. He was headed generally toward Bishopsgate, where there was a meeting to attend. He was pursued and harried the whole way by a feeling, difficult to identify, until at last he recognized it as a sort of jealousy. He did not know what Isaac was up to in the house/shop/laboratory/salon of M. LeFebure. He suspected Alchemy, Buggery, or some ripe warm concoction thereof: and if not, then a flirtation with same. Which was wholly Isaac's business and not Daniel's. Indeed, Daniel had no interest in either of those pastimes. To feel jealous was, therefore, foolish. And yet he did. Isaac had, somehow, found friends in whom he could confide things he hid from Daniel. There it was, simple and painful as a smack in the gob. But Daniel had friends of his own. He was going to see them now. Some were no less fraudulent, or foolish, than Alchemists. Perhaps Isaac was only giving him his just deserts for that.

Royal Society Meeting, Gresham's College

12 AUGUST 1670

❧

This Club of Vertuoso's, upon a full Night,
when some eminent Maggot-monger, for the
Satisfaction of the Society, had appointed to
demonstrate the Force of Air, by some hermet-
ical Pot gun, to shew the Difference of the
Gravity between the Smoak of Tobacco and
that of Colts-foot and Bittany, or to try some
other such like Experiment, were always com-
pos'd of such an odd Mixture of Mankind,
that, like a Society of Ringers at a quarterly
Feast, here sat a fat purblind Philosopher next
to a talkative Spectacle-maker; yonder a half-
witted Whim of Quality, next to a ragged Mathematician; on the other Side a consumptive
Astronomer next to a water-gruel Physician;
above them, a Transmutator of Metals, next to
a Philosopher-Stone-Hunter; at the lower End,
a prating Engineer, next to a clumsy-fisted Ma-
son; at the upper End of all, perhaps, an Atheistical Chymist, next to a whimsy-headed
Lecturer; and these the learned of the Wise-
akers wedg'd here and there with quaint Artifi-
cers, and noisy Operators, in all Faculties;

some bending beneath the Load of Years and indefatigable Labour, some as thin-jaw'd and heavy-ey'd, with abstemious Living and nocturnal Study as if, like *Pharaoh's* Lean Kine, they were designed by Heaven to warn the World of a Famine; others looking as wild, and disporting themselves as frenzically, as if the Disappointment of their Projects had made them subject to a Lunacy. When they were thus met, happy was the Man that could find out a new Star in the Firmament; discover a wry Step in the Sun's Progress; assign new Reasons for the Spots of the Moon, or add one Stick to the Bundle of Faggots which have been so long burthensome to the back of her old Companion; or, indeed, impart any crooked Secret to the learned Society, that might puzzle their Brains, and disturb their Rest for a Month afterwards, in consulting upon their Pillows how to straiten the Project, that it might appear upright to the Eye of Reason, and the knotty Difficulty to be rectify'd, as to bring Honour to themselves, and Advantage to the Public.

—NED WARD, *The Vertuoso's Club*

AUGUST 12. AT A MEETING of the SOCIETY,

MR. NICHOLAS MERCATOR and MR. JOHN LOCKE were elected and admitted.

The rest of Mr. BOYLE's experiments about light were read, with great satisfaction to the society; who ordered, that all should be registered, and that Mr. HOOKE should take care of having the like experiments tried before the society, as soon as he could procure any shining rotten wood or fish.

Dr. CROUNE brought in a dead parakeet.

Sir JOHN FINCH displayed an asbestos hat-band.

Dr. ENT speculated as to why it is hotter in summer than winter.

Mr. POWELL offered to be employed by the society in any capacity whatever.

Mr. OLDENBURG being absent, Mr. WATERHOUSE read a letter from a PORTUGUESE nobleman, most civilly complimenting the society for its successes in removing the spleens of dogs, without ill effect; and going on to enquire, whether the society might undertake to perform the like operation on his Wife, as she was most afflicted with splenetic distempers.

Dr. ENT was put in mind of an account concerning oysters.

Mr. HOOKE displayed an invention for testing whether a surface is level, consisting of a bubble of air trapped in a sealed glass tube, otherwise filled with water.

The Dog, that had a piece of his skin cut off at the former meeting, being enquired after, and the operator answering, that he had run away, it was ordered, that another should be provided against the next meeting for the grafting experiment.

The president produced from Sir WILLIAM CURTIUS a hairy ball found in the belly of a cow.

THE DUKE OF GUNFLEET produced a letter of Mons. HUYGENS, dated at Paris, mentioning a new observation concerning Saturn, made last spring at Rome by one CAMPANI, viz. that the circle of Saturn had been seen to cast a shadow on the sphere: which observation Mons. HUYGENS looked on as confirming his hypothesis, that Saturn is surrounded by a Ring.

A Vagabond presented himself, who had formerly received a shot into his belly, breaking his guts in two: whereupon one end of the colon stood out at the left side of his belly, whereby he voided all his excrement, which he did for the society.

Mr. POVEY presented a skeleton to the society.

Mr. BOYLE reported that swallows live under frozen water in the Baltic.

Dr. GODDARD mentioned that wainscotted rooms make cracking noises in mornings and evenings.

Mr. WALLER mentioned that toads come out in moist cool weather.

Mr. HOOKE related, that he had found the stars in Orion's belt, which Mons. HUYGENS made but three, to be five.

Dr. MERRET produced a paper, wherein he mentioned, that three skulls with the hair on and brains in them were lately found at Black-friars in pewter vessels in the midst of a thick stone-wall, with certain obscure inscriptions. This paper was ordered to be registered.

Mr. HOOKE made an experiment to discover, whether a piece of steel first counterpoised in exact scales, and then touched by a vigorous magnet, acquires thereby any sensible increase in weight. The event was, that it did not.

Dr. ALLEN gave an account of a person, who had lately lost a quantity of his brain, and yet lived and was well.

Dr. WILKINS presented the society with his book, intitled, An Essay Towards a Real Character and Philosophical Language.

Mr. HOOKE suggested, that it was worth inquiry, whether there were any valves in plants, which he conceived to be very necessary for the conveying of the juices of trees up to the height of sometimes 200, 300, and more feet; which he saw not how it was possible to be performed without valves as well as motion.

Sir ROBERT SOUTHWELL presented for the repository a skull of an executed person with the moss grown on it in Ireland.

THE BISHOP OF CHESTER moved, that Mr. HOOKE might be ordered to try, whether he could by means of the microscopic moss-seed formerly shewn by him, make moss grow on a dead man's skull.

Mr. HOOKE intimated that the experiment proposed by THE BISHOP OF CHESTER would not be as productive of new Knowledge, as a great many others that could be mentioned, if there were time enough to mention them all.

Mr. OLDENBURG being absent, Mr. WATERHOUSE read an extract, which the former had received from Paris, signifying that it was most certain, that Dr. DE GRAAF had unravelled testicles, and that one of them was kept by him in spirit of wine. Some of the physicians present intimating, that the like had been attempted in England many years before, but not with that success, that they could yet believe what Dr. DE GRAAF affirmed.

THE DUKE OF GUNFLEET gave of Dr. DE GRAAF an excellent Character; attesting that, while at Paris, this same Doctor had cured the Duke's son (now the EARL OF UPNOR) of the bite of a venomous *spyder*.

Occasion being given to speak of tarantulas, some of the members said, that persons bitten by them, though cured, yet must dance once a year: others, that different patients required different airs to make them dance, according to the different sorts of tarantulas which had bitten them.

THE DUKE OF GUNFLEET said, that the *Spyder* that had bitten his son in Paris, was not of the *tarantula* sort, and accordingly that the Earl does not under any account suffer any compulsion to dance.

The society gave order for the making of portable barometers, contrived by Mr. BOYLE, to be sent into several parts of the world, not only into the most distant places of England, but likewise by sea into the East and West Indies, and other parts, particularly to the English plantations in Bermuda, Jamaica, Barbados, Virginia, and New England; and to Tangier, Moscow, St. Helena, the Cape of Good Hope, and Scanderoon.

Dr. KING was put in mind of dissecting a lobster and an oyster.

Mr. HOOKE produced some plano-convex spherical glasses, as small as pin-heads, to serve for object-glasses in microscopes. He was desired to put some of them into the society's great microscope for a trial.

THE DUKE OF GUNFLEET produced the skin of a Moor tanned.

Mr. BOYLE remarked, that two very able physicians of his acquaintance gave to a woman desperately sick of the iliac passion above a pound of crude quicksilver which remained several days in her body without producing any fatal symptom; and afterwards dissecting the dead corpse, they found, that part of her gut, where the excrement was stopped, gangrened; but the quicksilver lay all on a heap above it, and had not so much as discoloured the parts of the gut contiguous to it.

Mr. HOOKE was put in mind of an experiment of making a body heavier than gold, by putting quicksilver to it, to see, whether any of it would penetrate into the pores of gold.

Dr. CLARKE proposed, that a man hanged might be begged of the King, to try to revive him; and that in case he were revived, he might have his life granted him.

Mr. WATERHOUSE produced a new telescope, invented by Mr. Isaac NEWTON, professor of mathematics in the university of Cambridge, improving on previous telescopes by contracting the optical path. THE DUKE OF GUN-FLEET, Dr. CHRISTOPHER WREN, and Mr. HOOKE, examining it, had so good opinion of it, that they proposed it be shown to the King, and that a description and scheme of it should be sent to Mons. HUYGENS at Paris, thereby to secure this invention to Mr. NEWTON.

The experiment of the opening of the thorax of a dog was suggested. Mr. HOOKE and Mr. WATERHOUSE having made this experiment formerly, begged to be excused for the duration of any such proceedings. Dr. BALLE and Dr. KING made the experiment but did not succeed.

A fifth Cabal, perhaps, would be a Knot of Mathematicians, who would sit so long wrangling about squaring the Circle, till, with Drinking and Rattling, they were ready to let fall a nauseous Perpendicular from their Mouths to the Chamber-Pot. Another little

Party would be deeply engaged in a learned
Dispute about Transmutation of Metals, and
contend so warmly about turning Lead into
Gold, till the Bar had a just Claim to all the Silver in their Pockets . . .

—NED WARD, *The Vertuoso's Club*

A FEW OF THEM ENDED UP at a tavern, unfortunately called
the Dogg, on Broad Street near London Wall. Wilkins (who
was the Bishop of Chester now) and Sir Winston Churchill
and Thomas More Anglesey, a.k.a. the Duke of Gunfleet,
amused themselves using Newton's telescope to peer into
the windows of the Navy Treasury across the way, where
lamps were burning and clerks were working late. Wheel-
barrows laden with lockboxes were coming up every few
minutes from the goldsmiths' shops on Threadneedle.

Hooke commandeered a small table, set his bubble-level
upon it, and began to adjust it by inserting scraps of paper
beneath its legs. Daniel quaffed bitters and thought that this
was all a great improvement on this morning.

"To Oldenburg," someone said, and even Hooke raised his
head up on its bent neck and drank to the Secretary's health.

"Are we allowed to know *why* the King put him in the
Tower?" asked Daniel.

Hooke suddenly became absorbed in table-levelling, the
others in viewing a planet that was rising over Bishopsgate,
and Daniel reckoned that the reason for Oldenburg's imprisonment was one of those things that everyone in London
should simply *know,* it was one of those facts Londoners
breathed in like the smoke of sea-coal.

John Wilkins brushed significantly past Daniel and
stepped outside, plucking a pipe from a tobacco-box on the
wall. Daniel joined him for a smoke on the street. It was a
fine summer eve in Bishopsgate: on the far side of London
Wall, lunaticks at Bedlam were carrying on vigorous disputes with angels, demons, or the spirits of departed rela-

tions, and on this side, the rhythmic yelping of a bone-saw came through a half-open window of Gresham's College as a cabal of Bishops, Knights, Doctors, and Colonels removed the rib-cage from a living mongrel. The Dogg's sign creaked above in a mild river-breeze. Coins clinked dimly inside the Navy's lockboxes as porters worried them up stairs. Through an open window they could occasionally glimpse Samuel Pepys, Fellow of the Royal Society, making arrangements with his staff and gazing out the window, longingly, at the Dogg. Daniel and the Bishop stood there and took it in for a minute as a sort of ritual, as Papists cross themselves when entering a church: to do proper respect to the place.

"Mr. Oldenburg is the heart of the R.S.," Bishop Wilkins began.

"I would give that honor to you, or perhaps Mr. Hooke . . ."

"Hold—I was not finished—I was launching a metaphor. Please remember that I've been preaching to rapt congregations, or at least they are *pretending* to be rapt—in any case, they *sit quietly* while I develop my metaphors."

"I beg forgiveness, and am now pretending to be rapt."

"Very well. Now! As we have learned by doing appalling things to stray dogs, the heart *accepts* blood returning from organs, such as the brain, through veins, such as the jugular. It *expels* blood *toward* these organs through arteries, such as the carotid. Do you remember what happened when Mr. Hooke cross-plumbed the mastiff, and connected his jugular to his carotid? And don't tell me that the splice broke and sprayed blood all around—this I remember."

"The blood settled into a condition of equilibrium, and began to coagulate in the tube."

"And from this we concluded that—?"

"I have long since forgotten. That bypassing the heart is a bad idea?"

"One *might* conclude," said the Bishop helpfully, "that an inert vessel, that merely *accepts* the circulating Fluid, but never *expels* it, becomes a stagnant back-water—or to put it otherwise, that the heart, by forcing it outwards, drives it around the cycle that in good time brings it back in from the organs and extremities. Hallo, Mr. Pepys!" (Shifting his focus to across the way.) "Starting a war, are we?"

"Too easy . . . winding one up, my lord," from the window.

"Is it going to be finished any time *soon*? Your diligence is setting an example for all of us—stop it!"

"I detect the beginnings of a lull . . ."

"Now, Daniel, anyone who scans the History of the Royal Society can see that, at each meeting, Mr. Oldenburg reads several letters from Continental savants, such as Mr. Huygens, and, lately, Dr. Leibniz . . ."

"I'm not familiar with that name."

"You *will* be—he is a mad letter-writer and a protégé of Huygens—a devotee of Pansophism—he has lately been *smothering* us with curious documents. You haven't heard about him because Mr. Oldenburg has been passing his missives round to Mr. Hooke, Mr. Boyle, Mr. Barrow, and others, trying to find someone who can even read them, as a first step towards determining whether or not they are nonsense. But I digress. For every letter Mr. Oldenburg *reads*, he *receives* a dozen—why so many?"

"Because, like a heart, he pumps so many *outwards*—?"

"Yes, precisely. Whole *sacks* of them crossing the Channel—driving the circulation that brings new ideas, from the Continent, back to our little meetings."

"Damn me, and now the King's clapped him in the Tower!" said Daniel, unable to avoid feeling a touch melodramatic—this kind of dialog not being, exactly, his metier.

"Bypassing the heart," said Wilkins, without a trace of any such self-consciousness. "I can already feel the Royal Society coagulating. Thank you for bringing Mr. Newton's telescope. Fresh blood! When can we see him at a meeting?"

"Probably never, as long as the Fellows persist in cutting up dogs."

"Ah—he's squeamish—abhors cruelty?"

"Cruelty to *animals*."

"Some Fellows have proposed that we borrow residents of . . ." said the Bishop, nodding towards Bedlam.

"Isaac might be more comfortable with that," Daniel admitted.

A barmaid had been hovering, and now stepped into the awkward silence: "Mr. Hooke requests your presence."

"Thank God," Wilkins said to her, "I was afraid you were going to complain he had *committed an offense* against your person."

The patrons of the Dogg were backed up against the walls in the configuration normally used for watching bar-fights, viz. forming an empty circle around Mr. Hooke's table, which was (as shown by the bubble instrument) now perfectly level. It was also clean, and empty except for a glob of quicksilver in the middle, with numerous pinhead-sized droplets scattered about in novel constellations. Mr. Hooke was peering at the large glob—a perfect, regular dome— through an optical device of his own manufacture. Glancing up, he twiddled a hog-bristle between thumb and index finger, pushing an invisibly tiny droplet of mercury across the table until it merged with the large one. Then more peering. Then, moving with the stealth of a cat-burglar, he backed away from the table. When he had put a good fathom between himself and the experiment, he looked up at Wilkins and said, "Universal Measure!"

"What!? Sir! You don't say!"

"You will agree," Hooke said, "that *level* is an absolute concept—any sentient person can make a surface level."

"It is in the Philosophical Language," said Bishop Wilkins—this signified *yes*.

Pepys came in the door, looking splendid, and had his mouth open to demand beer, when he realized a solemn ceremony was underway.

"Likewise mercury is the same in all places—in all worlds."

"Agreed."

"As is the number two."

"Of course."

"Here I have created a flat, clean, smooth, level surface. On it I have placed a drop of mercury and adjusted it so that the diameter is exactly two times its height. *Anyone, anywhere* could repeat these steps—the result would be a drop of mercury *exactly* the same size as *this* one. The diameter of the drop, then, can be used as the common unit of measurement for the Philosophical Language!"

The sound of men thinking.

Pepys: "Then you could build a container that was a certain number of those units high, wide, and deep; fill it with water; and have a standard measure of weight."

"Just so, Mr. Pepys."

"From length and weight you could make a standard pendulum—the time of its alternations would provide a universal unit of time!"

"But water beads up differently on different surfaces," said the Bishop of Chester. "I assume the same sorts of variations occur with mercury."

Hooke, resentful: "The surface to be used could be stipulated: copper, or glass . . ."

"If the force of gravity varies with altitude, how would that affect the height of the drop?" asked Daniel Waterhouse.

"Do it at sea-level," said Hooke, with a dollop of spleen.

"Sea-level varies with the tides," Pepys pointed out.

"What of other planets?" Wilkins demanded thunderously.

"Other *planets*!? We haven't finished with *this* one!"

"As our compatriot Mr. Oldenburg has said: 'You will please to remember that we have taken to task the whole Universe, and that we were obliged to do so by the nature of our Design!'"

Hooke, very stormy-looking now, scraped most of the quicksilver into a funnel, and thence into a flask; departed; and was sighted by Mr. Pepys (peering through the Newtonian reflector) no more than a minute later, stalking off towards Hounsditch in the company of a whore. "He's flown into one of his Fits of Melancholy—we won't see him for two weeks now—then we'll have to reprimand him," Wilkins grumbled.

Almost as if it were written down somewhere in the Universal Character, Pepys and Wilkins and Waterhouse somehow knew that they had unfinished business together—that they ought to be having a discreet chat about Mr. Oldenburg. A triangular commerce in highly significant glances and eyebrow-raisings flourished there in the Dogg, for the next hour, among them. But they could not all break free at once: Churchill and others wanted more details from Daniel about this Mr. Newton and his telescope. The Duke of Gunfleet got Pepys cornered, and interrogated him about dark matters concerning the Navy's finances. Blood-spattered, dejected Royal Society members stumbled in from Gresham's College, with the news that Drs. King and Belle had gotten lost in the wilderness of canine anatomy, the dog had died, and they really needed Hooke—where was he? Then they cornered Bishop Wilkins and talked Royal Society politics—would Comstock stand for election to President again? Would Anglesey arrange to have himself nominated?

BUT LATER—too late for Daniel, who had risen early, when Isaac had—the three of them were together in Pepys's coach, going somewhere.

"I note my Lord Gunfleet has taken up a sudden interest in *Naval*-gazing," said Wilkins.

"As our safety from the Dutch depends upon our Navy," Pepys said carefully, "and most of our Navy is arrayed before the Casbah in Algiers, *many* Persons of Quality share Anglesey's curiosity."

Wilkins only looked amused. "I did not hear him asking you of frigates and cannons," he said, "but of Bills of Exchange, and pay-coupons."

Pepys cleared his throat at length, and glanced nervously at Daniel. "Those who are responsible for *draining* the

Navy's coffers, must answer to those who are responsible for *filling* them," he finally said.

Even Daniel, a dull Cambridge scholar, had the wit to know that the coffer-drainer being referred to here was the armaments-maker John Comstock, Earl of Epsom—and that the coffer-filler was Thomas More Anglesey, Duke of Gunfleet, and father of Louis Anglesey, the Earl of Upnor.

"Thus C and A," Wilkins said. "What does the Cabal's second syllable have to say of Naval matters?"

"No surprises from Bolstrood* of course."

"Some say Bolstrood wants our Navy in Africa, so that the Dutch can invade us, and make of us a Calvinist nation."

"Given that the V.O.C.† is paying out dividends of forty percent, I think that there are many new Calvinists on Threadneedle Street."

"Is Apthorp one of them?"

"Those rumors are nonsense—Apthorp would rather build *his* East India Company, than invest in the *Dutch* one."

"So it follows that Apthorp wants a strong Navy, to protect our merchant ships from those Dutch East Indiamen, so topheavy with cannons."

"Yes."

"What of General Lewis?"

"Let's ask the young scholar," Pepys said mischievously.

Daniel was dumbstruck for a few moments—to the gurgling, boyish amusement of Pepys and Wilkins.

The telescope seemed to be watching Daniel, too: it sat in its box across from him, a disembodied sensory organ belonging to Isaac Newton, staring at him with more than human acuteness. He heard Isaac demanding to know what on

---

*Knott Bolstrood, a Barker and an old friend of Drake's, was rabidly Protestant and anti-French—the King had made him Secretary of State because no one in his right mind could possibly accuse him of being a crypto-Catholic.

†*Vereenigde Oostindische Compagnie,* or Dutch East India Company.

earth he, Daniel Waterhouse, could possibly be doing, riding across London in Samuel Pepys's coach—pretending to be a man of affairs!

"Err . . . a weak Navy forces us to keep a strong Army, to fight off any Dutch invasions," Daniel said, thinking aloud.

"But with a strong Navy, we can invade the Hollanders!" Wilkins protested. "More glory for General Lewis, Duke of Tweed!"

"Not without French help," Daniel said, after a few moments' consideration, "and my lord Tweed is too much the Presbyterian."

"Is this the same good Presbyterian who enjoyed a secret earldom at the exile court at St. Germaines, when Cromwell ruled the land?"

"He is a Royalist, that's all," Daniel demurred.

What was he doing in this carriage having this conversation, besides going out on a limb, and making a fool of himself? The real answer was known only to John Wilkins, Lord Bishop of Chester, Author of both the *Cryptonomicon* and the *Philosophical Language,* who encrypted with his left hand and made things known to all possible worlds with his right. Who'd gotten Daniel into Trinity College—invited him out to Epsom during the Plague—nominated him for the Royal Society—and now, it seemed, had something else in mind for him. Was Daniel here as an apprentice, sitting at the master's knee? It was shockingly prideful, and radically non-Puritan, for him to think so—but he could come up with no other hypothesis.

"Right, then, it all has to do with Mr. Oldenburg's letters abroad . . ." Pepys said, when some change in the baroscopic pressure (or something) signified it was time to drop pretenses and talk seriously.

Wilkins: "I assumed *that.* Which *one?*"

"Does it matter? All of the GRUBENDOL letters are intercepted and read before he even sees them."

"I've always wondered who does the reading," Wilkins reflected. "He must be very bright, or else perpetually confused."

"Likewise, all of Oldenburg's outgoing mail is examined—you knew this."

"And in some letter, he said something indiscreet—?"

"It is simply that the sheer *volume* of his foreign correspondence—taken together with the fact that he's from Germany—*and* that he's worked as a diplomat on the Continent—and that he's a friend of Cromwell's Puritanickal poet—"

"John Milton."

"Yes . . . finally, consider that no one at court understands even a tenth of what he's saying in his letters—it makes a certain type of person nervous."

"Are you saying he was thrown into the Tower of London on *general principles*?"

"As a precaution, yes."

"What—does that mean he has to stay in there for the *rest of his life*?"

"Of course not . . . only until certain very tender negotiations are finished."

"Tender negotiations . . ." Wilkins repeated a few times, as if further information could thus be pounded out of the dry and pithy words.

And here the discourse, which, to Daniel, had been merely confusing up to this point, plunged into obscurity perfect and absolute.

"I didn't know *he* had a tender bone in his body . . . oh, wipe that smirk off your face, Mr. Pepys, I meant nothing of the sort!"

"Oh, it is known that *his* feelings for *sa soeur* are most affectionate. He's writing letters to her *all the time* lately."

"Does she write back?"

"Minette spews out letters like a *diplomat*."

"Keeping his *hisness* well acquainted—I am guessing—with all that is new with her beloved?"

"The volume of correspondence is such," Pepys exclaimed, "that His Majesty can never have been so close to the man you refer to as he is today. Hoops of gold are stronger than bands of steel."

Wilkins, starting to look a bit queasy: "Hmmm . . . a good thing, then, isn't it, that *formal* contacts are being made through those two arch-Protestants—"

"I would refer you to Chapter Ten of your 1641 work," said Pepys.

"Er . . . stupid me . . . I've lost you . . . we're speaking now of Oldenburg?"

"I intended no change in subject—we're still on Treaties."

The coach stopped. Pepys climbed out of it. Daniel listened to the *whack, whack, whack* of his slap-soled boots receding across cobblestones. Wilkins was staring at nothing, trying to decrypt whatever Pepys had said.

Riding in a carriage through London was only a little better than being systematically beaten by men with cudgels—Daniel felt the need for a stretch, and so he climbed out, too, turned round—and found himself looking straight down a lane toward the front of St. James's Palace, a few hundred yards distant. Spinning round a hundred and eighty degrees, he discovered Comstock House, a stupefying Gothick pile heaving itself up out of some gardens and pavements. Pepys's carriage had turned in off of Piccadilly and stopped in the great house's forecourt. Daniel admired its situation: John Comstock could, if he so chose, plant himself in the center of his front doorway and fire a musket across his garden, out his front gate, across Piccadilly, straight down the center of a tree-lined *faux*-country lane, across Pall Mall, and straight into the grand entrance of St. James's, where it would be likely to kill someone very well-dressed. Stone walls, hedges, and wrought-iron fences had been cunningly arranged so as to crop away the view of Piccadilly and neighboring houses, and enhance the impression that Comstock House and St. James's Palace were all part of the same family compound.

Daniel edged out through Comstock's front gates and

House of Bourbon

The Bourbon-Orléans family tree is infinitely larger, more ramified, and more interlangled than can possibly be shown here, largely owing to the longevity, fertility, and polygamy of Louis XIV. One of the mistresses of Louis XIV produced six children who were made legitimate by fiat, and another produced two.

[1] Margaret of France ———— Henry IV ———— [2] Marie de Médicis
1553–1610
Henry of Navarre
KING OF FRANCE
FROM 1589

Anne of Austria ———— Louis XIII
1601–1643
KING OF FRANCE
FROM 1610

Four other
surviving children

Henrietta Maria
1609–1669
(See House of Stuart)

Charles I
1600–1649
KING OF ENGLAND
FROM 1625
(See House of Stuart)

Many wives and mistresses:
[1] Marie-Thérèse of Austria
[2] Madame de Maintenon
[m1] Louise de la Vallière
[m2] Marquise de Montespan

Louis XIV
1638–1715
KING OF FRANCE
FROM 1643

Louis
1661–1711
The Dauphin
"Monseigneur"

Philippe, duc d'Orléans
1640–1701
"Monsieur"
(See House of Stuart and
House of Orange-Nassau)

[1] Henrietta Anne of England
1644–1670
(See House of Stuart)

[2] Elisabeth Charlotte of
the Palatinate
1652–1722
(See House of Orange-Nassau)

The Houses of Bourbon and of Orléans
KINGS OF FRANCE TO 1848
KINGS AND QUEENS OF SPAIN TO THE TWENTIETH CENTURY
KINGS OF NAPLES AND SICILY
DUKES OF PARMA
SOVEREIGNS OF OTHER EUROPEAN STATES

stood at the margin of Piccadilly, facing south towards St. James's. He could see a gentleman with a bag entering the Palace—probably a doctor coming to bleed a few pints from Anne Hyde's jugular. Off to his left, in the general direction of the river, was an open space—a vast construction site, now—about a quarter of a mile on a side, with Charing Cross on the opposite corner. Since it was night, and no workers were around, it seemed as if stone foundations and walls were growing up out of the ground through some process of spontaneous generation, like toadstools bursting from soil in the middle of the night.

From here, it was possible to see Comstock House in perspective: it was really just one of several noble houses lined up along Piccadilly, facing towards St. James's Palace, like soldiers drawn up for review. Berkeley House, Burlington House, and Gunfleet House were some of the others. But only Comstock House had that direct Palace view down the lane.

He felt a giant door grinding open, and heard dignified murmurings, and saw that John Comstock had emerged from his house, arm in arm with Pepys. He was sixty-three years old, and Daniel thought that he was leaning on Pepys, just a bit, for support. But he had been wounded in battles more than once, so it didn't necessarily mean he was getting feeble. Daniel sprang to the carriage and got Isaac's telescope out of there and had the driver stow it securely on the roof. Then he joined the other three inside, and the carriage wheeled round and clattered out across Piccadilly and down the lane toward St. James's.

John Comstock, Earl of Epsom, President of the Royal Society, and advisor to the King on all matters Natural-Philosophic, was dressed in a Persian vest—a heavy coatlike garment that, along with the Cravate, was the very latest at Court. Pepys was attired the same way, Wilkins was in completely out-moded clothing, Daniel as usual was dressed as a penniless itinerant Puritan from twenty years ago. Not that anyone was looking at him.

"Working late hours?" Comstock asked Pepys, apparently reading some clue in his attire.

"The Pay Office has been extraordinarily busy," Pepys said.

"The King has been preoccupied with concerns of money—*until recently,*" Comstock said. "*Now* he is eager to turn his attentions back to his first love—natural philosophy."

"Then we have something that will delight him—a new Telescope," Wilkins began.

But telescopes were not on Comstock's agenda, and so he ignored the digression, and continued: "His Majesty has asked me to arrange a convocation at Whitehall Palace tomorrow evening. The Duke of Gunfleet, the Bishop of Chester, Sir Winston Churchill, you, Mr. Pepys, and I are invited to join the King for a demonstration at Whitehall: Enoch the Red will show us *Phosphorus.*"

Just short of St. James's Palace, the carriage turned left onto Pall Mall, and began to move up in the direction of Charing Cross.

"Light-bearer? What's that?" Pepys asked.

"A new elemental substance," Wilkins said. "All the alchemists on the Continent are *abuzz* over it."

"What's it made of?"

"It's not made of *anything*—that's what is meant by *elemental!*"

"What planet is it of? I thought all the planets were spoken for," Pepys protested.

"Enoch will explain it."

"Has there been any movement on the Royal Society's other concern?"

"Yes!" Comstock said. He was looking into Wilkins's eyes, but he made a tiny glance toward Daniel. Wilkins replied with an equally tiny nod.

"Mr. Waterhouse, I am pleased to present you with this order," Comstock said, "from my Lord Penistone,"* producing

---

*None other than Knott Bolstrood, who'd been ennobled, for protocol reasons, when the King had named him Secretary of State—the King had cho-

a terrifying document with a fat wax seal dangling from the bottom margin. "Show it to the guards at the Tower tomorrow evening—and, even as we are at *one* end of London, viewing the Phosphorus Demo', you and Mr. Oldenburg will be convened at the *other* so that you can see to his needs. I know that he wants new strings for his theorbo—quills—ink—certain books—and of course there's an enormous amount of unread mail."

"Unread by GRUBENDOL, that is," Pepys jested.

Comstock turned and gave him a look that must've made Pepys feel as if he were staring directly into the barrel of a loaded cannon.

Daniel Waterhouse exchanged a little glance with the Bishop of Chester. Now they knew who'd been reading Oldenburg's foreign letters: Comstock.

Comstock turned and smiled politely—but not pleasantly—at Daniel. "You're staying at your elder half-brother's house?"

"Just so, sir."

"I'll have the goods sent round tomorrow morning."

The coach swung round the southern boundary of Charing Cross and pulled up before a fine new town-house. Daniel, having evidently out-stayed his relevance, was invited in the most polite and genteel way imaginable to exit the coach, and take a seat on top of it. He did so and realized, without really being surprised, that they had stopped in front of the apothecary shop of Monsieur LeFebure, King's Chymist—the very same place where Isaac Newton had spent most of the morning, and had had an orchestrated *chance encounter* with the Earl of Upnor.

The front door opened and a man in a long cloak stepped out, silhouetted by lamplight from within, and approached the coach. As he got clear of the light shining out of the house, and moved across the darkness, it became possible to

---

sen to make him Count Penistone because that way, Bolstrood the ultra-Puritan could not sign his name without writing the word "penis."

see that the hem of his cloak, and the tips of his fingers, shone with a strange green light.

"Well met, Daniel Waterhouse," he said, and before Daniel could answer, Enoch the Red had climbed into the open door of the coach and closed it behind him.

The coach simply rounded the corner out of Charing Cross, which put them at one end of the long paved plaza before Whitehall. They drove directly towards the Holbein Gate, which was a four-turreted Gothic castle, taller than it was wide, that dominated the far end of the space. A huddle of indifferent gables and chimneys hid the big spaces off to their left: first Scotland Yard, which was an irregular mosaic of Wood Yards and Scalding Yards and Cider Houses, cluttered with coal-heaps and wood-piles, and after that, the Great Court of the Palace. On the right—where, during Daniel's boyhood, there'd been nothing but park, and a view towards St. James's Palace—there now loomed a long stone wall, twice as high as a man, and blank except for the gunslits. Because Daniel was up on top of the carriage he could see a few tree-branches over its top, and the rooves of the wooden buildings that Cromwell had thrown up within those walls to house his Horse Guards. The new King—perhaps remembering that this plaza had once been filled with a crowd of people come to watch his father's head get chopped off—had decided to keep the wall, and the gunslits, and the Horse Guards.

The Palace's Great Gate went by on the left, opening a glimpse of the Great Court and one or two big halls and chapels at the far end of it, down towards the river. More or less well-dressed pedestrians were going in and out of that gate, in twos and threes, availing themselves of a public right-of-way that led across the Great Court (it was clearly visible, even at night, as a rutted path over the ground) and that eventually snaked between, and through, various Palace Buildings and terminated at Whitehall Stairs, where watermen brought their little boats to pick up and discharge passengers.

The view through the Great Gate was then eclipsed by the corner of the Banqueting House, a giant white stone snuff-box of a building, which was kept dark on most nights so that torch- and candle-smoke would not blacken the buxom goddesses that Rubens had daubed on its ceiling. One or two torches were burning in there tonight, and Daniel was able to look up through a window and catch a glimpse of Minerva strangling Rebellion. But the carriage had nearly reached the end of the plaza now, and was slowing down, for this was an aesthetic cul-de-sac so miserable that it made even horses a bit woozy: the old quasi-Dutch gables of Lady Castle-maine's apartments dead ahead; the Holbein Gate's squat Gothic arch to the right and its medieval castle-towers loom-ing far above their heads; the Italian Renaissance Banquet-ing House still on their left; and, across from it, that blank, slitted stone wall, which was as close as Puritans had ever come to having their own style of architecture.

The Holbein Gate would lead to King Street, which would take them to a sort of pied-à-terre that Pepys had in that quarter. But instead the driver chivvied his team around a difficult left turn and into a dark downhill passage, barely wider than the coach itself, that cut behind the Banqueting House and drained toward the river.

Now, any Englishman in decent clothing could walk al-most anywhere in Whitehall Palace, even passing through the King's ante-chamber—a practice that European nobility considered to be far beyond vulgar, deep into the realm of the bizarre. Even so, Daniel had never been down this defile, which had always seemed Not a Good Place for a Young Pu-ritan to Go—he wasn't even sure if it had an outlet, and al-ways imagined that people like the Earl of Upnor would go there to molest serving-wenches or prosecute sword-duels.

The Privy Gallery ran along the right side of it. Now tech-nically a gallery was just a hallway—in this case, one that led directly to those parts of Whitehall where the King him-self dwelt, and toyed with his mistresses, and met with his counselors. But just as London Bridge had, over time, become covered over with houses and shops of haberdashers and glovers and drapers and publicans, so the Privy Gallery, tho' still an empty tube of air, had become surrounded by a jumbled encrustation of old buildings—mostly apartments that the King awarded to whichever courtiers and mistresses were currently in his favor. These coalesced into a bulwark of shadow off to Daniel's right, and seemed much bigger than they really were because of being numerous and confusing—as the corpse of a frog, which can fit into a pocket, seems to be a mile wide to the young Natural Philosopher who attempts to dissect it, and inventory its several parts.

Daniel was ambushed, several times, by explosions of laughter from candle-lit windows above: it sounded like sophisticated and cruel laughter. The passage finally bent round to the point where he could see its end. Apparently it debouched into a small pebbled court that he knew by reputation: the King, in theory, listened to sermons from the windows of various chambers and drawing-rooms that fronted on it. But before they reached that holy place the driver reined in his team and the carriage stopped. Daniel looked about, wondering why, and saw nothing except for a stone stairway that descended into a vault or tunnel beneath the Privy Gallery.

Pepys, Comstock, the Bishop of Chester, and Enoch the Red climbed out. Down in the tunnel, lights were now being lit. Consequently, through an open window, Daniel could see a banquet laid: a leg of mutton, a wheel of Cheshire, a dish of larks, ale, China oranges. But this room was not a dining-hall. In its corners he could see the gleam of retorts and quicksilver-flasks and fine balances, the glow of furnaces. He had heard rumors that the King had caused an alchemical laboratory to be built in the bowels of Whitehall, but until now, they had only been rumors.

"My coachman will take you back to Mr. Raleigh Waterhouse's residence," Pepys told him, pausing at the lip of the stairway. "Please make yourself comfortable below."

"You are very kind, sir, but I'm not far from Raleigh's, and I could benefit from the walk."

"As you wish. Please give my compliments to Mr. Olden-burg when you see him."

"I shall be honored to do so," Daniel answered, and just restrained himself from saying, *Please give mine to the King!*

Daniel now worked up his courage and walked down into the Sermon Court and gazed up into the windows of the King's chambers, though not for long—he was trying to look as if he came here all the time. A little side passage, un-der the end of the Privy Gallery, got him into the corner of the Privy Garden, which was a vast space. Another gallery ran along its edge, parallel to the river, and by going down it he could have got all the way to the royal bowling green and thence down into Westminster. But he'd had enough excite-ment for just now—instead he cut back across the great Gar-den, heading towards the Holbein Gate. Courtiers strolled and gossiped all round. Every so often he turned around and gazed back towards the river to admire the lodgings of the King and the Queen and their household rising up above the garden with the golden light of many beeswax candles shin-ing out of them.

If Daniel had truly been the man about town that, for a few minutes, he was pretending to be, he'd have had eyes only for the people in the windows and on the garden paths. He'd have strained to glimpse something—a new trend in the cut of Persian vests, or two important Someones ex-changing whispers in a shadowed corner. But as it was, there was one spectacle, and one only, that drew his gaze, like Po-laris sucking on a lodestone. He turned his back on the King's dwellings and looked south across the garden and the bowling green towards Westminster.

There, mounted up high on a weatherbeaten stick, was a sort of irregular knot of stuff, barely visible as a gray speck in the moonlight: the head of Oliver Cromwell. When the

King had come back, ten years ago, he'd ordered the corpse to be dug up from where Drake and the others had buried it, and the head cut off and mounted on a pike and never taken down. Ever since then Cromwell had been looking down helplessly upon a scene of unbridled lewdness that was Whitehall Palace. And now Cromwell, who had once dandled Drake's youngest son on his knee, was looking down upon him.

Daniel tilted his head back and looked up at the stars and supposed that seen from Drake's perspective up in Heaven it must all look like Hell—and Daniel right in the middle of it.

BEING LOCKED UP in the Tower of London had changed Henry Oldenburg's priorities all around. Daniel had expected that the Secretary of the Royal Society would jump headfirst into the great sack of foreign mail that Daniel had brought him, but all he cared about was the new lute-strings. He'd grown too fat to move around very effectively and so Daniel fetched necessaries from various parts of the half-moon-shaped room: Oldenburg's lute, extra candles, a tuning-fork, some sheet-music, more wood on the fire. Oldenburg turned the lute over across his knees like a naughty boy for spanking, and tied a piece of gut or two around the instrument's neck to serve as frets (the old ones being worn through), then replaced a couple of broken strings. Half an hour of tuning ensued (the new strings kept stretching) and then, finally, Oldenburg got what he really ached for: he and Daniel, sitting face to face in the middle of the room, sang a two-part song, the parts cleverly written so that their voices occasionally joined in chords that resonated sweetly: the curving wall of the cell acting like the mirror of Newton's telescope to reflect the sound back to them. After a few verses, Daniel had his part memorized, and so when he sang the chorus he sat up straight and raised his chin and sang loudly at those walls, and read the graffiti cut into the stone by prisoners of centuries past. Not your vulgar Newgate Prison graffiti—most of it was in Latin, big and solemn as gravestones, and there were astrological diagrams and runic incantations graven by imprisoned sorcerers.

Then some ale to cool the wind-pipes, and a venison pie and a keg of oysters and some oranges contributed by the R.S., and Oldenburg did a quick sort of the mail—one pile containing the latest doings of the Hotel Montmor salon in Paris, a couple of letters from Huygens, a short manuscript from Spinoza, a large pile of ravings sent in by miscellaneous cranks, and a Leibniz-mound. "This damned German will never shut up!" Oldenburg grunted—which, since Oldenburg was himself a notoriously prolix German, was actually a jest at his own expense. "Let me see . . . Leibniz proposes to found a *Societas Eruditorum* that will gather in young Vagabonds and raise them up to be an army of Natural Philosophers to overawe the Jesuits . . . here are his thoughts on free will versus predestination . . . it would be great sport to get him in an argument with Spinoza . . . he asks me here whether I'm aware Comenius has died . . . says he's ready to pick up the faltering torch of Pansophism*. . . . here's a light, easy-to-read analysis of how the bad Latin used by Continental scholars leads to faulty thinking, and in turn to religious schism, war, bad philosophy . . ."

"Sounds like Wilkins."

"Wilkins! Yes! I've considered decorating these walls with some graffiti of my own, and writing it in the Universal Character . . . but it's too depressing. 'Look, we have invented a new Philosophickal Language so that when we are imprisoned by Kings we can scratch a higher form of graffiti on our cell walls.'"

"Perhaps it'll lead us to a world where Kings can't, or won't, imprison us at all—"

"Now you sound like Leibniz. Ah, here are some new

---

*Pansophism was a movement among Continental savants, in which the said Comenius had been an important figure; it had influenced Wilkins, Oldenburg, and others to found the Experimental Philosophical Club and later the Royal Society.

mathematical proofs . . . nothing that hasn't been proved already, by Englishmen . . . but Leibniz's proofs are more elegant . . . here's something he has modestly entitled *Hypothesis Physica Nova*. Good thing I'm in the Tower, or I'd never have time to read all this."

Daniel made coffee over the fire—they drank it and smoked Virginia tobacco in clay-pipes. Then it was time for Oldenburg's evening constitutional. He preceded Daniel down a stack of stone pie-wedges that formed a spiral stair. "I'd hold the door and say 'after you,' but suppose I fell— you'd end up in the basement of Broad Arrow Tower crushed beneath me—and I'd be in the pink."

"Anything for the Royal Society," Daniel jested, marveling at how Oldenburg's bulk filled the helical tube of still air.

"Oh, you're more valuable to them than I am," Oldenburg said.

"Poh!"

"I am near the end of my usefulness. You are just beginning. They have great plans for you—"

"Until yesterday I wouldn't've believed you—then I was allowed to hear a conversation—perfectly incomprehensible to me—but it sounded frightfully important."

"Tell me about this conversation."

They came out onto the top of the old stone curtain-wall that joined Broad Arrow Tower to Salt Tower on the south. Arm in arm, they strolled along the battlements. To the left they could look across the moat—an artificial oxbow-lake that communicated with the Thames—and a defensive glacis beyond that, then a few barracks and warehouses having to do with the Navy, and then the pasture-grounds of Wapping crooked in an elbow of the Thames, dim lights out at Ratcliff and Limehouse—then a blackness containing, among other things, Europe.

"The Dramatis Personae: John Wilkins, Lord Bishop of Chester, and Mr. Samuel Pepys Esquire, Admiral's Secretary, Treasurer of the Fleet, Clerk of Acts of the Navy Board, deputy Clerk of the Privy Seal, Member of the Fishery Corporation, Treasurer of the Tangier Committee, right-hand-man of the Earl of Sandwich, courtier . . . am I leaving anything out?"

"Fellow of the Royal Society."

"Oh, yes . . . thank you."

"What said they?"

"First a brief speculation about who was reading your mail . . ."

"I assume it's John Comstock. He spied for the King during the Interregnum, why can't he spy for the King now?"

"Rings true . . . this led to some double entendres about tender negotiations. Mr. Pepys volunteered—speaking of the King of England, here—'his feelings for *sa soeur* are most affectionate, he's writing many letters to her.' "

"Well, you know that Minette is in France—"

"Minette?"

"That is what King Charles calls Henrietta Anne, his sister," Oldenburg explained. "I don't recommend using that name in polite society—unless you want to move in with me."

"She's the one who's married to the Duc d'Orléans*—?"

"Yes, and Mr. Pepys's lapsing into French was of course a way of emphasizing this. Pray continue."

"My Lord Wilkins wondered whether she wrote back, and Pepys said Minette was spewing out letters like a *diplomat*."

Oldenburg cringed, and shook his head in dismay. "Very crude work on Mr. Pepys's part. He was letting it be known that this exchange of letters was some sort of diplomatic negotiation. But he did not need to be so coarse with Wilkins . . . he must have been tired, distracted . . ."

---

*Philippe, duc d'Orléans, was the younger brother of King Louis XIV of France.

"He'd been working late—lots of gold going into the Navy Treasury under cover of darkness."

"I know it—behold!" Oldenburg said, and, tightening his arm, swung Daniel round so that both of them were looking west, across the Inmost Ward. They were near Salt Tower, which was the southeastern corner of the squarish Tower complex. The southern wall, therefore, stretched away from them, paralleling the river, connecting a row of squat round towers. Off to their right, planted in the center of the ward, was the ancient donjon: a freestanding building called the White Tower. A few low walls partitioned the ward into smaller quadrangles, but from this viewpoint the most conspicuous structure was the great western wall, built strong to resist attack from the always difficult City of London. On the far side of that wall, hidden from their view, a street ran up a narrow defile between it and a somewhat lower outer wall. Stout piles of smoke and steam were building from that street—which was lined with works for melting and working precious metals. It was called Mint Street. "Their infernal hammers keep me awake—the smoke of their furnaces comes in through the embrasures." Walls hereabouts tended to have narrow cross-shaped arrow-slits called embrasures, which was one of the reasons the Tower made a good prison, especially for fat men.

"So that's why kings live at Whitehall nowadays—to be upwind of the Mint?" Daniel said jestingly.

On Oldenburg's face, perfunctory amusement stamped out by pedantic annoyance. "You don't understand. The Mint's operations are extremely sporadic—it has been cold and silent for months—the workers idle and drunk."

"And now?"

"Now they are *busy* and drunk. A few days ago, as I stood in this very place, I saw a three-master, a man of war, heavily laden, drop anchor just around the river-bend, there. Small boats carrying heavy loads began to put in at the water-gate just there, in the middle of the south wall. On the same night, the Mint came suddenly to life, and has not slept since."

"And gold began to arrive at the Navy Treasury," Daniel said, "making much work for Mr. Pepys."

"Now, let us get back to this conversation you were allowed to hear. How did the Bishop of Chester respond to Mr. Pepys's rather ham-handed revelations?"

"He said something like, 'So Minette keeps his Majesty well acquainted with the doings of her beau?'"

"Now whom do you suppose he meant by that?"

"Her husband—? I know, I know—my naïveté is pathetic."

"Philippe, duc d'Orleans, owns the largest and finest collection of women's underwear in France—his sexual adventures are strictly limited to being fucked up the ass by strapping officers."

"Poor Minette!"

"She knew *perfectly well* when she married him," Oldenburg said, rolling his eyes. "She spent her honeymoon in bed with her new husband's elder brother: King Louis XIV. *That* is what Bishop Wilkins meant when he referred to Minette's *beau*."

"I stand corrected."

"Pray go on."

"Pepys assured Wilkins that, considering the volume of correspondence, King Charles couldn't help but be very close to the man in question—an analogy was made to hoops of gold . . ."

"Which you took to mean, matrimonial bliss?"

"Even I knew what Pepys meant by *that*," Daniel said hotly.

"So did Wilkins, I'm sure—how did he seem, then?"

"Ill at ease—he wanted reassurance that 'the two arch-Dissenters' were handling formal contacts."

"It is a secret—but generally known among the sort who rattle around London in private coaches in the night-time—

that a treaty with France is being negotiated by the Earl of Shaftesbury, and His Majesty's old drinking and whoring comrade, the Duke of Buckingham. Chosen for the job not because they are skilled diplomats but because not even your late father would ever accuse them of Popish sympathies."

A Yeoman Warder was approaching, making his rounds. "Good evening, Mr. Oldenburg. Mr. Waterhouse."

"Evening, George. How's the gout?"

"Better today, thank you, sir—the cataplasm seemed to work—where did you get the receipt from?" George then went into a rote exchange of code-words with another Beefeater on the roof of Salt Tower, then reversed direction, bade them good evening, and strolled away.

Daniel enjoyed the view until he was certain that the only creature that could overhear them was a spaniel-sized raven perched on a nearby battlement.

Half a mile upstream, the river was combed, and nearly dammed up, by a line of sloppy, boat-shaped, man-made islands, supporting a series of short and none too ambitious stone arches. The arches were joined, one to the next, by a roadway, made of wood in some places and of stone in others, and the roadway was mostly covered with buildings that sprayed in every direction, cantilevered far out over the water and kept from falling into it by makeshift diagonal braces. Far upstream, and far downstream, the river was placid and sluggish, but where it was forced between those starlings (as the man-made islands were called), it was all furious. The starlings themselves, and the banks of the Thames for miles downstream, were littered with wreckage of light boats that had failed in the attempt to shoot the rapids beneath London Bridge, and (once a week or so) with the corpses and personal effects of their passengers.

A few parts of the bridge had been kept free of buildings so that fires could not jump the river. In one of those gaps a burly woman stopped to fling a jar into the angry water below. Daniel could not see it from here, but he knew it would be painted with a childish rendering of a face: this a charm to ward off witch-spells. The water-wheels constructed in some of those arch-ways made gnashing and clanking noises that forced Waterhouse and Oldenburg, half a mile away, to raise their voices slightly, and put their heads closer together. Daniel supposed this was no accident—he suspected they were coming to a part of the conversation that Oldenburg would rather keep private from those sharp-eared Beefeaters.

Directly behind London Bridge, but much farther away round the river-bend, were the lights of Whitehall Palace, and Daniel almost convinced himself that there was a greenish glow about the place tonight, as Enoch the Red schooled the King, and his court, and the most senior Fellows of the Royal Society, in the new Element called Phosphorus.

"Then Pepys got too enigmatic even for Wilkins," Daniel said. "He said, 'I refer you to Chapter Ten of your 1641 work.'"

"The *Cryptonomicon?*"

"So I assume. Chapter Ten is where Wilkins explains steganography, or how to embed a subliminal message in an innocuous-seeming letter—" but here Daniel stopped because Oldenburg had adopted a patently fake look of innocent curiosity. "I think you know this well enough. Now, Wilkins apologized for being thick-headed and asked whether Pepys was speaking, now, of *you.*"

"Ho, ho, ho!" Oldenburg bellowed, the laughter bouncing like cannon-fire off the hard walls of the Inmost Ward. The raven hopped closer to them and screeched, *"Caa, caa, caa!"* Both humans laughed, and Oldenburg fetched a bit of bread from his pocket and held it out to the bird. It hopped closer and reared back to peck it out of the fat pale hand—but Oldenburg snatched it back and said very distinctly, "Cryptonomicon."

The raven cocked its head, opened its beak, and made a long gagging noise. Oldenburg sighed and opened his hand. "I have been trying to teach him words," he explained, "but that one is too much of a mouthful, for a raven." The bird's beak struck the bread out of Oldenburg's hand, and it hopped back out of reach, in case Oldenburg should change his mind.

"Wilkins's confusion is understandable—but Pepys's meaning is clear. There are some suspicious-minded persons upriver" (waving in the general direction of Whitehall) "who think I'm a spy, communicating with Continental powers by means of subliminal messages embedded in what purport to be philosophickal discourses—it being beyond their comprehension that anyone would care as much as I seem to about new species of eels, methods for squaring hyperbolae, *et cetera*. But Pepys was not referring to *that*—he was being ever so much more clever. He was telling Wilkins that the not-very-secret negotiations being carried on by Buckingham and Shaftesbury are like the innocuous-seeming message, being used to conceal the *truly* secret agreement that the two Kings are drawing up, using Minette as the conduit."

"God in Heaven," Daniel said, and felt obliged to lean back against a battlement so that his spinning head wouldn't whirl him off into the moat.

"An agreement whose details we can only guess at—except for this: it causes gold to appear there in the middle of the night." Oldenburg pointed to the Tower's water-gate along the Thames. Discretion kept him from speaking its ancient name: Traitor's Gate.

"Pepys mentioned in passing that Thomas More Anglesey was responsible for filling the Navy's coffers . . . I didn't understand what he meant."

"Our Duke of Gunfleet has much warmer connections with France than anyone appreciates," Oldenburg said—but then refused to say any more.

And because silver and gold have their value
from the matter itself; they have first this privilege, that the value of them cannot be altered
by the power of one, nor of a few common-
wealths; as being a common measure of the
commodities of all places. But base money,
may easily be enhanced, or abased.

—HOBBES, *Leviathan*

OLDENBURG GENTEELLY KICKED him out not much later, eager to get into that pile of mail. Under the politely curious
gaze of the Beefeaters and their semi-tame ravens, Daniel
walked down Water Lane, on the southern verge of the
Tower complex. He walked past a large rectangular tower
planted in the outer wall, above the river, and realized too
late that if he'd only turned his head and glanced to the left
at that point, he could've looked through the giant arch of
Traitor's Gate and out across the river. Too late now—
seemed a poor idea to go back. Probably just as well he
hadn't gawked—then whoever was watching him would suspect that Oldenburg had mentioned it.

Was he thinking like a courtier now?

The massive octagonal pile of Bell Tower was on his right.
As he got past it he dared to look up a narrow buffer between
two layers of curtain-walls no more than fifty feet apart. Half
of that width was filled up by the Mint's indifferent low
houses and workshops. Daniel glimpsed furnace-light radiat-
ing from windows, warming high stone walls, making silhou-
ettes of a congestion of carts bringing coal to burn. Men with
muskets gazed coolly back at him. Mint workers crossed from
building to building in the shambling gait of the exhausted.

Then he was underneath the great arch of the Byward
Tower, an elevated building thrown over Water Lane to control the Tower's land approach. A raven perched on a gar-
goyle and screeched "Cromwell!" at him as he passed

through onto the drawbridge that ran from Byward Tower out to Middle Tower, over the moat. Middle Tower gave way to Lion Tower—but the King's menagerie were all asleep and he did not hear the lions roar. From there he crossed over a last little backwater of the moat, over *another* drawbridge, and came into a little walled-in yard called the Bulwark—finally, then, through one last gate and into the world, though he had a lonely stroll over an empty moonlit glacis, past a few scavenging rats and copulating dogs, before he was among buildings and people.

But then Daniel Waterhouse was right in the City of London—slightly confused, as some of the streets had been straightened and simplifed after the Fire. He pulled a fat gold egg from his pocket—one of Hooke's experimental watches, a failed stab at the Longitude Problem, adequate only for landlubbers. It told him that the Phosphorus Demo' was not quite finished at Whitehall, but that it was not too late to call on his in-laws. Daniel did not especially like to just *call* on people—seemed presumptuous to think they'd want to open the door and see *him*—but he knew that this was how men like Pepys got to become men like Pepys. So to the house of Ham.

Lights burned expensively, and a coach and pair dawdled out front. Daniel was startled to discover his own family coat of arms (a castle bestriding a river) painted on the door of this coach. The house was smoking like a heavy forge—it was equipped with oversized chimneys, projecting tubes of orange light into their own smoke. As Daniel ascended the front steps he heard singing, which faltered but did not stop when he knocked: a very current melody making fun of the Dutch for being so bright, hard-working, and successful. Viscount Walbrook's* butler opened the door and recognized Daniel as a social caller—not, as sometimes happened, a nocturnal customer brandishing a goldsmith's note.

Mayflower Ham, neé Waterhouse—tubby, fair, almost

---

*Thomas Ham had been made Viscount Walbrook by the King.

fifty, looking more like thirty—gave him a hug that pulled
him up on tiptoe. Menopause had finally terminated her fantastically involved and complex relationship with her womb:
a legendary saga of irregular bleeding, eleven-month pregnancies straight out of the Royal Society proceedings, terrifying primal omens, miscarriages, heartbreaking epochs of
barrenness punctuated by phases of such explosive fertility
that Uncle Thomas had been afraid to come near her—dis-
turbing asymmetries, prolapses, relapses, and just plain
lapses, hellish cramping fits, mysterious interactions with
the Moon and other cœlestial phenomena, shocking imbal-
ances of all four of the humours known to Medicine plus a
few known only to Mayflower, seismic rumblings audible
from adjoining rooms—cancers reabsorbed—(incredibly)
three successful pregnancies culminating in four-day labors
that snapped stout bedframes like kindling, vibrated pictures
off walls, and sent queues of vicars, midwives, physicians,
and family members down into their own beds, ruined with
exhaustion. Mayflower had (fortunately for her!) been born
with that ability, peculiar to certain women, of being able to
talk about her womb in any company without it seeming in-
appropriate, and not only that but you never knew where in a
conversation, or a letter, she would launch into it, plunging
everyone into a clammy sweat as her descriptions and revelations forced them to consider topics so primal that they
were beyond eschatology—even Drake had had to shut up
about the Apocalypse when Mayflower had gotten rolling.
Butlers fled and serving-maids fainted. The condition of
Mayflower's womb affected the moods of England as the
Moon ruled the tides.

"How, er . . . *are you?*" Daniel inquired, bracing himself,
but she just smiled sweetly, made rote apologies about the
house not being finished (but no fashionable house ever *was*
finished), and led him to the Dining-Room, where Uncle
Thomas was entertaining Sterling and Beatrice Waterhouse,
and Sir Richard Apthorp and his wife. The Apthorps had a
goldsmith's shop of their own, and lived a few doors up

Threadneedle. The attire was not so aggressively fine, Daniel not so monstrously out of place, as at the coffee-house. Sterling greeted him warmly, as if saying, *Sorry old chap but the other day was business.*

They appeared to be celebrating something. Reference was made to all the work that lay ahead, so Daniel assumed it was some milestone in their grand shop-house-project. He wanted someone to ask him where he'd been, so that he could offhandedly let them know he'd been to the Tower waving around a warrant from the Secretary of State. But no one asked. After a while he realized that they probably would not care if they *did* know. The back door, fronting on Cornhill, kept creaking open, then booming shut. Finally, Daniel caught Uncle Thomas's eye, and, with a look, inquired what on earth was happening back there. A few minutes later, Viscount Walbrook got up, as if to use the House of Office, but tapped Daniel on the shoulder on his way out of the room.

Daniel rose and followed him down a hall—dark except for a convenient red glow at the far end. Daniel couldn't see around the tottering Punchinello silhouette of his host, but he could hear shovels crunching into piles of something, ringing as they flung their loads—obviously coal being fed to a furnace. But sometimes there was the icy trill of a coin falling and spinning on a hard floor.

The hall became sooty and extremely warm, and gave way to a brick-lined room where a laborer, stripped to a pair of drawers, was heaving coal into the open door of the House of Ham's forge—which had been hugely expanded when the house was reconstructed after the Fire. Another laborer was pumping bellows with his feet, climbing an endless ladder. In the old days, this forge had been a good size for baking tarts, which made sense for the sort of goldsmith who made earrings and teaspoons. Now it looked like something that could be used to cast cannon-barrels, and half the weight of the building was concentrated in the chimney.

Several black iron lock-boxes were open on the floor—

some full of silver coins and others empty. One of the Hams' senior clerks sat on the floor by one of these in a pond of his own sweat, counting coins into a dish out loud: "Ninety-eight . . . ninety-nine . . . hundred!" whereupon he handed the dish up to Charles Ham (the youngest Ham brother—Thomas being the eldest), who emptied it onto the pan of a scale and weighed the coins against a brass cylinder—then raked them off into a bucket-sized crucible. This was repeated until the crucible was nearly full. Then a glowing door was opened—knives of blue flame probed out into the dark room—Charles Ham donned black gauntlets, heaved a gigantic pair of iron tongs off the floor, thrust them in, hugged, and backed away, drawing out another crucible: a cup shining daffodil-colored light. Turning around very carefully, he positioned the crucible (Daniel could've tracked it with his eyes closed, by feeling its warmth shine on his face) and tipped it. A stream of radiant liquid formed in its lip and arced down into a mold of clay. Other molds were scattered about the floor, wherever there was room, cooling down through shades of yellow, orange, red, and sullen brown, to black; but wherever light glanced off of them, it gleamed silver.

When the crucible was empty, Charles Ham set it down by the scales, then picked up the crucible that was full of silver coins and put it into the fire. Through all of this, the man on the floor never paused counting coins out of the lock-box, his reedy voice making a steady incantation out of the numbers, the coins going *chink, chink, chink.*

Daniel stepped forward, bent down, took a coin out of the lock-box, and angled it to shine fire-light into his eyes, like the little mirror in the center of Isaac's telescope. He was expecting to see a worn-out shilling with a blurred portrait of Queen Elizabeth on it, or an old piece of eight or thaler that the Hams had somehow picked up in a money-changing transaction. What he saw was in fact the profile of King Charles II, very new and crisp, stamped on a limpid pool of brilliant silver—perfect. Shining that way in firelight, it brought back memories of a night in 1666. Daniel flung it back into the lock-box. Then, not believing his eyes, he thrust his hand in and pulled out a fistful. They were all the same. Their edges, fresh from Monsieur Blondeau's ingenious machine, were so sharp they almost cut his flesh, their mass blood-warm . . .

The heat was too much. He was out in the street with Uncle Thomas, bathing in cool air.

"They are *still warm*!" he exclaimed.

Uncle Thomas nodded.

"From the Mint?"

"Yes."

"You mean to tell me that the coins being stamped out at the Mint are, *the very same night*, melted down into *bullion* on Threadneedle Street?"

Daniel was noticing, now, that the chimney of Apthorp's shop, two doors up the street, was also smoking, and the same was true of diverse other goldsmiths up and down the length of Threadneedle.

Uncle Thomas raised his eyebrows piously.

"Where does it go *then*?" Daniel demanded.

"Only a Royal Society man would ask," said Sterling Waterhouse, who had slipped out to join them.

"What do you mean by that, brother?" Daniel asked.

Sterling was walking slowly towards him. Instead of stopping, he flung his arms out wide and collided with Daniel, embraced him and kissed him on the cheek. Not a trace of liquor on his breath. "No one knows where it goes—that is not the *point*. The point is *that it goes*—it moves—the movement ne'er stops—it is the blood in the veins of Commerce."

"But you must do something with the bullion—"

"We tender it to gentlemen who give us something in return" said Uncle Thomas. "It's like selling fish at Billingsgate—do the fishwives ask where the fish go?"

"It's generally known that silver percolates slowly eastwards, and stops in the Orient, in the vaults of the Great Mogul and the Emperor of China," Sterling said. "Along the way it might change hands hundreds of times. Does that answer your question?"

"I've already stopped believing I saw it," Daniel said, and went back into the house, his thin shoe-leather bending over irregular paving-stones, his dull dark clothing hanging about him coarsely, the iron banister cold under his hand—he was a mote bobbing in a mud-puddle and only wanted to be back in the midst of fire and heat and colored radiance.

He stood in the forge-room and watched the melting for a while. His favorite part was the sight of the liquid metal building behind the lip of the canted crucible, then breaking out and tracing an arc of light down through the darkness.

"Quicksilver is the elementary form of all things fusible; for all things fusible, when melted, are changed into it, and it mingles with them because it is of the same substance with them . . ."

"Who said that?" Sterling asked—keeping an eye on his little brother, who was showing signs of instability.

"Some damned Alchemist," Daniel answered. "I have given up hope, tonight, of ever understanding money."

"It's simple, really . . ."

"And yet it's not simple at all," Daniel said. "It follows simple rules—it obeys logic—and so Natural Philosophy should understand it, encompass it—and I, who know and understand more than almost anyone in the Royal Society, should comprehend it. But I don't. I never will . . . if money is a science, then it is a dark science, darker than Alchemy. It split away from Natural Philosophy millennia ago, and has gone on developing ever since, by its own rules . . ."

"Alchemists say that veins of minerals in the earth are twigs and offshoots of an immense Tree whose trunk is the center of the earth, and that metals rise like sap—" Sterling said, the firelight on his bemused face. Daniel was too tired at first to take the analogy—or perhaps he was underestimating Sterling. He assumed Sterling was prying for suggestions on where to look for gold mines. But later, as Sterling's coach was taking him off towards Charing Cross, he under-

stood that Sterling had been telling him that the growth of
money and commerce was—as far as Natural Philosophers
were concerned—like the development of that mysterious
subterranean Tree: suspected, sensed, sometimes exploited
for profit, but, in the end, unknowable.

THE KING'S HEAD TAVERN was dark, but it was not closed.
When Daniel entered he saw patches of glowing green light
here and there—pooled on tabletops and smeared on
walls—and heard Persons of Quality speaking in hushed
voices punctuated by outbreaks of riotous giggling. But the
glow faded, and then serving-wenches scurried out with
rush-lights and re-lit all of the lamps, and finally Daniel
could see Pepys and Wilkins and Comstock, and the Duke of
Gunfleet, and Sir Christopher Wren, and Sir Winston
Churchill, and—at the best table—the Earl of Upnor,
dressed in what amounted to a three-dimensional Persian
carpet, trimmed with fur and studded with globs of colored
glass, or perhaps they were precious gems.

Upnor was explaining phosphorus to three gaunt women
with black patches glued all over their faces and necks: "It is
known, to students of the Art, that each metal is created
when rays from a particular planet strike and penetrate the
Earth, *videlicet,* the Sun's rays create gold; the Moon's, silver; Mercury's, quicksilver; Venus's, copper; Mars's, iron;
Jupiter's, tin; and Saturn's lead. Mr. Root's discovery of a
new elemental substance suggests there may be another
planet—presumably of a green color—beyond the orbit of
Saturn."

Daniel edged toward a table where Churchill and Wren
were talking past each other, staring ever so thoughtfully at
nothing: "It faces to the east, and it's rather far north, isn't
it? Perhaps His Majesty should name it New Edinburgh . . ."

"That would only give the Presbyterians ideas!" Churchill
scoffed.

"It's not *that* far north," Pepys put in from another table.
"Boston is farther north by one and a half degrees of latitude."

"We can't go wrong suggesting that he name it after himself . . ."

"Charlestown? That name is already in use—Boston again."

"His brother then? But Jamestown was used in Virginia."

"What are you talking about?" Daniel inquired.

"New Amsterdam! His Majesty is acquiring it in exchange for Surinam," Churchill said.

"Speak up, Sir Winston, there may be some Vagabonds out in Dorset who didn't hear you!" Pepys roared.

"His Majesty has asked the Royal Society to suggest a new name for it," Churchill added, sotto voce.

"Hmmm . . . his brother sort of conquered the place, didn't he?" Daniel asked. He knew the answer, but couldn't presume to lecture men such as these.

"Yes," Pepys said learnedly, " 'twas all part of York's *Atlantic* campaign—*first* he took several Guinea ports, rich in gold, and richer in slaves, from the Dutchmen, and then it was straight down the trade winds to his next prize—New Amsterdam."

Daniel made a small bow toward Pepys, then continued: "If you can't use his Christian name of James, perhaps you can use his *title* . . . after all, York is a city up to the north on *our* eastern coast—and yet not *too* far north . . ."

"We have already considered that," Pepys said glumly. "There's a Yorktown in Virginia."

"What about 'New York'?" Daniel asked.

"Clever . . . but too obviously derivative of 'New Amsterdam,'" Churchill said.

"If we call it 'New York,' we're naming it after the *city* of York . . . the point is to name it after the *Duke* of York," Pepys scoffed.

Daniel said, "You are correct, of course—"

"Oh, come now!" Wilkins barked, slapping a table with the flat of his hand, splashing beer and phosphorus all directions. "Don't be pedantic, Mr. Pepys. Everyone will understand what it means."

"Everyone who is clever enough to matter, anyway," Wren put in.

"Err . . . I see, you are proposing a more *subtle* approach," Sir Winston Churchill muttered.

"Let's put it on the list!" Wilkins suggested. "It can't hurt to include as many 'York' and 'James' names as we can possibly think up."

"Hear, hear!" Churchill harrumphed—or possibly he was just clearing his throat—or summoning a barmaid.

"As you wish—never mind," Daniel said. "I take it that Mr. Root's Demonstration was well received—?"

For some reason this caused eyes to swivel, ever so briefly, toward the Earl of Upnor. "It went well," Pepys said, drawing closer to Daniel, "until Mr. Root threatened to spank the Earl. Don't look at him, don't look at him," Pepys continued levelly, taking Daniel's arm and turning him away from the Earl. The timing was unfortunate, because Daniel was certain he had just overhead Upnor mentioning Isaac Newton by name, and wanted to eavesdrop.

Pepys led him past Wilkins, who was good-naturedly spanking a barmaid. The publican rang a bell and everyone blew out the lights—the tavern went dark except for the freshly invigorated phosphorus. Everyone said "Woo!" and Pepys wrangled Daniel out into the street. "You know that Mr. Root makes the stuff from urine?"

"So it is rumored," Daniel said. "Mr. Newton knows more of the Art than I do—he has told me that Enoch the Red was following an ancient recipe to extract the Philosophic Mercury from urine, but happened upon phosphorus instead."

"Yes, and he has an entire tale that he tells, of how he found the recipe in Babylonia." Pepys rolled his eyes. "Enthralled the courtiers. Anyway—for this evening's Demo', he'd collected urine from a sewer that drains Whitehall, and boiled it—*endlessly*—on a barge in the Thames. I'll spare you the rest of the details—suffice it to say that when it was finished, and they were done applauding, and all of the courtiers were groping for a way to liken the King's splendor and radiance to that of Phosphorus—"

"Oh, yes, I suppose that would've been obligatory—?"

Wilkins banged out the tavern door, apparently just to *watch* the story being related to Daniel.

"The Earl of Upnor made some comment to the effect that some kingly essence—a royal humour—must suffuse the King's body, and be excreted in his urine, to account for all of this. And when all of the other courtiers were finished agreeing, and marveling at the Earl's *philosophick* acumen, Enoch the Red said, 'In truth, most of this urine came from the Horse Guards—and their horses.'"

"Whereat, the Earl was on his feet! His hand reaching for his sword—to defend His Majesty's honor, of course," Wilkins said.

"What was His Majesty's state of mind?" Daniel asked.

Wilkins made his hands into scale-pans and bobbled them up and down. "Then Mr. Pepys tipped the scales. He related an anecdote from the Restoration, in 1660, when he had been on the boat with the King, and certain members of his household—including the Earl of Upnor, then no more than twelve years old. Also aboard was the King's favorite old dog. The dog shit in the boat. The young Earl kicked at the dog, and made to throw it overboard—but was stayed by the King, who laughed at it, and said, 'You see, in some ways, at least, Kings are like other men!'"

"Did he really say such a thing!?" Daniel exclaimed, and instantly felt like an idiot—

"Of *course* not!" Pepys said, "I merely told the story that way because I thought it would be useful—"

"And was it?"

"The King laughed," Pepys said with finality.

"And Enoch Root inquired, whether it had then been necessary to give the Earl a spanking, to teach him respect for his elders."

"Elders?"

"The dog was older than the Earl—come on, pay attention!" Pepys said, giving Daniel a tremendous frown.

"Strikes me as an unwise thing to have said," Daniel muttered.

"The King said, 'No, no, Upnor has always been a civil fellow,' or some such, and so there was no duel."

"Still, Upnor strikes me as a grudge-holder—"

"Enoch has sent better men than Upnor to Hell—don't trouble yourself about *his* future," Wilkins said. "You need to tend to your own faults, young fellow—excessive sobriety, e.g. . . ."

"A tendency to fret—" Pepys put in.

"Undue chastity—let's back to the tavern!"

HE WOKE UP SOMETIME THE next day on a hired coach bound for Cambridge—sharing a confined space with Isaac Newton, and a load of gear that Isaac had bought in London: a six-volume set of *Theatrum Chemicum*,* numerous small crates stuffed with straw, the long snouts of retorts poking out—canisters of stuff that smelled odd. Isaac was saying, "If you throw up again, please aim for this bowl—I'm collecting bile."

Daniel was able to satisfy him there.

"Where Enoch the Red failed, you're going to succeed—?"

"I beg your pardon?"

"Going after the Philosophic Mercury, Isaac?"

"What else is there to do?"

"The R.S. adores your telescope," Daniel said. "Oldenburg wants you to write more on the subject."

"Mmm," Isaac said, lost in thought, comparing passages in three different books to one another. "Could you hold this for a moment, please?" Which was how Daniel came to be a human book-rest for Isaac. Not that he was in any condition to accomplish greater things. In his lap for the next hour was a tome: folio-sized, four inches thick, bound in gold and sil-

---

*A vast, turgid, incoherent compendium of alchemical lore.

ver, obviously made centuries before Gutenberg. Daniel was going to blurt, *This must have been fantastically expensive,* but on closer investigation found a book-plate pasted into it, bearing the arms of Upnor, and a note from the Earl:

> Mr. Newton—
> May this volume become as treasured by you, as the memory of our fortuitous meeting is to me—
>
> *UPNOR.*

❧

Aboard Minerva, Cape Cod Bay, Massachusetts

NOVEMBER 1713

❧

WHEN THEY'VE MADE it out of Plymouth and into Cape Cod Bay, van Hoek returns to his cabin and becomes Captain once more. He looks rather put out to find the place so discomposed. Perhaps this is a sign of Daniel's being a bitter old Atheistical crank, but he nearly laughs out loud. *Minerva*'s a collection of splinters loosely pulled together by nails, pegs, lashings, and oakum, not even large enough to count as a mote in the eye of the world—more like one of those microscopic eggs that Hooke discovered with his microscope. She floats only because boys mind her pumps all the time, she remains upright and intact only because highly intelligent men never stop watching the sky and seas around her. Every line and sail decays with visible speed, like snow in sunlight, and men must work ceaselessly worming, parceling, serving, tarring, and splicing her infinite network of hempen lines in order to prevent her from falling apart in mid-ocean with what Daniel imagines would be explosive suddenness. Like a snake changing skins, she sloughs away what is worn and broken and replaces it from inner reserves—evoluting as she goes. The only way to sustain this perpetual and necessary evolution is to replenish the stocks that dwindle from her holds as relentlessly as sea-water leaks in. The only way to do *that* is to trade goods from one port to another, making a bit of money on each leg of the perpetual voyage. Each day assails her with hurricanes and pirate-fleets. To go out on the sea and find a *Minerva* is like finding, in the desert, a Great Pyramid blanced upside-down on its tip. She's a baby in a basket—a book in a bonfire. And yet van Hoek has the temerity to appoint his cabin as if it were a gentleman's drawing-room, with delicate weather-glasses, clocks, optickal devices, a decent library, a painting or two, an enamel cabinet stocked with Chinese crockery, a respectable stock of brandy and port. He's got *mirrors* in here, for Christ's sake. Not only that, but when he enters to discover a bit of broken glass on the deck, and small impact-craters here and there, he becomes so outraged that Dappa doesn't need to tell Daniel they'd best leave him alone for a while.

"So the curtain has come down on your performance. Now, a man in your position *might* feel like a barnacle—unable to leave the ship—an annoyance to mariners—but on *Minerva* there is a job for everyone," says Dappa, leading him down the midships staircase to the gundeck.

Daniel's not paying attention. A momentous rearrangement has taken place since Daniel was last here. All of the obstructions that formerly cluttered the space have been moved elsewhere or thrown overboard to create rights-of-way for the cannons. These had been lashed up against the inside of the hull, but now they've been swung round ninety degrees and each aimed at its gunport. As they are maneuvering on Cape Cod Bay, miles from the nearest Foe, those gunports are all closed for now. But like stage-hands laboring in the back of a theatre, the seamen are hard at work with diverse arcane tools, viz. lin-stocks, quoins, gunner's picks, and worming-irons. One man's got what looks like a large magnifying-glass, except without the glass—it's an empty circle of iron on a handle. He sits astride a crate of cannonballs, heaving them out one at a time and passing them through the ring to gauge them, sorting them into other crates. Others whittle and file round blocks of wood, called sabots, and strap cannonballs to them. But anyone carrying a steel blade is distinctly un-welcome near the powder-barrels, because steel makes sparks.

One sailor, an Irishman, is talking to one of the Plymouth whaleboat pirates captured this morning. A cannon is be-tween the two men, and when a cannon is between two men, that is what they talk about. "This is Wapping Wendy, or W.W., or dub-dub as we sometimes dub her in the heat of battle, though you may call her 'darling' or 'love of my life' but never 'Wayward Wendy' as *that* lot—" glowering at the crew of another gun, "Mr. Foote," "—like to defame her."

"Is she? Wayward?"

"She's like any other lass, you must get to know her, and then what might seem inconstant is clearly revealed as a kind of consistency—faithfulness even. And so the first thing you must know about our darling girl is that her bore tends up and to larboard of her centerline. And she's a tight one, is our virginal Wendy, which is why we on the dub-dub crew must keep a sharp eye for undersized balls and husband 'em carefully . . ."

Someone on the crew of "Manila Surprise" nudges that gun's port open for a moment, and sun shines in. But Manila Surprise is on the larboard side of the ship. "We are sailing southwards!?" Daniel exclaims.

"No better way to run before a north wind," Dappa says.

"But in that direction, Cape Cod is only a few miles away! What sort of an escape route is that?"

"As you have reckoned, we shall have to work to windwards *eventually* in order to escape from Cape Cod Bay," Dappa says agreeably. "When we do, Teach's fleet will be tacking along with us. But his ships are fore-and-aft rigged and can sail closer to the wind, and make better headway, than our dear *Minerva,* a square-rigger. Advantage Teach."

"Shouldn't we head north while we can, then?"

"He would catch us in a matter of minutes—his entire fleet together, working in concert. We want to fight Teach's ships one at a time if we can. So southwards it is, for now. Running before the wind in full sail, we are faster than they. So Teach knows that if he pursues us to the south we may lose him. But he also knows that we must wheel about and work northwards before long—so he will spread out a sort of picket-line and wait for us."

"But will Teach not anticipate all of this, and take pains to keep his fleet together?"

"In a well-disciplined fleet, pursuing Victory, that's how it would go. But that is a pirate-fleet, in pursuit of plunder, and by the rules and account-books of piracy, the lion's share goes to the ship that takes the prize."

"Ah—so the captain of each ship has incentive to split away and attack us individually."

"Just so, Dr. Waterhouse."

"But would it not be foolhardy for a little sloop to engage a ship with all—this?" Daniel gestures down the length of the gundeck—a bustling bazaar where cannonballs, sabots, and powder-kegs, lies, promises, and witticisms are being exchanged lustily.

"Not if the ship is undermanned, and the captain a senile poltroon. Now, if you'll just follow me down into the hold— don't worry, I'll get this lantern lit, soon as we are away from the gunpowder—there, that's it. She's a tidy ship, wouldn't you agree?"

"Beg pardon? Tidy? Yes, I suppose, as ships go . . ." says Dr. Waterhouse, finding Dappa, sometimes, too subtle—an excess of quicksilver in the constitution.

"Thank you, sir. But 'tis a disadvantage, when we have to fight with blunderbusses. The virtue of a blunderbuss, as you may know, is to make a weapon out of whatever nails, pebbles, splinters, and fragments might be lying about—but here on *Minerva* we make a practice of sweeping that matter up, and throwing it overboard, several times daily. At times like this we *do* regret that we neglected to hoard it."

"I know more than you imagine of blunderbusses. What do you want me to do?"

"In a little while, one of the men'll be teaching you how to fuze mortar-bombs—but we're not quite ready for that just yet—now I would ask you to go down into the hold and—"

Dr. Waterhouse doesn't believe, until he's down there, what Dappa tells him next. He hasn't seen the hold yet, and reckons it'll be like the shambolic Repository at the Royal Society—but no. The great casks and bales are stacked, and lashed in place, with admirable neatness, and there is even a Diagram tacked to the staircase bulkhead in which the location of each object is specified, and notes made as to what's stored there and when it was done. Underneath, under a sub-heading labelled BILGE, van Hoek himself has scratched "out-moded china—keep handy."

Dappa has pulled two sailors away from what they've been doing the last half-hour: standing by a gunport carrying on a learned discourse about an approaching pirate-sloop. The sailors considered this to be time well spent, but Dappa felt otherwise. These two spend a minute consulting the Diagram, and Daniel realizes with moderate astonishment that they both know how to read, and interpret figures. They agree that the out-moded china is to be found forward, and so that's where they go—to the most beautiful part of the ship, where many ribs radiate from the up-curving keel,

forming an upside-down vault, so it's like being a fly exploring the ceiling of a cathedral. The sailors move a few crates
out of the way—they never stop talking, each trying to outdo
the other in bloodcurdling yarns about the cruelty of certain
infamous pirates. They pull up a hatch that gives access to
the bilge, and in no time at all two crates of markedly ugly
china have been fetched out. The crates themselves are
handsome productions of clear-grained red cedar, chosen
because it won't rot in the wet bilge. Into them the china has
been thrown with no packing material between items, so part
of Daniel's work is already done. He thanks the two sailors
and they look back at him queerly, then return abovedecks.
Daniel spreads an old hammock—two yards of sailcloth—
on the planking, tips a crate over, and then attacks its spilled
contents with a maul.

What is the optimal size (he wonders) of a shard of pottery for firing out of a blunderbuss? When the King's guards
shot him before his father's house during the Fire, he was
knocked down, bruised, cut, but not really *penetrated*. Probably the larger the better, which makes his job easier—one
would like to see great sharp triangles of gaudily-painted
porcelain spinning through the air, plunging into pirate-
flesh, severing major vessels. But too large and it won't pack
into the barrels. He decides to aim for a mean diameter of
half an inch, and mauls the plates accordingly, sweeping
chunks that are the right size off into small canvas bags, rak-
ing bigger ones toward him for more punishment. It is satis-
fying, and after a while he finds himself singing an old song:
the same one he sang with Oldenburg in Broad Arrow Tower.
He keeps time with his hammer, and draws out those notes
that make the cargo-hold resonate. All round him, water
seeps through the cracks between *Minerva*'s hull-planks (for
he is well below the water-line) and trickles down merrily
into the bilge, and the four-man pumps take it away with a
steady suck-and-hiss that's like the systole and diastole of a
beating heart.

Gresham's College, Bishopsgate, London
1672

> The Inquisitive Jesuit RICCIOLI has taken great
> pains by 77 Arguments to overthrow the Coper-
> nican Hypothesis. . . . I believe this one Discov-
> ery will answer them, and 77 more, if so many
> can be thought of and produced against it.
> —ROBERT HOOKE

DANIEL SPENT A GOOD PART of two months on the roof of
Gresham's College, working on a hole—making, not mending, one. Hooke could not do it because his vertigo had been
acting up, and if it struck while he was on top of the College,
he would plunge to the ground like a wormy apple from a
tree, his Last Experiment a study into the mysterious power
of Gravitation.

For a man who claimed to hate the appearance of sharp
things when viewed under a microscope, Hooke spent a
great deal of time honing jabs at Inquisitive Jesuits. While
Daniel was up on the roof making the hole, and a rain-hatch
to cover it, Hooke was safe at ground level, running up and
down a gallery. Strapped into his groin was a narrow hard
saddle, and projecting from the saddle a strut with a wheel
on the end, geared to a clock-work dial: a pedometer of his
own design, which enabled him to calculate how much distance he had covered going *nowhere*. The purpose—as he

explained to Daniel and diverse other aghast Fellows of the
R.S.—was not to get from point A to point B, but to sweat.
In some way, sweating would purge his body of whatever
caused his headaches, nausea, and vertigo. From time to
time, he would stop and refresh himself by drinking a glass
of elemental mercury. He had set up a table at one end of the
gallery where he stockpiled that and several of Mons.
LeFebure's fashionable medicines. There were various sorts
of quills, too. Some of them he used to tickle the back of his
throat and induce vomiting, others he sharpened, dipped in
ink, and used to note down data from his pedometer, or to
vent his spleen at Jesuits who refused to admit that the Earth
revolved around the Sun, or to sketch out plans for Bedlam,
or to write diatribes against Oldenburg, or simply to transact
the routine business of the City Surveyor.

The Inquisitive Jesuit Riccioli had pointed out that *if* the
heavens were sown with stars, some near and some far, and
if the Earth were looping round the Sun in a vast ellipse,
then the positions of those stars with respect to one another
should shift during the course of the year, as trees in a forest
changed their relative positions in the eyes of a traveler
moving past. But no such parallax had been observed, which
proved (to Riccioli, anyway) that the Earth must be fixed in
the center of the Universe. To Hooke it only proved that
good enough telescopes hadn't been built, nor precise
enough measurements made. To obtain the level of magnification he needed, he had to construct a telescope 32 feet
long. To annull the light-bending effects of the Earth's atmosphere (which were obvious from the fact that the Sun became an oval when it rose or set), he had to aim it straight
up—hence the demand for a vertical shaft to be bored
through Gresham's College. Gresham's antique mansion
was now like an ancient plaster wall that had been mended
so many times it consisted entirely of interlocked patches. It
was solid scar tissue. This made the work more interesting
for Daniel, and taught him more than he'd ever cared to

know about how buildings were put up, and what kept them from falling down.

The goal was to gaze straight *up* into Heaven, and count the miles to the nearest stars. But as Daniel did most of the work during the daytime, he spent most of his idle moments looking *down* into London—six years since the Fire now—but its reconstruction really just getting underway.

Formerly Gresham's College had huddled among buildings of about the same height, but the Fire had burnt almost to its front door, and so now it loomed like a manor house over a devastated fiefdom. If Daniel stood on the ridge of the roof, facing south toward London Bridge half a mile away, everything in his field of view bore marks of heat and smoke. Suppose the city were a giant Hooke-watch, with Gresham's College the central axle-tree, and London Bridge marking twelve o'clock. Then Bedlam was directly behind Daniel at six o'clock. The Tower of London was at about ten o'clock. The easterly wind, and its glacis, had preserved it from the flames. The wedge from the Tower to the Bridge was a tangle of old streets with charred spikes of old church-steeples jutting up here and there, like surveyor's stakes—literally. This to the chagrin of Hooke, who'd presented the City with a plan to rationalize the streets, only to be frustrated by a few such impediments that had survived the flames; for those who opposed his plans used the carbonized steeples as landmarks to shew where streets had once been, and ought to be remade, be they never so narrow and tortuous. The negative space between construction-sites defined new streets now, only a little wider and straighter than the old. Right in the center of this wedge was the place where the Fire had started—an empty moon-crater cordoned off so that Hooke and Wren could build a monument there.

Directly before Daniel, in the wedge from about noon to one o'clock, was the old goldsmiths' district of Threadneedle and Cornhill streets, which converged at the site of the Royal Exchange—all so close that Daniel could hear the eternal flame of buying and selling in the courtyard of the 'Change, fueled by the latest data from abroad, and he could look into the windows of Thomas Ham's house and see Mayflower (like a matron) plumping pillows and (like a schoolgirl) playing leapfrog with William Ham, her youngest child, her dear heart.

The west-bound street formed by the confluence of Threadneedle and Cornhill became Cheapside, which Hooke had insisted on making much wider than it had been before—eliciting screams of agony and near-apocalyptic rantings from many—attacks that Hooke, who cared less than anyone what people thought of him, was uniquely qualified to ignore. It ran straight as Hooke could make it to the once and future St. Paul's, now a moraine of blackened stones, congealed roofing-lead, and plague-victims' jumbled bones. Wren was still working on plans and models for the new one. The streets limning St. Paul's Churchyard were lined with printers' shops, including the ones that produced most Royal Society publications, so the trip up and down Cheapside had become familiar to Daniel, as he went there to fetch copies of Hooke's *Micrographia* or inspect the proofs for Wilkins's *Universal Character*.

Raising his sights a notch and gazing over the scab of St. Paul's (which stood at about two o'clock), he could see Bridewell on the far side of it—a former Royal palace, now tumbledown, where whores, actresses, and Vagabond-wenches picked oakum, pounded hemp, and carried out diverse other character-building chores, until they had become reformed. That marked the place where the Fleet River—which was simply a ditch full of shit—intersected the Thames. Which explained why the Royals had moved out of Bridewell and ceded it to the poor. The fire had jumped the ditch easily, and kept eating through the city until a shortage of fuel, and the King's and Lord Mayor's heroic house-bombing campaign, had finally drawn a lasso around it. So whenever he did this Daniel inevitably had to trace the dividing-line between burnt and unburnt parts of the city from the River up across Fleet Street as far as Holborn (three o'clock). Out back of the place where his father had been blown up six years ago, a quadrangle had been laid out, lined with houses and shops, and filled with gardens, fountains, and statues. Others just like it were going up all around, and starting to crowd in around the edges of those few great Houses along Piccadilly, such as Comstock House. But those developments, and the great successes they had brought to Sterling and Raleigh, were old news to Daniel, and didn't command his attention as much as certain strange new undertakings around the edges of the city.

If he turned and looked north over the bones of the old Roman wall he could look right into Bedlam less than a quarter of a mile away. It had not been burnt, but the city had hired Hooke to tear it down and rebuild it anyway, as long as they were rebuilding everything else. The joke being that London and Bedlam seemed to have exchanged places: for Bedlam had been emptied out and torn down in preparation for its reconstruction, and was a serene rock-garden now, whereas all of London (save a few special plots such as the Monument site and St. Paul's) was in the throes of building—stones and bricks and timbers moving through the city on streets so congested that watching them fill up in the morning was like watching sausage casings being stuffed with meat. Wrecked buildings being torn down, cellars being dug, mortar being mixed, paving-stones being flung off carts, bricks and stones being chiselled to fit, iron wheel-rims grinding over cobbles—all of it made noise that merged together into a mad grind, like a Titan chewing up a butte.

So: strange enough. But beyond Bedlam, to the north and northeast, and sweeping round beyond the Tower along the eastern skirts of the city, were several artillery-grounds and army camps. These had been busy of late, because of the Anglo-Dutch War. *Not* the same Anglo-Dutch war that Isaac had listened to from his orchard in Woolsthorpe six years ago, for that had concluded in 1667. This was a wholly new

and different Anglo-Dutch War, the third in as many decades. This time around, though, the English had finally gotten it right: they were allied with the French. Ignoring all
considerations of what was really in the best interests of England, and setting aside all questions of moral rightness (and
the current King was rarely troubled and little hindered by
either), this seemed like a much better plan than fighting
against France. Plenty of French gold had entered the country to bring Parliament around to Louis XIV's side, and to
pay for a lot of ships to be built. France had an immense
army and needed little help from England on land; what
Louis had bought, and paid for several times over, was the
Royal Navy, and its guns, and its gunpowder.

It was difficult, therefore, for Daniel to make any sense of
the project underway northeast of London. Over several
weeks Daniel watched a flat parade-ground develop pits and
wrinkles, which slowly grew to ditches and mounds, and
shaped and resolved themselves (as if he were adjusting the
focus of a prospective glass) into sharp neat earthworks.
Daniel had never seen such things because, until now, they
had not been built in England, but from books and siege-
paintings he knew them as ramparts, a bastion, ravelins, and
a demilune work. But if this were a preparation for Dutch invasion, it was poorly thought out, because these works stood
in isolation, protecting nothing save a pasture with a few
dozen befuddled, but extremely well-defended, cows. Nevertheless, guns were mustered out from the Ordnance store-
houses in the Tower, and hauled up onto the ramparts by
teams of straining oxen—hernias with legs. The cracks of
the teamsters' whips and the snorts and bellows of the beasts
were carried for miles on a sea breeze all the way across
Houndsditch and over the Wall and up the pitched roof of
Gresham's College into Daniel's ears. Daniel for his part
only stared in amaze.

Nearer the river, in the flat country beyond the Tower,
Naval works took over from Military ones: shipyards messy
with blond timber from Scotland or Massachusetts, splat-

tered planks drawing themselves up into the curved hulls of ships, dead firs resurrected as masts. Colossal plumes of black smoke spreading downwind, pointing to Comstock-forges where tons of iron were being melted down and poured into subterranean cannon-molds, and windmill-blades rolling on the horizon, turning the gear-trains of mighty Comstock-machines that bored holes down the centers of those cannons.

Which brought Daniel's gaze back to the Tower, where he'd started: the central mystery, where treasure-ships from (as everyone in London now knew) France brought in the gold to be minted into the guineas that paid for all of those ships and cannons, and for the services of England in its new role as a sort of naval auxiliary to France.

ONE DAY, HEARING CHURCH-BELLS RING two o'clock, Daniel descended the ladder through the telescope-shaft. Hooke had gone out to inspect some new pavement, leaving behind nothing but a faint metallic scent of vomit. Daniel walked directly across the street, dodging uncouth traffic of heavy carts. He climbed into Samuel Pepys's carriage and made himself comfortable. Several minutes passed. Daniel looked at passers-by out the window. A hundred yards south, the streets would be a-bustle with brokers of East India stocks and goldsmiths' notes, but this place, tucked up against London wall, was a queer eddy, or backwater, and Daniel observed a jumble of Navy men, Dissident preachers, Royal Society hangers-on, foreigners, and Vagabonds, stirring and shuffling about one another in no steady pattern. It was an inscrutable Gordian knot suddenly cleft by one Chase Scene: a scruffy barefoot boy came bolting up Broad Street, pursued by a bailiff with a cudgel. Glimpsing a side street that ran off to the left, between the Navy Treasury and the Dutch Church, the boy skidded round the corner—paused—considered matters—and freed himself of a burden by heaving a pale brick into the air. It sheared apart, the wind caught it, and it puffed into a cloud of fluttering rectangles, whirling mysteriously round their long axes. By the time Daniel or anyone else thought to look for him, the boy was gone. The bailiff shifted to a straddling gait, as if riding an invisible pony, and began trying to step on all of the libels at once, gathering them in his arms, stuffing them into his pockets. Several members of the Watch stormed up and exchanged monosyllabic gasping noises with the bailiff. They all turned and glared at the façade of the Dutch Church, then went back to rounding up handbills.

Samuel Pepys was preceded by his cologne and his wig, and pursued by a minion embracing a sheaf of giant rolled documents. "I thought it well played, on the boy's part," he said, climbing into the coach and handing Daniel one of the libels.

"An old trick of the trade," Daniel said.

Pepys looked delighted. "Drake put *you* out on the streets?"

"Of course . . . 'twas the common rite of passage for all Waterhouse boys."

The handbill was a cartoon depicting King Louis XIV of France with his breeches piled up round his ankles and hairy buttocks thrust out, shitting an immense turd into the mouth of an English sailor.

"Let's take it to Wilkins! It'll cheer him up enormously," Pepys suggested, and pounded on the ceiling. The coachman drove the horses forward. Daniel made his body go limp so that he would not accrue lacerations from the continual battering onslaughts of the vehicle's benches and bulkheads.

"Did you bring it?"

"I always have it with me," Pepys said, producing an irregular nodule about the size of a tennis ball, "as you have all *your* parts."

"To remind you of your own mortality?"

"Once a man's been cut for the stone, 'tis hardly *necessary.*"

"Why, then?"

"It is my conversation-starter of last resort. It gets *anyone* talking: Germans, Puritans, Red Indians . . ." He handed the object to Daniel. It was heavy. Heavy as a stone.

"I cannot believe this came out of your bladder," Daniel said.

"You see? Never fails!" Pepys answered.

But Daniel got no further response from Pepys, who'd already unrolled one of the large documents, creating a screen that divided the carriage in half. Daniel had assumed that they were all diagrams of men-of-war. But when they turned west on Cheapside the sun came in the carriage window and shone through the paper, revealing a grid of numbers. Pepys muttered things to his assistant, who jotted them down. Daniel was left to rotate the bladder-stone in his hand and gaze out at London, so different when seen at street-level. Passing through St. Paul's Churchyard, they saw the whole contents of a printer's shop turned out into the street—several bailiffs, and one of Sir Roger L'Estrange's lieutenants, pawing through stacks of unbound sheets, and holding wood-blocks up to mirrors.

Within a few minutes, anyway, they were at Wilkins's house. Pepys left his assistant and his papers below in the carriage and pounded up stairs holding the bladder-stone in his hand like a questing knight brandishing a fragment of the Cross.

He shook it in Wilkins's face. Wilkins only laughed. But it was good that he did, because his room was otherwise a horror—his dark breeches couldn't conceal that he had been pissing blood, sometimes sooner than he could get to the chamber-pot. He was both wizened and bloated at the same time, if that were possible, and the smell that came out of his flesh seemed to suggest his kidneys weren't keeping up their end of the bargain.

While Pepys exhorted the Bishop of Chester to allow himself to be cut for the stone, Daniel looked about, and was dispirited but not surprised to see several empty bottles from the apothecary shop of Monsieur LeFebure. He gave one a sniff. It was *Elixir Proprietalis LeFebure*—the same stuff

Hooke swallowed when headaches had brought him to the brink of suicide—the fruits of LeFebure's researches into certain remarkable properties of the poppy family. It was hugely popular at Court, even among those not afflicted with headaches or the Stone. But when Daniel saw Wilkins go into a bladder spasm—reducing the Lord Bishop of Chester, and Founder of the Royal Society, to a dumb animal for several minutes, convulsing and howling—he decided perhaps Monsieur LeFebure was not such a sinister fellow after all.

When it was over, and Wilkins was Wilkins again, Daniel showed him the handbill, and mentioned L'Estrange's raid on the printing-shop.

"The same men doing the same things as ten years ago," Wilkins pronounced.

From that—*the same men*—Daniel knew that the originator of the handbills, and ultimate target of L'Estrange's raids, must be Knott Bolstrood.

"And that is why I cannot stop what I am doing to be cut for the Stone," Wilkins said.

DANIEL ERECTED A BLOCK AND TACKLE above the Gresham shaft, Hooke put the rebuilding of London on hold for a day, and they put the long telescope into place, Hooke cringing and screaming every time it was bumped, as if the instrument were an extension of his own eyeball.

Meanwhile Daniel could never keep his attention fixed on the heavens, for the warm mutterings and nudgings of London would not leave him alone—notes slipped under his door, raised eyebrows in coffee-shops, odd things witnessed in the street all captured his attention more than they should've. Outside the city, scaffolding rose up from the glacis of those mysterious fortifications, and long benches began to shingle it.

Then, one afternoon, Daniel and all London's Persons of Quality and most of her pickpockets were there, sitting on those benches or milling about in the fields. The Duke of Monmouth rode out, in a Cavalier outfit whose magnificence was such as to refute and demolish every sermon ever preached by a Calvinist—because if those sermons were true, Monmouth ought to be struck dead on the spot by a jealous God. John Churchill—possibly the only man in England handsomer than Monmouth—therefore wore slightly less thrilling clothes. The King of France could not attend this event, as he was so busy conquering the Dutch Republic just now, but a strapping actor pranced out in his stead, dressed in royal ermine, and took up a throne on an artificial hillock, and occupied himself with suitable bits of stage-business, viz. peering at events through a glass; pointing things out to diverse jewelled mistresses draped all about his vicinity; holding out his Sceptre to order his troops forward; descending from his throne to speak a few kind words to wounded officers who were brought up to him on litters; standing up and striking a grave defiant pose during moments of crisis, whilst holding out a steady hand to calm his jittery *femmes*. Likewise an actor had been hired to play the role of D'Artagnan. Since everyone knew what was about to happen to him, he got the most applause when he was introduced—to the visible chagrin of the (real) Duke of Monmouth. In any event: cannons were discharged picturesquely from the ramparts of "Maestricht," and "Dutchmen" struck defiant poses on the battlements, creating among the spectators a *frisson* of righteous anger (how dare those insolent Dutchmen defend themselves!?)—rapidly transmuted into patriotic fervor as, at a signal from "Louis XIV," Monmouth and Churchill led a charge up the slope of the demilune work. After a bit of thrilling swordplay and much spattering-about of stage-blood, they planted French and English flags side by side on the parapet, shook hands with "D'Artagnan," and exchanged all manner of fond and respectful gestures with the "King" on his hillock.

There was an ovation. Daniel could hear nothing else, but he *saw* some odd sort of pratfall directly in front of him: a young man in severe dark clothing, who'd been standing in front of Daniel and blocking his view with a sort of Pilgrim-hat, turned round and splayed his limbs out like a squashed bug, let his head loll back on his white collar, stuck his tongue out, and rolled his eyes back in their sockets. He was mocking the pose of several "Dutch" defenders who were now *hors de combat* up on the demilune. He did not make a very pretty picture. Something was grievously wrong with his face: a dermatological catastrophe about the cheeks.

Behind him, a scene-change was underway: the dead defenders were resurrecting themselves and scurrying round back of the ramparts to prepare for the next act. Likewise the man in front of Daniel now recovered his balance and turned out not to be a dead Dutchman at all, just a young English bloke with a sour look about him. His attire was not just *any* drab garb but the *specific* drab garb worn, nowadays, by Barkers. But (now that Daniel thought about it slightly harder) it was very like the clothing worn by the mock-Dutchmen pretending to defend Maestricht. Come to think of it, those "Dutchmen" had looked a great deal more like English religious Dissenters than they had like actual Dutchmen, who (if the grapevine was to be believed) had long ago ditched their old Pilgrimish togs (which had been inspired by Spanish fashions anyway) and now dressed like everyone else in Europe. So in *addition* to being a re-enactment of the Siege of Maestricht, this show was *also* a parable about well-dressed rakes and blades overcoming dull severe Calvinists in the streets of London town!

The slowness with which Daniel realized all this was infuriating to the young Barker in front of him—who had the cannonball head and mighty jawbone of an authentic Bolstrood.

"Is that Gomer?" Daniel exclaimed, when the ovation had died away into a thrum of thirsty squires calling for beer. Daniel had known the son of Knott Bolstrood as a little boy, but hadn't set eyes on him in at least a decade.

Gomer Bolstrood answered the question by staring Daniel full in the face. On the front of each of his cheeks, just to either side of his nose, was an old wound: a complex of red trenches and fleshy ramparts, curved round into the crude glyph "S.L." These marks had been made by a branding iron in the open-air court before the Sessions House at the Old Bailey, a few moments after Gomer had been pronounced guilty of being a Seditious Libeller.

Gomer Bolstrood could not be more than twenty-five years old, but that munition-like head, combined with those brands, gave him the presence of a much older man. He aimed his chin significantly towards a location off behind the stands.

Gomer Bolstrood, son of His Majesty's Secretary of State Knott, son of ur-Barker Gregory, led Daniel into a Vagabond-camp of tents and wagons set up to serve and support this gala re-enactment. Some of the tents were for the actors and actresses. Gomer led Daniel between a couple of those, which meant fighting their way against a flood tide of "French Mistresses" coming back from the "Sun King's" throne. Even as the sensitive eyes of Isaac Newton had been semi-permanently branded with the image of the solar disk during his colors experiments, so Daniel's retinas were now stamped with a dozen or more cleavages. All of those cleavages must have had heads up above them somewhere—but the only one he *noticed* was speaking to one of the other girls in a French accent. From which he reckoned (in retrospect, somewhat simple-mindedly) that she must be French. But before Daniel could drift off into a full reverie, Gomer Bolstrood had grabbed his upper arm and pulled him 'tween the flaps of an adjoining beer tent.

The beer was Dutch. So was the man sitting at the table. But the *waffle* that the man was eating was indisputably Belgian.

Daniel sat in the chair indicated, and watched the Dutch gentleman eat the waffle for a while. He aimed his eyes in that direction, anyway. The image that still persisted before his eyes was cleavages, and the face of that "French" lass. But after a while this, sadly, faded, and was replaced by a waffle that had been put in front of him on a Delft china plate. And none of your crude heavy Pilgrim-ware, but the good stuff, export-grade.

He sensed an implicit demand that he should Partake. So he dissected a corner from the waffle, put it in his mouth, and began to chew it. It was good. His eyes were adjusting to the dimness of the tent, and he was noticing stacks of handbills piled up in the corners, neatly wrapped up in old proof-sheets. The words on the proof-sheets were in every language save English—these bills had been printed in Amsterdam and brought over on a beer-ship or perhaps a waffle-barge. Every so often the tent-flaps would part, and Gomer, or one of the taciturn, pipe-smoking Dutchmen in the corners, would peer out and thrust a brick of hand-bills through the gap.

"Whaat doo Belgian waffles and the cleavages of those girls haave in common?" said the Dutch Ambassador; for it was none other. He dabbed butter from his lips with a napkin. He was blond, and pyramidal, as if he consumed a lot of beer and waffles. "I saaw you staaring at them," he added, apologetically.

"I haven't the *merest* idea—sir!"

"Negateev Spaace," the Dutch Ambassador intoned, letting those double vowels resonate as only a heavyweight Dutchman could. "Have you heard of thees? It is an *aart woord*. Wee know about *negateev spaace* because we like *peectures soo muuch*."

"Is it anything like negative numbers?"

"Eet ees the spaace between twoo theengs," said the other, and put his hands on his chest and forced his pectorals together to create a poor impression of cleavage. Daniel watched with polite incredulity, and tried not to shudder. The Dutchman plucked a fresh waffle off a plate and held it up by one corner, like a rag soaked with something unpleasant. "Likewise—the waffle of Belgium is shaaped and defiined, not by its own essential naatuure, but by the hot plaates of haard iron that encloose it on toop and boottom."

"Oh, I see—you're making a point about the Spanish Netherlands!"

The Dutch Ambassador rolled his eyes and tossed the waffle back over his shoulder—before it struck the ground, a stout, disconcertingly monkey-like dog sprang into the air and snatched it, and began to masticate it—*literally*—for the sound it made was like a homunculus squatting on the floor muttering, "masticate masticate masticate."

"Traaped between Fraance and the Dutch Republic, the Spanish Netherlands is raapidly consuumed by Louis the Quatorze Bourbon. Fine. But when *Le Roi du Soleil* reaches Maestricht he touches—whaat?"

"The political and military equivalent of a hot iron plate?"

The Dutch Ambassador probed negative space with a licked finger, seemed to touch something, and drew back sharply, making a sizzling noise through his teeth. Perhaps by Dutch luck, perhaps by some exquisite sense of timing, Daniel felt the atmosphere socking him in the gut. The tent clenched inwards, then inflated. Waffle-irons chattered and buzzed in the dimness, like skeletons' teeth. The monkey-dog scurried under the table.

Gomer Bolstrood pulled back a tent-flap to provide a clear view to the top of the demilune-work, which had been ruptured by detonation of a vast internal store of gunpowder. It looked like a steaming loaf that had been ripped in half. Resurgent Dutchmen were prancing around on the top, trampling and burning those French and English flags. The spectators were on the brink of riot.

Gomer let the tent-flap fall shut again, and Daniel turned his attention back to the ambassador, who had never taken his gaze off of Daniel.

"Maybe Fraance taakes Maestricht—but not so easily—they lose the hero D'Artagnan. The war will be won by us, however."

"I am pleased to know that you will have success in Holland—now will you consider changing your tactics in London?" Daniel said this loudly so that Gomer could share in it.

"In whaat waay?"

"You know what L'Estrange has been doing."

"I know what L'Estrange has been *failing* to do!" the Dutch Ambassador chortled.

"Wilkins is trying to make London like Amsterdam—and I'm not speaking of wooden shoes."

"Many churches—no established religion."

"It is his life's work. He has given up on Natural Philosophy, these last years, to direct all of his energies toward that goal. He wants it because it is best for England—but the High Anglicans and Crypto-Catholics at Court are against anything that smacks of Dissidents. So Wilkins's task is difficult enough—but when those same Dissidents are linked, in the public mind, with the Dutch enemy, how can he hope for success?"

"In a year—when the dead are counted, and the true costs of the war are understood—Wilkins's task will be too easy."

"In a year Wilkins will be dead of the stone. Unless he has it cut out."

"I can recommend a chirurgeon-barber, very speedy with the knife—"

"He does not feel that he can devote several months to recovery, when the pressure is so immediate and the stakes so high. He is just on the verge of success, Mr. Ambassador, and if you would let up—"

"We will let up when the French do," the Ambassador said, and waved at Gomer, who pulled the flap open again to show the demilune being re-conquered by French and English troops, led by Monmouth. To one side, "D'Artagnan" lay wounded in a gap in the wall. John Churchill was supporting the old musketeer's head in his lap, feeding him sips from a flask.

The tent-flap remained open for rather a long time, and Daniel eventually understood that he was being shown the door. As he walked out he caught Gomer's elbow and drew him outside onto the dirt street. "Brother Gomer," he said, "the Dutch are deranged. Understandably. But *our* situation is not so desperate."

"On the contrary," said Gomer, "I say that *you* are in desperate peril, Brother Daniel."

Anyone else would have meant *physical* peril by that, but Daniel had spent enough of his life around Gomer's—which was to say, Daniel's—ilk to know that Gomer meant the spiritual kind.

"I don't suppose that's just because I was staring at a pretty girl's bosom just now—?"

Gomer did not much fancy the jest. Indeed, Daniel sensed before those words were out of his mouth that they would only confirm Gomer's opinion of him as Fallen, or at best, Falling fast. He tried something else: "Your own father is Secretary of State!"

"Then go and speak to my father."

"The point I am making is that there is no harm—or *peril,* if that is what you want to call it—in employing *tactics.* Cromwell used tactics to win battles, did he not? It did not mean he lacked faith. On the contrary—*not* to use the brains God gave you, and making every struggle into a frontal charge, is sinful—thou shalt not tempt the Lord thy God!"

"Wilkins has the stone," Gomer said. "Whether 'twas placed in his bladder by God, or the Devil, is a question for Jesuits. Anyway, he has it, and shall likely die of it, unless you and your Fellows can gin up a way to transmute it into some watery form that can be pissed out. In dread of his death, you have wrought in your mind this phant'sy that if I, Gomer Bolstrood, leave off distributing handbills in the streets of London, it shall set in motion a lengthy chain of consequences that shall somehow end in Wilkins's suffering some chirurgeon to cut him for the stone, him surviving the operation, and living happily ever after, as the kind father you never had. And *you* say that the *Dutch* are deranged?"

Daniel could not answer. The discourse of Gomer had struck him in the face with no less heat, force, and dumbfounding pain than the branding iron had Gomer's.

"As you phant'sy yourself a master of *tactics,* consider this whorish spectacle we have been witnessing." Gomer waved at the demilune-work. Up on the parapet, Monmouth was planting the French and English flags anew, to the cheers of the spectators, who broke into a lusty chorus of "Pikes on the

Dikes" even as "D'Artagnan" breathed his last. John Churchill carried him down the slope of the earthwork in his arms and laid him on a litter where his body was bedecked with flowers.

"Behold the martyr!" Gomer brayed. "Who gave his life for the cause, and is fondly remembered by all the Quality! Now *there* is a tactic for you. I am sorry Wilkins is sick. I would not put him in harm's way on any account, for he was a friend to us. But it is not in my power to keep Death from his door. And when Death does come, 'twill make of him a Martyr—not so romantick as D'Artagnan perhaps—but of more effect in a better cause. Beg your pardon, Brother Daniel." Gomer stalked away, tearing open the wrapper on a sheaf of libels.

"D'Artagnan" was being carried along the front of the bleachers in a cortege of gorgeously mussed and tousled Cavaliers, and spectators were doing business with roving flower-girls and showering bouquets and blossoms on those heroes living and "dead." But even as petals were fluttering down on the mock-Musketeer, Daniel Waterhouse found slips of paper coming down all around him, carried on a breeze from the bleachers. He slapped one out of the air and was greeted with a cartoon of several French cavaliers gang-raping a Dutch milkmaid. Another showed a cravated musketeer, silhouetted in the light of a burning Protestant church, about to catch a tossed baby on the point of his sword. All around Daniel, and up in the stands, spectators were passing these bills hand-to-hand, sometimes wadding them into sleeves or pockets.

So the matter was complicated. And it only become more so ten minutes later, when, during a bombardment of "Maestricht," a cannon burst in full view of all spectators. Most people assumed it was just a stage-trick until bloody fragments of artillerymen began to shower down all among them, mingling with the continual flurry of handbills.

Daniel walked back to Gresham's College and worked all night with Hooke. Hooke stayed below, gazing up at various stars, and Daniel remained on the roof, looking at a nova that was flaring in the west end of London: a Mobb of people with torches, milling around St. James's Fields and discharging the occasional musket. Later, he learned that they had attacked Comstock House, supposedly because they were furious about the cannon that had burst.

John Comstock himself showed up at Gresham's College the next morning. It took several moments for Daniel to recognize him, so altered was his countenance by shock, by outrage, and even by shame. He demanded that Hooke and the rest drop what they were doing and investigate the remnants of the burst cannon, which he insisted had been tampered with in some way "by mine enemies."

༄

College of the Holy and Undivided Trinity, Cambridge

1672

༈

There are few things, that are incapable of being represented by a fiction.

—HOBBES, *Leviathan*

Once More into the Breeches
A COMEDY

DRAMATIS PERSONAE

MEN: MR. VAN UNDERDEVATER, a *Dutchman*, founder of a great commercial empire in *sow's-ears* and *potatoes'-eyes*

NZINGA, a cannibal Neeger, formerly King of the Congo, now house-slave to Mr. van Underdevater

JEHOSHAPHAT STOPCOCK, the Earl of BRIMSTONE, an *enthusiast*

TOM RUNAGATE, a discharged soldier turned *Vagabond*

THE REV. YAHWEH PUCKER, a Dissident divine

EUGENE STOPCOCK, son of Lord Brimstone, a Captain of Foot

FRANCIS BUGGERMY, Earl of Suckmire, a *foppish courtier*

DODGE AND BOLT, two of Tom Runagate's accomplices

WOMEN: MISS LYDIA VAN UNDERDEVATER, the daughter and sole heiress of Mr. van Underdevater, recently returned from a *Venetian* finishing-school

LADY BRIMSTONE, wife to Jehoshaphat Stopcock

MISS STRADDLE, Tom Runagate's *companion*

SCENE: SUCKMIRE, a rural estate in Kent

ACT I. SCENE I.

SCENE: a Cabin in a Ship at Sea. Thunder heard, flashes of Lightning seen.

Enter Mr. van Underdevater in dressing-gown, with a lanthorn.

VAN UND: Boatswain!

       Enter Nzinga wet, with a Sack.

NZINGA: Here, master, what—

VAN UND: Odd's bodkins! Have you fallen into the tar-pot, boatswain?

NZINGA: It is I, Master—your slave, My Royal Majesty, by the Grace of the tree-god, the rock-god, river-god, and diverse other gods who have slipped my mem'ry, of the Congo, King.

VAN UND: So it is. What have you in the bag?

NZINGA: Balls.

VAN UND: Balls! Sink me! You have quite forgot your Civilizing Lessons!

NZINGA: Of ice.

VAN UND: Thank heavens.

NZINGA: I gathered 'em from the deck—where they are falling like grape-shot—and for this you thank heaven?

VAN UND: Aye, for it means the boatswain is still in possession of all his Parts. Boatswain!

Enter LYDIA in dressing-gown, dishevelled.

LYDIA: Dear father, why do you shout for the boatswain so?

VAN UND: My dear Lydia, I would fain pay him to bring this infernal storm to an end.

LYDIA: But father, the boatswain can't stop a tempest!

VAN UND: Perhaps he knows someone who can.

NZINGA: I know a weather-god in Guinea who can— and at rates very reasonable, as he will accept payment in rum.

VAN UND: Rum! You take me for a half-wit? If this is what the weather-god does when he is *sober*—

NZINGA: Cowrie-shells would do in a pinch. If master would care to despatch My Majesty on the next *southbound* boat, My Majesty would be pleased to broker the transaction—

VAN UND: You prove yourself a shrewd man of commerce. I am reminded of when I traded the holes in a million cannibals' ears, for the eyes of a million potatoes, and beat the market at both ends of the deal—

More thunder.

VAN UND: Too, slow, too slow! Boatswain!

Enter Lord Brimstone.

LORD BRIMSTONE: Here, here, what is this bawling?

LYDIA: Lord Brimstone—your servant.

VAN UND: The price of ending this tempest is too high, the market in Pagan Deities too remote—

LORD B: Then why, sir, do you call for the boatswain?

VAN UND: Why, sir, to tell him to be of good courage and to remain firm in the face of danger.

LYDIA: Oh, too late, father!

VAN UND: What mean you, child?

LYDIA: When the boatswain heard you, he lost what firmness he had, and fled in a panic.

VAN UND: How do you know it?

LYDIA: Why, he upset the hammock altogether, and tumbled me onto the deck!

VAN UND: Lydia, Lydia, I have spent a fortune sending you to that school in Venice, where you have been studying to become a virtuous maiden—

LYDIA: And I have studied hard, Father, but it is ever so difficult!

VAN UND: Has all that money been wasted?

LYDIA: Oh, no, Father, I learned some lovely songs from our dancing-master, Signore Fellatio.

*Sings.**

VAN UND: I've heard enough—Boatswain!

Enter Lady Brimstone.

LADY BRIMSTONE: My lord, have you found who is making that dreadful *noise* yet?

LORD B: M'lady, it's that *Dutchman.*

LADY B: So much for idle *investigations*—what have you *done* about it, my lord?

LORD B: Nothing, my lady, for they say that the only way to quiet one of these obstreperous Dutchmen is to drown him.

LADY B: Drown—why, my lord—you're not thinking of throwing him overboard—?

---

*Here, a moiety of the audience—mostly Cambridge undergraduates—stood up (if they weren't standing to begin with) and applauded. Admittedly they would've come erect and shown their appreciation for almost any human female recognizable as such who appeared on the grounds of their College, but more so in this case since the role of Lydia was being played by Eleanor (Nell) Gwyn—the King's Mistress.

LORD B: Every soul aboard is *thinking* of it, M'lady. But
with a Dutchman it isn't necessary, as they live below
sea-level to begin with. 'Tis merely a question of getting the sea to go back where the Good Lord put it in
the first place—

LADY B: And how d'you propose to effect *that*, my lord?

LORD B: I have been conducting experiments on a
novel engine to make windmills turn backwards, and
pump water *down-hill*—

LADY B: Experiments! Engines! I say the way to put
Dutchmen under water's with French gunpowder
and English courage!

Whatever the actor playing Lord Brimstone said was like
expectorating into the River Amazon. For the true SCENE of
these events was Neville's Court* on a spring evening, and the
true Dramatis Personae a roll that would've consumed many
yards of paper and drams of ink to set it out fully. The script
was an unpublished masterwork of courtly and collegiate intrigue, comprising hundreds of more or less clever lines being
delivered—mostly *sotto voce*—at the same instant, producing
a contrapuntal effect quite intricate but entirely too much for
young Daniel Waterhouse to grasp. He had been wondering
why persons such as these bothered to go to plays at all, when
every day at Whitehall provided more spectacle—now he
sensed that they did so because the stories in the theatre were
simple, and arrived at fixed conclusions after an hour or two.

Heading up the cast of tonight's performance was King
Charles II of England, situated on the upper floor of Trinity's miserable wreck of a library, where several consecutive
windows had been opened up and converted into temporary
opera-boxes. The Queen, one Catherine of Braganza, a Portuguese princess with a famously inoperative womb, was
seated to one side of His Majesty, pretending to understand
English as usual. The guest of honor, the Duke of Mon-

---

*A grassy quadrangle surrounded by buildings of Trinity College.

mouth (King Charles's son by his mistress Lucy Walter), was on the other side. The windows flanking the King's contained various elements of his court: one was anchored by Louise de Kéroualle, the Duchess of Portsmouth and the King's mistress. Another by Barbara Villiers, a.k.a. Lady Castlemaine, a.k.a. the Duchess of Cleveland, former lover of John Churchill, and the King's mistress.

Moving outwards from the three central windows, there was one all filled up with Angleseys: Thomas More Anglesey and his nearly indistinguishable sons, Philip, now something like twenty-seven years old, and Louis, who was twenty-four, but looking younger. For protocol dictated that, as the Earl of Upnor was visiting his *alma mater*, he had to wear academic robes. Though he'd mobilized a squadron of French tailors to liven them up, they were still academic robes, and the object infesting his wig was unmistakably a mortarboard.

Balancing this Anglesey-window was a window all crowded with Comstocks, specifically the so-called Silver branch of that race: John and his sons Richard and Charles foremost, all dressed likewise in robes and mortarboards. Unlike the Earl of Upnor they seemed comfortable dressed that way. Or at least *had* until the play had begun, and the character of Jehoshaphat Stopcock, Lord Brimstone, had come tottering out dressed precisely as they were.

The King's Comedians, performing on a temporary stage that had been erected in Neville's Court, had decided to plow onwards in spite of the fact that no one could hear a word they were saying. "Lord Brimstone" seemed to be upbraiding his wife about something—presumably, her reference to "French gunpowder," as opposed to "English," which, on some other planet, might have been a rhetorical figure, but here seemed very much like a stab at John Comstock. Meanwhile, most of the audience—who, if they had the good fortune to be seated, were seated on chairs and benches arranged in the corner of Neville's Court, beneath the windows of King and Court—were trying to break out into the opening stanza of "Pikes on the Dikes," the most widely plagiarized song in England: a rousing ditty about why it was an excellent idea to invade Holland. But the King held out one hand to silence them. Not that he was lacking in belligerence—but down on the stage, "Lydia van Underdevater" was delivering a line that looked like it was meant to be funny. And the King didn't like it when the buzz of Intrigue drowned out his Mistress.

All of the Comedians suddenly fell down, albeit in dramatickal and actorly ways—and that went double for Nell Gwyn, who wound up draped over a bench with one arm stretched out gracefully, displaying about a square yard of flawless pale armpits and bosoms. The audience were poleaxed. The long-called-for boatswain finally ran in and announced that the ship had run aground in sands just off Castle Suckmire. "Lord Brimstone" sent Nzinga out to fetch his trunk, which arrived with the immediacy that can only happen in stageplays. The owner pawed through its contents, spilling out a strange mixture of drab out-moded clothing and peculiar equipment, viz. retorts, crucibles, skulls, and microscopes. Meanwhile Lydia was picking up certain of his garments, such as farmers' breeches and cowherds' boots, holding them at arm's length and mugging. Finally, Lord Brimstone stood up, tucking a powder-keg under one arm, and slapping a frayed and bent mortarboard onto his head.

LORD B: What's wanted to move this ship is Gunpowder!

Among the groundlings in their chairs and on the grass, much uneasy shifting and muttering, and tassels flopping this way and that, as mortarboard-wearing scholars turned to each other to enquire as to just who was being made fun of here, or shook their heads, or bowed them low to pray for the souls of the King's Comedians, and of whomever had written this play, and of the King who'd insisted he couldn't make it through a one-night stand at Cambridge without being entertained.

Very different reactions, though, from the windows-cum-opera-boxes: the Duchess of Portsmouth was undone. Her bosom was heaving like a spritsail gone all a-luff, her head was thrown back to expose a whole lot of jewelled throat. These spectacles had already caused diverse groundling scholars to fall out of their chairs. She was being supported by a pair of young blades in huge curled and beribboned wigs, who were wiping tears of mirth away from their eyes with the fingertips of their kid gloves—having already donated their lace hankies to the Duchess.

Meanwhile, mortarboard-wearing gunpowder magnate John Comstock—who'd long opposed the Duchess of Portsmouth's efforts to introduce French fashions to the English court—was managing a thin, oddly distracted smile. The King—who, until tonight anyway, had generally sided with Comstock—was smiling, and the Angleseys were all having the times of their lives.

An elbow to the kidney forced Daniel to stop gaping at the Duchess's efforts to rupture her bodice, and to pay some attention to the rather homelier sight of Oldenburg, who was seated next to him. The hefty German had been released from the Tower as suddenly and as inexplicably as he'd been clapped into it. He glanced down toward the far end of Neville's Court, then frowned at Daniel and said, "Where *is* he? Or at least *it!*" meaning Isaac Newton and his paper on tangents, respectively. Then Oldenburg turned the other way and peeked up round the edge of his mortarboard toward the Angleseys' box, where Louis Anglesey, the Earl of Upnor, had somehow gotten his merriment under control and was giving Oldenburg a Significant Glare.

Daniel was glad to have a pretext for leaving. All through the play he had been trying and trying to suspend his disbelief, but the damned thing just wouldn't suspend. He rose to his feet, bunched his robes up, and sidestepped down a row of chairs, treading on diverse Royal Society feet. Sir Winston Churchill: *Cheers on your boy's Maestricht work, old chap.* Christopher Wren: *Let's get that cathedral up, what, no dilly-dallying!* Sir Robert Moray: *Let's have lunch and talk about eels.* Thank God Hooke had had the temerity to

not show up—too busy rebuilding London—so Daniel
didn't have to step on any of *his* parts. Finally, Daniel was
out on open grass. This was really a job for John Wilkins—
but the Bishop of Chester was lying on his bed down in London, ill of the stone.

Working his way round back of the stage, Daniel found
himself among several wagons that had been used to haul
dramaturgickal mysteries up from London. Awnings had
been rigged to them and tents pitched in between, so tent-
ropes were stretched across the darkness, thick as ship's rigging, and hitched round splintery wooden stakes piercing the
(until the actors had shown up, anyway) flawless lawn. Various items of what he could only assume were ladies' under-
garments (they were definitely *garments*, but he had never
seen their like—Q.E.D.) dangled from the ropes and occasionally surprised the hell out of him by pawing clammily at
his face. Daniel had to plot a devious course, then pursue it
slowly, to escape the tangle. So it was really—*really*—just an
accident that he found the two actresses, doing whatever the
hell it was that females do when they excuse themselves and
exchange warm knowing looks and go off in pairs. He caught
the very end of it: "What should I do w'th'old one?" said a
young lady with a lovely voice, and an accent from some part
of England with too many sheep.

"Fling it into the crowd—start a riot," suggested the
other—an Irish girl.

This touched off fiendish whooping. Clearly no one had
taught these girls how to titter.

"But they wouldn't even know what it was," said the girl
with the lovely voice, "we are the first women to set *foot* in
this place."

"Then neither will they know if you leave it where it lies,"
the Irish girl answered.

The other now dropped her rural accent and began talking
exactly like a Cambridge scholar from a good family. "I say,
what's this in the middle of my bowling-green? It would appear to be . . . fox-bait!"

More whooping—cut short by a man's voice out of a backstage caravan: "Tess—save some of that for the King— you're wanted on the stage."

The lasses picked up their skirts and exeunted. Daniel glimpsed them as they transited across a gap between tents, and recognized the one called Tess from the "Siege of Maestricht." She was the one he had taken for a French-woman, simply because he'd heard her talking that way. He now understood that she was really an Englishwoman who could talk any way she pleased. This might have been obvi-ous, since she was a professional actress; but it was new to him, and it made her interesting.

Daniel emerged from behind the tent where he'd been (it is fair to say) lurking, and—purely in a spirit of philosophi-cal inquiry—approached the spot where Tess of the beauti-ful voice and many accents had been (fair to say) squatting.

In a sort of hod projecting above the stage, more gunpow-der was lit off in an attempt to simulate lightning, and it made a pool of yellow light in front of Daniel for just a moment. Neatly centered in a patch of grass—grass that was almost phosphorus-green, this being Spring—was a wadded-up rag, steaming from the warmth of Tess, bright with blood.

> Of sooty coal the Empiric Alchimist
> Can turn, or holds it possible to turn
> Metals of drossiest Ore to perfet Gold
> As from the Mine.
>
> —MILTON, *Paradise Lost*

IT HAD BEEN A FULL DAY for the King. Or perhaps Daniel was being naïve to think so—more likely, it was a typical day for the King, and the only persons feeling exhausted were the Cantabrigians who had been trying to maintain the pretense that they could keep up with him. The entourage had appeared on the southern horizon in mid-morning, looking (Daniel sup-posed) quite a bit like the invasion that Louis XIV had recently flung into the Dutch Republic: meaning that it thundered and threw up dust-clouds and consumed oats and generated ramparts of manure like any Regiment, but its wagons were all gilded, its warriors were armed with jewelled Italian rapiers, its field-marshalls wore skirts and commanded men, or condemned them, with looks—this fell upon Cambridge, anyway, with more effect than King Louis had achieved, so far, in the Netherlands. The town was undone, dissolved. Bosoms everywhere, bare-assed courtiers spilling out of windows, the good Cambridge smell of fens and grass overcome by perfumes, not just of Paris but of Araby and Rajasthan. The King had abandoned his coach and marched through the streets of the town accepting the cheers of the scholars of Cambridge, who had formed up in front of their several Colleges, robed and arranged by ranks and degrees, like soldiers drawn up for review. He'd been officially greeted by the outgoing Chancellor, who had presented him with a colossal Bible—they said it was possible to see the royal nose wrinkling, and the eyes rolling, from half a mile away. Later the King (and his pack of demented spaniels) had dined at High Table in the College of the Holy and Undivided Trinity, under the big Holbein portrait of the college's Founder, King Henry VIII. As Fellows, Daniel and Isaac were accustomed to sitting at High Table, but the town was now stuffed with persons who ranked them, and so they'd been demoted halfway across the room: Isaac in his scarlet robes talking to Boyle and Locke about something, and Daniel shoved off in a corner with several vicars who—in violation of certain Biblical guidelines—plainly did not love one another. Daniel tried to stanch their disputatious drone and to pick up a few snatches of conversation from the High Table. The King had a lot to say about Henry VIII, all of it apparently rather droll.

At first, it was Old Hank's approach to polygamy: so ham-handed it was funny. All of it was veiled in royal wit, of course—he didn't come right out and say anything really, but the point seemed to be: why do people call me a libertine? At least I don't chop their heads off. If Daniel (or any other scholar in this place) had wanted to die instantly, he could have stood up at this point and hollered, "Well, at least *he* eventually got round to producing a legitimate male heir!" but this did not occur.

Several goblets later, the King moved on to some reflections on what a fine and magnificent and (not to put too fine a point on it) *rich* place Trinity College was, and how remarkable it was that such results could have been achieved by Henry VIII merely by defying the Pope, and sacking a few monasteries. So perhaps the coffers of Puritans, Quakers, Barkers, and Presbyterians might go, one day, towards building an even finer College! This was said as a jest, of course—he went on to say that of course he was speaking of *voluntary* contributions. Even so, it made the Dissenters in the room very angry—but (as Daniel later reflected) no more angry, really, than they'd been before. And it was a masterly bit of Catholic-bashing. In other words, all nicely calculated to warm the hearts and ease the fears of all the High Anglicans (such as John Comstock) in the hall. The King had to do a lot of that, because many assumed he was soft on Catholics, and some even thought he *was* one.

In other words, maybe he had just seen a little slice of Court politics as usual, and nothing of consequence had happened. But since John Wilkins had lost the ability to urinate, Daniel's job was to *pay attention* and report all of this to him later.

Then it was off to the chapel where the Duke of Monmouth, now a war hero as well as a renowned scholar and bastard, was installed as Chancellor of the University. After that, finally, the Comedy in Neville's Court.

DANIEL PAUSED IN THE CENTER of a Gothic arch and looked out over a spread of stone steps that led down into the Great Court of Trinity College: an area about four times the size of Neville's Court. In a strange way it reminded him of the 'Change in London, except that where the 'Change was a daytime place, all a-sparkle with Thomas Gresham's golden grasshoppers and vaulting Mercurys, and crowded with lusty shouting traders, *this* place was Gothickal in the extreme, faintly dusted with the blue light of a half-moon, sparsely populated by robed and/or big-wigged men skulking about the paths and huddling in doorways in groups of two or three. And whereas the 'Change-men made common cause to buy shares in sailing-ships or joint stock companies, and traded Jamaica sugar for Spanish silver, these men were transacting diverse small conspiracies or trading snatches of courtly data. The coming of Court to Cambridge was like Stourbridge Fair—an occasional opportunity for certain types of business, most of which was in some sense occult. He couldn't get in any trouble simply walking direct across the Great Court to the Gate. As a Fellow, he was allowed to tread on the grass. Most of these lurkers and strollers weren't. Not that they cared about the College's pedantic rules, but they preferred shadowy edges, having the courtier's natural affinity for joints and crevices. Across broad open space Daniel strode, so that no one could accuse him of eavesdropping. A line stretched from where he'd come in, to the Gate, would pass direct through a sort of gazebo in the center of the Great Court: an octagonal structure surmounting a little pile of steps, with a goblet-shaped fountain in the middle. Moonlight slanted in among the pillars and gave it a ghastly look—the stone pale as a dead man's flesh, streaked with rivulets of blood, pulsing from arterial punctures. Daniel reckoned it had to be some sort of Papist-style Vision, and was just about to lift up his hands to inspect them for Stigmata when he caught a whiff, and recollected that the fountain had been drained of water and filled with claret wine in honor of the King and of the new Chancellor: a decision that begged to be argued with. But no accounting for taste . . .

"The Africans cannot *propagate*," said a familiar voice, startlingly close.

"What do you mean? They can do so as well as anyone," said a *different* familiar voice. "Perhaps *better*!"

"Not without Neeger *women*."

"You don't say!"

"You must remember that the planters are short-sighted. They're all *desperate* to get out of Jamaica—they wake up every day expecting to find themselves, or their children, in the grip of some tropical fever. To import *female* Neegers would cost nearly as much as to import males, but the females cannot produce as much sugar—particularly when they are breeding." Daniel had finally recognized this voice as belonging to Sir Richard Apthorp—the second A in the CABAL.

"So they don't import females *at all?*"

"That is correct, sir. And a newly arrived male is only usable for a few years," Apthorp said.

"That explains *much* of the caterwauling that has been emanating lately from the 'Change."

The two men had been sitting together on the steps of the fountain, facing toward the Gate, and Daniel hadn't *seen* them until he'd drawn close enough to *hear* them. He was just getting ready to shift direction, and swing wide around the fountain, when the man who *wasn't* Sir Richard Apthorp stood up, turned around, and dipped a goblet into the fountain—and caught sight of Daniel standing there flat-footed. *Now* Daniel recognized him—he was only too easy to recognize in a dark Trinity courtyard with blood on his hands. "I say!" Jeffreys exclaimed, "is that a new statue over there? A Puritan saint? Oh, I'm wrong, it is moving now—what *appeared* to be a Pillar of Virtue, is revealed as Daniel Waterhouse—ever the keen observer—now making an empiric study of *us*. Don't worry, Sir Richard, Mr. Waterhouse *sees* all and *does* nothing—a model Royal Society man."

"Good evening, Mr. Waterhouse," Apthorp said, managing to convey, by the tone of his voice, that he found Jeffreys embarrassing and tedious.

"Mr. Jeffreys. Sir Richard. God save the King."

"The King!" Jeffreys repeated, raising his dripping goblet and then taking a swallow. "Stand and deliver like a good little scholar, Mr. Waterhouse. Why are Sir Richard's friends in the 'Change making such a fuss?"

"Admiral de Ruyter sailed down to Guinea and took away all of the Duke of York's slave-ports," Daniel said.

Jeffreys—one hand half-covering his mouth, and speaking in a stage-whisper: "Which the Duke of York had stolen from the Dutch, a few years before—but in Africa, who splits hairs?"

"During the years that the Duke's company controlled Guinea, many slaves were shipped to Jamaica—there they made sugar—fortunes were built, and will endure, as long as the attrition of slaves is replaced by new shipments. But the Dutch have now choked off the supply—so I'd guess that Sir Richard's clients at the 'Change can read the implications clearly enough—there must be some turmoil in the commodities markets."

Like a victim of unprovoked Battery looking for witnesses, Jeffreys turned toward Apthorp, who raised his eyebrows and nodded. Now Jeffreys had been a London barrister for some years. Daniel suspected that he knew of these events only as a mysterious influence that caused his clients to go bankrupt. "Some turmoil," Jeffreys said, in a dramatic whisper. "Rather dry language, isn't it? Imagine some planter's family in Jamaica, watching the work-force, and the harvest, dwindle—trying to stay one step ahead of bankruptcy, yellow fever, and slave rebellion—scanning the horizon for sails, praying for the ships that will be their salvation—some turmoil, you call it?"

Daniel could have said, *Imagine a barrister watching his moneybags dwindle as he drinks them away, scanning the Strand for a client who's got the wherewithal to pay his legal bills* . . . but Jeffreys was wearing a sword and was drunk. So he said: "If those planters are in church, and praying, then they've already found salvation. Good evening, gentlemen."

He headed for the Gate, swinging wide round the fountain so that Jeffreys wouldn't be tempted to run him through. Sir Richard Apthorp was applauding him politely. Jeffreys was mumbling and growling, but after a few moments he was able to get words out: "You are the same man as you were— or *weren't*—ten years ago, Daniel Waterhouse! You were ruled by fear *then*—and you'd have England ruled by it *now*! Thank God you are sequestered within these walls, and unable to infect London with your disgusting pusillanimity!"

And more in that vein, until Daniel ducked into the vault of the Great Gate of Trinity College. The gate was a hefty structure with crenellated towers at its four corners: a sort of mock-fortress, just the thing for retreating into when under attack by a Jeffreys. Between it and the side-wall of Trinity's shotgun chapel was a gap in the College's perimeter defenses about a stone's throw wide, patched with a suite of chambers that had a little walled garden in front of it, on the side facing towards the town. These chambers had been used to shield various Fellows from the elements over the years, but lately Daniel Waterhouse and Isaac Newton had been living there. Once those two bachelors had moved in their miserable stock of furniture, there had been plenty of unused space remaining, and so it had become the world's leading alchemical research facility. Daniel knew this, because he had helped build it—*was helping* build it, rather, for it was perpetually under construction.

Entering his home, Daniel pulled his robes close to his body so that they would not catch fire brushing against the glowing dome of the Reverberatory Furnace, wherein flames curled against the ceiling to strike downwards against the target. Then he pulled his skirts up so they wouldn't drag against the heap of coal that (though the room was dark) he knew would be piled on the floor to his right. Or, for that matter, the mound of horse dung on the left (when burnt, it made a gentle moist heat). He maneuvered down a narrow lead among stacks of wooden crates, an egglike flask of quicksilver packed into each one, and came round a corner into another room.

This chamber looked like a miniature city, built by outlandish stone-masons, and just in the act of burning down—

for each "building" had a peculiar shape, to draw in the air, channel flame, and carry away fumes in a particular way, and each one was filled with flames. Some of them smoked; some steamed; most gave off queer-smelling vapors. Rather than explaining what the place smelled like, 'twere easier to list what few things could *not* be smelled here. Lumps of gold lay out on tabletops, like butter in a pastry-shop—it being *de rigueur* among the higher sort of Alchemists to show a fashionable contempt for gold, as a way of countering the accusation that they were only in it for the money. Not all operations demanded a furnace, and so there were tables, too, sheathed in peened copper, supporting oil-lamps that painted the round bottoms of flasks and retorts with yellow flame.

Smudged faces turned towards Daniel, sequins of perspiration tumbled from drooping eyebrows. He immediately recognized Robert Boyle and John Locke, Fellows of the Royal Society, but, too, there were certain gentlemen who tended to show up at their garden-gate at perverse hours, robed and hooded—as if they really needed to conceal their identities when the King himself was practicing the Art at Whitehall. Viewing their petulant faces by fire-light, Daniel wished they'd kept the hoods on. For, alas, they weren't Babylonian sorcerers or Jesuit warrior-priests or Druidic warlocks after all, but an unmatched set of small-town apothecaries, bored noblemen, and crack-pated geezers, with faces that were either too slack or too spasmodical. One of them was markedly young—Daniel recognized him as Roger Comstock, he of the so-called Golden Comstocks, who'd been a scholar along with Daniel, Isaac, Upnor, Monmouth, and Jeffreys. Isaac had put Roger Comstock to work pumping a bellows, and the strain was showing on his face, but he was not about to complain. Too, there was a small and very trim raptor-faced man with white hair. Daniel recognized him as Monsieur LeFebure, the King's Chymist, who'd introduced John Comstock and Thomas More Anglesey and others—including the King himself—to the Art, when they'd been exiled in St.-Germain during the Cromwell years.

But all of these were satellites, or (like Jupiter's moons) satellites of satellites. The Sun stood at a writing-desk in the center of the room, quill in hand, calmly making notations in a large, stained, yellowed Book. He was dressed in a long splotched smock with several holes burnt through it, though the hem of a scarlet robe could be seen hanging beneath. His head was encased in a sort of leather sack with a window-pane let into it so that he could see out. Where Daniel stood, that rectangle of glass happened to be reflecting an open furnace-door, so instead of the bulging eyes, he saw a brilliant sheet of streaming flame. A breathing-tube, comprising segments of hollow cane plumbed together by the small intestine of some beast, was sewn through the bag. Isaac had tossed it back over his shoulder. It dangled down his back and ran across the floor to Roger Comstock, who pumped fresh air into it with a bellows. So they must be doing something with mercury this evening. Isaac had observed that quicksilver, absorbed into his body, produced effects like those of coffee or tobacco, only more so, and so he used the breathing apparatus whenever he had begun to feel especially twitchy.

The results of some experiment appeared to be cooling down on one of the tables—a crucible hanging in darkness giving off a sullen glow, like Mars—and Daniel reckoned it was as good a time as any to interrupt. He stepped into the middle of the room and held up the bloody rag. "The menstruum of a human female," he announced, "only a few minutes old!"

A bit melodramatic. But these men thrived on it. Why else would they conceal their persons in wizard-cloaks, and their knowledge in occult signs? *Some* of them, anyway, were deeply impressed. Newton turned round and glared significantly at Roger Comstock, who cringed and gave the bellows several brisk strokes. The sack around Isaac's head bulged and whistled. Isaac glared some more. One of the minions rushed up with a beaker. Daniel dropped the moist rag into it. Monsieur LeFebure approached and began to make calm observations in a fifty-fifty French-Latin mix. Boyle and Locke listened politely, the lesser Alchemists formed up in an outer circle, faces strained with the effort of decrypting whatever the King's Chymist was saying.

Daniel turned the other way to see Isaac peeling the wet sack off his head, then gathering his silver hair and holding it atop his skull to let the back of his neck cool down. He was gazing back at Daniel with no particular emotion. Of course he knew that the rag was just a diversionary tactic, but this did not affect him one way or the other.

"There's still time to see the second act of the play," Daniel said. "We're holding an empty seat for you—practically had to use muskets and pikes to keep scheming Londoners from it."

"You are taking the position, then, that God placed me on the earth, and in His wisdom supplied me with the resources that He has, so that I could interrupt my work, and spend my hours, watching a wicked atheistical play?"

"Of course not, Isaac, please don't impute such things to me, not even in private."

They were withdrawing to another room—which, therefore, in a more dignified sort of house would be called the w'drawing room—but here it was a workshop, the floor slick with wood-dust and shavings from a lathe, and a-crackle with failures from the glass-blowing bench, and cluttered with various hand-tools that they'd used to construct everything else. Isaac said nothing, only gazed at Daniel, all patient expectation. "From time to time—perhaps once a day—I prevail upon you to eat something," Daniel pointed out. "Does this mean I believe God put you here to stuff food into your mouth? Of course not. But in order for you to accomplish the work that you, and I, believe God shaped you for, you must put food into your body."

"Is it really your belief that watching *Once More into the Breeches* is comparable to eating?"

"To work, you require certain resources—nutrition is only *one*. A stipend, a workshop, tools, equipment—how do you get *them*?"

"Behold!" Isaac said, sweeping one arm over his empire of tools and furnaces. This caused the cuff of his robe to fly out from under his smock—catching sight of it, he grasped the smock's sleeve with the other hand and yanked it back to reveal the scarlet raiment of the Lucasian Professor of Mathematics. Coming from any other man this would have seemed dramatic and insufferably pompous, but from Isaac it was the simplest and most concise answer to Daniel's question.

"The Fellowship—the chambers—the laboratory—and the Lucasian Chair—all the best that you could hope for. You have all you need—for now. But how did you get those things, Isaac?"

"Providence."

"By which you mean *Divine* Providence. But how—"

"You wish to examine the workings of God's will in the world? I am pleased to hear it. For that is my sole endeavour. You are keeping me from it—let us go back into the other room and pursue an answer to your question together."

"By diverting your attention from those crucibles—for a few hours—you could gain a clearer understanding of, and a more profound gratitude for, what Providence has given you." Devising that sentence had required intense concentration on Daniel's part—he was gratified when it seemed to at least confuse Isaac.

"If there are some *data* I have overlooked, by all means edify me," Isaac said.

"Recall the Fellowship competition of several years ago. You'd been busy doing the work God put you here to do— *instead of* the work that Trinity College *expected* of you— consequently, your prospects seemed bleak—wouldn't you agree?"

"I have always placed my faith in—"

"In God, of course. But don't tell me you weren't worried you'd be sent packing, and live out your days as a gentleman farmer in Woolsthorpe. There were *other* candidates. Men who'd curried favor in the right places, and memorized all of the medieval claptrap we were expected to know. Do you remember, Isaac, what became of your competitors?"

"One went insane," Isaac recited like a bored scholar. "One passed out in a field from too much drink, caught a fever, and died. One fell down stairs drunk and had to withdraw because of injuries suffered. The fourth—" Here Isaac faltered, which was a rare event for him. Daniel seized the moment by stepping closer and adopting a curious and innocent look.

Isaac looked away and said, "The fourth one *also* fell down stairs drunk and had to withdraw! Now, Daniel, if you're trying to say that this was *incredibly improbable,* and fortunate for me, I have already given you my answer: Providence."

"But *in what form* did Providence exert itself? Some mysterious action at a distance? Or the earthly mechanics of colliding bodies?"

"Now you have quite lost me."

"Do you believe that God stretched out a finger from Heaven, and knocked those two down the staircase? Or did he put someone on Earth who arranged for these things to happen?"

"Daniel—surely you didn't—"

Daniel laughed. "Push them down stairs? No. But I think I know who *did.* You have the wherewithal to work, Isaac, because of certain Powers that Be—which is not to say that Providence isn't working *through* them. But what it all *means* is that you must, from time to time, pause in your labors, and spend a few hours maintaining friendly relations with those Powers."

Isaac had been pacing around the chamber during this lecture, and looking generally skeptical. More than one time he opened his mouth to make some objection. But at about the time Daniel finished, Isaac seemed to notice something.

Daniel thought it was one of many papers and note-books scattered upon a certain table. Whatever it might have been, the sight of it caused Isaac to reconsider. Isaac's face slackened, as if the internal flame were being banked. He began stripping off his smock. "Very well," he said, "please inform the others."

The others had already squeezed the rag out into a glass retort and were trying to distill from it whatever generative spirit they supposed must be exuded from a woman's womb. Roger Comstock and the other minions looked crestfallen to learn that Professor Newton would be leaving them, but Locke and Boyle and LeFebure took it in stride. Newton made himself presentable very quickly—this being why academics loved robes, and fops loathed them. A contingent of five Royal Society members—Boyle, Locke, LeFebure, Waterhouse, and Newton—set out across the Great Court of Trinity College. All were in long black robes and mortarboards save Newton, who led the way, a cardinal pursued by a flock of crows, a vivid red mark on the Trinity green.

"I HAVEN'T SEEN *THIS* PLAY," Locke said, "but I have seen one or two from which the story and characters of *this* one were . . . uh . . ."

Newton: "Stolen."

Boyle: "Inspired."

LeFebure: "Appropriated."

Locke: "Adapted, and so I can inform you that a ship has run aground in a storm, near a castle, the seat of a foppish courtier probably named something like Percival Kidney or Reginald Mumblesleeve—"

"Francis Buggermy, according to the Playbill," Daniel put in. Isaac turned around and glared at him.

"So much the better," Locke said. "But of course the fop's in London, never comes to the country—so a Vagabond named Roger Thrust or Judd Vault or—"

"Tom Runagate."

"And his mistress, Madeline Cherry or—"

"Miss Straddle, in this case."

"Are squatting there. Now, seeing a group of castaways from the ship coming ashore, these two Vagabonds dress up in the fop's clothing and impersonate Francis Buggermy and his mistress-of-the-moment—much to the surprise of a withered Puritan Bible-pounder who comes upon the scene—"

"The Reverend Yahweh Pucker," Daniel said.

"The rest we can see for ourselves—"

"Why's that old fellow all charred black?" Boyle demanded, catching sight of a performer up on the stage.

"He's a Neeger slave," Daniel said.

"Which reminds me," Locke put in, "I need to send a message to my broker—time to sell my stock in the Guinea Company, I fear—"

"No, no!" Boyle said, "I mean black as in *charred, burnt,* with smoke coming out of his hair!"

"No such thing was in the version *I* saw," Locke said.

"Oh . . . in an earlier scene, there was a hilarious misadventure, having to do with a keg of gunpowder," Daniel volunteered.

"Er . . . was this comedy written *recently*?"

"Since the . . . um . . . *events*?"

"One can only assume," Daniel said.

Significant chin-stroking and hemming now among the various R.S. Fellows (save Newton), who glanced up towards the Earl of Epsom as they made their way to their seats.

LYDIA: Is this walking, or swimming?

VAN UND: Fine muck—fine hurricanoe—throw up a dike there, and a windmill yonder, and I'll be able to join it to my estates in Flanders.

LYDIA: But it isn't *yours.*

VAN UND: Easily remedied—what's the name of the place?

LYDIA: That pretty boatswain said we were just off a place called Suckmire.

VAN UND: Don't pine for *him*, Lydia—yonder Castle's sure to house some Persons of Quality—why, I spy some now! Halloo!

TOM RUNAGATE: You see, Miss Straddle, they've already marked us as Courtiers. A few stolen rags are as good as Title and Pedigree.

MISS STRADDLE: Aye, Tom, true enough when we're barely within bowshot—but what's to come later?

TOM (*peering through spyglass*): What is to *come?* I have spied one candidate—

STRADDLE: That lass has breeding, my wayward Tom— she'll scorn you as a Vagabond, when she hears your voice—

TOM: I can do a fine accent well as any Lord.

STRADDLE: —and observes your uncouth manners.

TOM: Don't you know that bad manners are high fashion now?

STRADDLE: Stab me!

TOM: 'Tis truth! These fine people insult one another all day long—'tis called wit! Then they poke at one another with swords, and call it honor.

STRADDLE: Then 'tween Wit and Honor, the treasure on that wrack is as good as ours.

VAN UND: Halloo, there, sir! Throw us a line, we are sinking into your garden!

TOM: This one must be daft, he mistakes yonder mud-flat for a garden!

STRADDLE: Daft, or Delft.

TOM: You think he's Dutch!? Then I might levy a rope-climbing toll . . .

STRADDLE: What'll his daughter think of you then?

TOM: 'Tis well considered . . .

Throws rope.

LORD BRIMSTONE: Who's that Frenchman on the sea-wall? Has England been conquered? Heaven help us!

LADY B: He is no Frenchman, my lord, but a good En-

glish gentleman in *modern* attire—most likely it is
Count Suckmire, and that lady is his latest courtesan.

LORD B: You don't say!

To Miss Straddle. Good day, madam—I'm informed that
you are a Cartesian—here stands another!

STRADDLE: What's he on about?

TOM: Never mind—remember what I told you.

LORD B: *Cogito, ergo sum!*

STRADDLE: Air go some? Yes, the air goes some when
you flap your jaw, sir—I thought it was a sea-breeze,
until I smelled it.

To Tom. Is that the sort of thing?

TOM: Well played, my flower.

LADY B: That whore is most uncivil.

LORD B: No need to be vulgar, my dear—it means she
recognizes us as her equals.

>   *ENTER, from opposite, the Rev. Yahweh Pucker,*
>   *with BIBLE and SHOVEL.*

PUCKER: Here's proof the Lord works in mysterious
ways—I came expecting to find a ship-wrack, and
drownded bodies in need of burying—which service I
am ever willing to perform, for a small contribution—
group rates available—instead, it is a courtly scene. St.
James's Park on a sunny May morn ne'er was so.

TOM: Between the *Dutch* mercer, and the *English* lord,
there must be treasure aplenty on that wrack—if you
can divert them in the Castle, I'll get word to our
merry friends—they can steal the longboat these
rowed in on, and go fetch the goods.

STRADDLE: Whilst you salvage the Dutch girl's maiden-
head?

TOM: Lost at sea already, I fear.

NOW THERE WAS A CHANGE of scene to the interior of Castle
Suckmire. As things were being re-arranged upon the stage,
Oldenburg leaned close and said, "Is that him, then?"

"Yes, that's Isaac Newton."

"Well done—more than one Anglesey will be pleased— how did you flush him into the open?"

"I am not entirely sure."

"What of the tangents paper?"

"One thing at a time, please, sir . . ."

"I cannot understand his reticence!"

"He's only published one thing in his life—"

"The colors paper!? That was two years ago!"

"For you, two years of interminable waiting—for Isaac, two years of siege warfare—fending off Hooke on one front, Jesuits on the other."

"Perhaps if you would only relate to him how you have passed the last two months—"

Daniel managed not to laugh in Oldenburg's face.

UP ON THE STAGE IN Neville's Court, the plot was thickening, or, depending on how you liked your plots, expanding into a froth. Miss Straddle, played by Tess, was flirting with Eugene Stopcock, an infantry officer, who had rushed in from London to rescue his shipwrecked parents. Tom Runagate had already been to bed at least once with Lydia van Underdevater. The courtier Francis Buggermy had showed up incognito and begun chasing the slave Nzinga around in hopes of verifying certain rumors about the size of African men.

Isaac Newton was pinching the high bridge of his nose and looking mildly nauseated. Oldenburg was glaring at Daniel, and several important personages were glaring from On High at Oldenburg.

The play was entering Act V. Soon it would come to an end, triggering a plan, laid by Oldenburg, in which Isaac was finally going to be introduced to the King, and to the Royal Society at large. If Isaac's paper were not brought forth tonight, it never would be, and Isaac would be known only as an Alchemist who once invented a telescope. So Daniel excused himself and set out across Trinity's courtyards one more time.

The lurkers in the Great Court had thinned out, or perhaps he simply was not paying so much attention to them—he had decided what to do, and that gave him liberty, for the first time in months, to tilt his head back and look up at the stars.

It had turned out that Hooke, with his telescope project, had had much more on his mind than countering the ravings of some pedantic Jesuit. Sitting in the dark hole of Gresham's College, marking down the coordinates of various stars, he'd outlined the rudiments of a larger theory to Daniel: first that all cœlestial bodies attracted all others within their sphere of influence, by means of some gravitating power; second that all bodies put into motion moved forward in a straight line unless acted upon by some effectual power; third that the attractive power became more powerful as the body wrought upon came nearer to the center.

Oldenburg did not yet know the magnitude of Isaac's powers. Not that Oldenburg was stupid—he was anything but. But Isaac, unlike, say, Leibniz the indefatigable letter-writer or Hooke the Royal Society stalwart, did not communicate his results, and did not appear to socialize with anyone save daft Alchemists. And so in Oldenburg's mind, Newton was a clever though odd chap who'd written a paper about colors and then got into a fracas over it with Hooke. If Newton would only mingle with the Fellows a bit, Oldenburg seemed to believe, he would soon learn that Hooke had quite put colors out of his mind and moved on to matters such as Universal Gravitation, which of course would not interest young Mr. Newton in the slightest.

This entire plan was, in other words, an embryonic disaster. But it might not occur for another hundred years that most of the Royal Society, and a King with a passion for Natural Philosophy, would spend a night together in Cambridge, within shouting distance of the bed where Isaac slept and the table where he worked. Isaac had to be drawn out, and it had to happen tonight. If this would lead to open war with Hooke, so be it. Perhaps that was inevitable anyway, no matter what Daniel did in the next few minutes.

* * *

DANIEL WAS BACK in the chambers. Roger Comstock, left behind, Cinderella-like, to tidy up and tend the furnaces, had
apparently gotten bored and sneaked off to an alehouse, because the candles had all been snuffed, leaving the big room
lit only by the furnaces' rosy glow. Here Daniel would've
been at a stand, if not for the fact that he lived there, and could
find his way round in the dark. He groped a candle out of a
drawer and lit it from a furnace. Then he went into the room
where he'd conversed with Isaac earlier. Rummaging through
papers, trying to find the one about tangents—the first practical fruits of Isaac's old work about fluxions—he was reminded that the sight of something on this table had rattled
Isaac, and persuaded him to expose himself to the awful tor-
ment of watching a comedy. Daniel kept a sharp eye out, but
saw nothing except for tedious alchemical notes and recipes,
many signed not "Isaac Newton" but "Jeova Sanctus Unus,"
which was the pseudonym Isaac used for Alchemy work.

In any case—without solving the eternal mystery of why
Isaac did what he did—he spied the tangents paper on the far
corner of the table, and stepped forward to reach for it.

The place was suffused with odd sounds, mostly the
seething and hissing of diverse fuels burning in the furnaces,
and the endless popping and ticking of the wooden wall pan-
els. Another sound, faint and furtive, had reached Daniel's
ears from time to time, but that surly porter who bestrides
the gate of the conscious mind, spurning most of what is
brought in by the senses and admitting only perceptions of
Import or Quality, had construed this as a mouse sapping
and mining the wall, and shouldered it aside. Now, though, it
did come to Daniel's notice, for it grew louder: more rat than
mouse. Isaac's tangents paper was in his hand, but he stood
still for a few moments, trying to work out where this rat was
busy, so that he could come back in daylight and investigate.
The sound was resonating in a partition separating this room
from the big laboratory with the furnaces, which was not of
regular shape, but had several pop-outs and alcoves, built, by

men who'd long since passed away, for heaven only knew what reasons: perhaps to encase a chimney here, or add a bit of pantry space there. Daniel had a good idea of what lay on the opposite side of that wall that was making the grinding noises: it was a little sideboard, set into an alcove in the corner of the laboratory, probably used once by servants when that room had been a dining-hall. Nowadays, Isaac used the cabinets below it to store Alchemical supplies. The counter was stocked with mortars, pestles, &c. For certain of the things Isaac worked with had a marked yearning to burst into flame, and so he was at pains to store them in that particular alcove, as far as possible from the furnaces.

Daniel walked as quietly as he could back into the laboratory. He set the tangents paper down on a table and then picked up an iron bar that was lying next to a furnace door for use as a poker. There was more than one way to get rid of rats; but sometimes the best approach was the simplest, viz. ambush and bludgeon. He stalked down an aisle between furnaces, wiggling the poker in his hand. The alcove had been partitioned from the rest of the room by a free-standing screen such as ladies were wont to dress behind, consisting of fabric (now shabby) pleated and hung on a light wooden frame. This was to stop flying sparks, and to shield Isaac's fragile scales and fine powders from gusts of wind coming through open windows or down chimneys.

He faltered, for the gnawing had stopped, as if the rat sensed the approach of a predator. But then it started up again, very loud, and Daniel strode forward, stretched one toe out ahead of him, and kicked the screen out of the way. His poker-hand was drawn back behind his head, poised to ring down a death-blow, and the candle was thrust out before him to find and dazzle the rat, which he guessed would be out on the counter.

Instead he found himself sharing a confined space with another man. Daniel was so astonished that he froze, and sprang several inches into the air, at the same instant, if such a combination were possible, and dropped the poker, and fumbled the candle. He had nearly shoved the flame right into the face of this other chap: Roger Comstock. Roger had been working in the dark with a mortar and pestle and so the sudden appearance of this flame in his face not only startled him half out of his wits, but blinded him as well. And on the heels of those emotions came terror. He dropped what he had been working on: a mortar, containing some dark gray powder, which he had been pouring into a cloth bag at the instant Daniel surprised him. Indeed *drop* did not do justice to Roger's treatment of these two items; gravity was not nearly quick enough. He *thrust* them away, and at the same time flung himself backwards.

Daniel watched the flame of his candle grow to the size of a bull's head, enveloping his hand and arm as far as the elbow. He dropped it. The floor was carpeted with flame that leapt up in a great *FOOM* and disappeared, leaving the place perfectly dark. Not that all flames had gone, for Daniel could still hear them crackling; the darkness was because of dense smoke filling the whole room. Daniel inhaled some and wished he hadn't. This was gunpowder that Roger had been playing with.

Roger was out of the house in five heartbeats, notwithstanding that he did it on his hands and knees. Daniel crawled out after him and stood outside the door long enough to purge his lungs with several deep draughts of fresh air.

Roger had already scuttled across the garden and banged out the gate. Daniel went over to pull it closed, looking out first into the way. Some yards down, a couple of porters, shadowed under the vault of the Great Gate, regarded him with only moderate curiosity. It was *expected* that strange lights and noises would emanate from the residence of the Lucasian Professor of Mathematics. For shadowy figures to flee the building with smoke coming out of their clothes was only a little remarkable. Failing to close the garden gate was an egregious lapse; but Daniel saw to it.

Then, holding his breath, he ventured back in. He found the windows by grope and hauled them open. The flames had caught and spread in the fabric of the toppled screen, but gone no farther, owing to that Isaac suffered very little that was combustible to abide in the furnace-room. Daniel stomped out a few glowing edges.

In a more genteel setting, the smoke would have been accounted as a kind of damage to all the contents of the room that had been darkened and made noisome by it; but in a place such as this, it was nothing.

What had occurred was not an explosion—for the gunpowder, fortunately, had not been confined—but a very rapid burning. The screen was wrecked. The cabinetry in the alcove was blackened. A scale had been blown off the counter and was probably ruined. The mortar that Roger had dropped lay in fat shards at the epicenter of the black burst, making Daniel think of the cannon that had exploded at the "Siege of Maestricht," and other such disasters he had heard about lately aboard ships of the Royal Navy. Surrounding it were burnt scraps of linen—the bag into which Roger had been decocting the gunpowder when Daniel had set fire to it. It was, in other words, the least possible amount of devastation that could possibly result from deflagration of a sack of gunpowder inside the house. That said, this corner of the laboratory was a shambles, and would have to be cleaned up—a task that would fall to Roger anyway. Unless, as seemed likely, Isaac fired him.

One would think that being blown up would throw one's evening's schedule all awry. But all of this had passed very quickly, and there was no reason Daniel could not accomplish the errand that had brought him here. Indeed, the grave problems that had so burdened him on his walk over here were quite forgotten now, and would appear to be perfectly trivial seen against the stunning adventure of the last few minutes. His hand and, to a lesser degree, his face, were raw and red from flash-burns, and he suspected he might have to do without eyebrows for a few weeks. A quick change of robes and a wash were very much in order; no difficulty, as he lived upstairs.

But having done those, Daniel picked up the tangents paper, shook off the black grit that re-punctuated it, and headed out the door. This was no more than a tenth of everything Isaac had accomplished with fluxions, but it was at least a *shred* of evidence—better than nothing—and sufficient to keep most Fellows of the Royal Society in bed with headaches for weeks. The night overhead was clear, the view excellent, the mysteries of the Universe all spread out above Trinity College. But Daniel lowered his sights and plodded toward the cone of steamy light where everyone was waiting.

✥

London Bridge
1673

✥

Once the characteristic numbers of most notions are determined, the human race will have a new kind of tool, a tool that will increase the power of the mind much more than optical lenses helped our eyes, a tool that will be as far superior to microscopes or telescopes as reason is to vision.

—Leibniz, *Philosophical Essays*,
Edited and translated by
Roger Arlew and Daniel Garber

NEAR THE MIDPOINT of London Bridge, a bit closer to the City than to Southwark, was a firebreak—a short gap in the row of buildings, like a missing tooth in a crowded jawbone. If you were drifting down-river in a boat, so that you could see all nineteen of the squat piers that held the bridge up, and all twenty of the ragstone arches and wooden draw-bridges that let the water through, you'd be able to see that this open space—"the square," it was called—stood directly above an arch that was wider than any of the others—thirty-four feet, at its widest.

As you drew closer to the bridge, and it became more and more obvious that your life was in extreme danger, and your mind, therefore, became focused on practical matters, you'd notice something even more important, namely that the sluice between the starlings—the snowshoe-like platforms of rubble that served as footings for the piers—was also wider, in this place, than anywhere else on the bridge. Con-sequently the passage through it looked less like a boiling cataract than a river rushing down from mountains during the spring thaw. If you still had the ability to steer for it, you would. And if you were a passenger on this hypothetical boat, and you valued your life, you'd insist that the waterman tie up for a moment at the tip of the starling and let you out, so that you could pick your way over that jammed horde of more or less ancient piles and the in-fill of mucky rubble; take a stair up to the level of the roadway; run across the Square, not forgetting to dodge the carts rushing both ways; descend another stair to the other end of the starling; and then hop, skid, and stagger across it until you reached the end, where your waterman would be waiting to pick you up again if indeed his boat, and he, still existed.

This accounted, anyway, for much that was peculiar about the part of London Bridge called the Square. Persons who went east and west on watermen's boats on the Thames tended to be richer and more important than those who went north and south across the Bridge, and the ones who actually cared enough about their lives, limbs, and estates to bother with climbing out and hiking over the starling tended to be richer and more important yet, and so the buildings that stood atop the Bridge to either side of the Square constituted location! location! location! to the better sort of retailers and publicans.

Daniel Waterhouse spent a couple of hours loitering in the vicinity of the Square one morning, waiting for a certain man on a certain boat. However, the boat he waited for would be coming the other direction: working its way upstream from the sea.

He took a seat in a coffee-house and amused himself watching flushed and sweaty ferry-passengers appear at the head of the stairs, as if they'd been spontaneously generated from the fœtid waters of the Thames. They'd crawl into the nearby tavern for a pint, fortifying themselves for the traversal of the Bridge's twelve-foot-wide roadway, where passengers were crushed between carts a few times a week. If they survived that, then they'd pop into the glover's or the haberdasher's for a bit of recreational shopping, and then perhaps dart into this coffee-house for a quick mug of java. The remainder of London Bridge was getting down at the heels, because much more fashionable shops were being put up in other parts of the city by the likes of Sterling, but the Square was prosperous and, because of the continual threat of boat-wrack and drowning, the merriest part of town.

And in these days it tended to be crowded, especially when ships came across the Channel, and dropped anchor in the Pool, and their Continental passengers were ferried hither in watermen's boats.

As one such boat drew near the Bridge, Daniel finished his coffee, settled his bill, and ventured out onto the street. Cartage and drayage had been baffled by a crowd of pedestrians. They all wanted to descend to the starling on the downstream side, and had formed a sort of bung that stopped not only the stairs but the street as well. Seeing that they were by and large City men, intent on some serious purpose, and not Vagabonds intent on his purse, Daniel insinuated himself into this crowd and was presently drawn in to the top of the stairs and flushed down to the top of the starling along with the rest. He supposed at first that all of these well-dressed men had come to greet specific passengers. But as the boat drew within earshot, they began to shout, not friendly greetings, but questions, in several languages, about the war.

"As a fellow Protestant—albeit Lutheran—it is *my* hoping that England and Holland shall become reconciled and that the war you speak of will no more exist."

The young German was standing up in a boat, wearing French fashions. But as the boat drew closer to the turbulence downstream of the Bridge, he came to his senses, and sat down.

"So much for hopes—now what of your *observations,* sir?" someone fired back—one of a few dozen who had by now crowded onto the starling, trying to get as close to the incoming boats and ferries as they could without falling into the deadly chute. Others were perched up on the edge of the Square, like gargoyles, still others were out on the river in boats plotting intercept courses, like boca-neers in the Caribbean. None of them was having any of this Lutheran diplomacy. None even knew who the young German was—just a passenger on a boat from abroad who was willing to talk. There were several other travelers on the same boat, but all of them ignored the shouting Londoners. If these had information, they would take it to the 'Change, and tell the tale with silver, and propagate it through the chthonic channels of the Market.

"What ship were you on, sir?" someone bellowed.

"*Ste-Catherine,* sir."

"Where did that ship come from, sir?"

"Calais."

"Had you any conversation with Naval persons?"

"A little, perhaps."

"Any news, or rumor, of cannons bursting on English ships?"

"Oh, sometimes it happens. By everyone in the ships of the *melee,* it is seen, for the whole side of the hull is outblown, and out the bodies fly, or so they say. To all of the sailors, friend and enemy, it is a lesson of mortality, perhaps. Consequently they all talk about it. But in the present war it happens no more than usual, I think."

"Were they Comstock cannons?"

The German took a moment to understand that, without even having set foot on English soil yet, he had talked himself into deep trouble. "Sir! The cannons of my lord Epsom are reckoned the finest in the world."

But no one wanted to hear that kind of talk. The topic had changed.

"Whence came you to Calais?"

"Paris."

"Did you see troops moving on your journey across France?"

"A few ones, exhausted, south-going."

The gentlemen on the starling hummed and vibrated for a few moments, assimilating this. One broke away from the crowd, toiling back towards the stairs, and was engulfed in barefoot boys jumping up and down. He scribbled something on a bit of paper and handed it to the one who jumped highest. This one spun, forced a path through the others, took the stairs four at a time, broke loose onto the Square, vaulted over a wagon, spun a fishwife, and then began to build speed up the bridge. From here to the London shore was a hundred and some yards, from there to the 'Change was six hundred—he'd be there in three minutes. Meanwhile the interrogation continued: "Did you see Ships of Force in the Channel, *mein Herr*? English, French, Dutch?"

"There was—" and here the man's English gave way. He made a helpless, encompassing gesture.

"Fog!"

"Fog," he repeated.

"Did you hear guns?"

"A few—but very likely they were only signals. Coded *data* speeding through the *fog,* so opaque to light, but so transparent to sound—" and here he lost control of his intellectual sphincters and began to think out loud in French, for-

tified with Latin, working out a system for sending encrypted data from place to place using explosions, building
on ideas from Wilkins's *Cryptonomicon* but marrying them
to a practical plan that, in its lavish expenditure of gunpowder, would be sure to please John Comstock. In other words,
he identified himself (to Daniel anyway) as Dr. Gottfried
Wilhelm Leibniz. The watchers lost interest and began aiming their questions at another boat.

Leibniz set foot on England. He was closely followed by
a couple of other German gentlemen, somewhat older,
much less talkative, and (Daniel could only suppose) more
important. They in turn were pursued by a senior servant
who headed up a short column of porters lugging boxes
and bags. But Leibniz had burdened himself with a
wooden box he would not let go of. Daniel stepped forward
to greet them, but was cut off by some brusque fellow who
shouldered in to hand a sealed letter to one of the older
gentlemen, and whispered to him for a moment in Low-
Dutch.

Daniel straightened up in annoyance. As luck would have
it, he looked toward the London shore. His eye lingered on
a quay just downstream of the Bridge: a jumbled avalanche
of blackened rubble left over from the Fire. It *could* have
been rebuilt years ago, but hadn't, because it had been
judged more important to rebuild other things first. A few
men were doing work of a highly intellectual nature,
stretching lines about and drawing sketches. One of them—
incredibly—just happened to be Robert Hooke, City Surveyor, whom Daniel had quietly abandoned at Gresham's
College an hour ago. *Not* so incredibly (given that he was
Hooke), he'd noticed Daniel standing there on the starling
in the middle of the river, greeting what was quite obviously a foreign delegation, and was therefore glaring and
brooding.

Leibniz and the others discussed matters in High-Dutch.
The interloper turned round to glance at Daniel. It was one
of the Dutch Ambassador's errand-boys-*cum*-spies. The

Germans formed some sort of a plan, and it seemed to involve splitting up. Daniel stepped in and introduced himself.

The other Germans were introduced by their *names* but what mattered was their *ancestry:* one of them was the nephew of the Archbishop of Mainz, the other the son of Baron von Boineburg, who was the same Archbishop's Minister. In other words *very* important people in Mainz, hence *rather* important ones in the Holy Roman Empire, which was more or less neutral in the French/English/Dutch broil. It had all the signs of being some sort of peace-brokering mission, i.e.

Leibniz knew who he was, and asked, "Is Wilkins still alive?"

"Yes . . ."

"Thank God!"

"Though very ill. If you would like to visit him I would suggest doing it *now*. I'll escort you gladly, Dr. Leibniz . . . may I have the honor of assisting you with that box?"

"You are very civil," Leibniz said, "but I'll hold it."

"If it contains gold or jewelry, you'd best hold it *tight*."

"Are the streets of London not safe?"

"Let us say that the Justices of the Peace are mostly concerned with Dissenters and Dutchmen, and our cutpurses have not been slow to adapt."

"What this contains is infinitely more valuable than gold," Leibniz said, beginning to mount the stairs, "and yet it cannot be stolen."

Daniel lunged forward in an effort to keep step. Leibniz was slender, of average height, and tended to bend forward when he walked, the head anticipating the feet. Once he had reached the level of the roadway he turned sharply and strode towards the City of London, ignoring the various taverns and shops.

He did not *look* like a monster.

According to Oldenburg, the Parisians who frequented the Salon at the Hotel Montmor—the closest French equivalent to the Royal Society of London—had begun using the Latin word *monstro* to denote Leibniz. This from men who'd

personally known Descartes and Fermat and who considered exaggeration an unspeakably vulgar habit. It had led to
some etymological researches among some members of the
R.S. Did they mean Leibniz was grotesquely misshapen? An
unnatural hybrid of a man and something else? A divine
warning?

"He lives up this way, does he not?"

"The Bishop has had to move because of his illness—he's
at his stepdaughter's house in Chancery Lane."

"Then still we go this way—then left."

"You have been to London before, Dr. Leibniz?"

"I have been studying London-paintings."

"I'm afraid most of those became antiquarian curiosities
after the Fire—like street-plans of Atlantis."

"And yet viewing several depictions of even an imaginary
city, is enlightening in a way," Leibniz said. "Each painter
can view the city from only one standpoint at a time, so he
will move about the place, and paint it from a hilltop on one
side, then a tower on the other, then from a grand intersection in the middle—all on the same canvas. When we look at
the canvas, then, we glimpse in a small way how God understands the universe—for he sees it from every point of view
at once. By populating the world with so many different
minds, each with its own point of view, God gives us a suggestion of what it means to be omniscient."

Daniel decided to step back and let Leibniz's words rever-
berate, as organ-chords must do in Lutheran churches.
Meanwhile they reached the north end of the Bridge, where
the racket of the water-wheels, confined and focused in the
stone vault of the gatehouse, made conversation impossible.
Not until they'd made it out onto dry land, and begun to ascend the Fish Street hill, did Daniel ask, "I note you've already been in communication with the Dutch Ambassador.
May I assume that your mission is not entirely *natural-
philosophick* in nature?"

"A rational question—in a way," Leibniz grumbled. "We
are about the same age, you and I?" he asked, giving Daniel

a quick inspection. His eyes were unsettling. Depending on what *kind* of monster he was, either beady, or penetrating.

"I am twenty-six."

"So am I. We were born about sixteen forty-six. The Swedes took Prague that year, and invaded Bavaria. The Inquisition was burning Jews in Mexico. Similar terrible things were happening in England, I assume?"

"Cromwell crushed the King's army at Newark—chased him out of the country—John Comstock was wounded—"

"And we are speaking only of kings and noblemen. Imagine the sufferings of common people and Vagabonds, who possess equal stature in God's eyes. And yet you ask me whether my mission is *philosophick* or *diplomatic,* as if those two things can neatly be separated."

"Rude and stupid I know, but it is my duty to make conversation. You are saying that it should be the goal of all natural philosophers to restore peace and harmony to the world of men. This I cannot dispute."

Leibniz now softened. "Our goal is to prevent the Dutch war from growing into a general conflagration. Please do not be offended by my frankness now: the Archbishop and the Baron are followers of the Royal Society—as am I. They are Alchemists—which I am *not,* except when it is *politic.* They hope that through pursuit of Natural Philosophy I may make contacts with important figures in this country, whom it would normally be difficult to reach through *diplomatic* channels."

"Ten years ago I might have been offended," Daniel said. "Now, there's nothing I'll not believe."

"But my interest in meeting the Lord Bishop of Chester is as pure as any human motive *can* be."

"He will sense that, and be cheered by it," Daniel said. "The last few years of Wilkins's life have been sacrificed entirely to politics—he has been working to dismantle the framework of theocracy, to prevent its resurgence, in the event a Papist ascends to the throne—"

"Or already *has* done so," Leibniz said immediately.

The offhanded way in which Leibniz suggested that King Charles II might be a crypto-Catholic hinted to Daniel that it was common knowledge on the Continent. This made him feel hopelessly dull, naïve, and provincial. He had suspected the King of many crimes and deceptions, but never of baldly lying about his religion to the entire Realm.

He had plenty of time to conceal his annoyance as they were passing through the heart of the city, which had turned into a single vast and eternal building-site even as the normal business of the 'Change and the goldsmiths' shops continued. Paving-stones were whizzing between Daniel and the Doctor like cannonballs, shovels slicing the air around their heads like cutlasses, barrows laden with gold and silver and bricks and mud trundling like munition-carts over temporary walk-ways of planks and stomped dirt.

Perhaps reading anxiety on Daniel's face, Leibniz said, "Just like the Rue Vivienne in Paris," with a casual hand-wave. "I go there frequently to read certain manuscripts in the Bibliothèque du Roi."

"I've been told that a copy of every book printed in France must be sent to that place."

"Yes."

"But it was established in the same year that we had our Fire—so I ween that it must be very small yet, as it's had only a few years to grow."

"A few very good years in mathematics, sir. And it also contains certain unpublished manuscripts of Descartes and Pascal."

"But none of the classics?"

"I had the good fortune to be raised, or to raise myself, in my father's library, which contained all of them."

"Your father was *mathematickally* inclined?"

"Difficult to say. As a traveler comprehends a city only by viewing pictures of it drawn from differing standpoints, I know my father only by having read the books that he read."

"I understand the similitude now, Doctor. The Bibliothèque du Roi then gives you the closest thing that currently exists to God's understanding of the world."

"And yet with a bigger library we could come ever so much closer."

"But with all due respect, Doctor, I do not understand how *this* street could be anything *less* like the Rue Vivienne—we have no such Bibliothèque in England."

"The Bibliothèque du Roi is just a *house,* you see, a house Colbert happened to buy on the Rue Vivienne—probably as an investment, because that street is the center of gold-smiths. Every ten days, from ten in the morning until noon, all of the merchants of Paris send their money to the Rue Vivienne to be counted. I sit there in Colbert's house trying to understand Descartes, working the mathematical proofs that Huygens, my tutor, gives me, and looking out the windows as the street fills up with porters staggering under their back-loads of gold and silver, converging on a few doorways. Are you beginning to understand my riddle now?"

"Which riddle was that?"

"This box! I said it contained something infinitely more valuable than gold, and yet it could not be stolen. Which way do we turn here?"

For they'd come out into the hurricane where Threadneedle, Cornhill, Poultry, and Lombard all collided. Message-boys were flying across that intersection like quarrels from crossbows—or (Daniel suspected) like broad Hints that he was failing to Get.

LONDON CONTAINED A HUNDRED LORDS, bishops, preachers, scholars, and gentlemen-philosophers who would gladly have provided Wilkins with a comfortable sick-bed, but he had ended up in his stepdaughter's home in Chancery Lane, actually rather close to where the Waterhouses lived. The entrance to the place, and the street in front, were choked with sweating courtiers—not the sleek top-level ones but the dented, scarred, slightly too old and slightly too ugly ones who actually got everything done.* They were milling in the street around a black coach blazoned with the arms of Count Penistone. The house was an old one (the Fire had stopped a few yards short of it). It was one of those slump-shouldered, thatch-roofed, half-timbered Canterbury Tales productions, completely out-moded by the gleaming coach and the whip-thin rapiers.

"You see—despite the purity of your motives, you're immersed in politics already," Daniel said. "The lady of the house is Cromwell's niece."

"What!? *The* Cromwell?"

"The same whose skull gazes down on Westminster from the end of a stick. Now, the owner of that excellent coach is Knott Bolstrood, Count Penistone—his father founded a sect called the Barkers, normally lumped in with many others under the pejorative term of Puritans. The Barkers are *gratuitously* radical, however—for example, they believe that Government and Church should have naught to do with each other, and that all slaves in the world should be set free."

"But the gentlemen in front are dressed like courtiers! Are they getting ready to siege the Puritan-house?"

"They are Bolstrood's hangers-on. You see, Count Penistone is His Majesty's Secretary of State."

"I had heard that King Charles the Second made a Phanatique his Secretary of State, but could not believe it."

"Consider it—could Barkers exist in any other country? Save Amsterdam, that is."

"Naturally not!" Leibniz said, lightly offended by the very idea. "They would be extinguished."

"Therefore, whether or not he feels any loyalty toward the King, Knott Bolstrood has no choice but to stand for a free and independent England—and so, when Dissenters accuse the King of being too close to France, His Majesty need

---

*Pepys being a good example—but he wasn't there.

only point to Bolstrood as the living credential of his independent foreign policy."

"But it's all a farce!" Leibniz muttered. "All Paris knows
England's in France's pocket."

"All London knows it, too—the difference is that we have
three dozen theatres here—Paris has only one of them—"

Leibniz's turn, finally, to be baffled. "I don't understand."

"All I am saying is that we happen to *enjoy* farces."

"Why is Bolstrood visiting the niece of Cromwell?"

"He's probably visiting Wilkins."

Leibniz stopped and considered matters. "Tempting. But
the protocol is impossible. I cannot enter the house!"

"Of course you can—with me," Daniel said. "Just follow."

"But I must go back and fetch my companions—for I do
not have the *standing* to disturb the Secretary of State—"

"I do," Daniel said. "One of my earliest memories is of
watching him destroy a pipe organ with a sledgehammer.
Seeing me will give him a warm feeling."

Leibniz stopped and looked aghast; Daniel could almost
see, reflected in his eyes, the stained-glass windows and
organ-pipes of some fine Lutheran church in Leipzig. "Why
would he commit such an outrage!?"

"Because it was in an Anglican cathedral. He would have
been about twenty—a high-spirited age."

"Your family were followers of Cromwell?"

"It is more correct to say that Cromwell was a follower of
my father—may God rest both of their souls." But now they
were in the midst of the courtier-mob, and it was too late for
Leibniz to obey his instincts, and run away.

They spent several minutes pushing among progressively
higher-ranking and better-dressed men, into the house and
up the stairs, and finally entered a tiny low-ceilinged
bedchamber. It smelled as if Wilkins had already died, but
most of him still lived—he was propped up on pillows, with
a board on his lap, and a fine-looking document on the
board. Knott Bolstrood—forty-two years old—knelt next to
the bed. He turned round to look as Daniel entered. During

the ten years Knott had survived on the Common-Side of
Newgate Prison, living in a dark place among murderers and
lunaticks, he had developed a strong instinct for watching
his back. It was as useful for a Secretary of State as it had
been for a marauding Phanatique.

"Brother Daniel!"

"My lord."

"You'll do as well as anyone—better than most."

"Do for what, sir?"

"Witnessing the Bishop's signature."

Bolstrood got a quill charged with ink. Daniel wrapped
Wilkins's puffy fingers around it. After a bit of heavy
breathing on the part of its owner, the hand began to move,
and a tangle of lines and curves began to take shape on the
page, bearing the same relationship to Wilkins's signature as
a ghost to a man. It was a good thing, in other words, that
several persons were on hand to verify it. Daniel had no idea
what this document was. But from the way it was engrossed
he could guess that it was meant for the eyes of the King.

Count Penistone was a man in a hurry, after that. But before he left he said to Daniel: "If you have any stock in the
Duke of York's Guinea Company, sell it—for that Popish
slave-monger is going to reap the whirlwind." Then, for
maybe the second or third time in his life, Knott Bolstrood
smiled.

"Show it to me, Dr. Leibniz," Wilkins said, skipping over
all of the formalities; he had not urinated in three days and
so there was a certain urgency about everything.

Leibniz sat gingerly on the edge of the bed, and opened
the box.

Daniel saw gears, cranks, shafts. He thought it might be a
new sort of timepiece, but it had no dial and no hands—only
a few wheels with numbers stamped on them.

"It owes much to Monsieur Pascal's machine, of course,"
Leibniz said, "but this one can *multiply* numbers as well as
add and subtract them."

"Make it work for me, Doctor."

"I must confess to you that it is not finished yet." Leibniz frowned, tilted the box toward the light, and blew into it sharply. A cockroach flew out and traced a flailing parabola to the floor and scurried under the bed. "This is just a demo'. But when it is finished, it will be *magnifique*."

"Never mind," Wilkins said. "It uses denary numbers?"

"Yes, like Pascal's—but binary would work better—"

"You needn't tell *me*," Wilkins said, and then rambled for at least a quarter of an hour, quoting whole pages from relevant sections of the *Cryptonomicon*.

Leibniz finally cleared his throat and said, "There are mechanical reasons, too—with denary numbers, too many meshings of gears are necessary—friction and backlash play havoc."

"Hooke! Hooke could build it," Wilkins said. "But enough of machines. Let us speak of Pansophism. Tell me, now—have you met with success in Vienna?"

"I have written to the Emperor several times, describing the French king's Bibliothèque du Roi—"

"Trying to incite his Envy—?"

"Yes—but in his hierarchy of vices, Sloth would appear to reign unchallenged by Envy or anything else. Have you met with success here, my lord?"

"Sir Elias Ashmole is starting a brave library—but he's distracted and addled with Alchemy. I have had to attend to more fundamental matters—" Wilkins said, and gestured weakly toward the door through which Bolstrood had departed. "I believe that binary arithmetickal engines will be of enormous significance—Oldenburg, too, is most eager."

"If I could carry your work forward, sir, I would consider myself privileged."

"Now we are only being polite—I have no time. Waterhouse!"

Leibniz closed up his box. The Bishop of Chester watched the lid closing over the engine, and his eyelids almost closed at the same moment. But then he summoned up a bit more strength. Leibniz backed out of the way, and Daniel took his place.

"My Lord?"

It was all he could get out. Drake had been his father, but John Wilkins really *was* his lord in almost every sense of the word. His lord, his bishop, his minister, his professor.

"The responsibility now falls upon you to make it all happen."

"My Lord? To make *what* happen?"

But Wilkins was either dead or asleep.

THEY STUMBLED THROUGH a small dark kitchen and out into the maze of yards and alleys behind Chancery Lane, where they drew the attention of diverse roosters and dogs. Pursued by their hue and cry, Mr. Waterhouse and Dr. Leibniz emerged into a district of theatres and coffee-houses. Any one of those coffee-houses would have sufficed, but they were close to Queen Street—another of Hooke's paving-projects. Daniel had begun to feel like a flea under the Great Microscope. Hooke subtended about half of the cosmos, and made Daniel feel as if he were flitting from one place of refuge to another, even though he had nothing to hide. Leibniz was hale, and seemed to enjoy exploring a new city. Daniel got them turned back in the direction of the river. He was trying to make out what responsibility, specifically, had just been placed on his shoulders by Wilkins. He realized—after a quarter of an hour of being a very poor conversationalist—that Leibniz might have ideas on the subject.

"You said you wanted to carry Wilkins's work forward, Doctor. *Which* of his projects were you referring to? Flying to the moon, or—"

"The Philosophical Language," Leibniz said, as if this should have been obvious.

He knew that Daniel had been involved in that project, and seemed to take the question as a sign that Daniel wasn't especially proud of it—which was true. Noting Leibniz's respect for the project, Daniel felt a stab of misgivings that perhaps the Philosophical Language had some wonderful properties that he had been too stupid to notice.

"What more is there to be done with it?" Daniel asked. "You have some refinements—additions—? You wish to translate the work into German—? You're shaking your head, Doctor—what is it, then?"

"I was trained as a lawyer. Don't look so horrified, Mr. Waterhouse, it is respectable enough, for an educated man in Germany. You must remember that we don't have a Royal Society. After I was awarded my Doctor of Jurisprudence, I went to work for the Archbishop of Mainz, who gave me the job of reforming the legal code—which was a Tower of Babel—Roman and Germanic and local common law all mangled together. I concluded that there was little point in jury-rigging something. What was needed was to break everything down into certain basic concepts and begin from first principles."

"I can see how the Philosophical Language would be useful in breaking things down," Daniel said, "but to build them back up, you would need something else—"

"Logic," Leibniz said.

"Logic has a dismal reputation among the higher primates in the Royal Society—"

"Because they associate it with the Scholastic pedants who tormented them in university," Leibniz said agreeably. "I'm not talking about *that* sort of thing! When I say logic, I mean Euclidean."

"Begin with certain axioms and combine them according to definite rules—"

"Yes—and build up a system of laws that is as provable, and as internally consistent, as the theory of conic sections."

"But you have recently moved to Paris, have you not?"

Leibniz nodded. "Part of the same project. For obvious reasons, I need to improve my knowledge of mathematics— what better place for it?" Then his face got a distracted, brooding look. "Actually there was *another* reason—the

Archbishop sent me as an emissary, to tender a certain proposal to Louis XIV."

"So today is not the first time you have combined Natural Philosophy with Diplomacy—"

"Nor the last, I fear."

"What was the proposal you set before the King?"

"I only got as far as Colbert, actually. But it was that, instead of invading her *neighbors,* La France ought to make an expedition to Egypt, and establish an Empire there—creating a threat to the Turk's left flank—Africa—and forcing him to move some armies away from his right flank—"

"Christendom."

"Yes." Leibniz sighed.

"It sounds—er—audacious," Daniel said, now on a diplomatic mission of his own.

"By the time I'd arrived in Paris, and secured an appointment with Colbert, King Louis had already flung his invasion-force into Holland and Germany."

"Ah, well—'twas a fine enough idea."

"Perhaps some *future* monarch of France will revive it," Leibniz said. "For the Dutch, the consequences were dire. For me, it was fortuitous—no longer straining at *diplomatic* gnats, I could go to Colbert's house in the Rue Vivienne and grapple with *philosophick* giants."

"I've given up trying to grapple with them," Daniel sighed, "and now only dodge their steps."

They rambled all the way down to the Strand and sat down in a coffee-house with south-facing windows. Daniel tilted the arithmetickal engine toward the sun and inspected its small gears. "Forgive me for asking, Doctor, but is this *purely* a conversation-starter, or—?"

"Perhaps you should go back and ask Wilkins."

"Touché."

Now some sipping of coffee.

"My Lord Chester spoke correctly—in a way—when he said that Hooke could build this," Daniel said. "Only a few years ago, he was a creature of the Royal Society, and he *would* have. Now he's a creature of London, and he has artisans build most of his watches. The only exceptions, perhaps, are the ones he makes for the King, the Duke of York, and the like."

"If I can explain to Mr. Hooke the importance of this device, I'm confident he'll undertake it."

"You don't understand Hooke," Daniel said. "Because you are German, and because you have diverse foreign connections, Hooke will assume you are a part of the Grubendolian cabal—which in his mind looms so vast that a French invasion of Egypt would be only a corner of it."

"Grubendol?" Leibniz said. Then, before Daniel could say it, he continued, "I see—it is an anagram for Oldenburg."

Daniel ground his teeth for a while, remembering how long it had taken *him* to decipher the same anagram, then continued: "Hooke is convinced that Oldenburg is stealing his inventions—sending them overseas in encrypted letters. What is worse, he saw you disembarking at the Bridge, and being handed a letter by a known Dutchman. He'll want to know what manner of Continental intrigues you're mixed up in."

"It's not a secret that my patron is the Archbishop of Mainz," Leibniz protested.

"But you said you were a Lutheran."

"And I am—but one of the Archbishop's objectives is to reconcile the two churches."

"*Here* we say there are *more* than two," Daniel reminded him.

"Is Hooke a religious man?"

"If you mean 'does he go to church,' then no," Daniel admitted, after some hesitation. "But if you mean 'does he believe in God' then I should say yes—the Microscope and Telescope are his stained-glass windows, the animalcules in a drop of his semen, or the shadows on Saturn's rings, are his heavenly Visions."

"Is he like Spinoza, then?"

"You mean, one who says God is nothing more than Nature? I doubt it."

"What does Hooke want?"

"He is busy all day and night designing new buildings, surveying new streets—"

"Yes, and I am busy overhauling the German legal code—but it is not what I *want*."

"Mr. Hooke pursues various schemes and intrigues against Oldenburg—"

"But surely not because he *wants* to?"

"He writes papers, and lectures—"

Leibniz scoffed. "Not a tenth of what he knows is written down, is it?"

"You must keep in mind, about Hooke, that he is poorly understood, partly because of his crookedness and partly because of his difficult personal qualities. In a world where many still refuse to believe in the Copernican Hypothesis, some of Hooke's more forward ideas would be considered grounds for imprisonment in Bedlam."

Leibniz's eyes narrowed. "Is it Alchemy, then?"

"Mr. Hooke despises Alchemy."

"Good!" Leibniz blurted—most undiplomatically. Daniel covered a smile with his coffee-cup. Leibniz looked horrified, fearing that Daniel might be an Alchemist himself. Daniel put him at ease by quoting from Hooke: "'Why should we endeavour to discover Mysteries in that which has no such thing in it? And like Rabbis find out Cabalism, and ænigmas in the Figure, and placing of Letters, where no such thing lies hid: whereas in natural forms . . . the more we magnify the object, the more excellencies and mysteries do appear; and the more we discover the imperfections of our senses, and the Omnipotency and Infinite perceptions of the great Creator.'"

"So Hooke believes that the secrets of the world are to be found in some microscopic process."

"Yes—snowflakes, for example. If each snowflake is unique, then why are the six arms of a *given* snowflake the same?"

"If we assume that the arms grew outwards from the center, then there must be something in that center that imbues each of the six arms with the same organizing principle—just as all oak trees, and all lindens, share a common nature, and grow into the same general shape."

"But to speak of some mysterious *nature* is to be like the Scholastics—Aristotle dressed up in a doublet," Daniel said.

"Or in an Alchemist's robe—" Leibniz returned.

"Agreed. Newton would argue—"

"That fellow who invented the telescope?"

"Yes. He would argue that if you could catch a snowflake, melt it, and distill its water, you could extract some essence that would be the embodiment of its nature in the physical world, and account for its shape."

"Yes—that is a good *distillation,* as it were, of the Alchemists' mental habit—which is to believe that anything we cannot understand must have some physical residue that can in principle be refined from coarse matter."

"Mr. Hooke, by contrast, is convinced that Nature's ways are consonant to man's reason. As the beating of a fly's wings is consonant to the vibration of a plucked string, so that the sound of one, produces a sympathetic resonance in the other—in the same way, every phenomenon in the world can, in principle, be understood by human ratiocination."

Leibniz said, "And so with a sufficiently powerful microscope, Hooke might peer into the core of a snowflake at the moment of its creation and see its internal parts meshing, like gears of a watch made by God."

"Just so, sir."

"And this is what Hooke *wants*?"

"It is the implicit goal of all his researches—it is what *must* believe and *must* look for, because that is the nature of Hooke."

"Now *you* are talking like an Aristotelian," Leibniz jested.

Then he reached across the table and put his hand on the box, and said something that was apparently quite serious. "What a watch is to *time,* this engine is to *thought*."

"Sir! You show me a few gears that add and multiply numbers—well enough. But this is not the same as *thought*!"

"What is a number, Mr. Waterhouse?"

Daniel groaned. "How can you ask such questions?"

"How can you *not* ask them, sir? You are a philosopher, are you not?"

"A Natural Philosopher."

"Then you must agree that in the *modern* world, mathematicks is at the heart of Natural Philosophy—it is like the mysterious essence in the core of the snowflake. When I was fifteen years old, Mr. Waterhouse, I was wandering in the Rosenthal—which is a garden on the edge of Leipzig— when I decided that in order to be a Natural Philosopher I would have to put aside the old doctrine of substantial forms and instead rely upon Mechanism to explain the world. This led me inevitably to mathematicks."

"When *I* was fifteen, I was handing out Phanatiqual libels just down the street from here, and dodging the Watch—but in time, Doctor, as Newton and I studied Descartes at Cambridge, I came to share your view concerning the supreme position of mathematics."

"Then I repeat my question: What is a number? And what is it to multiply two numbers?"

"Whatever it is, Doctor, it is different from *thinking*."

"Bacon said, 'Whatever has sufficient differences, perceptible by the sense, is in nature competent to express cogitations.' You cannot deny that numbers are in that sense competent—"

"To *express* cogitation, yes! But to *express* cogitations is not to *perform* them, or else quills and printing-presses would write poetry by themselves."

"Can your mind manipulate this spoon directly?" Leibniz said, holding up a silver spoon, and then setting it down on the table between them.

"Not without my hands."

"So, when you think about the spoon, is your mind manipulating the spoon?"

"No. The spoon is unaffected, no matter what I think about it."

"Because our minds cannot manipulate physical objects—cup, saucer, spoon—instead they manipulate *symbols* of them, which are stored in the mind."

"I will accept that."

"Now, you yourself helped Lord Chester devise the Philosophical Language, whose chief virtue is that it assigns all things in the world positions in certain tables—positions that can be encoded by numbers."

"Again, I agree that numbers can *express* cogitations, through a sort of encryption. But *performing* cogitations is another matter entirely!"

"Why? We add, subtract, and multiply numbers."

"Suppose the number three represents a chicken, and the number twelve the Rings of Saturn—what then is three times twelve?"

"Well, you can't just do it at *random*," Leibniz said, "any more than Euclid could draw lines and circles at random, and come up with theorems. There has to be a formal system of rules, according to which the numbers are combined."

"And you propose building a machine to do this?"

"*Pourquoi non?* With the aid of a machine, truth can be grasped as if pictured on paper."

"But it is still not thinking. Thinking is what angels do—it is a property given to Man by God."

"How do you suppose God gives it to us?"

"I do not pretend to know, sir!"

"If you take a man's brain and distill him, can you extract a mysterious essence—the divine presence of God on Earth?"

"That is called the Philosophick Mercury by Alchemists."

"Or, if Hooke were to peer into a man's brain with a good enough microscope, would he see tiny meshings of gears?"

Daniel said nothing. Leibniz had imploded his skull. The gears were jammed, the Philosophick Mercury dribbling out his ear-holes.

"You've already sided with Hooke, and against Newton,

concerning snowflakes—so may I assume you take the same position concerning brains?" Leibniz continued, now with exaggerated politeness.

Daniel spent a while staring out the window at a point far away. Eventually his awareness came back into the coffee-house. He glanced, a bit furtively, at the arithmetical engine. "There is a place in *Micrographia* where Hooke describes the way flies swarm around meat, butterflies around flowers, gnats around water—giving the *semblance* of rational behavior. But he thinks it is all because of internal mechanisms triggered by the peculiar vapors arising from meat, flowers, *et cetera*. In other words, he thinks that these creatures are no more rational than a trap, where an animal seizing a piece of bait pulls a string that fires a gun. A savage watching the trap kill the animal might suppose it to be rational. But the *trap* is not rational—the man who *contrived* the trap is. Now, if you—the ingenious Dr. Leibniz—contrive a machine that gives the *impression* of thinking—is it *really* thinking, or merely reflecting your genius?"

"You could as well have asked: are *we* thinking? Or merely reflecting God's genius?"

"Suppose I *had* asked it, Doctor—what would your answer be?"

"My answer, sir, is both."

"Both? But that's impossible. It has to be one or the other."

"I do not agree with you, Mr. Waterhouse."

"If we are mere mechanisms, obeying rules laid down by God, then all of our actions are predestined, and we are not really thinking."

"But Mr. Waterhouse, you were raised by Puritans, who believe in predestination."

"Raised by them, yes . . ." Daniel said, and let it hang in the air for a while.

"You no longer accept predestination?"

"It does not resonate sweetly with my observations of the world, as a good hypothesis *ought* to." Daniel sighed. "Now I see why Newton has chosen the path of Alchemy."

"When you say he *chose* that path, you imply that he must

have *rejected* another. Are you saying that your friend Newton explored the idea of a mechanically determined brain,
and rejected it?"

"It may be he explored it, if only in his dreams and nightmares."

Leibniz raised his eyebrows and spent a few moments
staring at the clutter of pots and cups on the table. "This is
one of the two great labyrinths into which human minds are
drawn: the question of free will versus predestination. You
were raised to believe in the latter. You have rejected it—
which must have been a great spiritual struggle—and become a thinker. You have adopted a modern, mechanical
philosophy. But that very philosophy now seems to be leading you back towards predestination. It is most difficult."

"But you claim to know of a third way, Doctor. I should
like to hear of it."

"And I should like to tell of it," Leibniz said, "but I must
part from you now, and make rendezvous with my traveling
companions. May we continue on some other day?"

∽

Aboard Minerva, *Cape Cod Bay, Massachusetts*

NOVEMBER 1713

⚘

HE DISSECTED MORE than his share of dead men's heads
during those early Royal Society days, and knows that the
hull of the skull is all wrapped about with squishy rigging:
haul-yards of tendon and braces of ligament cleated to pin-

rails on the jawbone and temple, tugging at the corners of
spreading canvases of muscle that curve over the forehead
and wrap the old Jolly Roger in as many overlapping layers
as there are sails on a ship of the line. As Daniel trudges up
out of *Minerva*'s bilge, dragging a chinking sack of ammuni-
tion behind him, he feels all that stuff tightening up, steadily
and inexorably, each stairstep a click of the pawls, as if invisible sailors were turning capstans inside his skull. He's
spent the last hour below the water-line—never his favorite
place on shipboard, but safe from cannonballs anyway—
smashing plates with a hammer and bellowing old songs,
and never been so relaxed in all his life. But now he's
climbed back up into the center of the hull, just the sort of
bulky bull's-eye pirates might aim swivel-guns at if they
lacked confidence in their ability to pick off small fine tar-
gets from their wave-tossed platforms.

Minerva's got a spacious stairwell running all the way
down through the middle of her, just ahead of the mighty
creaking trunk of the mainmast, with two flights of stairs
spiraling opposite directions so the men descending don't
interfere with those ascending—or so doddering Doctors
with sacks of pottery-shards do not hinder boys running up
from the hold with—what? The light's dim. They appear to
be canvas sacks—heavy bulging polyhedra with rusty nails
protruding from the vertices. Daniel's glad they're going
up the other stairs, because he wouldn't want one of those
things to bump into him. It'd be certain death from lock-
jaw.

Some important procedure's underway on the gundeck.
The gunports are all closed, except for one cracked open a
hand's breadth on the starboard side—therefore, not far
from Daniel when he emerges from the staircase. Several
relatively important officers have gathered in a semicircle
around this port, as if for a baptism. There's a general commotion of pinging and thudding coming from the hull-
planks and the deck above. It could be gunfire. And if it
could be, it probably is. Someone grabs the sack from

Daniel and drags it to the center of the gundeck. Men with empty blunderbusses converge on it like jackals on a haunch.

Daniel's elbowed hard by a man hauling on a line that enters *Minerva* through a small orifice above the gunport. This has the effect of (1) knocking Daniel down on his bony pelvis and (2) swinging said gunport all the way open, creating a sudden square of light. Framed in it is part of the rigging of a smaller ship, so close that a younger man could easily jump to it. There is a man—a pirate—on that ship pointing a musket in Daniel's direction, but he's struck down by a gaudy spray of out-moded china fragments, fired down from Minerva's upperdeck. "Caltrops away!" says someone, and boys with sacks lunge toward the open gunport and hurl out a tinkling cosmos, down to the deck of the smaller ship. Moments later the same ceremony's repeated through a gunport on the larboard side—so there must be a pirate-vessel *there*, too. The gunports are hauled closed again, sporting new decorations: constellations of lead balls fired into 'em from below.

The screaming/bellowing ratio has climbed noticeably. Daniel (helping himself to his feet, thank you, and hobbling crabwise to a safe haven near the mainmast, to inventory his complaints) reckons that the screaming must originate from shoeless pirates with caltrop-spikes between their metatarsals—until he hears "Fire! Fire!" and notes a curl of smoke invading the gundeck through a cracked gunport, speared on a shaft of sunlight. Then some instinct makes Daniel forget his bruises and sprains—he's up the last flight of stairs, spry as any eight-year-old powder monkey, and out in the sail-dappled sunlight, where he'll happily risk musket-balls.

But it's the pirate-sloop, not *Minerva,* that's on fire. Lines are going slack all over the starboard half of the ship. Each of them happens to terminate in a rusty grappling-hook that's lodged in a ratline or a rail. The pirates are cutting themselves free!

Now comes a general rush of men to larboard, where a whaleboat is still pestering them. *Minerva* rolls that direction on a sea. The whaleboat comes into view, no longer eclipsed by the hull's tumblehome, and a score of muskets and blunderbusses fire down into it at once. Daniel only glimpses the result—appalling—then *Minerva* rolls starboard and hides it from view.

The men throw their weapons into lockers and ascend into the rigging, pursuant to commands from van Hoek, who's up on the poop deck bellowing into a shiny trumpet of hammered brass. There are plenty of men belowdecks who could be making contributions here, but they don't come up. Daniel, beginning to get the hang of pirate-fighting, understands that van Hoek wants to hide the true size of his crew from Teach.

They have been running before a north wind (though it seems to've shifted a few points westwards) for over an hour. The southern limb of Cape Cod is dead ahead, barring their path. But long before reaching the shore, *Minerva* would run aground in coarse brown sand. So they have to come about now and begin to work to windward, towards the open Atlantic. These simple terms—"come about," for example— denote procedures that are as complicated and tradition-bound as the installation of a new Pope. Great big strong men are running toward the bow: the foreyard loosers and furlers, and the headsail loosers and stowers. They take up positions on the forecastledeck or shinny out onto the bowsprit, but politely step aside for the wiry foretopmen who begin their laborious ascent up the fore shrouds to work the topsails and things higher up the foremast. It is a bristling and tangled thicket of nautical detail. Like watching fifty surgeons dissect fifty different animals at once—the kind of stuff that, half a century ago, would've fascinated Daniel, sucked him into this sort of life, made him a sea-captain. But like a captain reefing and striking his sails before too strong a wind, lest it drive his ship onto the shallows, Daniel ignores as much of this as he can get away with, and tries to understand what is happening in its general outlines: *Minerva* is coming round toward the wind. In her wake, a mile abaft, is the sloop, her sails lying a-shiver, leaving the little ship dead in the water, drifting slowly to leeward, as pirates try to beat out flames with sopped canvas whilst not stepping on any of those caltrops. Several miles north of that, four more ships are spread out on the bay, waiting.

A panic of luffing and shivering spreads through *Minerva*'s rig as all the sails change their relationship to the wind, then everything snaps tight, just as the sailors knew it would, and she's running as close-hauled as she can, headed northeast. In just a few minutes she's drawn abeam of that scorched sloop, which is now steaming, rather than smoking, and attempting to make sail. It's obvious that caltrops and flying crockery-shards have deranged the crew, in the sense that no man knows what to do when. So the sloop's movements are inconclusive.

All the more surprising that van Hoek orders a tack, when it isn't really necessary. *Minerva* comes about and sails directly toward the meandering sloop. Several minutes later, *Minerva* bucks once as she rams the sloop amidships, then shudders as her keel drives the wreckage under the sea. Those burly forecastlemen go out with cutlasses and hatchets to cut shreds of the sloop's rigging away from the bowsprit, where it has become fouled. Van Hoek, strolling on the poop deck, aims a pistol over the rail and, in a sudden lily of smoke, speeds a drowning pirate to Hell.

✣

Royal Society Meeting, Gunfleet House
1673

✣

"I RENEW MY OBJECTION—" said Robert Boyle. "It does not seem *respectful* to inventory the contents of our Founder's guts as if they were a few keepsakes left behind in a chest—"

"Overruled," said John Comstock, still President of the Royal Society—just barely. "Though, out of respect for our *remarkably generous* host, I will defer to *him*."

Thomas More Anglesey, Duke of Gunfleet, was seated at the head of his drawing-room, at a conspicuously new gilt-and-white-enamel table in the *barock* style. Other bigwigs, such as John Comstock, surrounded him, seated according to equally *barock* rules of protocol. Anglesey withdrew a large watch from the pocket of his Persian vest and held it up to the light streaming in through about half an acre of window-glass, exceptionally clear and colorless and bubble-free and recently installed.

"Can we get through it in *fifty seconds*?" he inquired.

Inhalations all round. In his peripheral vision, Daniel saw several old watches being stuffed into pockets—pockets that tended to be frayed, and rimmed with that nameless dark shine. But the Earl of Upnor and—of all people—Roger Comstock (who was sitting next to Daniel) reached into clean bright pockets, took out new watches, and managed to hold them up in such a way that most everyone in the room could see that each was equipped, not just with *two* but *three* hands, the third moving so quickly that you could *see* its progress round the dial—counting the *seconds*!

Many hunched glances, now, toward Robert Hooke, the Hephaestus of the tiny. Hooke managed to look as if he didn't care about how impressed everyone was—which was probably true. Daniel looked over at Leibniz, sitting there with his box on his lap, who had a soulful, distant expression.

Roger Comstock, noting the same thing: "Is that how a German looks before he bursts into tears?"

Upnor, following Roger's gaze: "Or before he pulls out his broadsword and begins mowing down Turks."

"He deserves our credit for showing up at all," Daniel murmured—hypnotized by the movement of Roger Comstock's second-hand. "Word arrived yesterday—his patron died in Mainz."

"Of embarrassment, most likely," hissed the Earl of Upnor.

A chirurgeon, looking deeply nervous and out of his depth, was chivvied up to the front of the room. It was a big room, this. Its owner, the Duke of Gunfleet, perhaps too much under the spell of his architect, insisted on calling it the *Grand Salon.* This was simply French for *Big Big Room;* but it seemed a little bigger, and ever so much grander, when the French nomenclature was used.

Even under the humble appellation of Big Big Room, it was a bit too big and too grand for the chirurgeon. "Fifty seconds!—?" he said.

There was a difficult interlude, lasting much longer than fifty seconds, as a helpful Fellow tried to explain the idea of fifty seconds to the chirurgeon, who had got stuck on the misconception that they were speaking of 1/52s—perhaps some idiom from the gambling world?

"Think of minutes of longitude," someone called out from the back of the Big Big Room. "One sixtieth of that sort of a minute is called what?"

"A second of longitude," said the chirurgeon.

"By analogy, then, one sixtieth of a minute of *time* is—"

"A second . . . of time," said the chirurgeon; then was suddenly mortified as he ran through some rough calculations in his head.

"One thirty-six-hundredth of an hour," called out a bored voice with a French accent.

"Time's up!" announced Boyle, "Let us move on—"

"The good doctor may have *another* fifty seconds," Anglesey ruled.

"Thank you, my lord," said the chirurgeon, and cleared his throat. "Perhaps those gentlemen who have been the *patrons* of Mr. Hooke's horologickal researches, and are now the *beneficiaries* of his so ingenious handiwork, will be so kind as to keep me informed, during my presentation of the results of Lord Chester's *post-mortem,* as to the passage of time—"

"I accept that charge—you have already spent twenty seconds!" said the Earl of Upnor.

"Please, Louis, let us show due respect for our Founder, and for this Doctor," said his father.

"It seems *too late* for the former, Father, but I assent to the latter."

"Hear, hear!" Boyle said. This made the chirurgeon falter—but John Comstock stiffened him up with a look.

"Most of Lord Chester's organs were normal for a man of his age," the chirurgeon said. "In one kidney I found two small stones. In the ureter, some gravel. Thank you."

The chirurgeon sat down very hastily, like an infantryman who has just seen puffs of smoke bloom from the powder-pans of opposing muskets. Buzzing and droning filled the room—suddenly it was like one of Wilkins's glass apiaries, and the chirurgeon a boy who'd poked it with a stick. But the Queen Bee was dead, and there was disagreement as to who was going to be stung.

"It is what I suspected—there was no stoppage of urine," Hooke finally announced, "only pain from small kidney-stones. Pain that induced Lord Chester to take solace in opiates."

Which was as good as flinging a glass of water in the face of Monsieur LeFebure. The King's Chymist stood up. "To have given comfort to the Lord Bishop of Chester in his time of need is the greatest honor of my career," he said. "It would be an infamous shame if any of those *other* medicines he took, led to his demise."

Now a great deal more buzzing, in a different key. Roger Comstock stood up and cut through it: "If Mr. Pepys would be so kind as to show us *his* stone . . ."

Pepys fairly erupted to his feet across the room and shoved a hand into a pregnant pocket.

John Comstock sent both men back down with cast-iron eyes. "It would not be a kindness, Mr., er, *Comstock,* as we've all *seen* it."

Daniel's turn. "Mr. Pepys's stone is colossal—yet he was able to urinate a *little*. Considering the smallness of the urinary passages, is it not possible that a *small* stone might block urine as well as a *large* one—and perhaps *better*?"

No more buzzing now, but a deep general murmur—the point was awarded, by acclamation, to Daniel. He sat down. Roger Comstock ejaculated compliments all over him.

"I've had stones in the kidney," Anglesey said, "and I will testify that the pain is beyond description."

John Comstock: "Like something meted out by the *Popish Inquisition?*"

"I cannot make out what is going on," said Daniel, quietly, to his neighbor.

"Well, you'd best make it out before you say anything else," Roger said. "Just a suggestion."

"First Anglesey and Comstock are united in disgracing Wilkins's memory—then next moment, at each other's throats over religion."

"Where does that put you, Daniel?" Roger asked.

Anglesey, unruffled: "I'm sure I speak for the entire Royal Society in expressing unbounded gratitude to Monsieur LeFebure for easing Lord Chester's final months."

"The *Elixir Proprietalis LeFebure* is greatly admired at

Court—even among young ladies who are *not* afflicted with exquisitely painful disorders," said John Comstock. "Some of them like it so well that they have started a new fashion: going to sleep, and never waking up again."

The conversation had now taken on the semblance of a lawn-tennis match played with sputtering granadoes. There was a palpable shifting of bodies and chairs as Fellows of the R.S. aligned themselves for spectation. Monsieur LeFebure caught Comstock's lob with perfect aplomb: "It has been known since ancient times that syrup of poppies, in even small doses, cripples the judgment by *day* and induces frightful dreams by *night*—would you not agree?"

Here John Comstock, sensing a trap, said nothing. But Hooke answered, "I can attest to that."

"Your dedication to Truth is an example to us all, Mr. Hooke. In *large* doses, of course, the medicine *kills*. The *first* symptom—destruction of judgment—can lead to the *second*—death by over-dosing. That is why the *Elixir Proprietalis LeFebure* should only be administered under *my* supervision—and that is why I have personally taken pains to visit Lord Chester several times each week, during the months that his judgment was crippled by the drug."

Comstock was annoyed by LeFebure's resilience. But (as Daniel realized too late) Comstock had *another* goal in sight besides denting LeFebure's reputation, and it was a goal that he shared with Thomas More Anglesey—normally his rival and enemy. A look passed between these two.

Daniel stood. Roger got a grip on his sleeve, but was not in a position to reach his tongue. "I saw Lord Chester several times in his final weeks and saw no evidence that his mental faculties were affected! To the contrary—"

"Lest someone come away with the foolish opinion that you are being *unkind,* Monsieur LeFebure," Anglesey said—shooting a glare at Daniel—"did Lord Chester not consider this mental impairment a fair price to pay for the opportunity to spend a few last months with his family?"

"Oh, he paid that price *gladly,*" Monsieur LeFebure said.

"I collect that this is why we've heard so little from him in the way of Natural Philosophy of late—" Comstock said.

"Yes—and it is why we should overlook any of his more recent, er . . ."

"Indiscretions?"

"Enthusiasms?"

"Impulsive ventures into the *lower* realm of *politics*—"

"His mental powers dimmed—his heart was as pure as ever—and sought solace in well-meaning gestures."

That was all the poisoned eulogies Daniel could stand to hear—then he was out in the garden of Gunfleet House watching a white marble mermaid vomit an endless stream of clear babble into a fish-pond. Roger Comstock was right behind him.

There were marble benches a-plenty, but he could not sit. Rage had taken him. Daniel was not especially susceptible to that passion. But he understood, now, why the Greeks had believed that Furies were angels of a sort, winged-swift, armed with whips and torches, rushing up out of Erebus to goad men unto madness. Roger, watching Daniel pace around the garden, might have convinced himself that his friend's wild lunges and strides were being provoked by invisible lashes, and that his face had been scorched by torches.

"O for a sword," Daniel said.

"Aw, you'd be dead right away if you tried that!"

"I know that, Roger. Some would say there are worse things than being dead. Thank god Jeffreys wasn't in the room—to see me running out of it like a thief!" And here his voice choked and tears rushed to his eyes. For this was the worst part. That in the end he had done nothing—*nothing*—except run out of the *Grand Salon*.

"You're clever, but you don't know what to do," Roger said. "I'm the other way round. We complement each other."

Daniel was annoyed. Then he reflected that to be the complement of a man with as many deficiencies as Roger Comstock was a high distinction. He turned and looked the other up and down, perhaps with an eye towards punching him in the nose. Roger was not so much *wearing* his wig as *embedded* in its lower reaches, and it was *perfect*—the sort of wig that had its own staff. Daniel, even if he were the punching sort, could not bring himself to ruin anything so perfect. "You are too modest, Roger—obviously you've gone out and done *something* clever."

"Oh, you've noticed my attire! I hope you don't think it's foppish."

"I think it's *expensive.*"

"For one of the Golden Comstocks, you mean . . ."

Roger came closer. Daniel kept being cruel to Roger, trying to make him go away, but Roger took it as honesty, implying profound friendship.

"Well, in any case it is certainly an improvement on your appearance the last time I saw you." Daniel was referring to the explosion in the laboratory, which was now far enough in the past that both Daniel and Roger had their eyebrows back. He had not seen Roger since that night because Isaac, upon coming back to find the lab blown up, had fired him, and sent him packing, not just out of the laboratory, but out of Cambridge. Thus had ended a scholarly career that had probably needed to be put out of its misery in any case. Daniel knew not whither their Cinderella had fled, but he appeared to have done well there.

Roger plainly had no idea what Daniel was talking about. "I don't recall that—did you meet me in the street, before I left for Amsterdam? I probably did look wretched then."

Daniel now tried the Leibnizian experiment of rehearsing the explosion in the laboratory from Roger's point of view.

Roger had been working in the dark: a necessity, as any open flame might set fire to the gunpowder. And not much of an inconvenience, since what he'd been up to was dead simple: grinding the powder in a mortar and dumping it into a bag. Both the sound, and the feel of the pestle in his hand, would tell when the powder had been ground to a fine enough consistency for whatever purpose Roger had in mind. So he had worked blind. Light was the one thing he prayed he wouldn't see, for it would mean a spark that would be certain to ignite the powder. Attent on work and worry, he had never known that Daniel had come back to the house— why should he, since he was supposed to be watching a play? And Roger had not yet heard the applause and the distant murmur of voices that would signal its end. Roger had never heard Daniel's approach, for Daniel, who'd phant'sied he was stalking a rat, had been at pains to move as quietly as possible. The heavy fabric screen had blocked the light of Daniel's candle to the point where it was no brighter than the ambient furnace-glow. Suddenly the candle-flame had been in Roger's face. In other circumstances he'd've known it for what it was; but standing there with a sack of gunpowder in his hands, he had taken it for what he'd most dreaded: a spark. He had dropped the mortar and the bag and flung himself back as quick as he could. The explosion had followed in the next instant. He could neither have seen nor heard anything until after he'd fled the building. So there was no ground to suppose he had ever registered as much as the faintest impression of Daniel's presence. He'd not seen Daniel since.

And so Daniel was presented with a choice between telling Roger the truth, and assenting to the lie that Roger had conveniently proffered: namely, that Daniel had spied Roger in the street before Roger had departed for Amsterdam. Telling the truth held no danger, so far as he could see. The lie was attended with a small peril that Roger—who was cunning, in a way—might be dangling it before him as some sort of test.

"I thought you knew," Daniel said, "I was in the laboratory when it happened. Had gone there to fetch Isaac's paper on tangents. Nearly got blown to bits myself!"

Astonishment and revelation came out of Roger's face like sudden flame. But if Daniel had owned a Hooke watch, he would have counted only a few seconds of time before the old look came back down over his face. As when a candle-snuffer pounces on a wild flame and the errant brilliance that had filled one's vision a moment ago is in an instant vanished, the only thing left in its place a dull sight of old silverwork, frozen and familiar.

"I *phant'sied* I'd heard someone moving about in there!" Roger exclaimed. Which was obviously a lie; but it made the conversation move along better.

Daniel was keen to ask Roger what he'd been doing with the gunpowder. But perhaps it would be better to wait for Roger to volunteer something. "So it was to Amsterdam you went, to recuperate from the excitements of that evening," Daniel said.

"Here first."

"Here to London?"

"Here to the Angleseys'. Lovely family. And socializing with them has its benefits." Roger reached up as if to stroke his wig—but dared not touch it.

"What, you're not in their *employ*—?"

"No, no! It's much better. I *know* things. Certain of the Golden Comstocks immigrated—all right, all right, some would say *fled*—to Holland in the last century. Settled in Amsterdam. I went and paid them a visit. From them, I knew that de Ruyter was taking his fleet to Guinea to seize the Duke of York's slave-ports. So I sold my Guinea Company shares while they were still high. Then from the Angleseys I learned that King Looie was making preparations to invade the Dutch Republic—but could never stage a campaign without purchasing grain first—purchasing it you'll never guess *where*."

"No!"

"Just so—the Dutch sold France the grain that King Looie is using to conquer them! At any rate—I took my money from the Guinea Company shares, and took a large position in Amsterdam-grain just before King Looie bid the price up! Voilà! Now I've a Hooke-watch, a big wig, and a lot on fashionable Waterhouse Square!"

"You own—" Daniel began, and was well on his way to saying *You own some of my family estate!?* when they were interrupted by Leibniz, stalking through a flower-bed, hugging his brain-in-a-box.

"Dr. Leibniz—the Royal Society were quite taken with your Arithmetickal Engine," Roger said.

"But they did not like my *mathematickal* proofs," said one dejected German savant.

"On the contrary—they were acknowledged to be unusually elegant!" Daniel protested.

"But there is no honor in *elegantly* proving a theorem in 1672 that some Scotsman proved *barbarously* in 1671!"

"You could not possibly have known that," Daniel said.

"Happens all the time," said Roger, a-bristle with bogus authority.

"Monsieur Huygens should have known, when he assigned me those problems as exercises," Leibniz grumbled.

"He probably *did*," Daniel said. "Oldenburg writes to him every week."

"It is well-known that GRUBENDOL is a trafficker in foreign intelligence!" announced Robert Hooke, crashing through a laurel bush and tottering onto a marble bench as vertigo seized him. Daniel gritted his teeth, waiting for a fist-fight, or worse, to break out between Hooke and Leibniz, but Leibniz let this jab at Oldenburg pass without comment, as if Hooke had merely farted at High Table.

"Another way of phrasing it might be that Mr. Oldenburg keeps Monsieur Huygens abreast of the latest developments from England," Roger said.

Daniel picked up the thread: "Huygens probably heard about the latest English theorems through that channel, and gave them to you, Doctor Leibniz, to test your mettle!"

"Never anticipating," Roger tidily concluded, "that fortunes of War and Diplomacy would bring you to the *Britannic* shore, where you would innocently present the same results to the Royal Society!"

"Entirely the fault of Oldenburg—who steals my latest watch-designs, and despatches 'em to that same Huygens!" Hooke added.

"Nonetheless—for me to present theorems to the Royal Society—only to have some gentleman in a kilt stand up in the back of the room, and announce that he proved the same thing a year ago—"

"Everyone who matters knows it was innocent."

"It is a blow to my reputation."

"Your reputation will outshine any, when you finish that Arithmetickal Engine!" announced Oldenburg, coming down a path like a blob of mercury in a trough.

"Any *on the Continent,* perhaps," Hooke sniffed.

"But all of the Frenchmen who are competent to *realize* my conception, are consumed with vain attempts to match the work of Mr. Hooke!" Leibniz returned. Which was a reasonably professional bit of flattery, the sort of thing that greased wheels and made reputations in small Continental courts.

Oldenburg rolled his eyes, then straightened abruptly as a stifled belch pistoned up his gorge.

Hooke said, "I have a design for an arithmetickal engine of my own, which I have not had the *leisure* to complete yet."

"Yes—but do you have a design for what you shall *do* with it, when it's finished?" Leibniz asked eagerly.

"Calculate logarithms, I suppose, and outmode *Napier's* bones . . ."

"But why concern yourself with anything so tedious as logarithms!?"

"They are a tool—nothing more."

"And for what purpose do you wish to *use* that tool, sir?" Leibniz asked eagerly.

"If I believed that my answer would remain within the walls of this fair garden, Doctor, I would say—but as matters stand, I fear my words will be carried to Paris with the *swiftness*—though surely not the *grace*—of the winged-footed messenger of the gods." Staring directly at Oldenburg.

Leibniz deflated. Oldenburg stepped closer to him, whilst turning his back on Hooke, and began trying to cheer the

Doctor up—which only depressed him more, as being claimed, by Oldenburg, as an ally, would condemn him forever in Hooke's opinion.

Hooke removed a long slim deerskin wallet from his breast pocket and unrolled it on his lap. It contained a neat row of slim objects: diverse quills and slivers of cane. He selected a tendril of whalebone—set the wallet aside—spread his knees wide—leaned forward—inserted the whalebone deep into his throat—wiggled it—and immediately began to vomit up bile. Daniel watched with an empiric eye, until he had made sure the vomit contained no blood, parasites, or other auspices of serious trouble.

Oldenburg was muttering to Leibniz in High-Dutch, of which Daniel could not understand a single word—which was probably why. But Daniel could make out a few names: first of Leibniz's late patron in Mainz, and then of various Parisians, such as Colbert.

He turned round hoping to continue his conversation with Roger, but Roger had quietly removed himself to make way for his distant cousin the Earl of Epsom—who was stalking directly toward Daniel looking as if he would be happy to settle matters with a head-butting duel. "Mr. Waterhouse."

"My Lord."

"You loved John Wilkins."

"Almost as a father, my lord."

"You would have him revered and respected by future generations of Englishmen."

"I pray that Englishmen will have the wisdom and discernment to give Wilkins his due."

"I say to you that those Englishmen will dwell in a country with one Established Church. If, God willing, I have my way, it will be Anglican. If the Duke of Gunfleet has his, it will be the Roman faith. Deciding *which* might require another Civil War, or two, or three. I might kill Gunfleet, Gunfleet might kill me—my sons or grandsons might cross swords with his. And despite these fatal differences, he and I are *as one* in the conviction that no nation can exist without one Established Church. Do you imagine that a few Phanatiques can overcome the combined power of all the world's Epsoms and Gunfleets?"

"I was never one for vain imaginings, my lord."

"Then you admit that England will have an Established Church."

"I confess it is likely."

"Then what does that make those who stand in opposition to an Established Church?"

"I don't know, my lord—eccentric Bishops?"

"On the contrary—it makes them heretics and traitors, Mr. Waterhouse. To change a heretic and a traitor into an eccentric Bishop is no mean task—it is a form of Transmutation requiring many Alchemists—hooded figures working in secret. The last thing they need is for a sorcerer's apprentice to stumble in and begin knocking things over!"

"Please forgive my ineptitude, my lord. I responded impulsively, because I thought he was being attacked."

"*He* was not being attacked, Mr. Waterhouse—*you* were."

DANIEL LEFT ANGLESEY HOUSE and wandered blindly along Piccadilly, realized he was in front of Comstock House, veered away from that, and fled into St. James's Fields—now parted into neat little squares where grass was trying to establish itself on the muck of construction. He sat on a plank bench, and slowly became aware that Roger Comstock had been following him the entire way, and that he'd (presumably) been talking the entire time. But he pointedly declined to bring his breeches into contact with the bench, a splintery improvisation strewn with pasty-flakes, pipe-ashes, and rat-shite.

"What were Leibniz and Oldenburg on about? Is German among the many things that you understand, Daniel?"

"I think it was that Dr. Leibniz has lost his patron, and needs a new one—with any luck, in Paris."

"Oh, most difficult for such a man to make his way in the world without a patron!"

"Yes."

"It seems as if John Comstock is cross with you."

"Very."

"His son is captain of one of the invasion-ships, you know. He is nervous, irritable just now—not himself."

"On the contrary, I think I have just seen the real John Comstock. It's safe to say that my career in the Royal Society is at an end—as long as he remains President."

"Informed opinion is that the Duke of Gunfleet will be president after the next election."

"That's no better—for in their hatred of me, Epsom and Gunfleet are one man."

"Sounds as though *you* need a patron, Daniel. One who sympathizes."

"*Is* there anyone who sympathizes?"

"I do."

This took a while to stop seeming funny, and to percolate inwards. The two of them sat there silently for a while.

Some sort of parade or procession seemed to be headed this general direction from Charing Cross, with beating of drums, and either bad singing or melodious jeering. Daniel and Roger got up and began wandering down towards Pall Mall, to see what it was.

"Are you making me some sort of proposal?" Daniel finally asked.

"I made a penny or two this year—still, I'm far from being an Epsom or a Gunfleet! I put most of my *liquid* capital into buying that parcel of land from your brothers . . ."

"Which one is it?"

"The large one on the corner there, just next to where Mr. Raleigh Waterhouse built *his* house . . . what think you of it, by the way?"

"Raleigh's house? It's, er . . . big, I suppose."

"Would you like to put it in the shade?"

"What can you possibly mean?"

"I want to erect a bigger house. But I didn't study my

mathematics at Trinity, as you know only too well, Daniel—
I need *you* to design it for me, and oversee the construction."

"But I'm not an architect—"

"Neither was Mr. Hooke, before he was hired to design
Bedlam and diverse other great Fabricks—you can bang out
a house as well as he, I wager—and certainly better than that
block-head who slapped Raleigh's together."

They'd come out into Pall Mall, which was lined with
pleasant houses. Daniel was already eyeing their windows
and roof-lines, collecting ideas. But Roger kept his eye on the
procession, which was nearly upon them: several hundred
more or less typical Londoners, albeit with a higher than
usual number of Dissident, and even a few Anglican, preachers. They were carrying an effigy, dangling from the top of a
long pole: a straw man dressed in ecclesiastical robes, but
whorishly colored and adorned, with a huge mitre affixed to
his head, and a long bishop's crook lashed to one mitt. The
Pope. Daniel and Roger stood to one side and watched for
(according to Roger's watch) a hundred and thirty-four seconds as the crowd marched by them and drained out of the
street into St. James's Park. They chose a place in clear view
of both St. James's Palace and Whitehall Palace, and planted
the pole in the dirt.

Soldiers were already headed toward them from the Horse
Guards' compound between the two Palaces: a few forerun-
ners on horseback, but mostly formations of infantrymen that
had spilled out too hastily to form up into proper squares.
These were in outlandish fantastickal attire, with long peaked
caps of a vaguely Polish style.* Daniel at first took them for
dragoons, but as they marched closer he could see nippled
cannonballs—granadoes!—dangling from their ox-hide belts
and bandoliers, thudding against their persons with each step.

---

*As King Louis XIV had guards dressed as Croats, so Charles might have
Poles; any nation whose survival depended on crossing swords with Turks
had a fearsome reputation nowadays.

That detail was not lost on the crowd of marchers, either. After a few hasty words, they held torches to the hem of the Pope's robe and set it afire. Then the crowd burst, granadoe-like. By the time those grenadiers arrived, the procession had been re-absorbed by London. There was nothing for the grenadiers to do but knock the effigy down and stamp out the flames—keeping them well away from the grenades, of course.

"'Twas well-conceived," was Roger Comstock's verdict. "Those were Royal Guards—the Duke of York's new regiment. Oh, they're commanded by John Churchill, but make no mistake, they are York's men."

"What on earth do you mean when you say something like this was well-conceived? I mean, you sound like a *connoisseur* sipping the latest port."

"Well, that Mobb could've burnt the Pope anywhere, couldn't they? But they chose here. Why here? Couldn't've chosen a more dangerous place, what with Grenadiers so near to hand. Well, the answer of course is that they wished to send a message to the Duke of York . . . to wit, that if he doesn't renounce his Papist ways, next time they'll be burning *him* in effigy—if not in *person*."

"Even *I* could see, that night at Cambridge, that Gunfleet and the younger Angleseys are the new favorites at Court," Daniel said. "While Epsom is lampooned in plays, and his house besieged by the Mobb."

"Not so remarkable really, given the rumors . . ."

"What rumors?" Daniel almost added *I am not the sort of person who hears or heeds such things,* but just now it was difficult to be so haughty.

"That our indifferent fortune in the war is chargeable to faulty cannon, and bad powder."

"What a marvellously convenient excuse for failure in war!"

Until that moment Daniel had not heard anyone say aloud that the war was going badly. The very idea that the English and the French together could not best a few Dutchmen was absurd on its face. Yet, now that Roger had mentioned it, there was a lack of good news, obvious in retrospect. Of course people would be looking for someone to blame.

"The cannon that burst at the 'Siege of Maestricht,'" Daniel said, "do you reckon 'twas shoddy goods? Or was it a scheme laid by Epsom's enemies?"

"He has enemies," was all Roger would say.

"*That* I see," said Daniel, "and, too, I see that the Duke of Gunfleet is one of them, and that he, and other Papists, like the Duke of York, are a great power in the land. What I do *not* understand is why those two enemies, Epsom and Gunfleet, a few minutes ago were as one man in heaping obloquy on the memory of John Wilkins."

"Epsom and Gunfleet are like two captains disputing command of a ship, each calling the other a mutineer," Roger explained. "The ship, in this similitude, is the Realm with its established church—Anglican or Papist, depending on as Epsom's or Gunfleet's faction prevails. There is a third faction belowdecks—dangerous chaps, well organized and armed, but, most unnervingly, under no distinct leader at the moment. When these Dissidents, as they are called, say, 'Down with the Pope!' it is music to the ears of the Anglicans, whose church is founded on hostility to all things Romish. When they say, 'Down with forced Uniformity, let Freedom of Conscience prevail,' it gladdens the hearts of the Papists, who cannot practice their faith under that Act of Uniformity that Epsom wrote. And so at different times both Epsom's and Gunfleet's factions phant'sy the Dissidents as allies. But when the Dissidents question the idea of an Established Church, and propose to make the whole country an Amsterdam, why then it seems to the leaders of both factions that these Dissident madmen are lighting fuzes on powder-kegs *to blow up the ship itself*. And *then* they unite to crush the Dissidents."

"So you are saying that Wilkins's legacy, the Declaration of Indulgence, is a powder-keg to them."

"It is a fuze that might, for all they know, lead to a powder-keg. They must stomp it out."

"Stomping on me as well."

"Only because you presented yourself to be stomped in the stupidest possible way—by your leave, by your leave."

"Well, what *ought* I to've done, when they were attacking him so?"

"Bit your tongue and bided your time," Roger said. "Things can change in a *second.* Behold this Pope-burning! Led by Dissidents, against Papists. If you, Daniel, had marched at the head of that Mobb, why, Epsom would feel you were on his side against Anglesey."

"Just what I need—the Duke of Gunfleet as personal enemy."

"Then prate about Freedom of Conscience! That is the excellence of your position, Daniel—if you would only open your eyes to it. Through nuances and shifts so subtle as to be *plausibly deniable,* you may have *either* Epsom *or* Gunfleet as your ally at any given moment."

"It sounds cavilling and pusillanimous," said Daniel, summoning up some words from the tables of the Philosophick Language.

Without disagreeing, Roger said: "It is the key to achieving what Drake dreamed of."

"How!? When all the power is in the hands of the Angleseys and the Silver Comstocks."

"Very soon you shall see how wrong you are in that."

"Oh? Is there some other source of power I am not aware of?"

"Yes," said Roger, "and your uncle Thomas Ham's cellar is full of it."

"But that gold is not his. It is the sum of his obligations."

"Just so! You have put your finger on it! There is hope for you," Roger said, and stepped back from the bench preparatory to taking leave. "I hope that you will consider my proposal in any event . . . Sir."

"Consider it under consideration, Sir."

"And even if there is no time in your life for houses—perhaps I could beg a few hours for my theatre—"

"Did you say *theatre*?"

"I've bought part interest in one, yes—the King's Comedians play there—we produced *Love in a Tub* and *The Lusty Chirurgeon*. From time to time, we need help making thunder and lightning, as well as demonic apparitions, angelic visitations, impalements, sex-changes, hangings, live births, *et cetera*."

"Well, I don't know what my family would think of my being involved in such things, Roger."

"Poh! Look at what *they* have been up to! Now that the Apocalypse has failed to occur, Daniel, you must find something to do with your several talents."

"I suppose the least I could to is keep you from blowing yourself to pieces."

"I can hide nothing from you, Daniel. Yes. You have divined it. That evening in the laboratory, I was making powder for theatrickal squibs. When you grind it finer, you see, it burns faster—more flash, more bang."

"I noticed," Daniel said. Which made Roger laugh; which made Daniel feel happy. And so into a sort of spiral they went. "I've an appointment to meet Dr. Leibniz at a coffee-house in the theatre district later . . . so why don't we walk in that direction now?" Daniel said.

"Perhaps you might have stumbled across my recent monograph, *On the Incarnation of God* . . ."

"Oldenburg mentioned it," Daniel said, "but I must confess that I have never attempted to read it."

"During our last conversation, we spoke of the difficulty of reconciling a *mechanical* philosophy with free will. This problem has any number of resonances with the *theological* question of incarnation."

"In that both have to do with spiritual essences being infused into bodies that are in essence mechanical," Daniel said agreeably. All around them, fops and theatre-goers were edging away towards other tables, leaving Leibniz and Waterhouse with a pleasant clear space in the midst of what was otherwise a crowded coffee-house.

"The problem of the Trinity is the mysterious union of the divine and human natures of Christ. Likewise, when we debate whether a mechanism—such as a fly drawn to the smell of meat, or a trap, or an arithmetickal engine—is *thinking* by itself, or merely *displaying the ingenuity* of its creator, we are asking whether or not those engines have, in some sense, been imbued with an *incorporeal principle* or, vulgarly, *spirit* that, like God or an angel, possesses free will."

"Again, I hear an echo of the Scholastics in your words—"

"But Mr. Waterhouse, you are making the common mistake of thinking that we must have Aristotle *or* Descartes—that the two philosophies are irreconcilable. On the contrary! We may accept modern, mechanistic explanations in physics, while retaining Aristotle's concept of self-sufficiency."

"Forgive me for being skeptical of that—"

"It is your *responsibility* to be skeptical, Mr. Waterhouse, no forgiveness is needed. The details of how these two concepts may be reconciled are somewhat lengthy—suffice it to say that I have found a way to do it, by assuming that every body contains an incorporeal principle, which I identify with *cogitatio*."

"Thought."

"Yes!"

"Where is this principle to be found? The Cartesians think it's in the pineal gland—"

"It is not spread out through space in any such vulgar way—but the *organization* that it causes is distributed throughout the body—it *informs* the body—and we may know that it exists, by observing that information. What is the difference between a man who has just died, and one who is going to die in a few ticks of Mr. Hooke's watch?"

"The Christian answer is that one has a soul, and the other does not."

"And it is a fine answer—it needs only to be translated into a new Philosophical Language, as it were."

"You would translate it, Doctor, by stating that the *living* body is informed by this organizing principle—which is the outward and visible sign that the mechanical body is, for the time being anyway, unified with an incorporeal principle called Thought."

"That is correct. Do you recall our discussion of symbols? You admitted that your mind cannot manipulate a spoon directly—instead it must manipulate a symbol of the spoon, inside the mind. God could manipulate the spoon directly, and we would name it a miracle. But *created* minds cannot—they need a passive element through which to act."

"The body."

"Yes."

"But you say that *Cogitatio* and *Computation* are the same, Doctor—in the Philosophical Language, a single word would suffice for both."

"I have concluded that they are one and the same."

"But your Engine does computation. And so I am compelled to ask, at what point does it become imbued with the incorporeal principle of Thought? You say that *Cogitatio* informs the body, and somehow organizes it into a mechanical system that is capable of acting. I will accept that for now. But with the Arithmetickal Engine, you are working backwards—constructing a mechanical system in the hopes that it will become impregnated from above—as the Holy Virgin. When does the Annunciation occur—at the moment you put the last gear into place? When you turn the crank?"

"You are too literal-minded," Leibniz said.

"But you have told me that you see no conflict between the notion that the mind is a mechanickal device, and a belief in free will. If that is the case, then there must be some point at which your Arithmetickal Engine will cease to be a collection of gears, and become the body into which some angelic mind has become incarnated."

"It is a false dichotomy!" Leibniz protested. "An incorpo-

real principle *alone* would not give us free will. If we accept—as we must—that God is omniscient, and has fore-
knowledge of all events that will occur in the future, then He
knows what we will do before we do it, and so—even if we
be angels—we cannot be said to have free will."

"That's what I was always taught in church. So the
prospects for your philosophy seem dismal, Doctor—free
will seems untenable both on grounds of theology and of
Natural Philosophy."

"So you say, Mr. Waterhouse—and yet you agree with
Hooke that there is a mysterious consonance between the
behavior of Nature, and the workings of the human mind.
Why should that be?"

"I haven't the faintest idea, Doctor. Unless, as the Alchemists have it, all matter—Nature and our brains together—are suffused by the same Philosophick Mercury."

"A hypothesis neither one of us loves."

"What is *your* hypothesis, Doctor?"

"Like two arms of a snowflake, Mind and Matter grew out
of a common center—and even though they grew *indepen-
dently* and without communicating—each developing according to its own internal rules—nevertheless they grew in
perfect harmony, and share the same shape and structure."

"It is rather Metaphysickal," was all Daniel could come
back with. "What's the common center? God?"

"God arranged things from the beginning so that Mind
could understand Nature. But He did not do this by continual
meddling in the development of Mind, and the unfolding of
the Universe . . . rather He fashioned the nature of both
Mind and Nature to be harmonious from the beginning."

"So, I have complete freedom of action . . . but God knows
in advance what I will do, because it is my nature to act in
harmony with the world, and God partakes of that harmony."

"Yes."

"It is odd that we should be having this conversation,
Doctor, because during the last few days, for the first time in
my life, I have felt as if certain possibilities have been set

before me, which I may reach out and grasp if I so choose."

"You sound like a man who has found a patron."

The notion of Roger Comstock as patron made Daniel's gorge rise a bit. But he could not deny Leibniz's insight. "Perhaps."

"I am pleased, for your sake. The death of my patron has left *me* with very few choices."

"There must be some nobleman in Paris who appreciates you, Doctor."

"I was thinking rather of going to Leiden to stay with Spinoza."

"But Holland is soon to be overrun . . . you could not pick a worse place to be."

"The Dutch Republic has enough shipping to carry two hundred thousand persons out of Europe, and around the Cape of Good Hope to the furthermost islands of Asia, far out of reach of France."

"That is entirely too phantastickal for me to believe."

"Believe. The Dutch are already making plans for this. Remember, they made half of their land with the labor of their hands! What they did once in Europe, they can do again in Asia. If the last ditch is stormed, and the United Provinces fall under the heel of King Louis, I intend to be there, and I will board ship and go to Asia and help build a new Commonwealth—like the New Atlantis that Francis Bacon described."

"For you, sir, such an adventure might be possible. For me, it can never be anything more than a romance," Daniel said. "Until now, I've always done what I *had* to, and this went along very well with the Predestination that was taught me. But now I may have choices to make, and they are choices of a *practical* nature."

"Whatever acts, cannot be destroyed," said the Doctor.

Daniel went out the door of the coffee-house and walked up and down London for the rest of the day. He was a bit like a comet, ranging outwards in vast loops, but continually drawn back toward certain fixed poles: Gresham's College, Waterhouse Square, Cromwell's head, and the ruin of St. Paul's.

Hooke was a greater Natural Philosopher than he, but Hooke was busy rebuilding the city, and half-deranged with imaginary intrigues. Newton was also greater, but he was lost in Alchemy and poring over the Book of Revelation. Daniel had supposed that there might be an opportunity to slip between those two giants and make a name for himself. But now there was a *third* giant. A giant who, like the others, was distracted by the loss of his patron, and dreams of a free Commonwealth in Asia. But he would not be distracted forever.

It was funny in a painful way. God had given him the desire to be a great Natural Philosopher—then put him on earth in the midst of Newton, Hooke, and Leibniz.

Daniel had the training to be a minister, and the connections to find a nice congregation in England or Massachusetts. He could walk into that career as easily as he walked into a coffee-house. But his ramble kept bringing him back to the vast ruin of St. Paul's—a corpse in the middle of a gay dinner-party—and not just because it was centrally located.

⚰

Aboard Minerva, Cape Cod Bay, Massachusetts

NOVEMBER 1713

⚕

These in thir dark Nativitie the Deep
Shall yield us pregnant with infernal flame,
Which into hallow Engins long and round
Thick-rammed, at th' other bore with touch of
    fire

Dilated and infuriate shall send forth
From far with thundring noise among our
    foes
Such implements of mischief as shall dash
To pieces, and oerwhelm whatever stands
Adverse, that they shall fear we have disarmd
The Thunderer of his only dreaded bolt.
                            —Milton, *Paradise Lost*

SNATCHING A FEW MINUTES' REST in his cabin between engagements, Daniel's mood is grave. It is the solemnity, not
of a man who's involved in a project to kill other men
(they've been doing that all day, for Christ's sake!), but of
one who's gambling his own life on certain outcomes. Or
having it gambled *for* him by a Captain who shows signs
of—what's a diplomatic way to put it—having a rich and
complicated inner life. Of course, whenever you board ship
you put your life in the Captain's hands—*but*—

Someone is *laughing* up there on the poop deck. The gaiety clashes with Daniel's somber mood and annoys him. It's
a derisive and somewhat cruel laugh, but not without sincere
merriment. Daniel's looking about for something hard and
massive to thump on the ceiling when he realizes it's van
Hoek, and what has him all in a lather is some sort of technical Dutch concept—the *Zog*.

Trundling noises from the upperdeck,* and all of a sudden
Minerva's a different ship: heeling over quite a bit more than
she was, but also rolling from side much more ponderously.
Daniel infers that a momentous shifting of weights has occurred. Getting up, and going back out on the quarterdeck, he
sees it's true: there are several short bulbous carronnades
here—nothing more or less than multi-ton blunderbusses,

---

*Which, remember, is one "storey" below the quarterdeck, where Daniel is
pretty much giving up on getting any relaxation.

with large-bore, short-range, miserable accuracy. But (not to put too fine a point on it) large bores, into which gunners are shoveling all manner of messy ironmongery: pairs of cannonballs chained together, nails, redundant crowbars, clusters of grapeshot piled on sabots and tied together with ostentatiously clever sailors' knots. Once loaded, the carronades are being run out to the gunwales—hugely increasing the ship's moment of inertia, accounting for the change in the roll period—

"Calculating our odds, Dr. Waterhouse?" Dappa inquires, descending a steep stair from the poop deck.

"What means *Zog,* Dappa, and why's it funny?"

Dappa gets an alert look about him as if it isn't funny at all, and points across half a mile of open water toward a schooner flying a black flag with a white hourglass. The schooner is on the weather bow* parallelling their course but obviously hoping to converge, and grapple, with *Minerva* in the near future. "See how miserably they make headway? We are outpacing them, even though we haven't raised the mainsail."

"Yes—I was going to inquire—*why* haven't we raised it? It *is* the largest sail on the ship, and we *are* trying to go fast, are we not?"

"The mainsail is traditionally raised and worked by the gunners. *Not* raising it will make Teach think we are short-handed in that area, and unable to man all our cannon at one time."

"But wouldn't it be worthwhile to tip our hand, if we could outrun that schooner?"

"We'll outrun her *anyway.*"

"But she *wants* us to draw abeam of her, does she not— that is the entire *point* of being a pirate—so perhaps she has thrown out drogues, and that is why she wallows along so pitiably."

---

*That is, ahead of them and off to the side from which the wind is blowing—at about ten o'clock.

"She doesn't *need* to throw out drogues because of her appalling *Zog.*"

"There it is again—what, I ask, is the meaning of that word?"

"Her wake, look at her wake!" Dappa says, waving his arm angrily.

"Yes—now that we are so, er, unsettlingly close, I can see that her wake's enough to capsize a whaleboat."

"Those damned pirates have loaded so many cannon aboard, she rides far too low in the water, and so she's got a great ugly *Zog.*"

"Is this meant to reassure me?"

"It is meant to answer your question."

"*Zog* is Dutch for 'wake,' then?"

Dappa the linguist smiles yes. Half his teeth are white, the others made of gold. "And a much better word it is, because it comes from *zuigen* which means 'to suck.'"

"I don't follow."

"Any seaman will tell you that a ship's wake sucks on her stern, holding her back—the bigger the wake, the greater the suck, and the slower the progress. That schooner, Doctor Waterhouse, sucks."

Angry words from van Hoek above—Dappa scurries down to the upperdeck to finish whatever errand Daniel interrupted. Daniel follows him, then goes aft, skirts the capstan, and descends a narrow staircase to the aftmost part of the gundeck. Thence he enters the room at the stern where he's been in the habit of taking his temperature measurements. He commences a perilous traversal of the room, headed towards that bank of undershot windows. To a landlubber the room would look pleasingly spacious, to Daniel it appears desperately short of handholds—meaning that as the ship rolls, Daniel stumbles for a greater distance, and builds up more speed, before colliding with anything big enough to stop him. In any case, he gets to the windows and looks down into *Minerva*'s *Zog.* She has one, to be sure, but compared to that schooner to windward, *Minerva* hardly sucks at all. The Bernoullis would have a field day with this—

There is also a pirate-ketch converging on them from leeward, in much the same way as the schooner is doing from windward, and Daniel is fairly certain that this ketch doesn't suck much at all. He is certain he saw drogues trailing behind her. *Minerva* is lying dead upon the wind, which is to say, she's as close-hauled as possible—she can fall off to leeward but she cannot turn into the wind any farther. Since the ketch is to leeward—downwind of *Minerva*—falling away from the wind will send *Minerva* straight into the musket-fire and grappling-irons that are no doubt being readied on her decks and fighting-tops. But the ketch, being fore-and-aft rigged, can sail closer to the wind anyway. So even if *Minerva* holds her course, the ketch will be able to cut her off—driving her into the sucking (because heavily armed) schooner.

All of which goes to explain Daniel's second reason for having gone to this room: it's as far from the fighting as he can get without jumping overboard. But he does not find the solace he wants, because from here he can see two *additional* pirate-ships gaining on them from astern, and they seem bigger and better than any of the others.

An explosion, then another, then a lot of them at once—obviously something organized. Daniel's still alive, *Minerva*'s still afloat. He flings open the door to the gundeck but it's dark and quiet, the gunners all convened around the cannons on the larboard side—none of which has been fired. It must have been those carronnades on the upperdeck firing their loads of junk.

Daniel turns round and looks out the window to see the ketch being left behind, fine on the lee quarter.* It is no longer recognizable as a ketch, though—just a hull heaped with tangled, slack rigging and freshly splintered blond

---

*At about five o'clock if he were facing toward the bow.

wood. One of her guns sparks and something terrible comes out of it, directly towards him—big and spreading. He begins to fall down, more out of vertigo than any coherent plan. All the glass in all those windows explodes toward him, driven on a wall of buckshot. Only some of it hits him in the face, and none in the eyes—more luck than a natural philosopher can comfortably account for.

The door's been flung open again, either by the blast of shot or by his falling back into it, so half of him is lying on the gundeck now. Suddenly, radiance warms his tightly closed eyelids. It could be a choir of angels, or a squadron of flaming devils, but he doesn't believe in any of that stuff. Or it could be *Minerva*'s powder magazine exploding—but that would involve loud noises, and the only noises he hears are the creaking and grumbling of gun-carriages being hauled forward. There's a refreshing sea breeze in his nostrils. He takes a big risk and opens his eyes.

All of the gunports on the larboard side have been opened at once, and all of the cannon rolled out. Gunners are hauling on blocks and tackles, slewing their weapons this way or that—others levering the guns' butts up with crowbars and hammering wedges underneath—there are, in short, as many feverish preparations as for a royal wedding. Then fire is brought out, the roll of the ship carefully timed, and Daniel—poor Daniel doesn't think to put his hands over his ears. He hears one or two cannon-blasts before going deaf. Then it's just one four-ton iron tube after another jerking backwards as lightly as shuttlecocks.

He is fairly certain that he is dead now.

Other dead men are around him.

They are lying on the upperdeck.

A couple of sailors are sitting on Daniel's corpse, while another tortures his deceased flesh with a needle. Sewing his dismembered parts back on, closing up the breaches in his abdomen so stuff won't leak out. So *this* is what it felt like to have been a stray dog in the clutches of the Royal Society!

As Daniel is lying flat on his back, his view is mostly sky-wards, though if he turns his head—an astonishing feat, for a dead man—he can see van Hoek up on the poop deck bellowing through his trumpet—which is aimed nearly straight down over the rail.

"What on earth can he be shouting at?" Daniel asks.

"Apologies, Doctor, didn't know you'd come awake," says a Looming Column of Shadow, speaking in Dappa's voice, and stepping back to block the sun from Daniel's face. "He's parleying with certain pirates who rowed out from Teach's flagship under a flag of truce."

"What do they want?"

"They want you, Doctor."

"I don't understand."

"You're thinking too hard—there's naught *to* understand—it is entirely simple," Dappa says. "They rowed up and said, 'Give us Dr. Waterhouse and all is forgotten.'"

Dr. Waterhouse now ought to spend a long time being dumbstruck. But his stupefaction lasts only a little while. The sensation of nubby silk thread being drawn briskly through fresh holes in his flesh, makes serious reflection all but impossible. "You'll do it—of course," is the best he can come up with.

"Any other captain would—but whoever arranged to put you aboard, must've known about Captain van Hoek's feelings concerning pirates. Behold!" and Dappa steps out of the way to give Daniel an unobstructed view of a sight stranger than anything gawkers would pay to view at St. Bartholomew's Fair: a hammer-handed man climbing up into the rigging of a ship. That is to say that one of his arms is terminated, not by a hand, and not by a hook, but by an actual hammer. Van Hoek ascends to a suitably perilous altitude, up there alongside the colors that fly from the mizzenmast: a Dutch flag, and below it, a smaller one depicting the Ægis. After getting himself securely tangled in the shrouds—weaving limbs through rope so that his body is spliced into the rigging—he begins to pluck nails out of his mouth and drive them through the hem of each flag into the wood of the mast.

It seems, now, that every sailor who's not sitting on Daniel is up in the rigging, unfurling a ludicrously vast array of sails. Daniel notes with approval that the mainsail's finally been hoisted—that charade is over. And now moreover *Minerva*'s height is being miraculously increased as the topmasts are telescoped upwards. An asymptotic progression of smaller and smaller trapezoids spreads out upon their frail-seeming yards.

"It's a glorious gesture for the Captain to make—now that he's sunk half of Teach's fleet," Daniel says.

"Aye, Doctor—but not the better half," Dappa says.

⚭

The City of London
1673

⚥

A fifth doctrine, that tendeth to the dissolution
of a commonwealth, is, *that every private man
has an absolute propriety in his goods; such, as ex-
cludeth the right of the sovereign.*

—Hobbes, *Leviathan*

DANIEL HAD NEVER been an actor on a stage, of course, but when he went to plays at Roger Comstock's theatre—especially when he saw them for the fifth or sixth time—he was struck by the sheer oddity of these men (and women!) standing about on a platform prating the words of a script for the hundredth time and trying to behave as if hundreds of persons weren't a few yards away goggling at them. It was strangely mannered, hollow, and false, and all who took part in it secretly wanted to strike the show and move on to something new. Thus London during this the Third Dutch War, waiting for news of the Fall of Holland.

As they waited, they had to content themselves with such smaller bits of news as from time to time percolated in from the sea. All London passed these rumors around and put on a great pompous show of reacting to them, as actors observe a battle or storm said to be taking place off-stage.

Queerly—or perhaps not—the only solace for most Londoners was going to the theatre, where they could sit together in darkness and watch their own behavior reflected back to them. *Once More into the Breeches* had become very popular since its Trinity College debut. It had to be performed in Roger Comstock's theatre after its first and second homes were set on fire owing to lapses in judgment on the part of the pyrotechnicians. Daniel's job was to simulate lightning-flashes, thunderbolts, and the accidental detonation of Lord Brimstone without burning down Roger's investment. He invented a new thunder-engine, consisting of a cannonball rolling down a Spiral of Archimedes in a wooden barrel, and he abused his privileges at the world's leading alchemical research facility to formulate a new variant of gunpowder that made more flash and less bang. The pyrotechnics lasted for a few minutes, at the beginning of the play. The rest of the time he got to sit backstage and watch Tess, who always dazzled him like a fistful of flash-powder going off right in the face, and made his heart feel like a dented cannonball tumbling down an endless hollow Screw. King Charles came frequently to watch his Nellie sing her pretty songs, and so Daniel took some comfort—or amusement at least—in knowing that he and the King both endured this endless Wait in the same way: gazing at the cheeks of pretty girls.

The small bits of news that *did* come in, while they waited for the *big* one, took various forms at first, but as the war went on they seemed to consist mostly of death-notices. It was not quite like living in London during the Plague; but more than once, Daniel had to choose between two funerals going on at the same hour. Wilkins had been the first. Many more followed, as if the Bishop of Chester had launched a fad.

Richard Comstock, the eldest son of John, and the model for the stalwart if dim Eugene Stopcock in *Breeches,* was on a ship that was part of a fleet that fell under the guns of Admiral de Ruyter at Sole Bay. Along with thousands of other Englishmen, he went to David Jones's Locker. Many of the survivors could now be seen hobbling round London on bloody stumps, or rattling cups on street-corners. Daniel was startled to receive an invitation to the funeral. Not from John, of course, but from Charles, who had been John's fourth son and was now the only one left (the other two had died young of smallpox). After his stint as laboratory assistant during the Plague Year at Epsom, Charles had matriculated at Cambridge, where he'd been tutored by Daniel. He had been well on his way to being a competent Natural Philosopher. But now he was the scion of a great family, and never could be aught else, unless the family ceased to be great, or he ceased being a part of it.

John Comstock got up in front of the church and said, "The Hollander exceeds us in industry, and in all things else, but envy."

King Charles shut down the Exchequer one day, which is to say that he admitted that the country was out of money, and that not only could the Crown not repay its debts, but it couldn't even pay *interest* on them. Within a week, Daniel's uncle, Thomas Ham, Viscount Walbrook, was dead—of a broken heart or suicide, no one save Aunt Mayflower knew—but it scarcely made a difference. This led to the most theatrickal of all the scenes Daniel witnessed in London that year (with the possible exception of the reenactment of the Siege of Maestricht): the opening of the Crypt.

Thomas Ham's reliable basement had been sealed up by

court officials immediately upon the death of its proprietor,
and musketeers had been posted all round to prevent Ham's
depositors (who had, in recent weeks, formed a small muttering knot that never went away, loitering outside; as others
held up libels depicting the atrocities of King Looie's army
in Holland, so these held up Goldsmiths's Notes addressed
to Thomas Ham) from breaking in and claiming their various plates, candlesticks, and guineas. Legal maneuverings
began, and continued round the clock, casting a queer
shadow over Uncle Thomas's funeral, and stretching beyond
it to two days, then three. The cellar's owner was already in
the grave, his chief associates mysteriously unfindable, and
rumored to be in Dunkirk trying to buy passage to Brazil
with crumpled golden punch-bowls and gravy-boats. But
those were rumors. The *facts* were in the famously safe and
sturdy Ham Bros. Cellar on Threadneedle.

This was finally unsealed by a squadron of Lords and Justices, escorted by musketeers, and duly witnessed by
Raleigh, Sterling, and Daniel Waterhouse; Sir Richard
Apthorp; and various stately and important Others. It was
three days exactly since King Charles had washed his hands
of the royal debts and Thomas Ham had met his personal
Calvary at the hands of the Exchequer. That statistic was
noted by Sterling Waterhouse—as always, noticer of details
par excellence. As the crowd of Great and Good Men shuffled
up the steps of Ham House, he muttered to Daniel: "I wonder
if we shall roll the stone aside and find an empty tomb?"

Daniel was appalled by this dual sacrilege—then reflected
that as he was now practically living in a theatre and moon-
ing over an actress every night, he could scarcely criticize
Sterling for making a jest.

It turned out not to be a jest. The cellar was empty.

Well—not empty. It was full, now, of speechless men,
standing flatfooted on the Roman mosaic.

RALEIGH: "I knew it would be bad. But—my God—
there's not even a *potatoe.*"

STERLING: "It is a sort of anti-miracle."

LORD HIGH CHANCELLOR OF THE REALM: "Go up and tell the musketeers to go and get more musketeers."

They all stood there for quite a while. Attempts to make conversation flared sporadically all round the cellar and fizzled like flashes in damp pans. Except—strangely—among Waterhouses. Disaster had made them convivial.

RALEIGH: "Our newest tenant informs me you've decided to turn architect, Daniel."

STERLING: "We thought you were going to be a savant."

DANIEL: "All the other savants are doing it. Just the other day, Hooke figured out how arches work."

STERLING: "I should have thought that was *known* by now."

RALEIGH: "Do you mean to say all existing arches have been built on *guesswork*?"

SIR RICHARD APTHORP: "Arches—and Financial Institutions."

DANIEL: "Christopher Wren is going to re-design all the arches in St. Paul's, now that Hooke has explained them."

STERLING: "Good! Maybe the *new* one won't become all bow-legged and down-at-heels, as the old one did."

RALEIGH: "I say, brother Daniel—don't you have some *drawings* to show us?"

DANIEL: "Drawings?"

RALEIGH: "In the w'drawing room, perhaps?"

Which was a bad pun and a cryptickal sign, from Raleigh the patriarch (fifty-five years comically aged, to Daniel's eyes seeming like a young Raleigh dressed up in rich old man's clothes and stage-makeup), that they were all supposed to Withdraw from the cellar. So they did, and Sir Richard Apthorp came with them. They wound up on the upper floor of Ham House, in a bedchamber—the very same one that Daniel had gazed into from his perch atop Gresham's College. A rock had already come in through a window and was sitting anomalously in the middle of a rug, surrounded by polygons of glass. More were beginning to thud against the walls, so Daniel swung the windows open to preserve the glazing. Then they all retreated to the center of the room and perched up on the bed and watched the stones come in.

STERLING: "Speaking of Guineas, or lack thereof—shame about the Guinea Company, what?"

APTHORP: "Pfft! 'Twas like one of your brother's theatrickal powder-squibs. Sold my shares of it long ago."

STERLING: "What of you, Raleigh?"

RALEIGH: "They owe me money, is all."

APTHORP: "You'll get eight shillings on the pound."

RALEIGH: "An outrage—but better than what Thomas Ham's depositors will get."

DANIEL: "Poor Mayflower!"

RALEIGH: "She and young William are moving in with me anon—and so you'll have to seek other lodgings, Daniel."

STERLING: "What fool is buying the Guinea Company's debts?"

APTHORP: "James, Duke of York."

STERLING: "As I said—what dauntless hero is, *et cetera* . . ."

DANIEL: "But that's nonsense! They are *his own* debts!"

APTHORP: "They are the Guinea Company's debts. But he is winding up the Guinea Company and creating a new Royal Africa Company. He's to be the governor and chief shareholder."

RALEIGH: "What, sinking our Navy and making us slaves to Popery is not sufficient—he's got to enslave all the Neegers, too?"

STERLING: "Brother, you sound more like Drake every day."

RALEIGH: "Being surrounded by an armed mob must be the cause of sounding that way."

APTHORP: "The Duke of York has resigned the Admiralty . . ."

RALEIGH: "As there's nothing left to be Admiral *of* . . ."

APTHORP: "And is going to marry that nice Catholic girl*
and compose his African affairs."

STERLING: "Sir Richard, this must be one of those things
that you know before anyone else does, or else there would
be rioters in the streets."

RALEIGH: "There *are,* you pea-wit, and unless I'm having
a Drakish vision, they have set fire to this very house."

STERLING: "I meant they'd be rioting 'gainst the Duke,
not our late bro-in-law."

DANIEL: "I personally witnessed a sort of riot 'gainst the
Duke the other day—but it was about his religious, not his
military, political, or commercial shortcomings."

STERLING: "You left out 'intellectual and moral.'"

DANIEL: "I was trying to be concise—as we are getting a
bit short of that spiritous essence, found in *fresh* air, for
which fire competes with living animals."

RALEIGH: "The Duke of York! What bootlicking courtier
was responsible for naming New York after him? 'Tis a perfectly acceptable *city.*"

DANIEL: "If I may change the subject . . . the reason I led
us to this room was yonder *ladder*, which in addition to being
an excellent Play Structure for William Ham, will also convey us to the roof—where it's neither so hot nor so smoky."

STERLING: "Daniel, never mind what people say about
you—you always have your *reasons.*"

[Now a serio-comical musical interlude: the brothers
Waterhouse break into a shouted, hoarse (because of smoke)
rendition of a Puritan hymn about climbing Jacob's Ladder.]

SCENE: The rooftops of Threadneedle Street. Shouts,
shattering of glass, musket-shots heard from below. They
gather round the mighty Ham-chimney, which is now vent-
ing smoke of burning walls and furniture below.

SIR RICHARD APTHORP: "How inspiring, Daniel, to gaze

---

*Mary Beatrice d'Este of Modena; for Anne Hyde had been winched into a
double-wide grave two years previously.

down the widened and straightened prospect of Cheapside and know that St. Paul's will be rebuilt there anon—'pon *mathematick* principles—so that it's likely to *stay up* for a bit."

STERLING: "Sir Richard, you sound ominously like a *preacher* opening his sermon with a commonplace observation that is soon to become one leg of a tedious and strained *analogy.*"

APTHORP: "Or, if you please, one leg of an arch—the other to be planted, oh, about *here.*"

RALEIGH: "You want to build, what, some sort of triumphal arch, spanning that distance? May I remind you that *first* we want some sort of *triumph*!?"

APTHORP: "It is only a similitude. What Christopher Wren means to do *yonder* in the way of a Church, I mean to do *here* with a *Banca.* And as Wren will use Hooke's principles to build that Church soundly, I'll use modern means to devise a *Banca* that—without in any way impugning your late brother-in-law's illustrious record—will not have armed mobs in front of it burning it down."

RALEIGH: "Our late brother-in-law was ruined, because the King borrowed all of his deposits—presumably at gunpoint—and then declined to pay 'em back—what *mathematick* principle will you use to prevent *that*?"

APTHORP: "Why, the same one that you and your co-religionists have used in order to maintain your faith: tell the King to leave us alone."

RALEIGH: "Kings do not love to be told that, or *anything.*"

APTHORP: "I saw the King yesterday, and I tell you that he loves being bankrupt even less. I was *born* in the very year that the King seized the gold and silver that Drake and the other merchants had deposited in the Tower of London for safekeeping. Do you recall it?"

RALEIGH: "Yes, 'twas a black year, and made rebels of many who only wanted to be merchants."

APTHORP: "Your brother-in-law's business, and the practice of goldsmith's notes, arose as a result—no one trusted the Tower any more."

STERLING: "And after today no one will trust goldsmiths, or their silly notes."

APTHORP: "Just so. And just as the Empty Tomb on Easter led, in the fullness of time, to a Resurrection . . ."

DANIEL: "I am stopping up mine ears now—if the conversation turns Christian, wave your hands about."

THE KNOWLEDGE THAT THE DUTCH had won the war percolated through London invisibly, like Plague. Suddenly everyone had it. Daniel woke up in Bedlam one morning knowing that William of Orange had opened the sluices and put a large part of his Republic under water to save Amsterdam. But he couldn't recall *whence* that knowledge had come.

He and his brothers had worked their way up Threadneedle by assailing one rooftop after another. They'd parted company with Apthorp on the roof of *his* goldsmith's shop, which was still solvent—yet there was an armed mob in front of *it*, too, and in front of the *next* goldsmith's, and the next. Far from *escaping* a riot, they understood, somewhat too late, that they were working their way toward the center of a much *larger* one. The obvious solution was to turn round and go back the way they'd come—but now a platoon of Quakers was coming toward them over the rooftops gripping matchlocks, each Quaker trailing a long thread of smoke from the smoldering punk in his fingers. Looking north across Threadneedle they could see a roughly equivalent number of infantrymen headed over the rooftops of Broad Street, coming from the direction of Gresham's College, and it seemed obvious enough that Quakers and Army men would soon be swapping musket-balls over the heads of the mob of Quakers, Barkers, Ranters, Diggers, Jews, Huguenots, Presbyterians, and other sects down below.

So it was down to the street and into the stone-throwing fray. But when they got down there, Daniel saw that these were not the young shin-kickers and head-butters of Drake's glory days. These were paunchy mercers who simply wanted to know where all of their money had got to. The answer was that it had gone to wherever it goes when markets crash. Daniel kept treading on wigs. Sometimes a hundred rioters would turn around and flee *en bloc* from sudden musket-fire and all of their wigs would fall off at once, as though this were a practiced military drill. Some of the wigs had dollops of brain in them, though, which ended up as pearly skeins on Daniel's shoes.

They pushed their way up Broad Street, away from the 'Change, which seemed to be the center of all disturbance. Those mock-Polish grenadiers were formed up in front of the building that had been the Guinea, and was soon to be the Royal Africa, Company. So the Waterhouses squirted past on the far side of the street, looking back to see whether any of those fatal spheres were trajecting after them. They tried to get in at Gresham's College. But many offices of the City of London had been moved into it after the fire, and so it was shut up and almost as well guarded as the Royal Africa Company.

So they had kept moving north and eventually reached Bedlam, and found an evening's refuge there amid piles of dressed stone and splats of mortar. Sterling and Raleigh had departed the next morning, but Daniel had remained: encamped, becalmed, drained, and feeling no desire to go back into the city. From time to time he would hear a nearby church-bell tolling the years of someone who'd died in the rioting.

Daniel's whereabouts became known, and messengers began to arrive, several times a day, bearing invitations to more funerals. He attended several of them, and was frequently asked to stand up and say a few words—not about the deceased (he scarcely knew most of them), but about more general issues of religious tolerance. In other words, he was asked to parrot what Wilkins would've said, and for Daniel that was easy—much easier than making up words of his own. Out of a balanced respect for his own father, he mentioned Drake, too. This felt like a slow and indirect form of suicide, but after his conversation with John Comstock he did not feel he had much of a life to throw away. He was strangely comforted by the sight of all those pews filled with men in white and black (though sometimes Roger Comstock would show up as a gem of color, accompanied by one or two courtiers who were sympathetic, or at least curious). More mourners would be visible through open doors and windows, filling the church-yard and street.

It reminded him of the time during his undergraduate days when the Puritan had been murdered by Upnor, and Daniel had traveled five miles outside of Cambridge to the funeral, and found his father and brothers, miraculously, there. Exasperating to his mind but comforting to his soul. His words swayed their emotions much more than he wanted, or expected—as two inert substances, mixed in an Alchemist's mortar, can create a fulminating compound, so the invocation of Drake's and Wilkins's memories together.

But this was not what he wanted and so he began to avoid the funerals after that, and stayed in the quiet stone-garden of Bedlam.

Hooke was there, too, for Gresham's College had become too crowded with scheming fops. Bedlam was years away from being done. The masons hadn't even begun work on the wings. But the middle part was built, and on top of it was a round turret with windows on all sides, where Hooke liked to retreat and work, because it was lonely and the light was excellent. Daniel for his part stayed down below, and only went out into the city to meet with Leibniz.

DOCTOR GOTTFRIED WILHELM LEIBNIZ picked up the coffee-pot and tipped it into his cup for the third time, and for the third time nothing came out of it. It had been empty for half an hour. He made a little sigh of regret, and then reluctantly stood up. "I beg your pardon, but I begin a long journey tomorrow. First the Channel crossing—then, between Calais and Paris, we shall have to dodge French regiments, straggling home, abject, starving, and deranged."

Daniel insisted on paying the bill, and then followed the Doctor out the door. They began strolling in the direction of the inn where Leibniz had been staying. They were not far from the 'Change. Paving-stones and charred firebrands still littered the unpaved streets.

"Not much divine harmony in evidence, here in London," Daniel said. "I can only hang my head in shame, as an Englishman."

"If you and France had conquered the Dutch Republic, you would have much more to be ashamed of," Leibniz returned.

"When, God willing, you get back to Paris, you can say that your mission was a success: there is no war."

"It was a failure," Leibniz said, "we did not prevent the war."

"When you came to London, Doctor, you said that your philosophick endeavours were nothing more than a cover for diplomacy. But I suspect that it was the other way round."

"My philosophick endeavours were a failure, too," Leibniz said.

"You have gained *one* adherent . . ."

"Yes. Oldenburg pesters me every day to complete the Arithmetickal Engine."

"Make that *two* adherents, then, Doctor."

Leibniz actually stopped in his tracks and turned to examine Daniel's face, to see if he was jesting. "I am honored, sir," he said, "but I would prefer to think of you not as an *adherent* but as a *friend*."

"Then the honor is all mine."

They linked arms and walked in silence for a while.

"Paris!" Leibniz said, as if it were the only thing that could get him through the next few days. "When I get back to the Bibliothèque du Roi, I will turn all of my efforts to mathematics."

"You don't want to complete the Arithmetickal Engine?"

It was the first time Daniel had ever seen the Doctor show annoyance. "I am a philosopher, not a watchmaker. The *philosophickal* problems associated with the Arithmetickal Engine have already been solved . . . I have found my way out of *that* labyrinth."

"That reminds me of something you said on your first day in London, Doctor. You mentioned that the question of free will versus predestination is one of the two great labyrinths into which the mind is drawn. What, pray tell, is the other?"

"The other is the composition of the continuum, or: what is space? Euclid assures us that we can divide any distance in half, and then subdivide each of them into smaller halves, and so on, *ad infinitum.* Easy to say, but difficult to understand . . ."

"It is more difficult for *metaphysicians* than for *mathematicians,* I think," Daniel said. "As in so many other fields, modern mathematics has given us tools to work with things that are infinitely small, or infinitely large."

"Perhaps I am too much of a metaphysician, then," Leibniz said. "I take it, sir, that you are referring to the techniques of infinite sequences and series?"

"Just so, Doctor. But as usual, you are overly modest. You have already demonstrated, before the Royal Society, that you know as much of those techniques as any man alive."

"But to me, they do not resolve our confusion, so much as give us a way to think about how confused we are. For example—"

Leibniz gravitated toward a sputtering lamp dangling from the overhanging corner of a building. The City of London's new program to light the streets at night had suffered from the fact that the country was out of money. But in this riotous part of town, where (in the view of Sir Roger L'Estrange, anyway) any shadow might hide a conspiracy of Dissidents, it had been judged worthwhile to spend a bit of whale-oil on street-lamps.

Leibniz fetched a stick from a pile of debris that had been a goldsmith's shop a week earlier, and stepped into the circle of brown light cast on the dirt by the lamp, and scratched out the first few terms of a series:

$$\frac{\pi}{4} = \frac{1}{1} - \frac{1}{3} + \frac{1}{5} - \frac{1}{7} + \frac{1}{9} - \frac{1}{11} + \frac{1}{13} - \frac{1}{15} + \frac{1}{17} \ \&c$$

"If you sum this series, it will slowly converge on pi. So we have a way to *approach* the value of pi—to *reach toward* it, but never to *grasp* it . . . much as the human mind can approach divine things, and gain an imperfect knowledge of them, but never look God in the face."

"It is not necessarily true that infinite series must be some sort of concession to the unknowable, Doctor . . . they can clarify, too! My friend Isaac Newton has done wizardly things with them. He has learned to approximate any curve as an infinite series."

Daniel took the stick from Leibniz, then swept out a curve in the dirt. "Far from *detracting* from his knowledge, this has *extended* his grasp, by giving him a way to calculate the tangent to a curve at any point." He carved a straight line above the curve, grazing it at one point.

A black coach rattled up the street, its four horses driven onwards by the coachman's whip, but veering nervously around piles of debris. Daniel and Leibniz backed into a doorway to let it pass; its wheels exploded a puddle and turned Leibniz's glyphs and Daniel's curves into a system of strange canals, and eventually washed them away.

"Would that *some* of our work last longer than *that,*" Daniel said ruefully. Leibniz laughed—for a moment—then walked silently for a hundred yards or so.

"I thought Newton only did Alchemy," Leibniz said.

"From time to time, Oldenburg or Comstock or I cajole him into writing out some of his mathematical work."

"Perhaps I need more cajoling," Leibniz said.

"Huygens can cajole you, when you get back."

Leibniz shrugged violently, as if Huygens were sitting astride his neck, and needed to be got rid of. "He has tutored me well, to this point. But if all he can do is give me problems that have already been solved by some Englishman, it must mean that he knows no more mathematics than I do."

"And Oldenburg is cajoling you—but to do the wrong thing."

"I shall endeavour to have an Arithmetickal Engine built in Paris, to satisfy Oldenburg," Leibniz sighed. "It is a worthy project, but for now it is a project for a mechanic."

They came into the light of another street-lamp. Daniel took advantage of it to look at his companion's face, and gauge his mood. Leibniz looked a good deal more resolute than he had beneath the *previous* street-lamp. "It is childish of me to expect older men to tell me what to do," the Doctor said. "No one *told* me to think about free will versus predestination. I plunged into the middle of the labyrinth, and became thoroughly lost, and then had no choice but to think my way out of it."

"The second labyrinth awaits you," Daniel reminded him.

"Yes . . . it is time for me to plunge into it. Henceforth, that is my only purpose. The next time you see me, Daniel, I will be a mathematician second to none."

From any other Continental lawyer these words would have been laughably arrogant; but they had come from the mouth of the monster.

> I laid the reins upon the neck of my lusts.
> —JOHN BUNYAN, *The Pilgrim's Progress*

DANIEL WAS AWAKENED one morning by a stifled boom, and supposed it was a piece being tested in the Artillery Yard outside of town. Just as he was about to fall back to sleep he heard it again: *thump,* like the period at the end of a book.

Dawn-light had flooded the turret of Bedlam and was picking its way down through struts and lashings, plankdecks and scaffolds, dangling ropes and angling braces, to the ground floor where Daniel lay on a sack of straw. He could hear movements above: not blunderings of thieves or vermin, but the well-conceived, precisely executed maneuvers of birds, and of Robert Hooke.

Daniel rose and, leaving his wig behind, so that the cool air bathed his stubbled scalp, climbed up toward the light, ascending the masons' ladders and ropes. Above his head, the gaps between planks were radiant, salmon-colored lines, tight and parallel as harpsichord-strings. He hoisted himself up through a hatch, rousting a couple of swallows, and found himself within the dome of the turret, sharing a hemispherical room with Robert Hooke. Dust made the air gently luminous. Hooke had spread out large drawings of wings and airscrews. Before the windows he had hung panes of glass, neatly scored with black Cartesian grids, plotted with foreshortened parabolae—the trajectories of actual cannonballs. Hooke liked to watch cannonballs fly from a stand-point next to the cannon, standing inside a contraption he had built, peering through these sheets of glass and tracing the balls' courses on them with a grease-pencil.

"Weigh out five grains of powder for me," Hooke said. He was paying attention to part of a rarefying engine: one of many such piston-and-cylinder devices he and Boyle used to study the expansion of gases.

Daniel went over to a tiny scale set up on a plank between two sawhorses. On the floor next to it was a keg branded with the coat of arms of the Silver Comstocks. Its bung was loose, and peppered with grains of coarse powder. Next to it rested a small cylindrical bag of linen, about the diameter of a fist, plump and round as a full sack of flour. This had once been sewn shut, but Hooke had snipped through the uneven stitches and teased it open. Looking in among the petals of frayed fabric, Daniel saw that it, too, was filled with black powder.

"Would you prefer I take it from the keg, or the little bag?" Daniel asked.

"As I value my eyes, and my Rarefying Engine, take it from the keg."

"Why do you say so?" Daniel drew the loose bung out and

found that the keg was nearly full. Taking up a copper spoon that Hooke had left near the scale (copper did not make sparks), he scooped up a small amount of powder from the bung-hole and began sprinkling it onto one of the scale's frail golden pans. But his gaze strayed towards the linen bag. In part this was because Hooke, who feared so little, seemed to think it was a hazard. Too, there was something about this bag that was familiar to him, though he could not place it in his memory.

"Rub a pinch between your fingers," Hooke suggested. "Come, there is no danger."

Daniel probed into the linen bag and got a smudge of the stuff on his fingertips. The answer was obvious. "This is much finer than that in the keg." And that was the clew that reminded him where he had seen such a bag before. The night that Roger Comstock had blown himself up in the laboratory, he had been grinding gunpowder very fine, and pouring it into a bag just like this one. "Where did this come from? A theatre?"

For once Hooke was flummoxed. "What a very odd question for you to ask. Why do you phant'sy such a thing should come from a theatre, of all places?"

"The nature of the powder," Daniel said. "Ground so exceedingly fine." He nodded at the bag, for his hands were busy. Having weighed out five grains of powder from the keg, he poured them from the scale-pan into a cupped scrap of paper and carried it over to Hooke. "Such powder burns much faster than this coarse stuff." He shook the paper for emphasis and it made a sandy rasp. He handed it to Hooke, who poured it into the cylinder of the Rarefying Engine. Some of these engines were wrought of glass, but this was a heavy brass tube about the size of a tobacco-canister: a very small siege-mortar, in effect. Its piston fit into it like a cannonball.

"I am aware of it," Hooke said. "That is why I do not wish to put five grains of it into the Rarefying Engine. Five grains of Comstock's powder burns slow and steady, and drives the piston up in a way that is useful to me. The same weight of that fine stuff from yonder bag would burn in an instant, and explode my apparatus, and me."

"That is why I supposed the bag might have come from a theatre," Daniel said. "Such powder may be unsuitable for the Rarefying Engine, but on the stage it makes a pretty flash and bang."

"That bag," said Hooke, "came from the magazine of one of His Majesty's Ships of War. The practice used to be, and still is on some ships, that powder is introduced into the bore of a cannon by scooping it up out of a keg and pouring it in. Similar to how a musketeer charges the barrel of his weapon. But in the heat of battle, our gunners are prone to mis-measure and to spill the powder on the deck. And to have open containers of powder near active cannon is to tempt disaster. A new practice is replacing the old. Before the battle, when it is possible to work calmly, the powder is carefully measured out and placed into bags, such as that one, which are sewn shut. The bags are stockpiled in the ship's magazine. During battle, as they are needed, they are ferried one at a time to the guns."

"I see," Daniel said, "then the gunner need only slash the bag open and pour its contents into the bore."

Hardly for the first time, Hooke was a bit irked by Daniel's stupidity. "Why waste time opening it with a knife, when fire will open it for you?"

"I beg your pardon?"

"Behold, the diameter of the bag is the same as the bore of the gun. Why open it then? No, the entire bag, sewn shut, is introduced into the barrel."

"The gunners never even see what is inside of it!"

Hooke nodded. "The only powder that the gunners need concern themselves with is the priming-powder that is poured into the touch-hole and used to communicate fire to the bag."

"Then those gunners are trusting the ones who sew up the bags—trusting them with their lives," Daniel said. "If the wrong sort of powder were used—" and he faltered, and went over and dipped his fingers once more into the bag before him to feel the consistency of the powder inside. The difference between it and the Comstock powder was like that between flour and sand.

"Your discourse is strangely like that of John Comstock when he delivered that bag and that keg to me," Hooke said.

"He brought them around *in person?*"

Hooke nodded. "He said he no longer trusted anyone to do it for him."

Whereat Daniel must have looked shocked, for Hooke held up a hand as if to restrain him, and continued: "I understood his state of mind too well. Some of us, Daniel, are prone to a sort of melancholy, wherein we are tormented by phant'sies that other men are secretly plotting to do us injury. It is a pernicious state for a man to fall into. I have harbored such notions from time to time about Oldenburg and others. Your friend Newton shows signs of the same affliction. Of all men in the world, I supposed John Comstock least susceptible to this disorder; but when he came here with this bag, he was very far gone with it, which grieved me more than anything else that has happened of late."

"My lord believes," Daniel guessed, "that some enemy of his has been salting the magazines of Navy ships with bags filled with finely milled powder, such as this one. Such a bag, sewn shut, would look the same, to a gunner, as an ordinary one; but when loaded into the bore, and fired—"

"It would burst the barrel and kill everyone nearby," Hooke said. "Which might be blamed on a faulty cannon, or on faulty powder; but as my lord manufactures *both,* the blame cannot but be laid on him in the end."

"Where did this bag come from?" Daniel asked.

"My lord said it was sent to him by his son Richard, who found it in the magazine of his ship on the eve of their sailing for Sole Bay."

"Where Richard was killed by a Dutch broadside," Daniel said. "So my lord desired that you would inspect this bag and render an opinion that it had been tampered with by some malicious conspirator."

"Just so."

"And have you done so?"

"No one has asked my opinion yet."

"Not even Comstock?"

"Nay, not even Comstock."

"Why would he bring you such evidence in person, and then not ask?"

"I can only guess," Hooke said, "that in the meantime he has come to understand that it does not really matter."

"What an odd thing to think."

"Not really," Hooke said. "Suppose I testified that this bag contained powder that was too fine. What would it boot him? Anglesey—for make no mistake, that's who's behind this—would reply that Comstock had made up this bag in his own cellar, as false evidence to exonerate himself and his faulty cannons. Comstock's son is the only man who could testify that it came from a ship's magazine, and he's dead. There might be other such bags in other magazines, but they are mostly on the bottom of the sea, thanks to Admiral de Ruyter. We have lost the war, and it must be blamed on someone. Someone other than the King and the Duke of York. Comstock has now come to understand that it is being blamed on him."

The daylight had become much more intense in the minutes Daniel had been up here. He saw that Hooke had rigged an articulated rod to the back of the piston, and connected the rod to a system of cranks. Now, by means of a tiny touch-hole in the base of the cylinder, he introduced fire to the chamber. *Thump.* The piston snapped up to the top of the bore much faster than Daniel could flinch away from it. This caused an instant of violent motion in the gear-train, which had the effect of winding a spring that spiraled around in a whirling hoop the size of a dinner-plate. A ratchet stopped this from unwinding. Hooke then re-arranged the gears so that the giant watch-spring was connected, by a string

wound around a tapered drum, to the drive-shaft of a peculiar helical object, very light-weight, made of parchment
stretched on a frame of steam-bent cane. Like a Screw of
Archimedes. The spring unwound slowly, spinning the
screw swiftly and steadily. Standing at one end of it, Daniel
felt a palpable breeze, which continued for more than a
minute—Hooke timed it with his latest watch.

"Properly wrought, and fed with gunpowder at regular intervals, it might generate enough wind to blow itself off the
ground," Hooke said.

"Supplying the gunpowder would be difficult," Daniel
said.

"I only use it because I *have* some," Hooke said. "Now
that Anglesey has been elected President of the Royal Society, I look forward to experimenting with combustible *vapors* in its stead."

"Even if I've moved to Massachusetts by then," Daniel
said, "I'll come back to London to watch you fly through the
air, Mr. Hooke."

A church-bell began ringing not far away. Daniel remarked that it was a bit early for funerals. But a few minutes
later another one started up, and another. They did not simply bong a few times and then stop—they kept pealing in
some kind of celebration. But the Anglican churches did not
seem to be sharing in the joy. Only the queer churches of
Dutchmen and Jews and Dissenters.

LATER IN THE DAY, Roger Comstock appeared at the gates
of Bedlam in a coach-and-four. The previous owner's coat of
arms had been scraped off and replaced with that of the
Golden Comstocks. "Daniel, do me the honor of allowing
me to escort you to Whitehall," Roger said, "the King wants
you there for the signing."

"Signing of *what*?" Daniel could imagine several possibilities—Daniel's death warrant for sedition, Roger's for
sabotage, or an instrument of surrender to the Dutch Republic, being three of the more plausible.

"Why, the Declaration! Haven't you heard? Freedom of conscience for Dissenters of all stripes—almost—just as Wilkins wanted it."

"That is very good news, if true—but why should His Majesty want *me* there?"

"Why, next to Bolstrood you are the leading Dissenter!"

"That is *not true.*"

"It doesn't matter," Roger said cheerfully. "He *thinks* it's true—and after today, it *will* be."

"Why does he think it's true?" Daniel asked, though he already suspected why.

"Because I have been telling everyone so," Roger answered.

"I haven't clothes fit to wear to a whorehouse—to say nothing of Whitehall Palace."

"There is very little practical difference," Roger said absent-mindedly.

"You don't understand. My wig's home to a family of swallows," Daniel complained. But Roger Comstock snapped his fingers, and a valet sprang out of the coach laden with diverse packages and bundles. Through the open door, Daniel glimpsed women's clothing, too—with women inside of it. Two *different* women. A *thump* from the turret, a muffled curse from Hooke. "Don't worry, it's nothing foppish," Roger said. "For a leading Dissident, it is entirely proper."

"Can the same be said of the *ladies*?" Daniel asked, following Roger and the valet into Bedlam.

"These aren't *ladies,*" Roger said, and other than that weak jest did not even try to answer the question. "Do London a favor and take those damned clothes off. I shall have my manservant burn them."

"The shirt is not so bad," Daniel demurred. "Oh, I agree that it is no longer fit for wearing. But it might be made into a powder-bag for the Navy."

"No longer in demand," Roger said, "now that the war is over."

"On the contrary, I say that a great many of them shall have to be made up now, as so many of the old ones are known to be defective."

"Hmm, you *are* well-informed, for a political naif. Who has been filling your head with such ideas? Obviously a supporter of Comstock."

"I suppose that supporters of Anglesey are saying that the powder-bags are all excellent, and it's Comstock's cannons that were made wrong."

"It is universally known, among the Quality."

"That may be. But it is known among you, and me, and a few other people, that bags were made up, containing powder that was ground fine."

Coincidentally or not, Daniel had reached the point of complete nakedness as he was saying these words. He had a pair of drawers on; but Roger tossed him fresh ones, and averted his gaze. "Daniel! I cannot bear to see you in this state, nor can I listen to any more of your needling suspicious discourse. I will turn my back on you, and talk for a while. When I turn round again, I will behold a new man, as well *informed* as he is *attired*."

"Very well, I suppose I've very little choice."

"None whatsoever. Now, Daniel. You saw me grinding the powder fine, and putting it into the bag, and there is no point in denying it. No doubt you think the worst of me, as has been your wont since we first studied together at Trinity. Have you stopped to ask yourself, how a man in my position could possibly manage to introduce bags of powder into the magazines of a ship of the Royal Navy? Quite obviously it is impossible. Someone else must have done it. Someone with a great deal more power and reach than I can even dream of possessing."

"The Duke of Gunfl—"

"Silence. Silence! And in silence ponder the similitudes between cannons and mouths. The simpleton beholds a cannon and phant'sies it an infallible destroyer of foes. But the veteran artilleryman knows that sometimes, when a cannon speaks, it bursts. Especially when it has been loaded in haste. When this occurs, Daniel, the foe is untouched. He may sense a distant gaseous exhalation, not puissant enough to ruffle his periwig. The eager gunner, *and all his comrades,* are blown to bits. Ponder it, Daniel. And for once in your life, show a trace of discretion. It does not really matter what the gentleman's name was who was responsible for causing those cannons to burst. What matters is that *I had no idea what I was doing.* What do *I,* of all people, know about naval artillery? All I knew was this: I met certain gentlemen at the Royal Society. Presently they became aware that I worked in Newton's laboratory as an assistant. One of them approached me and asked if I might do him a favor. Nothing difficult. He wanted me to grind up some gunpowder very fine and deliver it to him in wee bags. This I did, as you know. I made up half a dozen of those bags over the course of a year. One of them blew up on the spot, thanks to you. Of the other five, I now know that one was smuggled into the 'Siege of Maestricht,' where it caused a cannon to explode in full view of half of London. The other four went to the Royal Navy. One was detected by Richard Comstock, who sent it to his father. One exploded a cannon during a naval engagement against the Dutch. The other two have since found their way into David Jones's Magazine. As to my culpability: I did not understand until recently why the gentleman in question had made such an odd request of me. I did not know, when I was filling those bags, that they would be used to do murder."

Daniel, snaking his limbs through new clothes, believed every word of this. He had long ago lost count of Roger's moral lapses. Roger, he suspected, had broken as many of the ten commandments and committed as many of the seven deadly sins as it was in his power to do, and was actively seeking ways to break and commit those he had not yet ticked off the list. This had nothing to do with Roger's character. *Someone* was responsible for blowing up those poor gunners, as a ploy to dishonor the Earl of Epsom: as vile an act as Daniel could imagine. Thomas More Anglesey, Duke of Gunfleet, or one of his sons must have been at the head of the conspiracy, for as Roger had pointed out, Roger couldn't have done it all himself. The only question then was whether Roger had understood what was being done with those powder-bags. The Angleseys would never have told him, and so he'd have had to figure it out on his own. And Roger's career at Trinity gave no grounds to expect dazzling flashes of insight.

Believing in Roger's innocence lifted from Daniel's shoulders an immense weight that he had not been sensible of until it was gone. This felt so good that it triggered a few moments of Puritanical self-examination. Anything that felt so good might be a trick of the devil. Was he only *feigning* trust in Roger, *because* it felt good?

"How can you go on associating with those people when you know the atrocious thing they have done?"

"I was going to ask you."

"I beg your pardon?"

"You have been associating with them since the Plague Year, Daniel, at every meeting of the Royal Society."

"But I did not know they were doing murder!"

"On the contrary, Daniel, you have known it ever since that night at Trinity twelve years ago when you watched Louis Anglesey murder one of your brethren." Had he been a rather different sort of chap, Roger might have mentioned this in a cruelly triumphant way. Had he been Drake, he'd have said it sadly, or angrily. But being Roger Comstock, he proffered it as a witticism. He did it so well that Daniel let out a wee snort of amusement before coming to his senses and stifling himself.

The terms of the transaction finally were clear. Why did Daniel refuse to hate Roger? Not out of blindness to Roger's faults, for he saw Roger's moral cowardice as clearly as Hooke peering through a lens at a newt. Not out of Christian forgiveness, either. He refused to hate Roger because Roger saw moral cowardice in Daniel, had done so for years, and yet did not hate Daniel. Fair's fair. They were brothers.

As much as he had to ponder in the way of moral dilemmas vis-à-vis Roger, 'twas as nothing compared to half an hour later, when Daniel emerged, booted, bewigged, cravated, and jacketed, and equipped with a second-hand watch that Roger somehow begged off of Hooke, and climbed into the coach. For one of the women in there was Tess Charter. *Thump.*

When she and the other woman were finished laughing at the look on Daniel's face, she leaned forward and got her fingers all entangled with his. She was shockingly and alarmingly *alive*—somewhat more alive, in fact, than he was. She looked him in the eyes and spoke in her French accent: "Twooly, Daniel, eet eez ze hrole of a lifetime—portraying ze *mistress* of a gentlemen who eez too pure—too spiritual— to sink zee thoughts of zee flesh." Then a middling London accent. "But really I prefer the challenging parts. The ability to do them's what separates me from Nell Gwyn."

"I wonder what separates the *King* from Nell Gwyn?" said the other woman.

"Ten inches of sheepgut with a knot in one end—if the King knows what's good for him!" Tess returned. *Thump.*

This led to more in a similar vein. Daniel turned to Roger, who was sitting next to him, and said, "Sir! What on earth makes you believe I wish to appear to have a mistress?"

"Who said anything about *appearing* to have one?" Roger answered, and when Daniel didn't laugh, gathered himself up and said, "Poh! You could no more show up at Whitehall without a mistress, than at a duel without a sword! Come, Daniel! No one will take you seriously! They'll think you're hiding something!"

"And that he is—though none too effectively," Tess said, eyeing a new convexity in Daniel's breeches.

"I loved your work in *The Dutch Strumpet*," Daniel tried, weakly.

Thus, down London Wall and westwards, ho!—Daniel's every attempt to say anything *serious* pre-empted by a courtly witticism—more often than not, so bawdy he didn't even *understand* it, any more than Tess would understand the Proceedings of the Royal Society. Every jest followed by exaltations of female laughter and then a radical, and completely irrational, change in subject.

Just when Daniel thought he had imposed a bit of order on the conversation, the coach rattled into the middle of St. Bartholomew's Fair. Suddenly, outside the windows, bears were dancing jigs and hermaphrodites were tottering about on stilts. Devout men and well-bred ladies would avert their eyes from such sights, but Tess and the other woman (another Comedian, who gave every indication of being Roger's *authentic,* not *imaginary,* mistress) had no intentions of averting their gazes from *anything.* They were still chattering about what they'd seen ten minutes later as the coach moved down Holborn. Daniel decided to take his cue from Roger, who rather than trying to *talk* to the ladies merely sat and watched them, face smeared with a village idiot's grin.

They stopped by the corner of Waterhouse Square for ritual adoration of Roger's new lot, and to make sniping comments about Raleigh's house: that soon-to-be-o'ershadowed pile that Raleigh's architect had (it was speculated) blown out of his arse-hole during an attaque of the bloody phlux. The ladies made comments in a similar vein about the attire of the widow Mayflower Ham, who was descending from same, on her way to Whitehall, too.

Then down past any number of fields, churches, squares, *et cetera,* named after St. Giles, and a completely gratuitous detour along Piccadilly to Comstock House, where Roger had the coach stop so that he could spend several minutes savoring the spectacle of the Silver Comstocks moving out of the building that had served as their London seat since the Wars of the Roses. Colossal paintings, depicting scenes of hunting and of naval engagements, had been pulled out and leaned against the wrought-iron fence. Below them was a clutter of smaller canvases, mostly portraits, stripped of their gilded frames, which were going to auction. Making it appear that there was a whole crowd of Silver Comstocks, mostly in out-moded doublets or neck-ruffs, milling about down there and peering out grimly through the fence. "All behind bars where they should've been a hundred years ago!" Roger said, and then laughed at his own jest, loud enough to draw a look from John Comstock himself, who was standing in his forecourt watching some porters maneuver out the door a mainsail-sized painting of some Continental Siege. Daniel's eye fixed on this. Partly it was because looking at the Earl of Epsom made him melancholy. But also it was because he had been spending so much time with Leibniz, who often spoke of paintings such as this one when talking about the mind of God. On one piece of canvas, seemingly from one fixed point of view, the artist had depicted skirmishes, sallies, cavalry charges, and the deaths of several of the principals, which had occurred in different places at different times. And this was not the only liberty he had taken with the notion of time and space, for certain events—the digging of a mine beneath a bastion, the detonation of the mine, and the ensuing battle—were shown all together at once. The images stood next to each other like pickled larvae in the Royal Society's collection, sharing the same time for all time, and yet if you let your eye travel over them in the correct order you could make the story unfold within your mind, each event in its proper moment. This great painting did not, of course, stand alone, but was surrounded by all of the other paintings that had been carried out of the house before; its perceptions were ranged alongside others, this little Siege-world nested within a larger array of other things that the House of Comstock during its long history had perceived, and thought worthy to be set down on canvas. Now they were all being aired out and reshuffled, on a gloomy occasion. But to have this moment—the fall of the Silver Comstocks—embedded in so many old ones made it seem less terrible that it might have seemed if it had happened naked, as it were, and all alone in time and space.

* * *

THE EARL OF EPSOM TURNED his head and gazed across Piccadilly at his Golden cousin, but showed no particular emotion. Daniel had shrunk far down into the coach, where he hoped he'd be enshrouded in darkness. To him, John Comstock looked almost *relieved*. How bad could it be to live in Epsom and go hunting and fishing every day? That's what Daniel told himself—but later the sadness and haggardness in the Earl's face would appear in his mind's eye at the oddest times.

"Do not become stupid now, just because you are seeing his face," Roger said to him. "That man was a Cavalier. He led cavalry charges against the Parliamentarian foot-soldiers. Do you know what that means? Do you see that great bloody awful painting there of Comstock's great-uncle and his friends galloping after that fox? Replace the fox with a starving yeoman, unarmed, alone, and you have a fair picture of how that man spent the Civil War."

"I know all that," Daniel said. "And yet, and yet, somehow I still prefer him and his family to the Duke of Gunfleet and *his* family."

"John Comstock had to be cleared out of the way, and we had to lose a war, before *anything* could happen," Roger said. "As to Anglesey and his spawn, I love them even less than you do. Do not fret about them. Enjoy your triumph and your mistress. Leave Anglesey to me."

Then to Whitehall where they, and various Bolstroods and Waterhouses and many others, watched the King sign the Declaration. As penned by Wilkins, this document had given freedom of conscience to *everyone*. The version that the King signed today was not quite so generous: it outlawed certain extreme heretics, such as Arians who didn't believe in the Trinity. Nevertheless, it was a good day's work. Certainly enough to justify raising several pints, in several Drury Lane taverns, to the memory of John Wilkins. Daniel's pretend mistress accompanied him on every stage of this epochal pub-crawling campaign, which led eventually to Roger Comstock's playhouse, and, in particular, to a back-room of that playhouse, where there happened to be a bed.

"Who has been making sausages in here?" Daniel inquired. Which sent Tess into a fit of the giggles. She had just about got his new breeches off.

"I should say *you* have made a pretty one!" she finally managed to get out.

"I should say *you* are responsible for making it," Daniel demurred, and then (now that it was in plain view) added: "and it is anything but pretty."

"Wrong on both counts!" said Tess briskly. She stood up and grabbed it. Daniel gasped. She gave it a tug; Daniel yelped, and drew closer. "Ah, so it *is* attached to you. You shall have to accept responsibility for the making of it, then; can't blame the lasses for everything. And as for pretty—" she relaxed her grip, and let it rest on the palm of her hand, and gave it a good look. "You've never seen a *nasty* one, have you?"

"I was raised to believe they were *all* quite nasty."

"That may be true—it is all metaphysickal, isn't it? Quite. But please know some are nastier than others. And that is why we have sausage-casings in a bedchamber."

She proceeded to do something quite astonishing with ten inches of knotted sheepgut. Not that he needed ten inches; but she was generous with it, perhaps to show him a kind of respect.

"Does this mean it is not actually coitus?" Daniel asked hopefully. "Since I am not really touching you?" Actually he was touching her in a lot of places, and vice versa. But where it counted he was touching nothing but sheepgut.

"It is very common for men of your religion to say so," Tess said. "Almost as common as this irksome habit of talking while you are doing it."

"And what do *you* say?"

"I say that we are not touching, and not having sex, if it makes you feel better," Tess said. "Though, when all is finished, you shall have to explain to your Maker why you are at this moment buggering a dead sheep."

"Please do not make me laugh!" Daniel said. "It hurts somehow."

"What is funny? I simply speak the truth. What you are feeling is not hurting."

He understood then that she was right. Hurting wasn't the word for it.

When Daniel woke up in that bed, sometime in the middle of the following afternoon, Tess was gone. She'd left him a note (who'd have thought she was literate? But she had to read the scripts).

> Daniel,
> We shall make more sausages later. I am off to act. Yes, it may have slipped your mind that I am an actress.
>
> Yesterday I worked, playing the role of mistress. It is a difficult role, because dull. But now it has become fact, not farce, and so I shall not have to act any more; much easier. As I am no longer professionally engaged, pretending to be your mistress, I shall no longer be receiving my stipend from your friend Roger. As I am now your mistress in fact, some small gift would be appropriate. Forgive my forwardness. Gentlemen *know such things,* Puritans *must be instructed.*
>
> Tess
>
> P.S. You want instruction in acting. I shall endeavour to help.

Daniel staggered about the room for some minutes collecting his clothes, and tried to put them on in the right order. It did not escape his notice that he was getting dressed, like an actor, in the backstage of a theatre. When he was done he found his way out among sets and properties and stumbled out onto the stage. The house was empty, save for a few actors dozing on benches. Tess was right. He had found his place now: he was just another actor, albeit he would never appear on a stage, and would have to make up his own lines *ad libitum.*

His role, as he could see plainly enough, was to be a leading Dissident who also happened to be a noted savant, a Fellow of the Royal Society. Until lately he would not have thought this a difficult role to play, since it was so close to the truth. But whatever illusions Daniel might once have harbored about being a man of God had died with Drake, and been cremated by Tess. He very much phant'sied being a Natural Philosopher, but that simply was not going to work if he had to compete against Isaac, Leibniz, and Hooke. And so the role that Roger Comstock had written for him was beginning to appear very challenging indeed. Perhaps, like Tess, he would come to prefer it that way.

That much had been evident to him on that morning in 1673. But the ramifications had been as far beyond his wits as Calculus would've been to Mayflower Ham. He could not have anticipated that his new-launched career as actor on the stage of London would stretch over the next twenty-five years. And even if he had foreseen that, he could never have phant'sied that, after forty, he would be called back for an encore.

⚜

Aboard Minerva, Cape Cod Bay, Massachusetts

NOVEMBER 1713

☿

BLACKBEARD IS AFTER *HIM*! Daniel spent the day terrified even *before* he knew this—now's the time to be struck dead with fear. But he is calm instead. Partly it's that the surgeon's not sewing him together any more, and anything's an improvement on *that*. Partly it's that he lost some blood, and drank some rum, during the operation. But those are mechanistic explanations. Despite all that Daniel said to Wait Still concerning Free Will, *et cetera,* on the eve of his departure from Boston, he is not willing to believe, yet, that he is controlled by his balance of humours. No, Daniel is in a better mood (once he's had an hour or two to rest up, anyway) because things are beginning to make sense now. Albeit scantly. Pain scares him, death doesn't especially (he never expected to live so long!), but chaos, and the feeling that the world is not behaving according to rational laws, put him into the same state of animal terror as a dog who's being dissected alive but cannot understand why. To him the rolling eyes of those bound and muzzled dogs have ever been the touchstone of fear.

"Out for a stroll so soon, Doctor?"

Dappa's evidently recognized him by the tread of his shoes and walking-stick on the quarterdeck—he hasn't taken the spyglass away from his eye in half an hour.

"What about that schooner is so fascinating, Mr. Dappa? Other than that it's full of murderers."

"The Captain and I are having a dispute. I say it is a floaty and leewardly Flemish pirate-bottom. Van Hoek sees idioms in its rigging that argue to the contrary."

"*Bottom* meaning her hull—*floaty* meaning she bobs like a cork, with little below the water-line—which is desirable, I gad, for Flemings and pirates alike, as both must slip into shallow coves and harbors—"

"Perfect marks so far, Doctor."

"*Leewardly,* then, I suppose, means that because of that faintness in the keel, the wind tends to push her sideways through the water whenever she is sailing close-hauled—as she is now."

"And as are we, Doctor."

"*Minerva* has the same defect, I suppose—"

This slander finally induces Dappa to take the spyglass away from his eye. "Why should you assume any such thing?"

"All these Amsterdam-ships are flat-bottomed of necessity, are they not? For entering the Ijsselmeer . . ."

"*Minerva* was built on the Malabar coast."

"Mr. Dappa!"

"I would not dishonor you with jests, Doctor. It is true. I was there."

"But how—"

"'Tis an awkward time to be telling you the entire Narration," Dappa observes. "Suffice it to say that she is *not* leewardly. Her *apparent* course is as close as it can be to her *true* course."

"And you'd like to know, whether the same is true of yonder schooner," Daniel says. "It is not unlike the problem an astronomer faces, when—imprisoned as he is on a whirling and hurtling planet—he tries to plot the true trajectory of a comet through the heavens."

"Now it's *my* turn to wonder whether *you* are jesting."

"The water is like the Cœlestial Æther, a fluid medium through which all things move. Cape Cod, over yonder, is like the distant, fixed stars—by sighting that church-steeple in Provincetown, the High Land of Cape Cod to the south of it, the protruding mast of yonder wrack, and then by doing a bit of trigonometry, we may plot our position, and by joining one point to the next, draw our trajectory. The schooner, then, is like a comet—also moving through the æther—but by measuring the angles she makes with us and with the church-steeple, *et cetera,* we may find her *true* course; compare it with her *apparent* heading; and easily judge whether she is, or is not, leewardly."

"How long would it take?"

"If you could make sightings, and leave me in peace to make calculations, I could have an answer in perhaps half an hour."

"Then let us begin without delay," Dappa says.

Plotting it out on the back of an old chart in the common room, Daniel begins to understand the urgency. To escape the confines of Cape Cod Bay, they must clear Race Point at the Cape's northernmost tip. Race Point is northeast of them. The wind, for the last few hours, has been steady from northwest by north. *Minerva* can sail six points* from the wind, so she can just manage a northeasterly course. So leaving aside pirate-ships and other complications, she's in a good position to clear Race Point within the hour.

But as a matter of fact there are two pirate-ships paralleling her course, much as the schooner-that-sucked and the ketch were doing earlier. To windward (i.e., roughly northwest of *Minerva*) is a big sloop—Teach's flagship—which has complete freedom of movement under these circumstances. She's fast, maneuverable, well-armed, capable of sailing four points from the wind, and well to the north of the dangerous shallows, hence in no danger of running aground off of Race Point. The schooner, on the other hand, is to leeward, between *Minerva* and the Cape. She can also sail four points from the wind—meaning that she should be able to angle across *Minerva*'s course and grapple with her before Race Point. And if she does, there's no doubt that Teach's sloop will come in along the larboard side at the same moment, so that *Minerva* will be boarded from both sides at once. If that is all true, then *Minerva*'s best course is to turn her stern into the wind, fall upon the schooner, attack, and then come about (preferably before running aground on the Cape) and contend with the sloop.

But if Dappa is right, and the schooner suffers from the defect of leewardliness, then all's not as it seems. The wind will push her sideways, *away* from *Minerva* and *toward* the Race Point shallows—she won't be able to intercept *Minerva* soon enough, and, to avoid running aground, she'll have to tack back to the west, taking her out of the action. If that is true, *Minerva*'s best course is to maintain her present close-hauled state and wait for Teach's sloop to make a move.

It's all in the arithmetic—the same sort of arithmetic that Flamsteed, the Astronomer Royal, is probably grinding through at this very moment at the Observatory in Greenwich,

---

*There are thirty-two points on the compass rose.

toiling through the night in hopes of proving that Sir Isaac's latest calculation of the orbit of the moon is wrong. Except here *Minerva*'s the Earth, that schooner is Luna, and fixed Boston is, of course, the Hub of the Universe. Daniel passes an extraordinarily pleasant half-hour turning Dappa's steady observations into sines and cosines, conic sections and fluxions. Pleasant because it is imbued with the orderliness that taketh away his fear. Not to mention a fascination that makes him forget the throbbing and pulling stitches in his flesh.

"Dappa is correct. The schooner drifts to leeward, and will soon fall by the wayside or run aground," he announces to van Hoek, up on the poop deck. Van Hoek puffs once, twice, thrice on his pipe, then nods and goes into Dutch mutterings. Mates and messenger-boys disseminate his will into all compartments of the ship. *Minerva* forgets about the schooner and bends all efforts to the expected fight against Teach's wicked sloop-of-war.

In another half-hour, the leewardly schooner provides some coarse entertainment by actually running aground at the very knuckle of Cape Cod's curled fist. This is ignominious, but hardly unheard-of; these English pirates have only been in Massachusetts for a couple of weeks and can't expect to have all the sand-banks committed to memory. This skipper would rather run aground in soft sand, and refloat later, than flinch from battle and face Blackbeard Teach's wrath.

Van Hoek immediately has them come about to west by south, as if they were going to sail back to Boston. His intent is to cut behind Teach's stern and fire a broadside up the sloop's arse and along her length. But Teach has too much intelligence for that, and so breaks the other way, turning to the east to get clear of *Minerva*'s broadside, then wearing round to the south, pausing near the grounded schooner to pick up a few dozen men who might come in useful as boarders. After a short time he comes up astern of *Minerva*.

A tacking duel plays out there off of Race Point for an hour or so, Teach trying to find a way to get within musket-range of *Minerva* without being blown apart, van Hoek try-ing to fire just a single well-considered broadside. There are some paltry exchanges of fire. Teach puts a small hole in *Minerva*'s hull that is soon patched, and a cloud of hurtling junk from one of *Minerva*'s carronnades manages to carry away one of the sloop's sails, which is soon replaced. But with time, even van Hoek's hatred of pirates is worn down by the tedium, and by the need to get away from land while the sun is shining. Dappa reminds him that the Atlantic Ocean is just a mile or two that-a-way, and that nothing stands any more between them and it. He persuades van Hoek that there's no better way to humiliate a pirate than to leave him empty-handed, his decks crowded with boarders who have nothing to throw their grappling-hooks at. To out-sail a pi-rate, he insists, is a sweeter revenge than to out-fight him.

So van Hoek orders *Minerva* to come about and point her-self toward England. The men who've been manning the guns are told to make like Cincinnatus, walking away from their implements of war at the very moment of their victory so that they may apply themselves to peaceful toils: in this case, spreading every last sail that the ship can carry. Tired, smoke-smeared men lumber up into the light and, after a short pause to swallow ladles of water, go to work swinging wide the studdingsail booms. This nearly doubles the width of the ship's mightiest yards. The studdingsails tumble from them and snap taut in the wind. Like an albatross that has endured a long pursuit through a cluttered wilderness, te-diously dodging and veering from hazard to hazard, and that finally rises above the clutter, and sees the vast ocean stretching before it, *Minerva* spreads her wings wide, and flies. The hull has shrunk to a mote, dragged along below a giant creaking nebula of firm canvas.

Teach can be seen running up and down the length of his sloop with smoke literally coming out of his head, waving his cutlass and exhorting his crew, but everyone knows that *Queen Anne's Revenge* is a bit crowded, not to mention under-victualled, for a North Atlantic cruise in November.

Minerva accelerates into blue water with power that Daniel can feel in his legs, crashing through the odd rogue swell just as she rammed a pirate-boat earlier today, and, as the sun sets on America, she begins the passage to the Old World sailing large before a quartering wind.

✣

Dramatis Personae

✣

MEMBERS OF THE NOBILITY went by more than one name: their family surnames and Christian names, but also their titles. For example, the younger brother of King Charles II had the family name Stuart and was baptized James, and so might be called James Stuart; but for most of his life he was the Duke of York, and so might also be referred to, in the third person anyway, as "York" (but in the second person as "Your Royal Highness"). Titles frequently changed during a person's lifetime, as it was common during this period for commoners to be ennobled, and nobles of lower rank to be promoted. And so not only might a person have several names at any one moment, but certain of those names might change as he acquired new titles through ennoblement, promotion, conquest, or (what might be considered a combination of all three) marriage.

This multiplicity of names will be familiar to many readers who dwell on the east side of the Atlantic, or who read a lot of books like this. To others it may be confusing or even maddening. The following Dramatis Personae may be of help in resolving ambiguities.

If consulted too early and often, it may let cats out of bags by letting the reader know who is about to die, and who isn't.

The compiler of such a table faces a problem similar to the one that bedeviled Leibniz when trying to organize his patron's library. The entries (books in Leibniz's case, personages here) must be arranged in a linear fashion according to some predictable scheme. Below, they are alphabetized by name. But since more than one name applies to many of the characters, it is not always obvious where the entry should be situated. Here I have sacrificed consistency for ease of use by placing each entry under the name that is most commonly used in the book. So, for example, Louis-François de Lavardac, duc d'Arcachon, is under "A" rather than "L" because he is almost always called simply the duc d'Arcachon in the story. But Knott Bolstrood, Count Penistone, is under "B" because he is usually called Bolstrood. Cross-references to the main entries are spotted under "L" and "P," respectively.

Entries that are relatively reliable, according to scholarly sources, are in Roman type. Entries in *italics* contain information that is more likely to produce confusion, misunderstanding, severe injury, and death if relied upon by time travelers visiting the time and place in question.

⚭

ANGLESEY, LOUIS: 1648–. *Earl of Upnor. Son of Thomas More Anglesey. Courtier and friend of the Duke of Monmouth during the Interregnum and, after the Restoration, at Trinity College, Cambridge.*

ANGLESEY, PHILLIP: 1645–. *Count Sheerness. Son of Thomas More Anglesey.*

ANGLESEY, THOMAS MORE: 1618–1679. *Duke of Gunfleet. A leading Cavalier and a member of Charles II's court in exile during the Interregnum. After the Restoration, one of the A's in Charles II's CABAL (which see). Relocated to France during the Popish Plot troubles, died there.*

ANNE I OF ENGLAND: 1665–1714. Daughter of James II by his first wife, Anne Hyde.

APTHORP, RICHARD: 1631–. *Businessman and banker. One of the A's in Charles II's CABAL (which see). A founder of the Bank of England.*

D'ARCACHON, DUC: 1634–. *Louis-François de Lavardac. A cousin to Louis XIV. Builder, and subsequently Admiral, of the French Navy.*

D'ARCACHON, ÉTIENNE: 1662–. *Étienne de Lavardac. Son and heir of Louis-François de Lavardac, duc d'Arcachon.*

D'ARTAGNAN, CHARLES DE BATZ-CASTELMORE: C. 1620–1673. French musketeer and memoirist.

ASHMOLE, SIR ELIAS: 1617–1692. Astrologer, alchemist, autodidact, Comptroller and Auditor of the Excise, collector of curiosities, and founder of Oxford's Ashmolean Museum.

D'AVAUX, JEAN-ANTOINE DE MESMES, COMTE: French ambassador to the Dutch Republic, later an advisor to James II during his campaign in Ireland.

BOLSTROOD, GOMER: 1645–. *Son of Knott. Dissident agitator, later an immigrant to New England and a furniture maker there.*

BOLSTROOD, GREGORY: 1600–1652. *Dissident preacher. Founder of the Puritan sect known as the Barkers.*

BOLSTROOD, KNOTT: 1628–1682. *Son of Gregory. Ennobled as Count Penistone and made Secretary of State by Charles II. The B in Charles II's CABAL (which see).*

BOYLE, ROBERT: 1627–1691. Chemist, member of the Experimental Philosophical Club at Oxford, Fellow of the Royal Society.

VON BOYNEBURG, JOHANN CHRISTIAN: 1622–1672. An early patron of Leibniz in Mainz.

CABAL, THE: unofficial name of Charles II's post-Restoration cabinet, loosely modeled after Louis XIV's Conseil d'en-Haut, which is to say that each member had a general area of responsibility, but the boundaries were vague and overlapping (see table, p. 431).

CAROLINE, PRINCESS OF BRANDENBURG-ANSBACH: 1683–1737. Daughter of Eleanor, Princess of Saxe-Eisenach.

CASTLEMAINE, LADY: see Villiers, Barbara.

CATHERINE OF BRAGANZA: 1638–1705. Portuguese wife of Charles II of England.

CHARLES I OF ENGLAND: 1600–1649. Stuart king of England, decapitated at the Banqueting House after the victory of Parliamentary forces under Oliver Cromwell.

CHARLES II OF ENGLAND: 1630–1685. Son of Charles I. Exiled to France and later the Netherlands during the Interregnum. Returned to England 1660 and re-established monarchy (the Restoration).

CHARLES LOUIS, ELECTOR PALATINE: 1617–1680. Eldest surviving son of the Winter King and Queen, brother of Sophie, father of Liselotte. Re-established his family in the Palatinate following the Thirty Years' War.

CHARLES, ELECTOR PALATINE: 1651–1685. Son and heir to Charles Louis. War-gaming enthusiast. Died young of disease contracted during a mock siege.

CHESTER, LORD BISHOP OF: see Wilkins, John.

CHURCHILL, JOHN: 1650–1722. Courtier, warrior, duellist, cocksman, hero, later Duke of Marlborough.

CHURCHILL, WINSTON: Royalist, Squire, courtier, early Fellow of the Royal Society, father of John Churchill.

CLEVELAND, DUCHESS OF: see Villiers, Barbara.

COMENIUS, JOHN AMOS (JAN AMOS KOMENSKY): 1592–1670. Moravian Pansophist, an inspiration to Wilkins and Leibniz among many others.

THE CABAL

Responsible party	General area[s] of responsibility	Corresponding roughly to formal position of*
C COMSTOCK, JOHN (EARL OF EPSOM)	(Early in the reign) domestic affairs and justice. Later retired	Lord High Chancellor
A ANGLESEY, LOUIS (DUKE OF GUNFLEET)	(Early) the Exchequer and (covertly) foreign affairs, especially vis-a-vis France. Later Apthorp came to dominate the former. After Comstock's retirement, but before the Popish Plot, domestic affairs, and the Navy.	Various, including Lord High Admiral
B BOLSTROOD, KNOTT (COUNT PENISTONE)	Foreign affairs (ostensibly)	Secretary of State
A APTHORP, SIR RICHARD	Finance	Chancellor of the Exchequer
L LEWIS, HUGH (DUKE OF TWEED)	Army	Marshal, or (though no such position existed at the time) Defense Minister

*But sometimes they formally held these positions and sometimes they didn't.

❧

COMSTOCK, CHARLES: 1650–1708. *Son of John. Student of Natural Philosophy. After the retirement of John and the death of his elder brother, Richard, an immigrant to Connecticut.*

COMSTOCK, JOHN: 1607–1685. *Leading Cavalier, and member of Charles II's court in exile in France. Scion of the so-called Silver branch of the Comstock family. Armaments maker. Early patron of the Royal Society. After the Restoration, the C in Charles II's CABAL (which see). Father of Richard and Charles Comstock.*

COMSTOCK, RICHARD: 1638–1673. *Eldest son and heir of John Comstock. Died at naval battle of Sole Bay.*

COMSTOCK, ROGER: 1646–. *Scion of the so-called Golden branch of the Comstock family. Classmate of Newton, Daniel Waterhouse, the Duke of Monmouth, the Earl of Upnor, and George Jeffreys at Trinity College, Cambridge, during the early 1660s. Later, a successful developer of real estate, and Marquis of Ravenscar.*

DE CRÉPY: *French family of gentlemen and petty nobles until the Wars of Religion in France, during which time they began to pursue a strategy of aggressive upward mobility. They intermarried in two different ways with the older but declining de Gex family. One of them (Anne Marie de Crépy, 1653–) married the much older duc d'Oyonnax and survived him by many years. Her sister (Charlotte Adélaide de Crépy 1656–) married the Marquis d'Ozoir.*

CROMWELL, OLIVER: 1599–1658. Parliamentary leader, general of the anti-Royalist forces during the English Civil War, scourge of Ireland, and leading man of England during the Commonwealth, or Interregnum.

CROMWELL, ROGER: 1626–1712. Son and (until the Restoration) successor of his much more formidable father, Oliver.

EAUZE, CLAUDE: see *d'Ozoir, Marquis.*

ELEANOR, PRINCESS OF SAXE-EISENACH: D. 1696. Mother (by her first husband, the Margrave of Ansbach) of Caroline, Princess of Brandenburg-Ansbach. Late in life, married to the Elector of Saxony.

ELISABETH CHARLOTTE: 1652–1722. Liselotte, *La Palatine.* Known as Madame in the French court. Daughter of Charles Louis, Elector Palatinate, and niece of Sophie.

Married Philippe, duc d'Orléans, the younger brother of Louis XIV. Spawned the House of Orléans.

EPSOM, EARL OF: see *Comstock, John.*

FREDERICK V, ELECTOR PALATINATE: 1596–1632. King of Bohemia ("Winter King") briefly in 1618, lived and died in exile during the Thirty Years' War. Father of many princes, electors, duchesses, etc., including Sophie.

FREDERICK WILLIAM, ELECTOR OF BRANDENBURG: 1620–1688. Known as the Great Elector. After the Thirty Years' War created a standing professional army, small but effective. By playing the great powers of the day (Sweden, France, and the Hapsburgs) against each other, consolidated the scattered Hohenzollern fiefdoms into a coherent state, Brandenburg-Prussia.

DE GEX: *A petty-noble family of Jura, which dwindled until the early seventeenth century, when the two surviving children of Henry, Sieur de Gex (1595–1660), Francis and Louise-Anne, each married a member of the more sanguine family de Crépy. The children of Francis carried on the de Gex name. Their youngest was Édouard de Gex. The children of Louise-Anne included Anne Marie de Crépy (later duchesse d'Oyonnax) and Charlotte Adélaide de Crépy (later marquise d'Ozoir).*

DE GEX, FATHER ÉDOUARD: 1663–. *Youngest offspring of Marguerite Diane de Crépy (who died giving birth to him) and Francis de Gex, who was thirty-eight years old and in declining health. Raised at a school and orphanage in Lyons by Jesuits, who found in him an exceptionally gifted pupil. Became a Jesuit himself at the the age of twenty. Was posted to Versailles, where he became a favorite of Mademoiselle. de Maintenon.*

GREAT ELECTOR: see Frederick William.

GUNFLEET, DUKE OF: see *Anglesey, Thomas More.*

GWYN, NELL: 1650–1687. Fruit retailer and comedienne, one of the mistresses of Charles II.

HAM, THOMAS: 1603–. *Money-goldsmith, husband of May-*

flower Waterhouse, leading man of Ham Bros. Goldsmiths. Created Earl of Walbrook by Charles II.

HAM, WILLIAM: 1662–. *Son of Thomas and Mayflower.*

HENRIETTA ANNE: 1644–1670. Sister of Charles II and James II of England, first wife of Philippe, duc d'Orléans, Louis XIV's brother.

HENRIETTA MARIA: 1609–1669. Sister of King Louis XIII of France, wife of King Charles I of England, mother of Charles II and James II of England.

HOOKE, ROBERT: 1635–1703. Artist, linguist, astronomer, geometer, microscopist, mechanic, horologist, chemist, optician, inventor, philosopher, botanist, anatomist, etc. Curator of Experiments for the Royal Society, Surveyor of London after the fire. Friend and collaborator of Christopher Wren.

HUYGENS, CHRISTIAAN: 1629–1695. Great Dutch astronomer, horologist, mathematician, and physicist.

HYDE, ANNE: 1637–1671. First wife of James, Duke of York (later James II). Mother of two English queens: Mary (of William and Mary) and Anne.

JAMES I OF ENGLAND: 1566–1625. First Stuart king of England.

JAMES II OF ENGLAND: 1633–1701. Duke of York for much of his early life. Became King of England upon the death of his brother in 1685. Deposed in the Glorious Revolution, late 1688–early 1689.

JAMES VI OF SCOTLAND: see James I of England.

JEFFREYS, GEORGE: 1645–1689. Welsh gentleman, lawyer, solicitor general to the Duke of York, lord chief justice, and later lord chancellor under James II. Created Baron Jeffreys of Wem in 1685.

JOHANN FRIEDRICH: 1620–1679. Duke of Braunschweig-Lüneburg, book collector, a patron of Leibniz.

JOHN FREDERICK: see Johann Friedrich.

KÉROUALLE, LOUISE DE: 1649–1734. Duchess of Portsmouth. One of the mistresses of Charles II.

KETCH, JACK: Name given to executioners.

LAVARDAC: *A branch of the Bourbon family producing various hereditary dukes and peers of France, including the duc d'Arcachon* (see).

LEFEBURE: French alchemist/apothecary who moved to London at the time of the Restoration to provide services to the Court.

LEIBNIZ, GOTTFRIED WILHELM: 1646–1716. Refer to novel.

LESTRANGE, SIR ROGER: 1616–1704. Royalist pamphleteer and (after the Restoration) Surveyor of the Imprimery, hence chief censor for Charles II. Nemesis of Milton. Translator.

LEWIS, HUGH: 1625–. *General. Created Duke of Tweed by Charles II after the Restoration, in recognition of his crossing the River Tweed with his regiment (thenceforth called the Coldstream Guards) in support of the resurgent monarchy. The L in Charles II's CABAL (which see).*

LISELOTTE: *see* Elisabeth Charlotte.

LOCKE, JOHN: 1632–1704. Natural Philosopher, physician, political advisor, philosopher.

DE MAINTENON, MME.: 1635–1719. Mistress, then second and last wife of Louis XIV.

MARY: 1662–1694. Daughter of James II and Anne Hyde. After the Glorious Revolution (1689), Queen of England with her husband, William of Orange.

MARY OF MODENA: 1658–1718. Second and last wife of James II of England. Mother of James Stuart, aka "the Old Pretender."

MAURICE: 1621–1652. One of the numerous princely offspring of the Winter Queen. Active as a Cavalier in the English Civil War.

DE MESMES, JEAN-ANTOINE: see d'Avaux.

MINETTE: see Henrietta Anne.

MONMOUTH, DUKE OF (JAMES SCOTT): 1649–1685. Bastard of Charles II by one Lucy Walter.

MORAY, ROBERT: C. 1608–1673. Scottish soldier, official, and courtier, a favorite of Charles II. Early Royal Society figure, probably instrumental in securing the organization's charter.

NEWTON, ISAAC: 1642–1727. Refer to novel.

OLDENBURG, HENRY: 1615–1677. Emigrant from Bremen. Secretary of the Royal Society, publisher of the *Philosophical Transactions,* prolific correspondent.

D'OYONNAX, ANNE MARIE DE CRÉPY, DUCHESSE: 1653–. *Lady in Waiting to the Dauphine, Satanist, poisoner.*

D'OZOIR, CHARLOTTE ADÉLAIDE DE CRÉPY, MARQUISE: 1656–. *Wife of Claude Eauze, Marquis d'Ozoir.*

D'OZOIR, CLAUDE EAUZE, MARQUIS: 1650–. *Illegitimate son of Louis-François de Lavardac, duc d'Arcachon, by a domestic servant, Luce Eauze. Traveled to India in late 1660s as part of ill-fated French East India Company expedition. In 1674, when noble titles went on sale to raise funds for the Dutch war, he purchased the title Marquis d'Ozoir using a loan from his father secured by revenues from his slaving operations in Africa.*

PENISTONE, COUNT: see *Bolstrood, Knott.*

PEPYS, SAMUEL: 1633–1703. Clerk, Administrator to the Royal Navy, Member of Parliament, Fellow of the Royal Society, diarist, man about town.

PETERS, HUGH: 1598–1660. Fulminant Puritan preacher. Spent time in Holland and Massachusetts, returned to England, became Cromwell's chaplain. Poorly thought of by Irish for his involvement with massacres at Drogheda and Wexford. For his role in the regicide of Charles I, executed by Jack Ketch, using a knife, in 1660.

PHILIPPE, DUC D'ORLÉANS: 1640–1701. Younger brother of King Louis XIV of France. Known as Monsieur to the French Court. Husband first of Henrietta Anne of England, later of Liselotte. Progenitor of the House of Orléans.

PORTSMOUTH, DUCHESS OF: see Kéroualle, Louise de.

QWGHLM: *Title bestowed on Eliza by William of Orange.*

RAVENSCAR, MARQUIS OF: see *Comstock, Roger.*

ROSSIGNOL, ANTOINE: 1600–1682. "France's first full-time cryptologist" (David Kahn, *The Codebreakers*, which buy and read). A favorite of Richelieu, Louis XIII, Mazarin, and Louis XIV.

ROSSIGNOL, BONAVENTURE: D. 1705. Cryptanalyst to Louis XIV following the death of his father, teacher, and collaborator Antoine.

RUPERT: 1619–1682. One of the numerous princely offspring of the Winter Queen. Active as a Cavalier in the English Civil War.

DE RUYTER, MICHIEL ADRIAANSZOON: 1607–1676. Exceptionally gifted Dutch admiral. Particularly effective against the English.

VON SCHÖNBORN, JOHANN PHILIPP: 1605–1673. Elector and Archbishop of Mainz, statesman, diplomat, and early patron of Leibniz.

SHEERNESS, COUNT: see *Anglesey, Phillip*.

SOPHIE: 1630–1714. Youngest daughter of the Winter Queen. Married Ernst August, who later became duke of Braunschweig-Lüneburg. Later the name of this principality was changed to Hanover, and Ernst August and Sophie elevated to the status of Elector and Electress. From 1707 onwards, she was first in line to the English throne.

SOPHIE CHARLOTTE: 1668–1705. Eldest daughter of Sophie. Married Frederick III, elector of Brandenburg and son of the Great Elector. In 1701, when Brandenburg-Prussia was elevated to the status of a kingdom by the Holy Roman Emperor, she became the first Queen of Prussia and spawned the House of Prussia.

STUART, ELIZABETH: 1596–1662. Daughter of King James I of England, sister of Charles I. Married Frederick, Elector Palatine. Proclaimed Queen of Bohemia briefly in 1618, hence her sobriquet "the Winter Queen." Lived in exile during the Thirty Years' War, mostly in the Dutch Republic. Outlived her husband by three decades. Mother of many children, including Sophie.

STUART, JAMES: 1688–1766. Controversial but probably legitimate son of James II by his second wife, Mary of Modena. Raised in exile in France. Following the death of his father, styled James III by the Jacobite faction in England and "the Old Pretender" by supporters of the Hanoverian succession.

UPNOR, EARL OF: see *Anglesey, Louis*.

VILLIERS, BARBARA (LADY CASTLEMAINE, DUCHESS OF CLEVELAND): 1641–1709. Indefatigable mistress of many satisfied Englishmen of high rank, including Charles II and John Churchill.

WALBROOK, EARL OF: see *Ham, Thomas*.

WATERHOUSE, ANNE: 1649–. *Née Anne Robertson. English colonist in Massachusetts. Wife of Praise-God Waterhouse.*

WATERHOUSE, BEATRICE: 1642–. *Née Beatrice Durand. Huguenot wife of Sterling.*

WATERHOUSE, CALVIN: 1563–1605. *Son of John, father of Drake.*

WATERHOUSE, DANIEL: 1646–. *Youngest (by far) child of Drake by his second wife, Hortense.*

WATERHOUSE, DRAKE: 1590–1666. *Son of Calvin, father of Raleigh, Sterling, Mayflower, Oliver, and Daniel. Independent trader, political agitator, leader of Pilgrims and Dissidents.*

WATERHOUSE, ELIZABETH: 1621–. *Née Elizabeth Flint. Wife of Raleigh Waterhouse.*

WATERHOUSE, EMMA: 1656–. *Daughter of Raleigh and Elizabeth.*

WATERHOUSE, FAITH: 1689–. *Née Faith Page. English colonist in Massachusetts. (Much younger) wife of Daniel, mother of Godfrey.*

WATERHOUSE, GODFREY WILLIAM: 1708–. *Son of Daniel and Faith in Boston.*

WATERHOUSE, HORTENSE: 1625–1658. *Née Hortense Bowden. Second wife (m. 1645) of Drake Waterhouse, and mother of Daniel.*

WATERHOUSE, JANE: 1599–1643. *Née Jane Wheelwright. A pilgrim in Leiden. First wife (m. 1617) of Drake, mother of Raleigh, Sterling, Oliver, and Mayflower.*

WATERHOUSE, JOHN: 1542–1597. *Devout early English Protestant. Decamped to Geneva during reign of Bloody Mary. Father of Calvin Waterhouse.*

WATERHOUSE, MAYFLOWER: 1621–. *Daughter of Drake and Jane, wife of Thomas Ham, mother of William Ham.*

WATERHOUSE, OLIVER I: 1625–1646. *Son of Drake and Jane. Died in Battle of Newark during English Civil War.*

WATERHOUSE, OLIVER II: 1653–. *Son of Raleigh and Elizabeth.*

WATERHOUSE, PRAISE-GOD: 1649–. *Eldest son of Raleigh and Elizabeth. Immigrated to Massachusetts Bay Colony. Father of Wait Still Waterhouse.*

WATERHOUSE, RALEIGH: 1618–. *Eldest son of Drake, father of Praise-God, Oliver II, and Emma.*

WATERHOUSE, STERLING: 1630–. *Son of Drake. Real estate developer. Later ennobled as Earl of Willesden.*

WATERHOUSE, WAIT STILL: 1675–. *Son of Praise-God in Boston. Graduate of Harvard College. Congregational preacher.*

WEEM, WALTER: 1652–. *Husband of Emma Waterhouse.*

WHEELWRIGHT, JANE: see *Waterhouse, Jane.*

WILHELMINA CAROLINE: see Caroline, Princess of Brandenburg-Ansbach.

WILKINS, JOHN (BISHOP OF CHESTER): 1614–1672. Cryptographer. Science fiction author. Founder, first chairman, and first secretary of the Royal Society. Private chaplain to Charles Louis, Elector Palatinate. Warden of Wadham (Oxford) and Master of Trinity (Cambridge). Prebendary of York, Dean of Ripon, holder of many other ecclesiastical appointments. Friend of Nonconformists, Supporter of Freedom of Conscience.

WILLESDEN, EARL OF: see *Waterhouse, Sterling.*

WILLIAM II OF ORANGE: 1626–1650. Father of the better-known William III of Orange. Died young (of smallpox).

WILLIAM III OF ORANGE: 1650–1702. With Mary, daugher of James II, co-sovereign of England from 1689.

WINTER KING: see Frederick V.

WINTER QUEEN: see Stuart, Elizabeth.

WREN, CHRISTOPHER: 1632–1723. Prodigy, Natural Philosopher, and Architect, a member of the Experimental Philosophical Club and later Fellow of the Royal Society.

YORK, DUKE OF: The traditional title of whomever is next in line to the English throne. During much of this book, James, brother to Charles II.

DE LA ZEUR: *Eliza was created Countess de la Zeur by Louis XIV.*

KING OF THE VAGABONDS
continues The Baroque Cycle with the chronicle
of the breathtaking exploits of "Half-Cocked
Jack" Shaftoe—London street urchin turned
swashbuckling adventurer and legendary King
of the Vagabonds—risking life and limb for fortune and love while slowly maddening from the
pox.

Read on for the continuation of Neal Stephenson's extraordinary saga of a remarkable age and
its momentous events . . . Available now wherever
books are sold.

The Mud Below London
1665

MOTHER SHAFTOE KEPT TRACK of her boys' ages on her fingers, of which there were six. When she ran short of fingers—that is, when Dick, the eldest and wisest, was nearing his seventh summer—she gathered the half-brothers together in her shack on the Isle of Dogs, and told them to be gone, and not to come back without bread or money.

This was a typically East London approach to child-rearing and so Dick, Bob, and Jack found themselves roaming the banks of the Thames in the company of many other boys who were also questing for bread or money with which to buy back their mothers' love.

London was a few miles away, but, to them, as remote and legendary as the Court of the Great Mogul in Shahjahan-abad. The Shaftoe boys' field of operations was an infinite maze of brickworks, pig yards, and shacks crammed sometimes with Englishmen and sometimes with Irishmen living ten and twelve to a room among swine, chickens, and geese.

The Irish worked as porters and dockers and coal-haulers during the winter, and trudged off to the countryside in hay-making months. They went to their Papist churches every chance they got and frittered away their silver paying for the services of scribes, who would transform their sentiments into the magical code that could be sent across counties and seas to be read, by a priest or another scrivener, to dear old Ma in Limerick.

In Mother Shaftoe's part of town, that kind of willingness to do a day's hard work for bread and money was taken as proof that the Irish race lacked dignity and shrewdness. And this did not even take into account their religious practices and all that flowed from them, e.g., the obstinate chastity of their women, and the willingness of the males to tolerate it. The way of the mudlarks (as the men who trafficked through Mother Shaftoe's bed styled themselves) was to voyage out upon the Thames after it got dark, find their way aboard anchored ships somehow, and remove items that could be exchanged for bread, money, or carnal services on dry land.

Techniques varied. The most obvious was to have someone climb up a ship's anchor cable and then throw a rope down to his mates. This was a job for surplus boys if ever there was one. Dick, the oldest of the Shaftoes, had learnt the rudiments of the trade by shinnying up the drain-pipes of whorehouses to steal things from the pockets of vacant clothing. He and his little brothers struck up a partnership with a band of these free-lance longshoremen, who owned the means of moving swag from ship to shore: they'd accomplished the stupendous feat of stealing a longboat.

After approaching several anchored ships with this general plan in mind, they learned that the sailors aboard them—who were actually supposed to be on watch for mudlarks—expected to be paid for the service of failing to notice that young Dick Shaftoe was clambering up the anchor cable with one end of a line tied round his ankle. When the captain found goods missing, he'd be sure to flog these sailors, and they felt they should be compensated, in advance, for the loss of skin and blood. Dick needed to have a purse dangling from one wrist, so that when a sailor shone a lantern down into his face, and aimed a blunderbuss at him, he could shake it and make the coins clink together. That was a music to which sailors of all nations would smartly dance.

Of course the mudlarks lacked coins to begin with. They wanted capital. John Cole—the biggest and boldest of the fellows who'd stolen the longboat—hit upon another shrewd plan: they would steal the only parts of ships that could be reached without actually getting aboard first: namely, anchors. They'd then sell them to the captains of ships who had found their anchors missing. This scheme had the added attraction that it might lead to ships' drifting down the current and running aground on oh, say, the Isle of Dogs, at which point their contents would be legally up for grabs.

One foggy night (but all nights were foggy) the mudlarks set off in the longboat, rowing upstream. The mudlark term for a boat's oars was *a pair of wings*. Flapping them, they flew among anchored ships—all of them pointed upriver, since the anchor cables were at their bows, and they weathercocked in the river's current. Nearing the stern of a tubby Dutch *galjoot*—a single-masted trader of perhaps twice their longboat's length, and ten times its capacity—they tossed Dick overboard with the customary rope noosed around his ankle, and a knife in his teeth. His instructions were to swim upstream, alongside the *galjoot*'s hull, towards the bow, until he found her port side anchor cable descending into the river. He was to lash his ankle-rope to said cable, and then saw through the cable above the lashing. This would have the effect of cutting the *galjoot* free from, while making the longboat fast to, the anchor, effecting a sudden and silent transfer of ownership. This accomplished, he was to jerk on the rope three times. The mudlarks would then pull on the rope. This would draw them upstream until they were directly over the anchor, and if they hauled hard enough, the prize would come up off the riverbed.

Dick slopped away into the mist. They watched the rope uncoil, in fits and starts, for a couple of minutes—this meant Dick was swimming. Then it stopped uncoiling for a long while—Dick had found the anchor cable and gone to work! The mudlarks dabbled with rag-swathed oars, flapping those wings against the river's flow. Jack sat holding the rope, waiting for the three sharp jerks that would be Dick's signal. But no jerks came. Instead the rope went slack. Jack, assisted by brother Bob, pulled the slack into the boat. Ten yards of it passed through their hands before it became taut again, and then they felt, not three sharp jerks, exactly, but a sort of vibration at the other end.

It was plain that something had gone wrong, but Jack Cole was not about to abandon a good rope, and so they hauled in what they could, drawing themselves upstream. Somewhere along the flank of the *galjoot,* they found a noose in the rope, with a cold pale ankle lodged in it, and out came poor Dick. The anchor cable was knotted to that same noose. While Jack and Bob tried to slap Dick back into life, the mudlarks tried to pull in the anchor. Both failed, for the anchor was as heavy as Dick was dead. Presently, choleric Dutchmen up on the *galjoot* began to fire blunderbusses into the fog. It was time to leave.

Bob and Jack, who'd been acting as journeyman and apprentice, respectively, to Dick, were left without a Master Rope-Climber to emulate, and with a tendency to have extraordinarily bad dreams. For it was clear to them—if not right away, then eventually—that they had probably caused their own brother's death by drawing the rope taut, thereby pulling Dick down below the surface of the river. They were out of the mudlark trade for good. John Cole found a replacement for Dick, and (rumor had it) gave him slightly different instructions: take your ankle out of the noose *before* you cut the anchor cable.

Scarcely a fortnight later, John Cole and his fellows were caught in the longboat in broad daylight. One of their schemes had succeeded, they'd gotten drunk on stolen grog, and slept right through sunrise. The mudlarks were packed off to Newgate.

Certain of them—newcomers to the judicial system, if not to crime—shared their ill-gotten gains with a starving parson, who came to Newgate and met with them in the Gigger. This was a chamber on the lower floor where prisoners could thrust their faces up to an iron grate and be heard, if they shouted loudly enough, by visitors a few inches away. There, the parson set up a sort of impromptu Bible study class, the purpose of which was to get the mudlarks to memorize the 51st Psalm. Or, failing that, at least the first bit:

> *Have mercie upon me, o God, according to they loving kindenes: according to the multitude of thy compassions put awaie mine iniquities.*
>
> *Wash me throughly from mine iniquities, and clense me from my sin. For I knowe mine iniquities, & my sinne is ever before me.*
>
> *Against thee, against thee onely have I sinned, & done evil in thy sight, that thou maiest be just when thou speakest, and pure when thou judgest.*
>
> *Behold, I was borne in iniquitie, and in sinne hath my mother conceived me.*

Quite a mouthful, that, for mudlarks, but these were more diligent pupils than any Clerke of Oxenford. For on the day that they were marched down the straight and narrow passage to the Old Bailey and brought below the magistrate's balcony, an open Bible was laid in front of them, and they recited these lines. Which, by the evidentiary standards then prevailing in English courts, proved that they could read. Which proved that they were clergymen. Which rendered them beyond the reach of the criminal courts; for clergymen were, by long-hallowed tradition, subject only to the justice of the ecclesiastical courts. Since these no longer existed, the mudlarks were sent free.

It was a different story for John Cole, the oldest of the group. He had been to Newgate before. He had stood in the holding-pen of the Old Bailey before. And in that yard, below that balcony, in the sight of the very same magistrate, his hand had been clamped in a vise and a red-hot iron in the shape of a T had been plunged into the brawn of his thumb, marking him forever as Thief. Which by the evidentiary standards then prevailing, *et cetera,* made it most awkward for him to claim that he was a clergyman. He was sentenced, of course, to hang by the neck until dead at Tyburn.

Bob and Jack did not actually see any of this. They heard
the narration from those who had mumbled a few words of
Psalm 51 and been released and made their way back to the
Isle of Dogs. To this point it was nothing they had not heard
a hundred times before from friends and casual acquain-
tances in the neighborhood. But this time there was a new
twist at the end of the story: John Cole had asked for the two
surviving Shaftóe boys to meet him at the Triple Tree on the
morning of his execution.

They went out of curiosity more than anything. Arriving
at Tyburn and burrowing their way through an immense
crowd by artful shin-kicking, instep-stomping, and groin-
elbowing, they found John Cole and the others on a cart beneath the Fateful Nevergreen, elbows tied behind their
backs, and nooses pre-knotted around their throats, with
long rope-ends trailing behind them. A preacher—the Ordinary of Newgate—was there, urgently trying to make them
aware of certain very important technicalities in the Rules
of Eternity. But the condemnees, who were so drunk they
could barely stand up, were saying all manner of rude and
funny things back to him, faster than he could talk back.

Cole, more solemn than the others, explained to Jack and
Bob that when the executioner "turned him off," which was
to say, body-checked him off the cart and left him to hang
by his neck, Cole would very much appreciate it if Jack
could grab his left leg and Bob his right, or the other way
round if they preferred, and hang there, pulling him down
with their combined weight, so that he'd die faster. In exchange for this service, he told them of a loose board in the
floor of a certain shack on the Isle of Dogs beneath which
they could find hidden treasure. He laid out the terms of this
transaction with admirable coolness, as if he were hanged by
the neck until dead every Friday.

They accepted the commission. Jack Ketch was now the
man to watch. His office, the gallows, was of admirably simple and spare design: three tall pilings supporting a triangle
of heavy beams, each beam long enough that half a dozen

men could be hanged from it at once, or more if a bit of crowding could be overlooked.

Jack Ketch's work, then, consisted of maneuvering the cart below a clear space on one of the beams; selecting a loose rope-end; tossing it over the beam; making it fast with a bit of knot-work; and turning off the bloke at the opposing end of the rope. The cart, now one body lighter, could then be moved again, and the procedure repeated.

John Cole was the eighth of nine men to be hanged on that particular day, which meant that Jack and Bob had the opportunity to watch seven men be hanged before the time came for them to discharge their responsibilities. During the first two or three of these hangings, all they really noticed was the obvious. But after they grew familiar with the general outlines of the rite, they began to notice subtle differences from one hanging to the next. In other words, they started to become connoisseurs of the art, like the ten thousand or so spectators who had gathered around them to watch.

Jack noticed very early that men in good clothes died faster. Watching Jack Ketch shrewdly, he soon saw why: when Jack Ketch was getting ready to turn a well-dressed man off, he would arrange the noose-knot behind the client's left ear, and leave some slack in the rope, so that he'd fall, and gather speed, for a moment before being brought up short with an audible crack. Whereas men in ragged clothing were given a noose that was loose around the neck (at first, anyway) and very little room to fall.

Now, John Cole—who'd looked a bit of a wretch to begin with, and who'd not grown any snappier, in his appearance and toilette, during the months he'd languished in the Stone Hold of Newgate—was the shabbiest bloke on the cart, and obviously destined for the long slow kicking style of hanging. Which explained why he'd had the foresight to call in the Shaftoe boys. But it did not explain something else.

"See here," Jack said, elbowing the Ordinary out of the way. He was on the ground below the cart, neck craned to look far up at Jack Ketch, who was slinging John Cole's neck-rope over the beam with a graceful straight-armed hooking movement. "If you've got hidden treasure, why didn't you give it to him?" And he nodded at Jack Ketch, who was now peering down curiously at Jack Shaftoe through the slits in his hood.

"Er—well I din't have it *on* me, did I?" returned John Cole, who was a bit surly in his disposition on the happiest of days. But Jack thought he looked a bit dodgy.

"You could've sent someone to fetch it!"

"How's I to know they wouldn't nick it?"

"Leave off, Jack," Bob had said. Since Dick's demise, he had been, technically, the man of the family; at first he'd made little of it, but lately he was more arrogant every day. "He's s'posed to be saying his prayers."

"Let him pray while he's kicking!"

"He's not going to be doing any kicking, 'cause you and I are going to be hanging on his legs."

"But he's lying about the treasure."

"I can see that, you think I'm stupid? But as long as we're here, let's do a right job of it."

While they argued, Cole was turned off. He sprawled against the sky just above their heads. They dodged instinctively, but of course he didn't fall far. They jumped into the air, gained hand-holds on his feet, and ascended, hand-over-hand.

After a few moments of dangling from the rope, Cole began to kick vigorously. Jack was tempted to let go, but the tremors coming down Cole's legs reminded him of what he'd felt in the rope when poor Dick had been dragged down beneath the river, and he held on by imagining that this was some kind of vengeance. Bob must've had the same phant'sy, for both boys gripped their respective legs like stranglers until Cole finally went limp. When they realized he was pissing himself, they both let go at once and tumbled into the fœtid dust below the gibbet. There was applause from the crowd. Before they'd had time to dust themselves off, they were approached by the sister of the one remaining condemned man—also a slow-hanging wretch, by his looks—who offered them cash money to perform the same service. The coins were clipped, worn, and blackened, but they were coins.

John Cole's loose board turned out not to be loose, and when pried up, to cover shit instead of treasure. They were hardly surprised. It didn't matter. They were prosperous tradesmen now. On the eve of each hanging-day, Jack and Bob could be found in their new place of business: Newgate Prison.

It took them several visits just to understand the place. *Gate* in their usage meant a sort of wicket by which humans could pass through a fence around a hog-yard without having to vault over—not that vaulting was such a difficult procedure, but it was dangerous when drunk, and might lead to falling, and being eaten by the hogs. So gates they knew.

They had furthermore absorbed the knowledge that in several parts of London town were large fabricks called Gates, viz. Ludgate, Moorgate, and Bishopsgate. They had even passed through Aldgate a few times, that being their usual way of invading the city. But the connexion between gates of that type, and hog-yard-wickets, was most obscure. A gate in the hog-yard sense of the word made no sense unless built in a wall, fence, or other such formal barrier, as its purpose was to provide a means of passage through same. But none of the large London buildings called Gates appeared to have been constructed in any such context. They bestrode important roads leading into the city, but if you didn't want to pass through the actual gate, you could usually find a way round.

This went for Newgate as well. It was a pair of mighty fortress-turrets built on either side of a road that, as it wandered in from the countryside and crossed over Fleet Ditch, was named Holborn. But as it passed between those turrets, the high road was bottlenecked down to a vaulted passageway just wide enough for a four-horse team to squeeze through. Above, a castle-like building joined the turrets, and bridged the road. An iron portcullis made of bars as thick as Jack's leg was suspended within that castle so that it could be dropped down to seal the vault, and bar the road. But it was all show. For thirty seconds of scampering along side streets and alleys would take Jack, or anyone else, to the other side. Newgate was not surrounded by walls or fortifications, but rather by buildings of the conventional sort, which was to say, the half-timbered two- and three-story dwellings that in England grew up as quick and as thick as mushrooms. This Gothick fortress of Newgate, planted in the midst of such a neighborhood, was like a pelvis in a breadbasket.

If you actually did come into the city along Holborn, then when you ducked beneath that portcullis and entered the vaulted passageway beneath Newgate you'd see to the right a door leading into a porter's lodge, which was where new prisoners had their chains riveted on. A few yards farther along, you'd emerge from beneath the castle into the uncovered space of what was now called Newgate Street. To your right you would see a gloomy old building that rose to a height of three or four stories. It had only a few windows, and those were gridded over with bars. This was a separate piece of work from the turret-castle-vault building; rumor had it that it had once done service as an inn for travelers coming into the city along Holborn. But the prison had, in recent centuries, spread up Newgate Street like gangrene up a thigh, consuming several such houses. Most of the doorways that had once welcomed weary travelers were bricked up. Only one remained, at the seam between the castle and the adjoining inn-buildings. Going in there, a visitor could make a quick right turn into the Gigger, or, if he had a candle (for it grew dark immediately), he could risk a trip up or down a stairway into this or that ward, hold, or dungeon. It all depended on what sort of wretch he was coming to visit.

On Jack and Bob's first visit they'd neglected to bring a light, or money with which to buy one, and had blundered down-stairs into a room with a stone floor that made crackling noises beneath their feet as they walked. It was impossible to breathe the air there, and so after a few moments of blind panic they had found their way out and fled back into Newgate Street. There, Jack had noticed that his feet were bloody, and supposed that he must have stepped on broken glass. Bob had the same affliction. But Bob, unlike Jack, was wearing shoes, and so the blood could not have come from him. On careful inspection of the soles of those shoes, the mystery was solved: the blood was not smeared about, but spotted his soles, an array of little bursts. At the center of each burst was a small fleshy gray tube: the vacant corpse of an engorged louse that Bob had stepped on. This accounted for the mysterious crackling noise that they had heard while walking around in that room. As they soon learned, it was called the Stone Hold, and was accounted one of the lowest and worst wards of the prison, occupied only by common felons—such as the late John Cole—who had absolutely no money. Jack and Bob never returned to it.

Over the course of several later sallies into the prison they learned its several other rooms: the fascinating Jack Ketch his Kitchen; the so-called Buggering Hold (which they avoided); the Chapel (likewise); the Press-Yard, where the richest prisoners sat drinking port and claret with their periwigged visitors; and the Black Dogge Tavern, where the cellarmen—elite prisoners who did a brisk trade in candles and liquor—showed a kind of hospitality to any prisoners who had a few coins in their pockets. This looked like any other public house in England save that everyone in the place was wearing chains.

There were, in other words, plenty of lovely things to discover at the time and to reminisce about later. But they were not making these arduous trips from the Isle of Dogs to Newgate simply for purposes of sightseeing. It was a business proposition. They were looking for their market. And eventually, they found it. For in the castle proper, on the north side of the street, in the basement of the turret, was a spacious dungeon that was called the Condemned Hold.

Here, timing was everything. Hangings occurred only

eight times a year. Prisoners were sentenced to hang a week or two in advance. And so most of the time there were no condemned people at all in the Condemned Hold. Rather, it was used as a temporary holding cell for new prisoners of all stripes who had been frog-marched to the Porter's Lodge across the street and traded the temporary ropes that bound their arms behind their backs, for iron fetters that they would wear until they were released. After being ironed (as this procedure was called) with so much metal that they could not even walk, they would be dragged across the vault and thrown into the Condemned Hold to lie in the dark for a few days or weeks. The purpose of this was to find out how much money they really had. If they had money, they'd soon offer it to the gaolers in exchange for lighter chains, or even a nice apartment in the Press-Yard. If they had none, they'd be taken to some place like the Stone Hold.

If one paid a visit to the Condemned Hold on a day chosen at random, it would likely be filled with heavily ironed newcomers. These were of no interest to Jack and Bob, at least not yet. Instead, the Shaftoe boys came to Newgate during the days immediately prior to Tyburn processions, when the Condemned Hold was full of men who actually had been condemned to hang. There they performed.

Around the time of their birth, the King had come back to England and allowed the theatres, which had been closed by Cromwell, to open again. The Shaftoe boys had been putting their climbing skills to good use sneaking into them, and had picked up an ear for the way actors talked, and an eye for the way they did things.

So their Newgate performances began with a little mum-show: Jack would try to pick Bob's pocket. Bob would spin round and cuff him. Jack would stab him with a wooden poniard, and Bob would die. Then (Act II) Bob would jump up and 'morphosize into the Long Arm of the Law, put Jack in a hammerlock, (Act III) don a wig (which they had stolen, at appalling risk, from a side-table in a brothel near the Temple), and sentence him to hang. Then (Act IV) Bob would exchange the white wig for a black hood and throw a noose round Jack's neck and stand behind him while Jack would motion for silence (for by this point all of the Condemned Hold would be in a state of near-riot) and clap his hands together like an Irish child going to First Communion, and (Act V) utter the following soliloquy:

John Ketch's rope doth decorate my neck.
  Though rude, and cruel, this garland chafes me not.
  For, like the Necklace of Harmonia,
  It brings the one who wears it life eternal.
  The hangman draweth nigh—he'll turn me off
  And separate my soul from weak'ning flesh.
  And, as I've made my peace with God Almighty,
  My spirit will ascend to Heaven's Door,
  Where, after brief interrogation, Christ will—
  Bob steps forward and shoves Jack, then yanks the rope up
                    above Jack's head.
HAWKKH! God's Wounds! The noose quite strangleth
    me!
  What knave conceived this means of execution?
  I should have bribed John Ketch to make it quick.
  But, with so many lordly regicides
  Who've lately come to Tyburn to be penalized,
  The price of instant, painless death is quite
  Inflated—far beyond the humble means
  Of common condemnees, who hence must die
  As painf'lly as they've lived. God damn it all!
  And damn Jack Ketch; the late John Turner; and
  The judges who hath sent so many rich men to
  The gallows, thereby spurring said inflation.
  And damn my frugal self. For, at a cost
  That scarce exceeds an evening at the pub,
  Might I have hired those exc'llent Shaftoe boys,
  Young Jack, and Bob, the elder of the pair,
  To dangle from my legs, which lacking ballast,
  Do flail most ineffectu'lly in the air,

And make a sort of entertainment for
The *mobile.*
> *Bob removes the noose from Jack's neck.*

But soft! The end approaches—
Earth fades—new worlds unfold before my eyes—
  Can this be heaven? It seemeth warm, as if
  A brazier had been fir'd 'neath the ground.
  Perhaps it is the warmth of God's sweet love
  That so envelops me.

Bob, dressed as a Devil, approaches with a long pointed Stick.

How now! What sort
Of angel doth sprout Horns upon his pate?
  Where is thy Harp, O dark Seraph?
  Instead of which a Pike, or Spit, doth seem
  To occupy thy gnarled claws?

Devil: I am
  The Devil's Turnspit. Sinner, welcome home!

Jack: I thought that I had made my peace with God.
  Indeed I had, when I did mount the scaffold.
  If I had but died then, at Heaven's Gate
  I'd stand. But in my final agony,
  I took God's name in vain, and sundry mortal
  Sins committed, and thus did damn myself
  To this!

Devil: Hold still!
> *Devil shoves the point of his Spit up Jack's arse-hole.*

Jack: The pain! The pain, and yet,
  It's just a taste of what's to come.
  If only I had hired Jack and Bob!

*Jack, by means of a conjuror's trick, causes the point of the
spit, smeared with blood, to emerge from his mouth, and is led
away by the Devil, to violent applause and foot-stomping from
the Crowd.*

After the applause had died down, Jack, then, would circu-
late among the condemned to negotiate terms, and Bob, who
was bigger, would watch his back, and mind the coin-purse.